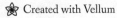 Created with Vellum

KERI ARTHUR

Magic Misled

A LIZZIE GRACE NOVEL

CHAPTER ONE

Samuel Kang was the picture of classic male perfection —oval-shaped face, chiseled cheekbones, and an extremely engaging smile. His shoulders were lovely and wide, his frame lean but muscular, and he had long legs that looked damn fine in close-fitting jeans—the very first thing I'd noticed when he'd walked through our café's door.

The second thing I'd noticed—when my gaze had finally wandered back to his face—were his eyes. They were mono-lidded and the most glorious shade of emerald green, which meant—despite the fact he had the crimson hair of a royal witch—there was a smidge of human somewhere in his background. Full-blood witches had silver eyes—even mine were now that color, though they'd initially been the exact same shade as his.

Unfortunately, Samuel Kang hadn't walked into our café to enjoy a coffee or a cake, and he certainly wasn't in the Faelan Reservation to spend time in one of the famous spa resorts.

He was here to catch a killer.

And I was very much a suspect.

With good reason, of course. I might not have actually killed Clayton Marlowe, but I'd certainly helped orchestrate it.

"I have to say, Mrs. Marlowe," his voice deliciously deep and melodic, "that you're the furthest thing from a grieving widow I've ever seen."

I raised an eyebrow. "He was my husband in name only. The marriage was never consummated and was recently annulled—as you're no doubt aware. And my name is Grace. Lizzie Grace."

"Indeed." Another smile flirted with his lips. I tried my best to ignore it, as I suspected he used his charm and good looks to disarm. "Tell me, in your own words, what happened that night."

"Why?" My voice was flat. "Hasn't a 'death by unknown supernatural entity' verdict been given?"

"By the coroner, yes. That doesn't mean the case is closed or that all parties involved should not be brought to justice."

Great. Just great. I picked up my hot chocolate and took a sip. Belle—who was not only my best friend and co-owner of the café, but also my familiar—had liberally laced it with whiskey, and it burned all the way down. While it did help ease the inner uncertainty, it was a damn good thing I wasn't driving home tonight. The mug was large, and drinking it all might well put me over the limit.

"You've no doubt heard the recordings by the Black Lantern investigators," I said, "so you already know everything I did and said that evening."

The Black Lantern Society was a group of witches, werewolves, and vampires who worked behind the scenes to right wrongs and bring justice to those who escaped it—via whatever means necessary. They also had an arm that worked openly in the courts, and had both psychic auditors and truth seekers on their books. The latter pairing had not only recorded my memories of the events leading up to my disastrous marriage, but also everything that had led to Clayton's bloody and brutal death.

Technically, you didn't actually tell them everything. Belle's comment whispered through my mind, her tone gently amused. *Because you totally omitted the vital part Gabe, Katie, and the wild magic played in it all. How you managed to conceal all that, I have no idea. At the very least, they should have been aware there were memories they couldn't access.*

Maybe our connection had something to do with it. I wasn't telepathic by any means, but she was my familiar. That not only made mind-to-mind communication possible, but also allowed us to draw on each other's strength—something we'd been forced to do more than a few times over the past months. *Maybe, after all these years, some of your expertise has rubbed off.*

Magic might work that way, but psychic powers don't. She paused. *Or, at least, they shouldn't. But this reservation doesn't seem to like the words "shouldn't" and "impossible."*

Considering you gained precognition after we merged to oust the White Lady from your body, it's not beyond the realms of possibility.

No, but it could also be the presence of the wild magic.

Which was another distinct possibility. My mother had unknowingly been pregnant with me when she'd been sent to control a newly formed wellspring. Though she'd been successful, the effort had almost killed her. It most certainly should have killed me. Instead, the wild magic had somehow infused with my DNA, becoming a deeply hidden force that had waited years to be unlocked and unleashed.

The first cracks in those inner locks had appeared the night Clayton tried to rape me. They'd been utterly smashed the night he'd died.

I had no idea what the true consequences of that would be, but I could feel the wild magic within even now. It was a river of white heat that pulsed through my body like blood.

"I have indeed heard everything the Society have in their possession," Samuel said. "But I'd still like to hear it all again, this time in your own words rather than as a telepathic memory recording."

"To repeat, why?"

He raised an eyebrow. "Because the High Witch Council wishes their own record of events."

"So they can twist the facts to suit whatever decisions have already been made, no doubt."

"You have a rather cynical view of the council."

I snorted softly. "My parents are—or were—members of that council. I like to think my views are realistic."

Another smile tugged at his lips. They were really lovely lips. "The sooner you comply with the request, the sooner I'll be out of your way."

Annoyance flickered through me, but I nevertheless gave him a rundown of everything that had happened during the final confrontation between Clayton and me, but once again omitting the part Katie and Gabe had played in it all. I'd rather be arrested than reveal the fact that not only was there a ghost guarding a second wellspring here in the reservation, but that ghost had bonded the soul of his werewolf wife to the wild magic itself. Her influence and power were now spreading across to the reservation's main wellspring, but none of us knew what would happen if she gained full control over both—or indeed if that was even possible.

"You were aware of the vampire's presence when you walked out of that house, were you not?" Samuel said.

It was interesting he didn't actually name said vampire. I'd certainly made no attempt to hide Maelle's part in all this. "Yes."

"Then why didn't you stop it?"

"For one, I didn't have the physical or magical strength to fight a gnat let alone a very old and very powerful vampire. And two, why on earth would I? The bastard deserved exactly what he got." My quick smile held little humor. "If I'd been present when he'd died, I would have danced with glee through his fucking remains."

"Because of what he did to you the night of your marriage?"

"Because of what he did to Belle."

He made a show of checking the file in front of him, though I doubted it was necessary. "That would be Isabelle Sarr?"

"Legally, her surname is Kent."

And though Belle was seriously considering reverting back to her birth name, I never would. Between Clayton's actions and my father's, the thought of becoming a Marlowe again was vomit inducing.

"But Clayton didn't only torture Belle," I continued evenly, "he was responsible for the explosion at Émigré that killed eight people and injured dozens of others."

"That connection has yet to be determined."

I snorted again. "Because the council's not actually trying all that hard to do so, are they? Let's be honest here— Clayton would never have faced justice for what he did to me or Belle or anyone else. He was too powerful—and had far too many friends in high places—for the case to have ever reached the council's court of justice."

"That's not actually true, given your father was one of his victims, but even so, you had no right to be judge and jury."

I studied him for a second. "Have you got a familiar, Samuel?"

Surprise flitted briefly through his expression. I suspected it was the first "honest" one I'd seen.

"Please, call me Sam, and yes, I do. But I don't see—"

"And you're connected telepathically to your familiar?"

"Of course, but—"

"Then imagine a scenario where your familiar is being tortured, and every ounce of their pain and suffering echoes through you. How would you feel? How would you react? Would you sit back and wait for the law to show up? Or would you do everything in your power to free your familiar, even if that means sidestepping the law?"

His expression gave very little away. I wished I knew what he was thinking, but the damn man was wearing the latest electronic gadget that guarded against telepathic intrusion.

I could probably get past it, Belle said. She was hiding in the reading room—where we did the psychic portion of our business—to keep out of his sight. *But it'd take more time and effort than is probably worthwhile at the moment. Besides, it's not like he's hiding all that much—not when it comes to those jeans or indeed the investigation.*

A comment backed by the fact the file sitting wide open on the table in front of him not only contained the coroner's report *and* his own notes, but various witness reports. He didn't seem to care if I could see them.

It does make me wonder if it's deliberate. Maybe he

wants me to check them out so I can fashion my answers to suit.

That hardly makes sense given the statements you've already made.

It does if my father is placing pressure on them to drop the investigation.

Her snort echoed sharply through my brain. *I doubt even your father has the gumption to interfere with this investigation—not when his own actions are also being looked at.*

Those actions being forcing me into a marriage against my will when I was still underage. *Why else would Samuel bother mentioning my father, then? Remember, the last thing he actually wants is me being charged as an accessory to Clayton's murder. It'd play havoc with his latest scheme to marry me off for the benefit of the family.*

Knowing your father, you landing in jail wouldn't actually stop his machinations.

That, sadly, was all too true. The only thing that really mattered to him was the family's position as the most powerful in Canberra. Of course, he also cared—rather greatly—about his own reputation, which was no doubt why he'd temporarily stepped down from the council and was now playing the "my best friend tried to kill me" card. It was simply all an effort to garner sympathy and overshadow the fact he'd illegally forced his underage daughter to marry his second cousin.

But even if they do decide to arrest you—and I seriously doubt Samuel's here to do that—it's not like he can get you off the reservation.

Thanks in large part to my connection with the wild magic within the reservation—and yet it was a restriction we'd never really tested. I'd certainly left the reservation for a day or so, but we only had the word of a ghost and my own intuition saying anything more permanent would be rejected.

I'd still rather avoid being arrested, thanks very much.

I'd rather you avoid that, too. Having to visit you in jail would get old real quick. Not to mention play havoc with my social life.

Because you have such a busy dating schedule these days.

My voice was dry, and she laughed. *I'm working on it, but I'm also totally over werewolves at the moment.*

Shame we're in a werewolf reservation, then. I paused. *I guess there is always Monty.*

Who wasn't only the reservation's resident witch, but also my cousin—and the only relative I actually liked.

I'll ignore that comment.

Which was a step up from her usual threat to do me damage after similar teasing comments in the past. And while it might not be an admission she actually liked him, their relationship had certainly taken a giant leap forward after Monty had not only stepped up to protect Belle, but had floored Clayton with the best punch I'd ever seen anyone throw. She was now openly going out with him, even if she wasn't yet willing to admit they were dating or an item.

"I guess in such a situation, there are very few of us who wouldn't act as you did," Sam said. "That does not make it right, however."

I took another sip of chocolate. "Does that mean you're here to arrest me?"

"No, I'm here to question all parties involved and to examine the various crime scenes. Nothing more, nothing less."

"But your recommendations will determine what happens next?"

"In part." He pressed a button on his phone and stopped the recording. "In truth, there has been some pressure on the council to let the matter slide."

"From my father?"

He smiled. It really was a lovely smile. Just as well my heart was taken, or I might have been tempted to flirt. "Surprisingly, no. It's actually coming from Clayton's family, who do not wish his behavior to become a matter of public record."

"Because it would reflect badly on them."

"Yes."

I studied him curiously for a second. "I suspect I'm not supposed to know that, so why say it?"

He made a small shrug. "Because I can sympathize with your situation."

"Really?"

My disbelief was evident, and he smiled again. "Perhaps I'll explain why over coffee one afternoon."

"I work most afternoons."

"I meant here, of course. I'm told you make the best coffee in town."

"We do."

"Then we'll talk again soon." He rose, gathered his files, and headed for the front door.

I followed him—my gaze admittedly more on the butt his jeans hugged so damn lovingly—and locked the door once he'd left.

"Well, that was all very odd." I made my way back to my chair and picked up my hot chocolate. "I think he needs to grab some lessons from Aiden on how to properly interview a suspect."

"It's not like they haven't already got a full record of your actions when it comes to Clayton." Belle came out of the reading room and went behind the serving counter. Like most Sarr witches, her black hair was long and straight, and her eyes bright silver. She was a smidge over six feet tall and had the build of an Amazon. Stunning was a word often used to describe her and one that was well deserved. "Maybe he really *is* here to follow up on what happened at Émigré and interview all the victims. The resulting reports might just be enough for the council to decide justice—however brutal—had been dispensed. You want a piece of cake?"

"If that's not the stupidest question of the year, I'm not sure what is."

She grinned. "Hey, it was only yesterday that you actually said no to a brownie."

"Because it was eight in the morning and I had a hangover."

"Serves you right for partying all night."

"It wasn't *all* night."

Just most of it. It wasn't every day your boyfriend turned thirty, after all, and it had to be celebrated in style. So I'd booked us a luxurious room and an eight-course dining experience with never-ending champagne at a five-star hotel down in Melbourne. To say it was a glorious evening would be another of those understatements.

Of course, there *was* a "proper" party this weekend with all his friends and family, but it was being held within the grounds of the O'Connor compound. I wasn't a werewolf, so I definitely wasn't on the invite list—which was no doubt the plan when his bitch of a mother had presented it as a fait accompli two weeks ago, just as I'd been getting out of hospital. I suspected she'd hoped I'd be so upset that I'd split with him but, in reality, it was just another indication that she really didn't know me—or even her son—all that well. The more she tried to pry us apart, the closer we became.

"Speaking of newly ancient boyfriends," Belle said, reaching for another mug. "Yours is just about to shove his key in the door."

I frowned and glanced at the clock. It was just gone six. "He was supposed to be working until eight."

"Maybe he decided to leave early so he could rush you home and have his wicked way with you."

Home now being his house in Argyle. We'd moved most of my stuff there a few days after I'd gotten out of hospital, and he'd spent the rest of that week cosseting me.

I rather liked being cosseted.

"A girl can only hope." I rose and headed for the door, then basically threw myself into his muscular arms the minute he stepped through.

He caught me with a grunt, kissed me thoroughly, and then said, with a wicked twinkle in his blue eyes, "Now *that* is a welcome a man can get used to."

"I wouldn't," Belle said. "I mean, you're old now. All that excitement and passion can't be good for your heart."

"I'll remind you of that when you turn thirty."

His voice was dry, and she laughed. "Which is a good year off yet. Plenty of time to get some action in before the senile years set in."

"Senility isn't generally a problem werewolves face, thank God." He pulled out the chair next to mine and sat down, his nostrils flaring lightly. "That drink is more whiskey than hot chocolate. Any reason why?"

I wrinkled my nose. "We just had a visit from the high council's chief investigator."

"I'm guessing that would be the witch I just saw leaving, then?"

"Deliciously *hot* witch would be a more correct term," I said.

He raised an eyebrow. "I have competition?"

The smile playing around his lips was warm and confident. A man who knew *exactly* where he stood in my affections.

"If you don't play your cards right, yes. Especially when he wears a pair of jeans almost as well as you."

"I'm relieved by the modifier." He thanked Belle as she placed a coffee and a plate of brownies in front of him. "What did he want?"

"He's here to interview witnesses and follow up on the bombing. I dare say he'll probably want to speak to you at some point."

"I dare say." He didn't look overly concerned by the prospect, and with good reason. Werewolf reservations were self-governing *and* self-policing. Had Aiden taken an active part in delivering Clayton to Maelle, there might have been problems, but he hadn't even known about it. He'd been too busy dealing with the bloody mess left behind at Émigré by Clayton's bomber. "Though the witch council *is* in full receipt of all our reports to date."

"The council apparently does not want to rely on the conclusions of others." Belle returned with her drink and two cakes—black forest for me, and a banana bread cheesecake for her—and sat down. "We suggested it's because they want to twist the facts to suit their already drawn conclusions, but Sam denied it."

Aiden raised his eyebrows again. "Sam?"

She nodded. "He was very quick to get on first-name

terms with our girl here. I suspect he was more intent on flirting than fact finding."

"Suspect? You didn't read his mind?" Aiden's expression was offended, though his blue eyes twinkled. "And why not, when you have no compunction raiding my mind willy-nilly?"

"Sadly, he was protected against telepathic invasion."

"So was Monty when he first arrived here, but that didn't stop you."

She grinned. "The effort wasn't worth it this time. He was being very upfront with his intentions."

"He basically said," I added, just in case Aiden was wondering if those intentions were more sexual in nature, "that Clayton's family is putting pressure on the council to drop the investigation. They want the coroner's 'death by unknown supernatural entity' verdict to stand as the overall official verdict."

"Which would please Maelle no end." He picked up his coffee and took a drink, his gaze on mine. We'd already had "the conversation"—the one about me not being open and honest about information he had a right to know—and he hadn't been too pleased by my response that it hadn't been my damn place to tell him about Maelle but rather the werewolf council's. The same council on which his father was a major player. "Have you heard from her?"

I frowned. "Why on earth would I?"

He shrugged. "You seem to be on better terms with her than most."

"She owed me a favor, and that favor is now repaid. I really don't expect to hear from her again." And if I put that statement out there often enough, maybe the universe would take note. "I don't think the reservation has seen the last of her, though. She's put too much time and effort into Émigré to walk away."

He grimaced. "I can't say I'd be unhappy if she did."

"She kept to her word, Aiden. She hasn't killed within the reservation."

"She *has* dined, though."

"Only on the willing, just as she promised."

He studied me for a moment. "Why are you defending her?"

I shrugged. "I'm just stating facts. Trust me, I'd be over the moon if we have seen the last of her and Roger."

"I gather he's her thrall?"

I nodded. A thrall was a human who—via a magical ceremony in which he or she shared a piece of the vampire's flesh—was given eternal life in return for eternal service. Roger wasn't dead; he'd simply been forced into a period of stasis. Basically, he'd been so badly injured that he'd placed himself into a coma to help his body heal and recover. I did sometimes wonder if part of his problem had been Maelle draining his strength in order to maintain her own.

"I daresay he'll come back to life when Maelle decides to make an appearance. From what I've read, thralls are very hard to kill."

"That seems to be a common theme here of late when it comes to supernatural nasties."

"As long as you're not blaming us for that," Belle said, "because we all know where the true fault lies."

"Yes, and you've mentioned it multiple times. Can we at least forgive the council even if we can't forget?"

She pursed her lips thoughtfully, but her mischievously glinting silver eyes somewhat spoiled the effect. "Okay—but only because you asked so nicely."

He rolled his eyes and returned his gaze to mine. "If you

do hear from Maelle, let me know. We need access to her security recordings."

I frowned. "Wouldn't they be in the security office? It's not like she had time to take them after the explosion."

"That's the trouble—we can't find the security office."

"Meaning it was destroyed in the bombing?"

"We don't think so. We think it's actually off site."

"That makes sense, given she had other services available off site," Belle said.

"Other services?" Aiden said, eyebrows rising.

Belle smiled. "Apparently, there's quite a few wolves in this reservation who don't mind a bit of BDSM. Heard and saw some interesting things the few nights I was there under her protection."

He blinked. "Really?"

"Ha!" Belle's tone was delighted. "I actually managed to shock a werewolf—who'd have thought *that* was even possible."

"Oh, I'm not shocked about the whole BDSM thing—people can get their rocks off however they choose as far as I'm concerned. I'm just surprised that the council allowed it to operate within the reservation without strict oversight and control."

"How do you know they didn't have oversight?" I asked mildly. "It's not like they mentioned who owned Émigré until they absolutely had to."

"True. And we've gotten way off track." He paused for a moment, his expression suddenly serious. "I actually came here to tell you—"

He cut the rest off as his phone rang sharply. He dragged it out of his pocket and hit the answer button. "Tala, what's up?"

Tala was his second-in-command and the very definition of a no-nonsense werewolf. She and I hadn't exactly gotten off on the right foot, mainly because she'd utterly believed all psychics were charlatans, but she had eventually—and graciously—admitted she was wrong. We might never be firm friends, but we were at least on friendlier terms these days.

"I'm here with her now. Hang on." He lowered the phone, his gaze on mine. "There's been a report of a kid wandering up near Fryer's Ridge. Tala and Mac have spent the last few hours scouting the area, with little success. They did find a torn bit of shirt, but there's no scent attached and no trail or prints to follow. Do you mind going out there to see if you can help?"

I frowned. "Has anyone reported a kid missing?"

"No."

"Then why is Tala so sure it's not a prank of some kind?"

"Because the report came from Patrick Sinclair, a friend of mine."

"Ah. Okay."

As he gave Tala the affirmative, I quickly gulped down the rest of my hot chocolate and pushed the half-eaten cake toward Belle. "I'll be back for that later."

"No, you won't," Aiden said, "You live with me now, remember?"

"Oh yeah." I grinned. "Tomorrow then."

"You might also want to rug up—it's getting damn cold up in the hills now that autumn is on the wane."

"Winter's only five days away." Belle said, amused. "That's a little more than 'on the wane.'"

"Maybe to you soft city types."

I rolled my eyes as their banter continued, and ran up the stairs to grab not only a coat, but also gloves, a wooly hat, and a scarf. Thankfully, I still had plenty of them here in my wardrobe, simply because I actually owned a ton of them. I hated winter. Or rather, hated being cold. Which was a bit of a laugh considering we'd settled in one of the coldest areas in country Victoria.

Once rugged up, I headed back downstairs to grab the backpack—which we now kept fully stocked and ready to go with all manner of potions, charms, and my silver knife—then returned to the café's dining area.

Aiden swung around and offered me his arm, then said over his shoulder as we left, "Hope you and Monty have a good night, Belle."

"It's not a date. We're only going to the movies together," she said, voice dry.

"Every would-be couple has to start somewhere," he said.

A spoon came flying across the room, and he ducked, laughing. As he opened the door, I bent to pick it up and then tossed it back. "I'll see you tomorrow."

"It's *just* the movies."

"Of course it is."

I followed Aiden out the door, locked it behind me, and then tucked my arm through his again. He'd parked his truck farther up the road, as there was a no-standing zone at the front of the café. As head ranger, he couldn't be seen to be breaking the rules. Not too often, anyway.

Seriously, Belle continued, *it's not.*

Why does it actually matter either way?

Because I once swore to hate blue-blood males for all eternity and to never go out with one.

I blinked. *You did? When was this?*

After Tommy Kang sprayed me with white dye.

I don't remember that. Or Tommy Kang, for that matter.

17

It happened before we were matched as witch and familiar.

I hope you gave him a piece of your mind.

My mind wasn't as strong then. He got my fist instead.

I smiled. *For what it's worth, Monty's already told me in great detail his grand plans for the first official "we are an item" date. A jaunt to the movies pales in comparison.*

There was a long mental pause. *Care to detail said grand plan?*

No. You'll have to officially date him to find out.

You're annoying, you know that?

I grinned but didn't bother replying. Sooner or later, she'd admit the truth everyone else already knew.

Aiden opened the truck's door, ushering me inside before running around to the driver side.

Once we were on the road and heading out of Castle Rock, I said, "So, what did you come to tell me?"

He glanced at me. "It can wait."

There was an edge to his voice that had my eyebrows rising. "If that's the case, you wouldn't have come to see me, but would have waited until we were both home."

A smile tugged at his lips. "True. But I didn't have anything else to do, and now I have. It'll wait."

"I hate waiting."

His glance was somewhat heated. "So I've discovered."

I smiled at the smoky note in his deep voice. "Where in Fryer's Ridge is the kid lost? It's a fairly large area, isn't it?"

He nodded. "It's near the Oven Rock campground."

"So called because it contains an oven?"

He laughed. "There *is* a natural rock formation that forms an oven, and campers do often use it to make damper, barbeque food, or boil water."

"I'm gathering there's nothing much in the way of facilities there."

"Camping isn't about facilities. It's about the experience."

"If there isn't a proper loo and at least a lake to bathe in, I'm not interested."

He cast me an amused glance. "I'll keep a note for future holidays."

"Then also consider that anything under four stars is akin to camping in my opinion."

He laughed. "This from the woman who spent how many years on the run and often living in less than salubrious surroundings?"

A smile tugged at my lips. "It was all part of the disguise. Neither my father nor Clayton would have ever thought of looking for us in a hostel or boarding house."

"At least now you're free from all that."

"I'm free from Clayton. Don't for an instant think my father has finished with me."

In fact, I wouldn't actually be surprised if he was the reason for Sam's presence here. Many of the Kangs were renowned lawyers, often holding prominent positions in the judiciary system. It would certainly be a worthwhile connection in my father's eyes, and he was astute enough to realize the fact Sam's branch of the family had a human ancestor somewhere in their past might make him far more attractive to me.

If that *was* the case, then it certainly meant he'd at least learned something from the whole Clayton disaster.

"Perhaps not," Aiden said, "but you're no longer underage, and he can't spell you into anything anymore."

I wasn't so sure about the latter, but I didn't bother admitting that. Live for the moment, worry about future

19

heartbreak when it rolls around was the new motto I was trying to live by.

But it was damnably hard after all those years of worrying over every little detail or action.

A few kilometers outside Louton, he turned right onto a graveled road that—once we went over the rail bridge—got progressively narrower and rougher. I hung on to the hand-grip in an effort to stop being tossed around, but it didn't really help.

We eventually pulled into the camping area, although in truth it looked little different to the other scrubby, tree-filled areas we'd driven past in the last twenty minutes or so. Two green-striped, white SUVs were parked off in the trees to the right, but neither Tala nor Mac were visible.

Aiden parked his truck, and we both climbed out. I moved to the back of the vehicle and studied the area through slightly narrowed eyes. Though we were a long way from either of the wellsprings, tiny filaments of wild magic floated through the air. That seemed to be happening more and more of late, and it was decidedly odd. Layers of spells now protected the main wellspring, and it *should* have stopped any fragments of magic escaping. Unless, of course, these filaments were from Katie's wellspring.

I raised a hand, and the nearest couple immediately deviated toward me. They curled around my fingers and wrists, fragile moonbeams that pulsed with power. Within that power was a sense of acknowledgment. Of kinship—and it had nothing to do with Katie, even though these threads *were* sourced from her wellspring. They were acknowledging the power within me—a power that burned so brightly it momentarily felt as if I was being consumed by fire.

But these filaments *were* her eyes and ears; they were

her means of knowing what was happening within the reservation without having to leave the safety of her wellspring.

And though it wasn't a direct connection to her, I could sense through them that nothing untoward had happened in the immediate area.

Which didn't mean nastiness hadn't happened in the wider area. Not even the wild magic could cover the entire reservation.

I hoped that wasn't the case, though. The reservation—and certainly its witches—could really do with a break from the supernatural nastiness.

And of course, now that I'd put that thought out there in the wilder world, fate would no doubt take it as a challenge.

I turned and followed Aiden through the trees. He moved with the lithe grace of a predator; I was more like an uncoordinated elephant. While my merges with Katie had resulted in an odd sort of bleed over of her wolf abilities, resulting in a sharpening of my senses and even added strength, I doubted I'd ever be able to step werewolf-light through the scrub.

Tala had obviously heard me coming, because she appeared at the top of the ridge. Like most werewolves, she was on the slender side but whip strong. She was around the same height as me, with the dark skin and black hair of the Sinclair pack. She was also a lot older than either Aiden or me, having become a ranger only after trying several other careers first.

"Anything?" Aiden asked, stopping beside her.

She shook her head. "I tried contacting Patrick, but he's not answering."

Aiden grunted. "They've been having reception issues out his way of late."

"Tell me about it," Tala muttered. She gave me a nod of greeting. "Sorry to drag you out in the cold like this, but it may be our only shot of finding this damn kid."

"There's no guarantee I'll have any better luck, especially if that bit of cloth you found is hours old." I stopped beside Aiden, my breath condensing lightly on the air. It was going to be a bitter night.

"It's still worth a shot. This way."

She turned and led us along a path that was little more than a rough kangaroo track. Even with the deep shadows of night now falling, I could clearly see where I was going—an unexpected consequence of my merges with Katie.

Another figure appeared on the trail ahead—Mac. He had the typical rangy build of a werewolf, with brown skin and hair. "Still no luck getting hold of Patrick. Mari says he hasn't come home yet."

"Meaning he's probably still out here." Aiden scanned the bush with a frown. "Odd that he's made no move to contact either of you."

"He might have just made the report and not stayed," Tala said.

Aiden shook his head. "Patrick's not the type to leave a kid out here alone. He'll be out there trying to find him. Where's the material remnant?"

"This way."

Mac spun on a heel and led the way off the roo track into the deeper scrub. About thirty feet in, we came across the scrap of material—and it really was just a scrap. It was only a few inches long, and half that in width, and had been snagged by the thorns of a rather nasty-looking bush. It also was at hip height, which suggested we weren't dealing with a littlie, but rather someone older. Relief stirred; an older kid might be just as afraid as a toddler, but they'd be a little more capable of survival. Or, at least, I hoped they were.

Aiden stepped to one side and motioned me forward. I squatted in front of the piece of material and studied it through narrowed eyes. If there was one thing I'd learned over the last few months, it was to never take anything at face value—not when it came to dealing with the machinations of supernatural entities, at any rate.

There was no immediate indication that's what we were dealing with here—no caress of magic or supernatural foulness immediately evident on the blue scrap—but unease nevertheless stirred.

As usual, the psychic part of my soul had no answers as to *why*.

I tentatively reached out and touched the strip of material. Nothing. I drew in a deep breath, then opened the psychometry "gates." On a surface level, the talent let me trace misplaced items and sense emotions via touch. On a deeper level, I could track missing people or slip into the mind of whoever owned the item I was holding, allowing me to see and experience whatever was happening to them at the time. The latter was not something I did very often—I'd discovered the hard way just how dangerous being locked into the mind of another could be.

However, both sides of the talent needed some form of connectivity to work—like constant use or the wearer only recently having stripped the item off—and that didn't appear to be the case here.

"Anything?" Aiden asked.

"No. It's been at least six hours since this scrap was torn away."

A flicker caught my attention. A filament of wild magic

spun around the material, darted toward me, and then returned to the material.

Katie, using the wild magic to make a suggestion.

But if she knew what was going on or where the missing kid was, why didn't she just use the filament to connect with me? Or was it more a matter that she knew something was off, but didn't know the specifics? She might be the reservation's true guardian but not even she could be every-where or see everything.

I took a deep breath and released it slowly. "There is one more thing I can try, though I'm not sure it'll actually work."

"Is it dangerous?" Aiden asked.

I glanced up. "It may be the only chance we have of finding this kid quickly."

He hesitated and then nodded sharply. Not happy about the unspoken risk but also not willing to let a kid wander around an area filled with old mine shafts any longer than necessary.

I just hoped the idea would work. I'd certainly woven wild magic through my spells often enough—even if it had mostly been unintentional—so it was theoretically possible that I could use it to enhance my psychic abilities.

But there were no guidebooks when it came to this sort of thing. One of Monty's connections in Canberra had found an old book titled *Earth Magic: Its Uses and Dangers* —earth magic being the original name for wild magic—that held the promise of being a font of forgotten information, but it hadn't yet arrived. Things tended to move slowly in Canberra's dusty halls.

I took another deep breath and then carefully pulled a filament of power from the fiery inner river and directed it toward my fingers and the cloth. For several seconds, nothing happened. Then tiny sparks of white began to dance across the material, weaving in and out of its threads as if sewing itself into the material. The whole scrap began to glow, and in the outer recesses of my mind, shadows stirred. I frowned and psychically reached for them, but the fragile wisps of memory spun away from my grasp. I swore softly and pushed harder. The shadows abruptly solidified, and images slammed into my mind so hard and fast it tore a gasp from my throat.

What I saw was death.

But it wasn't a kid or even a teenager.

It was an adult. A werewolf.

Patrick Sinclair, to be exact.

CHAPTER TWO

I released the scrap of material and pushed back, landing with a grunt on my butt.

"You okay?" Aiden squatted in front of me, his expression concerned.

"Yes. No." I took a deep breath and then met his gaze. "It's not good news. He's dead."

He scraped a hand across his bristly chin, the sound like sandpaper in the still evening. "An accident? Or something worse?"

"Worse." I hesitated and gently touched his arm. "It's not a kid, Aiden. It's Patrick."

The wave of disbelief, pain, and sorrow hit so hard, it had me gasping for air even as tears sprang to my eyes. I was generally well shielded against the onslaught of emotion that sometimes came with an unguarded touch, but there was no shielding against this—and not just because of its crushing strength. Our connection—and the growing depth of my feelings for him—had made it virtually impossible.

Who knew love could have such a brutal consequence?

I quickly let go of his arm and flexed my fingers in a vague effort to release the lingering wash of his emotions.

"I'm sorry, Aiden—"

He nodded, short and sharp. His expression was stony, the emotions I could feel so sharply well hidden. "Are you able to lead us to him?"

"I think so." Though I was no longer touching the fabric, the images I'd accessed still burned in my mind. While I doubted they'd be enough to guide me directly, sparks still flickered across the material remnant. Once again, unease stirred. Not because of what I'd just done, but because there were undoubtedly a lot more surprises in store when it came to the inner wild magic.

I swallowed heavily. I could tell myself all I wanted not to worry about the changes and what they might mean, but the truth of the matter was, it scared the hell out of me. And while I *did* need to understand what was happening, I also feared taking that step would send me down a path from which there was no retreat.

I'd say retreat hasn't been an option for a while now came Belle's comment. *Besides, ignoring a problem—or running from it—never leads to anything good.*

Depends on the problem. Running from Clayton had given us the time—and, in the end, the power—to deal with him.

That was a somewhat unique situation, though.

In terms of uniqueness, I think my connection to the wild magic would be so far off the scale it'd be in space. And why are you listening to my thoughts? Where's Monty?

Running late, apparently. Her tone was somewhat peeved, though I was well aware she was in fact only talking to keep my mind off the death I'd soon be finding. *If he doesn't hurry up, we'll miss the start of the movie.*

I'm sure he has a good reason.

He hasn't. A phone call delayed him, apparently.

He does have to work occasionally—although I will admit it's odd that he's chosen a call over a date with his future wife.

I could almost see her eye roll. *Seriously? Enough with that crap.*

Okay. But only if you promise to block my thoughts and just enjoy your night out.

She sighed. It was a very put-upon sound. *Fine. I promise.*

Aiden's hand appeared in front of my nose. "Let's go."

I took another of those deep breaths that didn't do jack-squat to ease the inner tension, then clasped his hand. He pulled me up easily, but the pulse of his sorrow once again echoed through me.

I blinked back the sting of tears and ducked away from his gaze. "Am I able to take the cloth with me?"

"Yes." He quickly untangled it and handed it to me. "How far away is he?"

"Some distance."

I wrapped my fingers around the material and reached again for the inner wild magic. Though I directed it back onto the cloth, slivers also shot down my legs, only to pool around my toes.

As if blocked.

Instinct stirred again. My boots ...

I swore, sat back down, and quickly pulled them off.

"What the hell are you doing?" Aiden asked.

"I'll explain later."

Though I wasn't entirely sure there *was* any way to explain the sudden certainty I needed to be barefoot. But it wasn't the first time I'd buried my toes into the earth to draw on her power—I'd done the same thing up in Kalimna Park when I'd summoned a will-ó-the-wisp to light the way the night I'd unsuccessfully tried to save a teenager from a vampire.

And perhaps the reason the wisp had answered me— and had, in fact, interacted with me several times since, even though they had a well-deserved reputation for mischief—was due not so much to a decision to be helpful, but rather the connection we both shared to the energy of the earth. Perhaps it had sensed what I hadn't then begun to suspect.

I shoved my socks into my boots, then tied the laces together and rose. The minute my toes dug into the ground, the pooling magic slipped deep into the earth. A heartbeat later—with my body acting as a conduit—a connection formed between the strip of material gripped in my right hand and the energy of the earth. It was a connection that would lead me directly to death.

I could feel it. "See" it. In my mind, if not yet in reality.

"Liz." Aiden's voice held an edge of uncertainty and concern. "What are you doing?"

"Finding." My reply was soft. Distracted.

I handed him my shoes and walked away, concentrating on what I was seeing in my mind rather than where each step was going. I had no real awareness of my surroundings, and yet I didn't trip. I didn't stumble. My feet moved unerringly over the rough ground as I led the rangers deeper and deeper into the forest.

Eventually, we reached the top of a deep ravine. I paused and stared at the shadows haunting the steep, heavily treed slope. Death waited for us below. I couldn't see the full extent of that death, but I could certainly feel its weight on the earth. Could taste the bitterness of the blood that had leached into the soil.

I swallowed heavily, then blinked as the ravine and the trees began to fade in and out of existence. The pulsing connection between the earth and me briefly faltered, and I became aware of the unnatural racing of my heart and of the fierce pounding in my head. Moisture trickled over my eyelashes and dribbled down my cheeks. Not tears. Blood. I had to break the connection. *Now*. Before it was too late.

Before the sheer force of it tore me apart.

"He's in the ravine." The words were little more than a ragged croak. My throat was raw and scratchy, and speaking hurt. "Directly below this point. I have to rest."

I dropped heavily onto a nearby rock, ignored the pain that slithered up my spine, and drew my knees up to my chest. The connection to the earth snapped as my feet left the ground, and the force of it rebounded so hard, my whole body shook. A tide of weakness threatened to wash me away, and it was all I could do to remain upright. To not collapse into unconsciousness and escape the tear-inducing pain pounding through every part of me.

"Tala, Mac, go," Aiden said. "I'll be with you in a minute."

As the two of them moved off, he squatted in front of me and gently touched my bruised and icy feet. His hands were so warm they felt like a furnace, but maybe that was because I was suddenly so cold.

His gaze searched my face—a heat I could feel rather than see. "What the hell just happened, Liz? Your eyes are bleeding again, and you were glowing."

"I was using the wild magic to find your friend."

"It was more than that," he growled. "I'm well aware of the toll using the wild magic takes on you, but this was something else. It was almost as if you were fading in front of our eyes."

Because I probably was. I swallowed again. It didn't help my throat. "There's always a price to pay when it comes to using magic, Aiden. Wild magic is no different."

"Yes, but this—" He stopped, and sucked in a breath. "This frightened the hell out of me."

Me too. At least it did now that I had a chance to actually think about it. I finally opened my eyes and met his gaze. "I was using the earth's energy as a sort of magical GPS, and that shouldn't be possible. Doing the impossible does tend to take a little more effort."

I said the last part lightly, but he didn't look at all amused.

"I'll be fine, Aiden," I added. "Go do your job. I'll wait here until you can spare someone to take me home."

His gaze searched mine for several seconds, then he rose, stripped off his coat, and wrapped it around my shoulders.

"You forget I'm a werewolf and can smell your utter exhaustion. I've also got a very high detection rate when it comes to bullshit."

A smile tugged at my lips. "Maybe one of these days I'll learn to lie better."

"Or maybe just learn to stop lying." He kissed the top of my head. "Put your shoes and socks back on and warm your damn feet up. I won't be long."

"But the investigation—"

"If it *is* Patrick down there—and I don't for an instant doubt your certainty—then someone will have to inform his parents. I've known them all my life—it wouldn't be right to give someone else the task."

I shifted a hand and briefly gripped his. His sorrow and

grief were now well under control, but tears nevertheless stung my eyes. "I'm so sorry, Aiden."

"So am I." He grimaced. "It's the one part of this job that I absolutely hate. Back soon."

He turned and disappeared into the ravine's darkness. I tugged his coat closer, letting its length fold over my toes rather than going to the effort of pulling on either my socks or boots. I just didn't have the strength right now. Instead, I concentrated on my breathing, drawing in the musky, smoky scent that clung to the coat's inner lining and finding an odd sort of comfort in it. In very many ways, he was my rock, as important to me as Belle.

Belle would not only always be in my life, she was in fact as vital as life to me.

Neither could be truly said about Aiden.

It took a while for the world to stop spinning and my heart rate to calm. The eye-watering ache in my head wasn't showing any sign of abating, but that was no real surprise given I'd pushed to the utter limits of my strength, both physical and magical.

Had I pushed beyond them, what would have happened?

Could it have actually torn me apart?

That had certainly been Gabe's fate, but we'd always presumed it was a combination of the spell he'd been using and the forces he'd unleashed in the process. But what if the spell hadn't been the problem? What if it had been the wild magic itself? Had it formed a connection to the earth's energy via the spell in much the same manner as my inner wild magic?

Gabe had warned that if I kept using the wild magic in extreme ways—such as when I'd propped up Émigré's collapsing ceiling and walls to save Aiden and the others trapped in the basement—it would, each time, take me longer to recover. What he hadn't mentioned was whether it could do to me what it had done to him. But maybe he figured he didn't need to, given my own nebulous certainty at the time that the connection made me more even as it made me less.

Which *did* tie in somewhat to Aiden's comment. Perhaps it wasn't so much an all-consuming explosion of flesh I had to worry about, but rather using so much energy that it consumed every part of me, gradually *dissolving* flesh until I became nothing more than a spirit.

After what had happened here tonight, it did seem a more likely scenario. I guessed the question then was, how far could I safely push its use before that eventuated?

To which Belle would no doubt have replied, *quit trying to test the limit and just live in the safety zone.*

Which was sensible, of course. Problem was, I wasn't entirely sure this reservation would allow sensible.

I grimaced, then carefully brushed a sleeve across my eyes, wiping away the tears and the lingering remnants of blood. My eyes were aching—no doubt the aftereffect of blood vessels erupting—but my vision was at least clearing. I couldn't help wondering if the faster pace of healing was a result of the wild magic or my merges with Katie.

Of course, those merges would never make me a full werewolf, which was a damn shame given it was probably the only thing that would save my relationship with Aiden.

I once again thrust the thought away. *Live for the moment*, I admonished myself sternly. *Enjoy what you have rather than worrying about what might be.*

Which was fine in theory, but I'd spent most of my adult life doing the latter rather than the former. It was damnably hard to switch direction.

I sighed, then carefully bent and picked up my boots. After tugging on my socks, I pulled on my boots, wincing as my bruised and battered feet protested the tight confines. The earth magic might have allowed me to travel without tripping, but it sure as hell hadn't offered any form of protection.

It was a good half hour before Aiden returned, though I smelled him well before I heard or saw him. The faint breeze sweeping up from the valley below not only filled my nostrils with his warm, musky scent, but also the stench of blood and death.

Which only made me wonder exactly how Patrick had died. I might have felt the weight of his body and his blood on the earth, but the manner in which he'd died hadn't been revealed in any of the images I'd been given. Maybe that was because I'd been seeking a location rather than a cause. Even so, it was pretty evident his death had been neither quick nor easy.

Aiden appeared, his face in shadows but his hair glinting silver in the moon's wan light. While most Australian wolf packs were amber-eyed and brown, red, or black in color, the O'Connors were the rarer blue-eyed gray wolves. Their hair—and their coats when in wolf form—ran the full gamut of that color, from being so dark it could be mistaken for brown to the lightest of silvers. Aiden's pack tended toward the brighter end of the scale.

"It *was* Patrick." Though his voice was even, his hands were clenched. Fighting for control. To not react in anger or hurt or pain. To keep all those things distant so he could keep doing his job.

"Bad?"

"Yes." He paused. "You didn't see it in your visions?"

I shook my head. "Just that he was dead and that it hadn't been natural."

"I guess that's something." He drew in a breath and released it slowly. "It actually looks as if he's been attacked by an animal. Teeth and claw marks everywhere."

"Could they have been done after death?"

"Possibly, but I personally doubt it. There's too much blood staining the ground for it to be an after-death assault."

"Does that mean he was attacked by another wolf?"

Aiden scraped a hand across his jaw. "It's a possibility. It certainly wouldn't be the first time we've had wolves go rogue in the reservation."

"But?" There obviously was one there.

"But if it was a rogue, we would have smelled him. Or, at least, seen his tracks on the ground."

"There are ways and means of covering both scent and tracks, though."

"True. You ready to go?"

I nodded and carefully rose. The minute my feet touched the ground, sharp pain hit, and a hiss escaped. Aiden made a low sound in the back of his throat, then swept me up into his arms.

"Aiden, you can't carry me all the way back to your truck."

"Watch me."

"Damn it, I'm too heavy—"

"Rubbish."

"But—"

"Shut up, woman, and enjoy the ride."

A laugh escaped. "I can think of more fitting situations for a comment like that."

"So can I." A smile flirted with his lips, but just as

quickly faded. "Unfortunately, said situations probably won't be happening tonight."

"No." I rested my head against his chest. With his arms holding me so securely and his heart beating so steadily against my ear, I felt unbelievably safe. I always would be with him, no matter what happened between us. "Are rogue werewolves much of a problem? I remember seeing an article once in a South Australian newspaper that mentioned a wolf rampaging through the Barossa Valley, but that was years ago."

"It doesn't happen often, which is just as well given the damage a rogue can do to the human population."

And to werewolves, if Patrick *was* the victim of such an attack. "Why does it happen at all, then?"

He didn't answer immediately, concentrating instead on traversing a tricky bit of slope. By the time we reached the other side and were on even ground again, his breathing was heavier.

"Sometimes it's drugs or alcohol," he said. "While our metabolic rate generally means we process both faster than a human and therefore shouldn't be affected by them, there are always outliers."

Because everyone's metabolic rate was different, even when it came to werewolves. "And the other times?"

"Faulty genetics, though it's more a theory than confirmed fact, as no study has ever been undertaken of the phenomena."

He stepped carefully over a fallen tree and continued up the old roo track. No wonder my feet were all cut and bruised—the track was a stone-filled, debris-littered mess. It was a damn wonder I didn't break something.

"In general," he continued, "it's thought that in some wolves, there's a fault in the DNA adaption that allows us to heal wounds as we switch from one shape to another. Somehow, at some point, that fault is flicked from inactive to active, and instead of repairing the body, it begins to attack it. This inevitably leads to madness."

"And is possibly the basis for all the werewolf legends?"

"Yes. The changes that make them mad also force them into a half-human, half-wolf hybrid with almost super-human strength."

I shivered at the thought. "Do you think we do have one?"

"Until Ciara does the autopsy, we won't know for sure. But I hope not."

So did I. While I might have wanted an end to super-natural nasties, a homegrown mad half wolf definitely didn't sound as if it'd be much of an improvement.

"What else could it have been, though?"

He briefly glanced down at me, something I felt more than saw. "You tell me. You're the one with the supernatural radar."

A smile tugged at my lips. "I think the radar's currently offline. I certainly didn't feel anything that makes me suspect we've another demon or occult beastie on the reservation."

He grunted. "Let's just hope it remains that way."

We finally reached the camping area. Aiden placed me down, then opened the truck's door and helped me into the cabin. The drive home was a quiet one. I suspected his mind was on the grim news he'd soon have to deliver, and I was just too damn tired to muster any attempt at conversation.

It took us just on half an hour to reach Argyle. His house lay at the far end of a six-unit complex built close to the sandy shoreline of the vast Argyle Lake. It was a two-story, cedar-clad building with a wall of glass that over-looked the water. Most of the big trees that surrounded it were deciduous, which meant it was protected from the worst of the summer heat but the winter light could shine through.

Aiden stopped in front, then climbed out and ran over to the door to open it. Then he came back for me, picking me up and carrying me inside despite my protests.

The house's layout was pretty basic—this level was a long room divided by the open wooden staircase. In the front half there was an old-fashioned fireplace, around which sat a C-shaped, hugely comfortable leather sofa. The TV—a monster of a thing—was tucked into the corner between the fireplace and the glass wall. The kitchen–diner lay on the other side of the staircase, and there were now a lot more kitchen utensils and cooking paraphernalia in the drawers and on the benches than there had been before I'd moved in. It was the only real alteration I'd made to the place. However much Aiden might deny it, we both knew I was only a temporary rather than a permanent resident in his home and, as such, I didn't feel it was right to redecorate. But long term or short, there was no way known I was going to put up with the meager scraps he laughingly called his cooking and baking ware.

The fire had gone out over the course of the day, but warmth still lingered in the big room. He walked across to the stairs and carried me up. There were two bedrooms up here, each with their own en suite. Ours was the one with the long view over the water and a balcony on which to sit. Or, on the odd occasion, do something far more exciting —*not* that there'd be much of that going on now that winter was almost upon us.

"Shower or bed?" he said, pausing in the middle of the room.

"I believe a shower might be in order."

"I believe you're right."

I lightly slapped the muscular arm holding me so tenderly. "I'm not the only one who smells right now, Ranger."

"Yes, but mine is good honest sweat. Yours is mingled with blood and pain."

"I didn't know pain had a smell."

"Then now you do." He placed me down carefully, but kept hold of my arm until I was balanced. My feet immediately started their protests again, and though I managed to curtail the instinctive gasp of pain, he obviously sensed it. "Will you be all right? Or do you want some help to undress and shower?"

"Go do what you have to do." I leaned forward and kissed him tenderly. "I'll be fine."

"You keep making that statement. One of these days, I might actually believe you." He cupped my cheek, his smile sweet and eyes full of gentle amusement. "I'm not sure what time I'll be home, so don't wait up for me."

"I don't think I could even if I wanted to."

Concern flickered through his eyes, but he didn't say anything. He simply brushed a gentle kiss across my lips, then turned and left. I waited until his truck had reversed out and sped away, then slowly stripped off. In the bathroom's bright light, my feet looked even worse than they felt. Aside from the multiple minor cuts and bruises, there was a deep puncture wound in my right heel and a colorful bruise forming around the arch of my left foot. Unless Katie's werewolf capacity to fast heal made an unexpected overnight appearance, there was no way I'd be able to waitress tomorrow. I dragged out my phone and made a call to Celia—who was the niece of our regular waitress, Penny, and who now worked a permanent three days a week for us —to ask if she could fill in for me tomorrow.

With that done, I turned on the water and stepped in, letting the steaming heat wash away at least some of the aches and pain. It didn't do a lot for my feet, however. I rubbed antiseptic all over them, pulled on some socks to stop said antiseptic getting all over the sheets, then climbed into bed. I was asleep almost as soon as my head hit the pillow.

Aiden wasn't beside me when I woke the next morning, though the dent in the pillow suggested he'd at least made it home last night. I stretched to ease the muscle kinks, winced as my feet protested the movement, and then grabbed my phone to check the time. It was barely six, which surprised me. Given the toll using the wild magic generally took on my strength, I'd been expecting to sleep much later.

I tentatively reached out for Belle, but was stopped by a soft barrier of magic. It meant she was in her room and still asleep. I'd placed a ton of spells around both bedrooms when we'd first moved in—not so much to keep evil out, but to give her some mental space from the constant barrage of my thoughts. She might be my familiar, but she didn't need to be on call twenty-four seven. *That* would likely drive even the strongest person insane.

Of course, I *could* push past the barrier if I absolutely had to, but it wasn't necessary in this particular case. I might not be able to waitress but I could still work, even if I did so propped up on a stool in either the kitchen or behind the serving counter.

I flicked off the blankets, sat up, and then carefully pulled off my socks to inspect my feet. Surprisingly, many of the smaller cuts *had* healed, but the puncture wound remained sore and ugly-looking, and the big bruise around the arch of my left foot was now even more colorful. I put my socks back on, then carefully rose. Putting any sort of weight on my feet hurt, but not as badly as I'd feared. I hobbled over to the wardrobe, got dressed, and then carefully negotiated the stairs.

Aiden wasn't in the kitchen, and his truck wasn't in its usual position out front. No real surprise there. While he technically wasn't rostered on until later in the day, he'd always considered it his duty to be present during any major investigation. He *had* left me a note, however: *Early meeting with Ciara. Will see you tonight. Dinner is on me.*

Such a romantic, I thought with a wry smile.

I shoved a couple of crumpets into the toaster then made a coffee to go. Once I'd smeared the crumpets with Vegemite and then melted cheese over the top of them—the best way to eat crumpets, in my opinion—I slung my backpack over my shoulder, then grabbed my keys, coat, and breakfast, and headed out.

A few days ago, I'd bought a little yellow-and-black Suzuki Swift to tootle back and forth from the café to Aiden's. While the council had replaced the SUV we'd destroyed, it cost an arm and a leg to run, so we used it mainly for business purposes. Me having the Suzi also meant Belle could use the SUV should she need it.

Aiden wasn't entirely impressed with the car—more because of the bright color, I suspected—but jumping into it always made me smile. And there were definitely some days in this damn reservation when that sort of boost was needed.

I reversed out and, once on the main highway, turned the music up loud. It took just over half an hour to reach

Castle Rock, and Belle was awake and cheerily singing in the kitchen by the time I hobbled in.

"Sounds like a good time was had last night." I shoved my bag under the counter and then headed into the kitchen.

"The movie was average, but we headed over to that new pub in—" She stopped abruptly. "What the hell did you do? Why are you limping?"

I wrinkled my nose. "I bruised my left foot and cut my right."

"And how did you manage that?"

"Long story short, running barefoot through a forest." I snagged a carrot from the pile she was cutting and happily munched on it.

"That's what I get for staying out of your thoughts," she muttered. "Damn it, woman—"

"I'm fine, and there's nothing you could have done to help. I will be limited in what I can do today, however." I glanced at my watch. "Celia's coming in at eight to help out."

"Ah. Good." She scraped the carrot sticks into a metal container. "Did you find the kid?"

"No. We did, however, find a dead and mutilated man."

"How the hell did we go from a lost kid to a murdered man?" She held up a hand. "Don't answer that. It's this place again."

Indeed. "There's evidence of an animal attack, but until Ciara's finished her examination, we won't know for sure."

"So the dead man is human?"

"Wolf."

"I can't imagine an ordinary animal getting the better of a werewolf."

"Aiden thought it might be the result of a rogue wolf attack. Apparently it's happened in the past." I propped my butt against the stove to take the weight off my bruised foot. Which, of course, only made the punctured foot protest. "So, the pub? Details are required."

She grinned. "It's the old Walker Street Pub. The new owners have turned it into a funky ale bar with live music. And Monty, I have to say, is a fabulous dancer."

"So a good time was had?"

"Indeed."

Given how firmly her thoughts were currently shut down, I was thinking a *very* good time was had. "So, when's the first official date?"

She rolled her eyes. "Never. And you promised to drop the subject."

I grinned. "Does that mean you're going to roll into an actual relationship with the man without ever admitting it?"

"I'm not dumb enough to answer *that* particular question."

"Monty will be very disappointed if his grand plans never get an airing, you know."

"He'll get over it. You want to grab a knife and start helping?"

"Grab me a stool, and I will."

She did so, and for the next half hour we finished the remaining bits of prep for the day. Our crew came in just before eight, and we had a fairly steady flow of customers for the rest of the day. While I hadn't been expecting Aiden to make an appearance, I was rather surprised Monty didn't —his afternoon coffee and cake breaks had become something of a ritual. But he *was* the reservation witch, and we did have a dead body on our hands.

Not knowing what was happening with that investigation was frustrating. I'd become rather accustomed to helping out with—or at least discussing—investigations when they were related to magic or the supernatural, and there was a large part of me that hated being out of the loop.

The café was closed and we were on the final stages of cleaning up when the bell above the front door rang cheerfully and Monty stepped through. He was the same height as Belle and very well built, with crimson hair that gleamed like dark fire in the late sunlight streaming through the windows and features that were easy enough on the eye.

"If you want coffee, you'll have to settle for instant," I said. "I've just cleaned down the machine."

"That's fine, but I'm not specifically here for that."

I raised an eyebrow at the odd note of excitement in his voice. "Then what are you here for?"

"I brought a present for Belle."

He stepped to one side and opened the door wider. A woman stepped past him. Shock coiled through me, but was swiftly followed by utter happiness.

She was tall and slender, with dark skin and silver eyes. A thick strip of white now dominated the front section of her long black hair, and her beautiful face was more lined than I remembered.

But her smile was as warm and welcoming as ever.

Ava Sarr.

Belle's mom.

CHAPTER THREE

There was a loud crash in the kitchen, followed by a thick wave of disbelief and joy. A heartbeat later, Belle appeared, gripping the kitchen doorframe tightly with one hand, as if to keep herself upright. Or to stop her rushing forward only to find disappointment.

"Mom?" It was little more than an incredulous whisper. After all these years of desperately wishing she could see her mother just one more time, she now feared taking the evidence standing in front of her at face value.

"Yes, my darling girl, it's me." Ava's voice, like Belle's, was tremulous.

A sob escaped Belle's lips, then she flew across the room and into her mother's arms. For several minutes, the two of them just stood there, arms wrapped tightly around each other and sobbing onto each other's shoulders.

Monty moved around them and walked over to me. He looked decidedly pleased with himself.

"I take it this was your doing?"

He nodded. "We've been making arrangements for the

last week, but I only got confirmation of her flight details last night."

"Which was why you were late to pick Belle up," I guessed. "She wasn't happy about that, you know."

He grinned. "So she said, but it was totally worth a few minutes of grief."

"How the hell did you manage to keep it a secret from her?"

He airily waved a hand. "Ways and means."

"In other words, you're not telling in case you have to use the method again."

"Precisely."

I snorted. "I take it you picked Ava up from the airport?"

He nodded and leaned against the counter. "I hope you don't mind, but I said she'd be able to stay in your room now that you're over at Aiden's."

"Good idea." It'd give them more time together, if nothing else. "Does this mean you haven't yet gotten the autopsy results from last night's murder?"

"Yes, but only because they weren't ready this morning." He glanced at his watch. "I'm actually due over at the morgue—would you like to come along?"

My eyebrows rose. "Why the sudden willingness to share your job?"

"Have I ever been unwilling to share it? Besides, as the saying goes, more hands, lighter work."

"I'm thinking *that* doesn't apply in this particular case. You're the reservation witch, not me."

"Officially yes, but we both know that means jack-squat to the reservation's magic. I've very sensibly come to the conclusion that when there's the possibility of a death via supernatural means, you might as well be included from the get-go. I'm appointing you my deputy."

I snorted. "And you don't have to get clearance from Canberra for this? Or is it very much an 'off the books' and unpaid position?"

He slapped a hand against his chest. "You do me great injustice by thinking I'd stoop that low."

I merely raised an eyebrow. He grinned and added, "In other words, no. I approached both the High Witch Council *and* the reservation's council, telling them that—given the supernatural shit that keeps happening here—an assistant position was needed and that *you* had to fill it—"

"What?" Alarm slithered through me—although really, the cat was well and truly out of the bag when it came to my ability to use the wild magic. "What reason did you give them?"

"Not the wild magic, though the High Witch Council will undoubtedly be aware of your ability to interact with it now, thanks to your father. I simply said it was your psychic skills that had saved this reservation on numerous occasions now and it's about time you received an official status *and* remuneration for the amount of time you're away from your café."

"And did they all laugh hysterically at the prospect?"

He smiled. "No. They actually agreed it would be a good move. You're to be officially employed on a part-time basis as of last night. I have a heap of forms for you to fill in to make it official, but pay will be backdated."

"Huh," I said, surprised. Although, in truth, I shouldn't have been, given my dreams and premonitions had long ago warned that I would become reservation witch. They just didn't predict this variation. "Well, I'm not going to say no, because I absolutely *hated* being left out of the loop."

He laughed. "I did get that impression on the few occasions you weren't directly involved in investigations."

"And what about Belle? I mean, shouldn't she be getting consultant fees or something, given how often she helps out with ghosts and the like?"

"To be honest, I hadn't thought about it, but yeah, good idea. I'll see what I can do. Ready to go?"

I nodded and glanced at Ava and Belle. "I don't think we're going to get much sense out of either of them for a while, anyway."

"I think you might be right."

I slid off the stool, slung my purse over my shoulder, and then hobbled around the counter.

"I heard about your feet," he said. "From Aiden's description, I expected you to be on crutches."

"Aiden exaggerates."

"Our ranger does have his faults, but I wouldn't have said exaggeration was one of them." He studied me for a moment. "The wild magic accelerated the healing, didn't it?"

I shrugged. I couldn't admit that it was my merges with Katie's soul that were enhancing not only my sight and olfactory sense, but also my body's ability to heal. He still didn't know about the second wellspring, and I intended to keep it that way for as long as possible. "Who can really say?"

It was an answer that didn't please him, if his expression was anything to go by. "The sooner that fucking book gets here, the better."

"With that, I agree. I'd rather read about any problems that could arise from fusing with the wild magic than discover them the hard way."

I followed him across the room, but when I neared Ava

and Belle, Ava caught my arm and dragged me into their huddle.

"It's so good to see you again, Lizzie dearest. You have no idea how much I've missed you." Though Ava's voice was soft, it was filled with such emotion that tears stung my eyes. God, how I wished my own mother was capable of emoting even *half* as much. "Thank you for taking such good care of my baby girl."

I returned her hug fiercely. "I missed you too, but I'm afraid you've got that last part the wrong way around. I wouldn't be here if not for Belle."

Her arm briefly tightened. "We've all got so much to catch up on—"

"Yes, and you don't need me or Monty hanging about for the initial bit." I dropped a kiss on her wet cheek. "We'll see you both in a few hours."

Thank you, thank you, thank you. It was a litany that washed through my mind, though Belle was speaking to Monty rather than me. *I can never repay you for this.*

"I don't need repayment, Belle," he answered softly. "I just wanted to see you happy."

I am. Though how the hell you managed to keep this from me—

"Trade secret," he said. "Now, stop speaking to me and start catching up with your mom. Lizzie, you coming?"

"Absolutely."

I kissed both women, then followed him out the door. He'd parked directly out the front, in the no-standing zone, and must have seen my expression because he grinned unrepentantly. "It says 'no standing except for deliveries.' I was delivering."

I laughed and climbed into his old Ford. "When on

earth are you going to start using your Mustang rather than this old rattletrap?"

"Considering the condition of many roads in this reservation, absolutely never. She's a cruiser; a dirt road and her tires will never meet."

"The rattletrap isn't going to be great on a lot of those roads either."

"True." He did a U-turn and headed toward the hospital, where the morgue was situated. "But given the record this place has of destroying cars, the rattletrap is a mighty good move—especially given you've already destroyed two SUVs, and both Aiden and Ashworth lost their trucks. It's doubtful there'll be an endless supply of cash for new cars coming from the council's coffers, even in a reservation as rich as this one."

He did have a point. I crossed mental fingers that we didn't lose another SUV, let alone my little Suzi. I might not have had her for very long, but I was already attached.

It didn't take us long to get across to the hospital. Monty parked out the front of the morgue—which had only recently reopened after a spell bomb had torn it apart—and then led the way inside.

The blonde receptionist looked up with a smile. "They're waiting for you in morgue one."

"Thanks, Betty." Monty immediately headed left.

We were buzzed through the door and then walked down a corridor to a door at the far end. Monty opened it and ushered me inside. The smell of antiseptic and death hit so strongly, it felt like it was coating the back of my throat. I blinked and did my best to ignore it.

Aiden and Ciara were examining a body on the middle table of the three in the room, but glanced up as we walked over.

"Lizzie," Ciara said. "It's lovely to see you, but it's also somewhat surprising."

"She's now officially my deputy, on a part-time basis, so expect her presence more often."

Aiden raised his eyebrows. "When did this happen?"

"Agreement came through yesterday—"

"I wasn't informed—"

"Because it's not a ranger decision." Monty stopped beside Ciara. "We got a cause of death yet?"

"Initial blood and tox results only, but there are no indications that he'd been drugged or drunk."

"Which is what we expected," Aiden added.

He did *not* look happy, which no doubt meant he and I would be having a "discussion" later about my new position. I loved the damn man, but there were times when his protective tendencies got tedious.

I did my best to ignore the radiating annoyance and studied Patrick's body. He lay in three pieces, his left arm and the opposite leg having been torn from his body. "The teeth marks and bruising would seem to indicate he was still alive when he was torn apart."

Amusement touched Ciara's expression. "Are you now gunning for the position of coroner's assistant?"

"Hardly, especially given the smell in this place. I'm not entirely sure how you stand it all the time."

"You get used to it." She studied me speculatively. "And it shouldn't be all that noticeable to a human nose."

"I'm not human, per se. I'm a wild-magic-enhanced witch."

"True." She motioned to several bite marks on the upper portion of his attached thigh. "I've sent images to a forensic odontologist for a second opinion, but I believe these are caused by human teeth rather than wolf or anything else."

"So, does that mean we're *not* dealing with a rogue werewolf?" Monty asked.

"Not necessarily," Aiden said. "It would depend on what stage of degradation he or she is at. It's possible the body has mutated but not yet the facial structure."

"Which, aside from being an unpleasant situation," Ciara said, "would tip the rogue further into madness. Human teeth are not designed to rip fresh flesh, and his morphing state wouldn't make it viable to interact or even remain with his pack."

"So he or she *is* from one of our packs?" Monty said.

Aiden shook his head. "We'd have been informed at the first sign of it happening. The reservation relies too heavily on tourism now to risk a rogue on the loose."

"How do you explain the tears across his stomach?" I said. "They don't look clean enough to be knife wounds—unless, of course, a serrated knife was used. And don't give me that look, Ciara—I'm a cook. Knives are part of my business."

She smiled. "That is where things get interesting. They appear to be the result of both claws and fangs."

"So, a different attacker to whoever caused the bites on the legs and arms?" Monty asked.

"Unknown, as the saliva results are inconclusive."

I frowned. "Wolves don't use claws to attack, and canines would have resulted in a different type of wound," I said. "So wouldn't that confirm there *are* two attackers?"

Aiden nodded. "Unless the stomach wounds were inflicted after the initial attack."

"But," Ciara said, "a wolf the size of Patrick should have been able to repel—or at least curtail—such an attack."

"But rogues have almost supernatural strength, don't they?" Monty asked.

She nodded. "But if he was morphing between forms, it would have addled his—or her—senses. That would have given Patrick the advantage."

"Then there's the whole lack of scent or print factor," Aiden said. "I know there're means of disguising both, but we did a wide search and weren't able to pick anything up."

Monty frowned. "Not even the kid Patrick said he'd heard?"

"No—and it's that fact that makes me think something else might be going on. Patrick wouldn't have made a false report, so even if the kid somehow made it home, we should have found their scent in the wider searches, at least."

Monty glanced at me. "You didn't feel anything to suggest we're dealing with a supernatural or demonic entity?"

"No, but I didn't get down to the murder site, either."

"Ah well, maybe we'd better head across and check it out."

I wrinkled my nose. "As much as I'd love to do just that, my feet aren't in any condition to take another long hike. Besides, there wouldn't be much left in the way of magical clues now given how much time has passed, surely?"

"Probably not, but it's still worth checking." He frowned. "If we *are* dealing with some sort of supernatural entity, it might be worth doing a search through your library."

Meaning the supernatural and spell library Belle had inherited from her grandmother. "I think we're probably going to need a bit more information than simply 'an entity that mimics a kid crying' to have any hope of finding anything, but I can look."

"Good." His gaze moved to Aiden. "I'll need someone to take me out there, Ranger."

"I will." Aiden glanced at his sister. "You'll send the full report as soon as it's available?"

"As ever," she said with a smile.

"Thanks." Aiden pressed a hand lightly to my spine and gently ushered me out after Monty. I breathed deeply once we were all outside, but it didn't do a whole lot to erase the taste of death and antiseptic. Sharper senses, I thought sourly, weren't everything they were cracked up to be.

"Do you mind driving Liz back to the café?" Monty said. "I'll need to zip home and grab some things."

Aiden nodded. "I'll meet you there, if you like. Your car wouldn't take the roads around Fryer's Point too well anyway."

"His car," I said, voice severe but a smile twitching my lips, "would disintegrate on those damn roads."

Monty laughed, jumped into his car, and headed off.

"He seems in an extraordinarily good mood today," Aiden commented, helping me into his truck.

"Good doesn't even begin to describe his mood. He arranged for Belle's mom to come visit and somehow managed to keep the whole thing from Belle."

"Now *that* is an impressive achievement." He turned the truck around and headed for the café.

"I know, right?" I shifted in my seat to study him. "So, what were you going to tell me last night before that phone call interrupted?"

He cast me a wry look. "We'll be outside your café in a minute—that's hardly enough time to go into any sort of detail—"

"Why is detail needed?"

He hesitated. "Because it involves wolf politics, my mother, and the fact she's my alpha."

"Oh, that's never a good combination."

"No." A smile twisted his lips. "I'll explain later tonight. Promise."

"*If* you don't get sidetracked by whatever Monty discovers up on the ridge and have to work late."

"I won't." He pulled up in front of our café.

I sighed, undid my seat belt, then leaned across and kissed him, long and lingering. "Don't be late with dinner, or I'll get grouchy."

He laughed softly. "I've swapped shifts with Mac, so I should be home by seven."

"Excellent."

I kissed him again, then grabbed my purse and climbed out. Once he'd driven off, I hobbled down the lane that ran down the side of our café to the parking area at the rear. As much as I wanted to know what had happened to my "other" family in the years since we'd fled, Belle needed time alone with her mom.

I jumped into the Suzi, reversed her out, and then headed over to the storage facility where we kept the majority of the books. It was situated a little outside Castle Rock, behind a busy industrial estate. We'd taken one of their "household" storage sections—the largest available—and layered it with so many different spells that even a gnat wasn't getting through. We'd also had a secondary fire- and flood-proof room built inside our unit, just to be doubly safe. While floods generally weren't a problem in this area, fires could be, and the storage facility sat on the edge of what amounted to a wilderness area along an old train line.

I shoved my card into the reader to open the gates and then drove to the end of the long building on the left. Our unit was the very last one. I parked in front of the roller door, then climbed out and glanced around. No one else was here, and there were no lights on in the office—which sat at the rear of the block, in between the two storage buildings, enabling them to see who was coming and going. I glanced at my watch; it was close to five thirty, so that wasn't unexpected, and it wasn't as if the office was manned full-time anyway.

But for some damn reason, instinct stirred. Something was wrong—though as usual, said instinct wasn't supplying any information as to what.

I pocketed my keys and walked over to the office. No one answered my knock, and a quick peer through the windows revealed there was no one inside and nothing out of place.

I frowned and headed back to our storage unit. It was then I noticed the roller door's lock had been jimmied, and the thick padlock the facility's owner insisted we use as additional security was sitting on the concrete in front of the door rather than being locked in place.

My gaze dropped to the bottom of the door; the edge had been bent upwards in a couple of places.

Someone had tried to get inside.

I knelt and carefully ran my hand across the door's bottom edge. Energy caressed my fingers, which meant the spells remained active, and that was a huge relief. They were undoubtedly the reason the would-be thieves hadn't succeeded. Roller doors—even locked ones—were easy enough to get into if you knew how. I *didn't*, but I'd certainly seen plenty of newspaper articles warning those in high-crime-rate areas about it.

I rose and took several steps back to study the roofline. There was no evidence the thieves had tried to get in from up top, so I turned and walked around to the rear of the unit. Again, there was nothing to suggest they'd tried to get in there, either, which was odd given there was only one camera watching the six-foot-wide strip of land between the razor-wire topped chain wire fence and the building. It would have been the easiest camera to disable, but from where I was standing, there was no evidence it had been tampered with in any way.

There was also no evidence that the would-be thieves had gained access into the storage yard through the fence—the razor wire might have meant they couldn't have climbed it, but the right wire cutter would have gotten through the fence easily enough.

I walked back to the front of our unit and studied the forecourt area again. There were multiple cameras in this area, and at least two of them were trained on our unit—one of the reasons we'd chosen it. They would have captured the persons behind the attempted break-in, so why weren't we notified?

I had no idea, but I very much intended to find out. I grabbed the phone out of my purse and quickly rang the after-hours number.

Harry, the owner and manager, answered on the third ring. "Castle Rock Ultimate Storage," he said. "How may I help you?"

"Harry, it's Lizzie Grace. I just arrived at my storage unit and discovered someone has tried to break in. Did you notice anything on the cameras over the last couple of nights?"

"No—anything taken?" His voice was sharp.

"No, because they didn't get in."

"At least that's something. I'll be there in five—I'll have to check the other units, then look at the day's recording."

"Do you want me to call the rangers?"

He hesitated. "Let's wait and see if any of the other units have been hit."

"Shall I do a walk around while I'm waiting for you to arrive?"

"Probably best not to, just in case you foul any evidence if there have been other break-ins."

I resisted the urge to point out that I probably knew more about preserving evidence than he ever would, given who I was dating and how often I'd worked with the rangers, but maybe he was one of the rare few in this reservation who didn't actually know about me and Aiden.

"I'll be in my unit if you need to speak to me, then," I said, and hung up.

After shoving my phone into my pocket, I locked my car, then keyed open the roller door and lifted it up. The threads of magic protecting the contents of the unit were a swirling river of silver, gold, and a hint of red—which was the anti-fire spell we'd recently woven in. They reacted as I stepped inside, briefly resisting my presence before acknowledging and allowing me in. The inner space was dominated almost entirely by a secondary unit. It had been built on a metal platform one foot off the ground, and there was a three-foot gap between its walls and the main unit's. Though there was a door, there was no handle or lock. Like the storage units hidden behind the bookcase in our reading room, the door here used a magical version of a fingerprint scanner—one that would respond to only Belle and me.

I pressed my hand against the middle of the door. Energy caressed across my skin, then the door softly clicked open. I pushed it wider and stepped inside. Bookcases lined three walls and were filled to the brim with books of all ages and sizes. Belle might not have inherited all of her grandmother's books, but she'd certainly gotten a good percentage of them. In the center of the room was a small wooden table on which another dozen books sat—Nell's handwritten index system. Unfortunately, she'd had a very haphazard method of recording what information lay where, which made it somewhat difficult to find things. We were currently in the process of not only converting all the books to an electronic format—a long and somewhat laborious process—but also trying to make sense of the indexes.

Of course, making things easier to find wasn't the only reason for the conversion. It also gave us a backup in case the High Witch Council ever discovered we had the majority of Nell's library—which should, for all intents and purposes, have been gifted to the National Library in Canberra on her death.

Belle had initially asked a techie friend of hers to help with the conversion process, but after some serious misgivings over just how interested he was becoming in the old books, she'd decided we'd be better off doing it ourselves. And while it *was* undoubtedly safer, it would also now take a whole lot longer.

I sat on the table, crossed my legs, and then pulled the top index onto my knees. I was barely halfway through when I heard the gates open; a few seconds later, Harry's red four-wheel drive drove past and stopped outside the office. I carefully placed the index down and headed out of the inner unit, ensuring the door was locked before walking over.

"Hey, Lizzie," he said. He was a thin, rather dapper-looking man in his mid-fifties. "Sorry about this. Not sure why the alarms wouldn't have gone off—the sensors are set to trip if there's an un-carded entry."

I swung around and walked beside him as he headed for

my unit. "Maybe whoever did this managed to get hold of a card."

"I wouldn't have thought so, given it's in the contract that we be notified immediately if a card goes missing. Otherwise, our responsibility for damages is voided."

I was betting a lot of renters here didn't actually read the fine print. "The fence behind this building wasn't cut; I did check that."

He grunted and pulled down the roller door, studying the bent sections intently for a few minutes. "Certainly looks as if a pry bar has been used, and that suggests they didn't really know what they were doing. A determined thief could have gotten through easy enough."

A statement that echoed my earlier thoughts, and one I'm betting he didn't say too often. The security in this place was top-notch, but I knew for a fact the old couple who rented the smaller unit next to ours believed the roller door and the attached padlock made the unit impregnable. I doubted they'd be the only renters here thinking that.

"Maybe they were disturbed, which is why they didn't get through." Harry was well aware I was a witch, but he had no idea how extensive our protections were. Few did, in fact.

"Maybe." His expression suggested he didn't think so. "I'd better check the rest of them."

I tagged along. It turned out that three other units had been hit—their padlocks cut and their doors unsuccessfully jimmied.

"It's a rather random pattern of attack, isn't it?" I commented.

"Yes, which means it's probably the kids again." He shook his head. "I'm going to kill the little bastards when I catch them."

I raised my eyebrows. "Kids?"

He grimaced. "Yeah. There's a gang of teenagers that have been hitting the businesses around these parts for the last few weeks. They broke into next door a few days ago."

"The rangers haven't been able to track them?"

"They wear head-to-foot protective gear, apparently. Cunning little bastards."

"Who obviously aren't werewolves, as they surely wouldn't need to use a pry bar on the door."

A smile tugged at his lips, lending warmth to his otherwise stern features. "That is indeed true. I'll head up and check the cameras, but if it follows the same pattern as the other locations they've hit, I won't find anything."

"If you do, can you let me know?"

"Sure, but why?"

I shrugged. "Just curious."

He nodded and headed for the office. I returned to our unit and continued reading the index. I was about to pack up and leave when, on the second-to-last page, I found the slightest mention of a mischievous ghost that used the crying of a child to make travelers get lost.

I doubted what we were dealing with here was an actual ghost, but it was at least a start. Besides, Nell had a habit of making side notes about similar entities in the margins.

It only took a few minutes to find the book in question. I locked up both units, then walked over to the office.

Harry glanced up, his face lit by the small computer screen. "Nothing untoward as yet, but I've hours of tape to check yet."

I nodded. "Just in case you report it to the rangers, I left the cut lock on the ground. If we are dealing with kids, there might be prints."

"They haven't been that daft in their other break-ins, but I guess there's always a first time. Thanks."

I nodded and headed out. Dusk had given way to night, and the stars were gloriously bright, which meant it was going to be bitterly cold. Hopefully, I could get the fire alight when I got home—though it was an art I hadn't yet really mastered. As much as I loved his house *and* log fires, I couldn't help wishing he had central heating or even one of those wall gas units. But his body ran a lot hotter than mine, and he didn't see the necessity of having any other means of heating. Which meant that unless we kept the fire going constantly, the bedrooms tended to be icy on cold nights.

Of course, that wasn't so much of a problem when you were lying in bed next to a man who burned hot. It was a different matter entirely when it came to a middle of the night pee break.

I pulled into my parking spot at Aiden's house, then grabbed the book and my purse and headed in, dropping everything onto the coffee table before kneeling in front of the fire. The gods of warmth were obviously feeling kindly toward me tonight, because the kindling caught straight away, and I soon had the fire roaring. I held my hands in front of it for a few seconds to warm them up, then headed upstairs for a quick shower.

I was drying off when I heard his truck pull up. I wrapped the towel around my body, shoved on my slippers, and hobbled down—though it had to be said, the pain in my feet was nowhere near as bad as it had been this morning.

His gaze slid slowly down my length and came up heated. "I do love it when you greet me in a mostly naked state."

"It was too damn cold upstairs to risk greeting you in a wholly naked state. Things would have frozen and fallen off." I rose on my toes and dropped a kiss on his luscious lips. "What did you bring for dinner?"

He raised an eyebrow. "You can't smell it?"

"All I can smell is you. You smell good, by the way."

He chuckled softly. "I decided on Chinese, so we have beef in black bean sauce, lemon chicken, Mongolian lamb, and special fried rice."

"And dessert?"

"Was an extremely difficult decision, given you and Belle make the best cakes ever. I settled on burned fig and chunky caramel ice cream, with caramel and almond dark chocolate crisps as backup if you decided it was too cold for ice cream."

"A very good selection all round—especially since the chocolate can be added to the ice cream."

The smile that twitched his lips was decidedly cheeky. "I do aim to please—and in more ways than just in the bedroom."

"To which I will say, some of your best work is actually done *out* of the bedroom. In the shower, for instance. Or the balcony, or the rug in front of the fire, etcetera, etcetera."

He chuckled. "Can't have you getting bored on me now, can I?"

"No danger of that, Ranger."

I followed him across to the kitchen and got out the plates and cutlery while he opened all the containers. "Did Monty find anything helpful down in the ravine?"

"Nothing to suggest there was a supernatural entity involved." He picked up a plate and began to fill it. "But as you said, that was to be expected given the time that had passed. What's the book on the table?"

"It's one of Nell's—according to the index, it has some mentions of a supernatural being that uses crying as a lure." I shrugged. "Worth a shot, even if it comes to nothing."

He grunted and began filling his plate. "So when, exactly, did you learn Monty had received permission for you to become his deputy?"

"About ten minutes before you did." I regarded him steadily. "I wouldn't keep something like that secret, Aiden."

His gaze rose to mine and, after a second or two, he nodded. Annoyance stirred. "You keep saying that I need to trust you more, but that *is* a two-way street, you know."

"Yes. Old habits—"

"Are no excuse."

"Indeed. I vow to try harder."

"Good."

It was primly said, and his smile broke loose again. "Shall we retreat to the fire? You're in danger of being overrun by goose bumps if we stand here much longer."

"If you had gas heating in this place, it wouldn't be so much of a problem."

"Winter only lasts three months, and the fire is on twenty-four seven during that period. You won't freeze, trust me."

"Winter may only last three months," I said, voice dry, "but the wintery conditions certainly don't. Remember, Castle Rock isn't all that far away from Ballarat, one of the coldest spots in Victoria outside the Alps."

He grinned. "Then I shall endeavor to keep you toasty warm at all times."

I rolled my eyes, then sat next to him on the well-padded sofa, one leg tucked underneath me. It was a position that had the towel riding up my thigh, but I didn't really care given the heat now coming from the fire. And he certainly didn't, if his appreciative expression was anything to go by.

We ate our meal and chatted easily about our day—he updated me on the various investigations, and I made him chuckle with the many weird snippets of conversation I'd overheard in the café. Dessert had been consumed and we'd moved on to coffee when I finally asked the question that had been niggling all day.

"So, this important bit of news you needed to impart yesterday and have been avoiding ever since. Give, Ranger."

He sighed, placed his coffee on the table, and then shifted position to fully face me. His expression was serious, and my stomach did its usual acrobatic dance.

"Oh, this is looking ominous," I added. "Hang on while I put my coffee down in preparation."

"It's not that bad. Really."

A wry smile tugged at my lips. "Your expression and body language say otherwise, Ranger."

"Maybe I should have said, it's not that bad for you. Or me, really, for that matter."

A statement that only had my stomach churning harder, because the only reason he'd have *any* sort of problem with his pack would be because of me.

"Quit avoiding the issue and tell me."

"Fine." His voice was flat, but a fuse of anger and determination flared in his eyes. "I finally gave my mother an ultimatum a few days ago—either you're included in my birthday celebrations or I won't be there."

CHAPTER FOUR

D isbelief, joy, hope, and fear all tumbled through me,
constricting my throat and making it hard to breathe.
That he was doing this for me was big—and, in the end, very
dangerous, as it had the possibility of jeopardizing his position within the pack hierarchy. Humans were banned from
pack compounds; the one time I *had* entered, it was via a
special dispensation to aid Jeni, the werewolf who'd
witnessed Byron being torn apart by an Empusae. No
matter how long he and I were together—hell, even if by
some miraculous event we had kids together—I would never
be a participant in his life or his family there.

And family was *everything* to a werewolf. He risked
destroying his future for the sake of his present, and that
was something I just couldn't allow.

"Aiden, you can't—"

He gently pressed a finger against my lips. "I know
what you're going to say, and you're wrong. This is nothing
to do with my position in the pack, but rather my mother's
personal dislike for my partner and her determination to get
rid of said partner by fair means or foul."

I pulled away from his gentle touch, my silly heart singing over the fact he hadn't added the "current" modifier. "Yes, but she's not just your mother. She's your pack alpha, and you're bound to obey."

A smile tugged at his lips. "Only to a point—and only when my actions endanger the pack's safety. Neither is the case here."

"That doesn't mean there won't be repercussions for standing your ground on a matter as trivial as this."

His expression darkened as he grabbed my hands and shook them a little. "*We* are not trivial. This relationship is *not* trivial."

Damn it, don't do this to me. Don't make me hope when the words mean nothing long term. "You know what I meant, Aiden."

"Yes, and I don't care about a future that may or may not eventuate." A somewhat self-deprecating smile twisted his lips. "It would hardly be fair for me to keep advising *you* to live for the present if I wasn't doing the same myself."

"In defying your mother over this, you risk the pack declining to make you alpha if something ever happened to your parents, and we both know it."

"That's something I can worry about if and when it happens, but they're both hale and hearty and in no danger of dying for at least another fifty years."

"They won't step down once they're older?"

"They may, but that's still decades off yet."

"Aiden, I don't want to be the reason for a fracture forming between you and your parents."

"You won't. My father is fine with the whole situation. It's only my mother."

"One parent offside—especially when it's one half of

your pack's ruling couple—is more than enough, I'm thinking."

"Then you're overthinking. Besides, it wouldn't be the first time I've clashed with my mother, and it won't be the last."

"Yes, but she already hates me. This isn't going to help matters."

"Let me worry about my mother."

He couldn't be around twenty-four seven, and I very much doubted the bitch would take an ultimatum such as this lying down. I also had absolutely no doubt she'd make it a personal mission to ensure I was well aware of her feelings on the matter.

"Does that mean the party is off?" I touched his bristly cheek. "I know turning thirty is a big celebration for werewolves—"

"No more so than turning twenty-one is for humans." He shrugged. "I've never been a huge fan of parties. The more intimate type of celebration is more my speed."

"Aiden—"

He placed his hand over mine. "There *is* a party planned—it's outside the compound, but all those I actually care about will be there."

I studied him doubtfully. "Your parents?"

"My father, brothers, sisters, friends." A smile touched his lips. "Even a few witches I know."

But not his mother. That was not a good sign. "I wonder if there's a spell to ward off murderous thoughts? Because I'm thinking your mother will be sending a few my way."

He laughed and kissed me. "By the time Saturday comes around, she'll be over her snit. Ask Katie if you don't believe me. She went through much the same thing before Mom finally accepted Gabe."

"There's a huge difference in the situation, Aiden."

He raised an eyebrow. "Do you really think—had Katie not been dying—that she *wouldn't* have married Gabe?"

"Well, no, but—"

The rest of the protest died as his lips caught mine again. His kiss was a long, slow assault on my mouth and my senses, and it left me dizzy and heated and wanting him like crazy. Which was undoubtedly the point.

"You don't play fair, Ranger," I murmured when he finally pulled back.

His blue eyes glimmered with amusement and desire. "As the saying goes, all's fair in love and war. And speaking of loving—I'm thinking you're a little overdressed."

I raised an eyebrow. "I'm only wearing a towel. You're fully dressed. If anyone needs to be shedding clothes, it's you."

"A situation that is easily fixed."

He immediately rose, but he didn't strip off in any great hurry. Instead, he made it a tease, removing each item of clothing so slowly that I just wanted to scream for him to get on with it.

He was absolutely beautiful naked. The fire's lights caressed the lean but powerful planes of his body and lovingly played over the length of his erection. My fingers itched to do the same.

He held out a hand. I placed mine in it, and he tugged me up easily, freeing the towel from my body before tossing it nonchalantly onto the sofa. Then he drew me into his arms. His kiss was as hot as his skin and, oh, it was glorious.

From that moment on, there was no talking. We touched and teased, exploring each other, tasting each other, until the air burned with the thick heat of desire and my body was trembling with the need to have him deep inside.

When he finally was, it felt so damn good—so damn right—that I groaned and wrapped my arms around him, holding him still, delaying the moment of completion. For several seconds, neither of us moved. Then his lips caught mine, and he kissed me passionately.

"You," he whispered eventually, his breath so warm against my mouth and his gaze swirling with emotions he'd never acknowledge, "are all that matters to me. Not my pack, not my parents. *You.*"

He began to move, the rhythm one as old as time, and the ability to reply—or even think—slipped away as the tide of utter pleasure built and built and then finally crashed over me.

It was only much later, when we finally made it up to the bedroom and he was asleep beside me, that the words came back to haunt me.

Would he remember them when Mia finally came back to the reservation?

Would they make him hesitate when it came to going back to her?

Yes, an inner voice said. *But it won't make a difference.*

I closed my eyes and took a deep, somewhat shuddery breath. Damn it, *no.* I might not be able to fight what destiny had already lain out, but if the bitch wanted him back then she was in for a fight.

There was no way known I was going to make it easy for either of them.

Belle came down the stairs to the coffee shop the next morning, deep shadows under her eyes but her smile wide and her thoughts buzzing with happiness.

I handed her a cup of coffee. "Long night catching up, hey?"

"It was brilliant." She took a sip and leaned back against the counter. "Did you know Alison already has two kids—a nine-month-old named Beth, and Eddie, a three-year-old boy named after Dad?"

I blinked. Alison was just over five years younger than Belle and hadn't even been a teenager when we'd left. "Surely not—she's still a baby herself!"

Belle laughed. "She always did want a big family. She married Dylan Fitzgerald—you remember him? The scrawny kid that kept showing up unannounced at our house."

"Can't say that I do. I didn't actually live at your place, you know, even if I spent more time there than at home." I slid the bacon and eggs I'd been cooking onto two plates, then handed her one. "What about Josh? What's he up to these days?"

"He's apparently in London on an exchange program and is working for the PSI center there."

Josh was the middle child, three years younger than Belle and, like her, an extremely strong telepath. Unlike his older sister, however, his secondary talent was energy medicine—a rare and much sought after ability that could heal with one's own empathic, etheric, astral, mental, or spiritual energy. It wasn't surprising he'd been headhunted by the London unit—they were the biggest PSI center in the world.

"Has he hooked up with anyone?"

"Not in any permanent fashion, as far as Mom knows.

Sounds like he's utterly enjoying the freedoms and lifestyle of such a big modern city."

I smiled. Canberra—or Melbourne or Sydney for that matter—could never be described as anything other than a modern city, and Sydney was certainly more densely populated. But there was something about the sheer age of London that gave the place a grandeur and style that no Australian city could ever hope to achieve. According to my parents, anyway. I'd never actually been there.

I followed Belle across to our table and sat down. "I take it your mom is sleeping in?"

Belle nodded. "I told her to rest up for the day—she hates flying, and it always takes it out of her."

"I hope you're planning to take a few days off. The rest of us will cope just fine."

Especially given the skies had opened up early this morning and, according to the forecasters, were going to remain that way for the next few days. Shitty weather generally made for slow days in the café.

"I was planning to—though it's no fun touring around when it's colder than a fucking freezer."

I laughed. "You might want to cast your mind back and remember just how damn cold it got in Canberra in winter and spring."

"Yeah, but we've been in a lot of warmer climes since then, and I've grown unaccustomed to it."

"Then you'd better hope Castle Rock's weather isn't as horrendous as they're predicting."

"Indeed." She scooped up a bit of bacon and munched on it. "So, what happened between you and Aiden? There're all sorts of weird vibrations coming from you."

I grimaced and updated her on Aiden's ultimatum and party plans in between eating my meal.

"Whoa," she said. "That's big."

"Yeah. You can imagine how momma wolf is going to take it all."

Belle wrinkled her nose. "Anything she does will have repercussions. She can't threaten you—or even this business, in truth—without being considered unreasonable by everyone else. I know *that* for a fact."

Meaning she'd been skimming the thoughts of the council elders who occasionally came in here. "Do you think she cares?"

"Actually yeah, I do. A great deal."

"But do you actually think it'll stop her from threatening me?" Because I certainly didn't.

"Words are one thing, actions another. I doubt she'll do more than say her piece. Anything else would only harden Aiden's resolve, and that's the one thing she'll be desperate to avoid."

I hoped Belle was right, but I had a niggling suspicion Karleen was up in her den right now, brewing all sorts of retribution.

Belle chuckled. "She's not a witch, and she certainly can't brew anything that'll threaten us."

"I wouldn't bet on that." I mopped up the last bit of egg with a crust of toast, then sighed and picked up the plate and my coffee. "I'll go finish the prep. You want to do the cakes and the coffee machine?"

A smile twitched her lips. "Anyone would think you don't trust me to handle a knife after such a late night."

"Your mom's upstairs. If her baby girl gets all bloody, she's going to blame me."

Belle grinned. "No, she'd say it serves me right for consuming so much champagne when I knew I had to work the next day."

"And she'd be right."

Belle tossed a bit of toast at me. I laughed and ducked, then scooped it up off the floor and headed into the kitchen.

The day went from bad to worse weather wise, and customers were few and far between. Once the so-called lunchtime rush—all of a dozen people—was over, we left Penny in charge and headed upstairs.

The rest of the afternoon was spent reminiscing about old times and new over coffee, cake, many tears, and even more laughter.

It was, I thought happily, good to be back with family, even if it wasn't blood family.

My phone rang at five, the tone telling me it was Monty. Which meant something was up, because if he was just being social, he'd have rung Belle.

"What's happened?" I asked without preamble.

"Reports of another lost and crying kid." His voice was grim. "Given what happened last time, we're heading straight out. Can you be ready in five minutes?"

"Sure."

He immediately hung up, and I pushed to my feet.

"Am I missing some vital piece of information?" Belle said, confusion evident. "Why is he suddenly ringing you when he's the reservation witch?"

"You haven't gleaned the info from my thoughts? I'm shocked."

She lightly whacked my leg. "I've been otherwise occupied."

I grinned and quickly updated her. "I'll give you a mental shout if we happen to find a fresh death or a soul that needs help, but otherwise, enjoy your night."

"Fresh death?" Ava glanced at the two of us. "You're not kidding, are you?"

"Sadly, no." Belle glanced up at me. "Be careful out there."

"Careful is my middle name."

Her snort followed me down the stairs. I grabbed my coat, purse, and the backpack, then headed out the front to wait for Monty under the shop's old front veranda. His old wagon came clattering around the corner a few minutes later and pulled to a halt in the no-parking zone.

I jumped in and did up the seat belt as he zoomed off.

"Where are we headed?" The rain drummed so loudly on the wagon's roof that I practically had to shout the question. The wipers were not coping, which was somewhat scary given the speed he was going.

"The bush behind the motocross track."

I frowned. "I wasn't aware Castle Rock had one."

He cast an amused look my way. "It may be a smallish country town, but it's not lacking facilities, you know."

"This from the man who was only a few days ago bemoaning the absence of a decent cinema complex."

"And quite rightly. Ashworth might love the retro styling and movies the Royal shows, but I prefer pictures that are a little more *this* century."

So did I, to be honest. "I gather Aiden is meeting us there?"

"Tala is. Aiden and Jaz are over near Welshman's Reef —bad car accident, from the sound of it."

"I hope there're no fatalities."

"Tala didn't say."

"Who reported the crying child then?"

"One of the motocross riders. Apparently he was taking a break when he heard it."

"He didn't go investigate?"

"A couple of them did, but the kid kept moving deeper

into the scrub, even though the riders were shouting out to remain where he was."

"Were they human or wolf?"

"A mix, but the kid who reported it wasn't able to catch the kid's scent."

"Same problem the rangers had."

"Yeah, but that was hours after the fact. This is fresh, and there should be some sort of trail."

With this rain? That was doubtful. "It does suggest we might be dealing with some sort of supernatural entity after all."

"Or the entity is working with the rogue."

I frowned. "I wouldn't have thought that likely. Werewolves aren't generally known for making pacts with the supernatural."

"Which doesn't mean it can't happen. I guess it depends entirely on what sort of supernatural creature we're dealing with." He glanced at me. "Are you checking Belle's books to see if there's anything there?"

"Ha!" I said. "That's why you insisted I become your helper—you want to get your hands on those books."

He grinned. "You forget I'm going to marry that woman, so I can clearly bide my time when it comes to checking out the library."

I snorted. "Did you tell Ava these grand plans?"

"I did. She wished me luck and gave me her blessing."

I studied him for a second, uncertain if I should believe him or not. "Seriously?"

"Hell, yeah." The look he cast me was amused. "I may be lower in the power scale than my parents wished, but I'm still an Ashworth with high-flying parents. A catch, in other words."

I laughed. "Nothing like beating your own drum."

"Especially when it's nothing but the truth." A self-deprecating smile touched his lips. "Of course, I've yet to convince Belle of that."

"Play the long game, Monty."

"Oh, I am."

I smiled. "Did Tala say if there's a report of a missing kid? Or is that like last time too?"

"No reports, but the call only came in fifteen minutes ago, so it may be too early."

"If there's a kid young enough to be lost and crying in the bush, you'd think *someone* would be missing him."

"But you and I are sensible. Not all parents are."

"You being such an expert in the matter."

My voice was dry, and he chuckled softly. "You forget I haunt the café daily. It really *is* a microcosm of the wider community."

"Only on days when the weather hasn't unleashed."

He glanced at me, eyebrows raised. "Meaning I'll have to come in and consume more cake to keep the profits up?"

"You don't pay for said cake."

"You want me to start? Happy to, you know."

"I know, and we're fine, Monty."

Silence fell—to the extent it could be silent with the drumming rain and furiously swishing wipers, at any rate. We moved out of Castle Rock and sped a couple of miles down the road that led to Maldoon. The entrance into the motocross area was so simply signposted that we almost missed it, and was little more than a double farm gate and a dirt track that led up to the parking area and basic facilities.

Tala was talking to a couple of teenagers in bike leathers as we pulled up but immediately walked over. I climbed out of the wagon, then quickly zipped up my coat and pulled on the hood. Thankfully, I'd invested in a coat that went down to my knees, so at least most of me would remain warm and dry. I wasn't sure how long my boots would hold out in this weather, though.

"Danny says they walked a couple of kilometers in before he came back to make the phone call." Tala stopped in front of us. "We've still got two of them out there."

"Two is better than one," Monty commented. "They can watch each other's back."

"That depends entirely on what we're actually dealing with." Tala's voice was grim. "The crying kid was moving wolf fast, but didn't appear to hear their shouts."

Which wasn't surprising if we were dealing with something *other* than a wolf. Of course, it could also be the damn weather—my hearing was better than most, but the drumming rain made it difficult to catch what Tala was saying, and she was only a few feet away. "You think we're dealing with someone who's playing a game?"

"I think it highly likely."

"Patrick being torn apart wasn't a game," Monty said.

Tala's expression darkened. "I'm well aware of that. But there's no evidence as yet of the two being connected. It might simply be a case of him being in the wrong spot at the wrong time."

It was pretty evident she didn't believe that any more than I did. I just hoped that what happened to Patrick *didn't* happen to the two teenagers.

"It's probably going to be a long hike—you two got water and trail rations in those packs?" She paused and glanced down at my feet. "Will you be able to keep up? Your feet were quite a mess the other night."

"They looked worse than they were. I'll be fine. And yes, we have rations if needed."

She didn't look convinced but, with a quick "follow me," moved off briskly.

I swung my pack over my shoulders and hurried after her. Thankfully, the terrain here was relatively flat and the scrub wasn't thick. We moved in single file, at speed, along what amounted to little more than a snake track. A good twenty or so minutes passed before we hit a four-wheel drive track.

Tala swung onto it. "This heads for the rail line about ten kilometers away, but the kid veered off again not far up the road. That's when Danny retreated."

"Are you catching the scent of the other two teenagers yet?" Monty asked.

Tala shook her head. "But not only is the wind at our back, the rain's so bad it'll have washed away any prints."

"Which is the reason Danny and his mates didn't find a scent trail."

"No doubt. Annoying though, given night is moving in fast and this damn storm shows no sign of abating."

"The two motocross riders wouldn't walk on through the night, would they?" I asked.

Tala shrugged. "They're teenage boys, and teenage boys generally think themselves invincible. Anything is possible."

"When did you become an expert on teenage boys?" Monty asked.

"I have brothers." Her voice was wry. "Five of them, to be exact. I know *all* about the idiocy of boys, trust me."

Monty laughed, the sound echoing lightly through the trees. Somewhere out there in the gathering shadows, something stirred. Something that didn't quite feel right. I frowned and scanned the trees to the right of the track. There was nothing to see—nothing beyond the driving rain and bedraggled tree shadows, at any rate. And yet, unease stirred. Or maybe it was just fear of the unknown and what we might be running toward.

The track was now treacherous, the dirt turning to thick mud that either slid away from underneath or clung to the soles of my boots, making every step that much harder. Moisture seeped through the boot leather, but my socks were at least woolen so I was in no danger of getting iced toes. Squishing feet was no fun, however.

We eventually swung off the track and trudged on. The daylight was fading fast, and long shadows haunted the trees. I shivered, although, again, I wasn't sure if it was due to the increasing chill in my bones or the thought that it was the perfect night for evil to be hunting. Us finding anything out here was getting ever more unlikely, but Tala showed no sign of giving up. And that meant that we couldn't. There was no way known we could leave her alone up here; while it *was* possible we were dealing with kids playing tricks, it was just as likely we weren't.

"How much longer are we going to do this?" Monty swung his pack around and pulled out a flashlight. Its sudden brightness had me blinking rapidly. "There's no trail, no chance of a trail, and—"

He cut the rest off as Tala's phone rang. She quickly answered. "Danny? What's happened?"

She listened for a few minutes and then added, "Good. Thanks for letting me know."

"What?" I asked the minute she hung up.

"Danny's two mates just returned to the motocross site. They're all heading home."

Relief stirred. "Did they say anything else about the lost kid?"

"Only that he appeared to be heading to the old open

cut mining site, which isn't great news. That area is fucking dangerous."

"I take it that means we're still continuing on?"

She eyed the darkness doubtfully for a second. "Given I've not heard anything to indicate there's a kid out—" She cut the sentence off abruptly. "Did you hear that?"

"What?" Monty said, voice tense.

"*Listen.*"

I cocked my head, trying to catch whatever Tala had heard. The rain was fierce, and the wind had picked up, whipping through the tree branches and making them creak and groan in protest.

There was nothing ... The thought froze as I heard it—a shout. It was not only distant, but hadn't come from the throat of a kid. The voice was too deep—too masculine—to be that of a kid.

"It came from the left," I said.

Monty glanced at me sharply. "I'm not hearing anything, so why are you?"

"Enhanced senses, remember?" My gaze went to Tala. "It's a man, not a kid."

"That's what I thought." Her voice was flat. Hard. "Let's move."

She took off fast. The light from Monty's flashlight bobbed across the shadows, briefly illuminating the thorny bits of scrub that tore at our clothes and faces. I slipped on the muddy ground more than once, but I was managing to keep up with Tala, and that was the main thing.

Another shout, this time etched with fear.

Tala swore, and her form shimmered, moving easily from human to wolf.

"Tala, no!" I shouted. "Not without us."

She didn't listen. I swore, quickly created a tracking

spell, and tossed it after her. The spell caught the very end of her tail just as she went around a stand of saplings, and immediately began to spool out, giving us a glittering thread of silver to follow.

We raced on, slipping on the treacherous ground, the rain belting into our faces and the flashlight doing little now to light the way. The thread of my spell continued to run out in front of us, a lone line of hope in the bitterly dark night.

There were no more shouts; we might well have been alone out here. And I wondered if *that* had been the whole point. If we *were* dealing with a supernatural entity, then maybe he was after something juicier than a mere werewolf this time.

I shivered and thrust the thought away. I didn't need the fear of it. Not now. Not when Tala was out there alone, facing who knows what.

Five minutes later, the spell stopped spooling out. I slowed and wrapped a repelling spell around my fingers. Monty did the same, and as one, we walked on cautiously. The trail led upwards, the ground becoming stonier and harder to traverse. We were obviously nearing the open cut mining site.

A silhouette appeared against the skyline above us. My heart leapt into my throat a second before I realized it was Tala.

I released the tracking spell. As the bright remnants floated away on the wind, I clambered up the rest of the slope and stopped beside her. "Anything?"

"Yeah." Her voice was grim. "We've got another fucking body."

CHAPTER FIVE

"Not a kid, I hope," Monty said.

"No, but that doesn't make the situation any better." Tala's voice was curt. "There's no fucking phone reception in this area, so I'll have to go back a few klicks to call it in. Will you two be all right up here?"

"We're more than capable of protecting ourselves," Monty said. "But there's no reason for you to be haring off—Lizzie can simply contact Belle and get her to ring the rest of your team."

Tala glanced at me, eyebrow raised in question.

"Give me the precise location," I said, "and I'll contact her."

She did so. I passed the information on to Belle and then added, "She's on it now."

"Thanks," Tala said. "That'll at least save us some time."

"Where's the body?" Monty asked. "We might as well make sure there's no magical clues or party tricks left behind."

"It's just off this ridge, about halfway around, crammed between a boulder and a tree. Follow me."

I wiped the moisture from my face—a useless gesture in the force of the storm—and followed the two of them along the ridgeline. The flashlight's beam highlighted the sheeting rain and emphasized the deep, dark nothingness that encased whatever lay below us.

"How dangerous is this area?" I asked, somewhat nervously.

"It's an old open cut mine, so the area is littered with unstable mounds of refuse," she replied. "But there's no actual mineshafts to fall down, if that's what you're worried about."

"Good. Because it might be a case of third time unlucky."

"If your luck was going to fail," Monty commented, "it would have done so way before now."

"Luck is always guaranteed to run out when you truly need it," I muttered. Especially when, in my particular case, I'd already had so much of it.

We slowly moved forward; every step had stones rolling toward the edge on either side, suggesting that while the ridge might look stable, it actually wasn't. It was also decidedly narrow in parts. With the darkness barely lit by the flashlight's yellow puddle of light and the storm howling through the trees either side of us, it would have been very easy to slip and fall.

We were halfway around what seemed to be a long curve when a soft glimmer caught my attention.

"Monty, Tala, stop."

They immediately did so. "Why?"

"There's a soul in the trees ahead."

Monty swore softly. "The death wasn't ordained."

"Does that mean," Tala asked, "that he was killed before his time?"

"Yes." Monty carefully stepped to one side, then handed me the flashlight. "You'd better go first. You've got more experience when it comes to souls."

A smile tugged at my lips. "Souls generally aren't dangerous, especially those that have just risen."

"So the books say, but I've heard tales of souls having major snits and causing a storm of flying objects."

My smile grew. "That's more the province of ghosts than souls."

Monty blinked. "I thought souls and ghosts were one and the same?"

"Well, technically, they are." I gave him an amused look. "There was a whole subject at school on spirits, ghosts, and whatnot. Weren't you paying attention?"

"Obviously not."

I snorted. "Well then, generally speaking, we have three levels of apparitions. The faintest is the soul who is simply confused by their sudden death. They are also the easiest to deal with, as they generally just need help to move on. Then there's ghosts, who can be souls trapped in this world because of an unwillingness to move on, or even the desire to complete unfinished business. The worst are specters, who are nearly always out for vengeance of one kind or another."

"Do you know which one we're dealing with here?" Tala asked.

"Not as yet—I've only seen a glimmer. We'll know a lot more once Belle is on board to talk to him."

"And to calm him down if he happens to be the vengeance-seeking type," Monty added.

"Hopefully."

The flicker became brighter, which meant we were close to his body. I stopped and shone the flashlight down the slope. After a couple of seconds, I spotted the edge of a brown boot sticking out from the end of a large rock. I moved the light to study the ground between him and us. There were a lot of tailings littering the ground, which meant we needed to be careful going down. But Tala had gotten down—and up—in one piece already, so it shouldn't be too difficult.

I went down sideways in an effort to get more traction and to avoid going ass over tit if I did slip, and made it to the tree in one piece. The glimmer that was the soul backed away, and its confusion rolled over me. Which was odd, because I wasn't the one who was overly sensitive to souls. But maybe it was just another indicator of the changes the wild magic was causing not only in me, but also in the link I had with Belle, and maybe even Belle herself.

I shone the light into the gap between the tree and the rock. Our victim appeared to be middle-aged, with salt-and-pepper hair and a handlebar moustache. He was thin in build and was wearing a long Driza-Bone jacket, though it had been torn open across his stomach to reveal a paunch and ... *oh God*. I took a step back before I could stop it. His stomach had been ripped open, and his intestines were spilling over the ground. But they weren't whole. Far from it.

I'd very definitely seen much worse in my short time in this reservation, but the fact that someone—some*thing*—had been feasting on this man's innards very, very recently had the flight instinct rising.

"Well, that's a little different to Patrick's murder." Monty's voice was grim. "He might have had his limbs torn off but at least nothing had dined on him."

"His gut *had* been cut open," Tala said, "so it might simply mean the killer didn't have the time to do anything else."

I shifted my feet, bracing against the continuing desire to run. "Whoever did this certainly used the same method of concealing the body."

"Yes." Tala crossed her arms, the movement a touch impatient. "There's also no other obvious wounds, but he *is* lying on his side, so that may not mean anything. We'll learn more once Ciara gets here and we can move him. Of course, by the time she does get here, the rain might well have washed all evidence away."

Monty glanced at her. "There's an umbrella spell I can place over the body and its immediate surrounds that'll fix that."

I raised my eyebrows. "If there is such a thing as umbrella spells, why the hell didn't we use it to get up here?"

"Because they're stationary in design; us walking through the scrub would have ripped them apart in seconds." He shrugged off his backpack. "Why don't you create a protective circle while I do the umbrella?"

I nodded and pulled the small silk bag that contained my spell stones out of my backpack. These particular ones were rough-cut clear quartz; while most royal witches tended to use diamonds, quartz was cheaper while possessing very similar properties. I placed each stone carefully onto the ground, then added a glimmer spell to the top of each. It'd make finding them afterward easier while not affecting the overall strength of the protection circle. Once I'd completed the circle around the tree and the rock, I stepped inside and studied the ground, looking for somewhere to sit. Ashworth might have taught me to raise a protection spell while standing, but we also had a soul to contend with, and that meant connecting with Belle on a deeper level than usual. Sitting meant neither of us had to expend additional energy or conscious thought on remaining upright.

I spotted a strip of ground that wasn't overly stony and tucked the back of my coat under my butt to keep it dry as I sat cross-legged. A surge of power had my gaze snapping to the right. Monty's umbrella spell flared out across the gap between rock and tree in a slightly convex manner, which allowed the rain that did get through the canopy to slide off harmlessly to either side.

"Right." He squatted in front of me. "You ready?"

"Yes." I glanced at Tala. "Once Belle and I are merged, I'll narrate Belle's questions and the soul's answers so you can record it."

She nodded and tugged her phone out of her pocket. I took a deep breath to center my energy, then began weaving multiple layers of protections across the stones and attaching them lightly. When that was done, I activated the spell. The air thrummed with its power; the inner wild magic was coming through even the simplest of spells now.

"Nothing will be getting through *that*," Monty muttered. "Your spelling power is definitely increasing."

Which wasn't necessarily a good thing. Not when we had no idea where it might all end.

I took another deep breath and then reached for Belle.

Her response was immediate; she'd obviously been expecting to hear from me.

Of course I was, she said. *You might have closed the link but I've nevertheless been getting a faint wash of horror. I take it you need my ghostly expertise?*

If you're not doing anything too exciting, yes.

That entirely depends on whether you'd class sitting here with Mom consuming cake and drinking an Irish hot chocolate as exciting. Hang on while I put my drink down and get comfortable. The line went blank for several seconds. *Right, I'm ready. Let's do this.*

I told Tala to start recording, then immediately deepened the connection between Belle and me. There was a rush of warmth as her being flowed through mine and fused us as one, though the connection wasn't deep enough that her soul left her body. She could, however, use her talents while seeing through my eyes.

The glimmer that was the soul immediately jumped into focus. He was tall and, paunch aside, relatively thin. He looked to be in his mid-fifties and, for some reason, I suspected he was human.

What is your name? Belle asked.

Jackson. Jackson Pike. He looked around, his expression confused. *What's happened? Why do I feel so different?*

I quietly began relaying the conversation, though my concentration remained on the soul.

I'm afraid you're dead, Jackson—

No! That can't be. His gaze fell on his body, and his expression went from denial to horrid fascination. *That's me, isn't it?*

I'm afraid so. Belle's reply was gentle. It was hard to guess how some souls would react to such news, but I suspected Jackson wasn't one of the more violent ones. *I can help you move on, Jackson, but I need to ask you some questions first.*

Move on? Like, become an angel or something?

Belle's smile teased my lips. *If that is your destiny, then yes.*

He frowned. *Meaning it could the other place?*

89

Purgatory is certainly real enough, Belle said, *but mostly it isn't the hellfire and brimstone deal some religions depict.*

Then what is it?

Belle shrugged. *Sometimes, it's simply making amends for the mistakes you made in this life in the next.*

Like rebirth? That's a thing?

Yes.

Huh. He studied his body for a moment. *How did it happen?*

That's what I need you to tell me, Jackson.

He frowned. *But I don't know—*

Let's start at the beginning. Why were you out here in the first place?

He grimaced and waved a hand. As far as new souls went, he was pretty animated, suggesting he'd been like that in life. *Doing a bit of detecting. Storms like this often wash down the scree, exposing bits of missed gold.*

Why didn't you leave the area when darkness came in, then?

Because I set up for the night in one of the old buildings.

What's the last thing you can remember?

Slipping on the scree and falling on my ass. Bloody hurt, it did.

Which scree pile? Here, or elsewhere?

He looked around again, confusion evident. *Not here. The other side, near the old quartz crusher building. How did I get here?*

We don't know, Jackson. Did you hear anything odd before you fell? Any strange sounds?

I heard some kids calling out. They seemed to be chasing someone. He shrugged. *Not my business.*

Did you hear anything else? A kid crying, for instance?

No. He paused and frowned. *I did see something*

moving really fast through the trees. It was small and pale, but it disappeared before I could really see what it was. I figured it was just a bit of rubbish being tossed on the wind.

Where was this?

At the base of the ridge, in the trees behind the remnants of the tubular boiler.

Did it actually move like rubbish?

His frown deepened. *Well, no, but it didn't move like a person, either. Besides, it was too fast.*

Could it have been a werewolf?

An upright wolf? There's no such thing.

So it didn't resemble either a human or a wolf, but it ran upright?

I don't know. As I said, it moved really fast. It was there, and then it was gone. Irritation filled his tone. *Why all these questions?*

Because we need to know what killed you so we can find and stop it before it attacks again.

Oh.

What did you do after you fell, Jackson?

Belle's weariness began to seep down the line. Remote spirit talking always took a toll on her. I pushed a little strength her way and felt the wash of her thanks. *No more, though,* she added, *otherwise you'll be wiped out as well.*

Picked myself up, of course. Jackson's tone suggested it was a dumb question. *Unfortunately, the fall did something to the detector, so I headed back to the building.*

But did you make it back there?

He frowned again. *I can remember seeing it.*

Meaning you didn't actually get inside?

I don't know.

I need you to think back, Jackson. It's really important.

But I don't— He stopped, and something flickered

through his expression. Fear. He was remembering. *I was about twenty feet away from the intake opening.*

And?

There was a sound.

What sort of sound?

An odd sound.

Describe it.

It was a rasp. Like someone was having trouble breathing.

Where was it coming from?

From behind me. I spun around, and there were dots. Two red dots. And then ... and then I was looking down and there was blood on my stomach and my guts were in my hands ... His voice rose. *Oh God, oh God, it's eating me ...*

It can't hurt you anymore, Jackson, Belle said soothingly. *There's no pain and nothing to fear in this form, and only joy ahead.*

He took a deep shuddering breath—an instinctive measure that spoke of his newness to the afterlife. *I want to go now.*

Just one more question and then you're free.

I don't know what it was, he instantly said. *I never really saw it. I just felt something slice my stomach and then saw the blood.*

You said it was eating you. I know it's terrifying to remember, but as I've said, I need to know what you saw in order to stop this happening to someone else.

He hesitated and then reluctantly said, *I saw hair. Dark hair. And a face—a small face.*

A human face?

He hesitated. *I think so. It all happened so fast. One minute I was trying to contain my intestines and the next I was up here, unable to move away from this damn tree. It's like I've been chained here.*

You are, because that's where death actually claimed you. Are you ready to move on, Jackson?

He obviously was, but she had to formally ask the question before she could proceed. The spirit world was very strict when it came to this sort of stuff.

Well, I certainly don't want to stay in this godforsaken place.

Then you wish me to help you? Yes or no, Jackson.

Yes.

Then may fate bless you with happiness and old age in your next life.

As his thank-you rolled around us, Belle silently whispered the words that would set him on the path to rebirth.

His form faded as his soul moved on.

Not a lot of information in all that, Belle said wearily.

But a little more than what we had. You'd better go.

Yes, if only because there's a freshly made Irish coffee waiting for me. I'll see you tomorrow.

I blew her a mental kiss and broke the connection, then swiped the dripping hair out of my face and climbed stiffly to my feet. My butt was not only freezing but also numb.

"Well, he obviously wasn't killed here." Monty glanced at Tala. "Do you know the building he mentioned?"

"He probably meant the remnants of the crusher building, as not much else is standing. We'd better get over there, just in case there's evidence that needs preserving."

She strode away. I hastily wove an exception into the circle to allow Monty and me to get out, then followed her around the rest of the ridge. Her movements were quick and fast on the uneven ground—the benefit of being a werewolf, I suppose—but both Monty and I were far more cautious. It no doubt frustrated her, given she had to keep waiting for us.

We eventually reached the end of the ridge and slid carefully down the slope. Dark water lapped at the edge of a path that ran from the ridge to several uneven shapes. The remnants of the gold mine's buildings, no doubt.

Tala paused and once again waited for us to catch up. "The crusher building is the largest of the three you can see. How far away from it was he hit?"

"He said about twenty feet from the intake, if that makes any sense."

"He probably meant the section where a conveyer belt transporting the rock into the crusher went into the building. It's this way."

She strode off again but didn't get very far, stopping so abruptly I was forced to jump sideways in order to avoid running into her.

"Here," she said. "He died here."

I studied the ground. It was a mass of mud and dark pools of water that might or might not have been blood. "How can you tell?"

"I'm trained to see these things. Plus, I can smell the blood, even if the rain has done a damn fine job of washing most of it away." Her tone was annoyed. Not at me, but rather the weather. "Monty, can you protect this area the same way you did the body?"

"Yes," he said, "but you need to move back."

She immediately did so, then squatted to study the rain-soaked ground. "There looks to be two sets of footprints—one wolf, and the other Jackson's."

"He wasn't a wolf?" Monty asked.

"No, but all three packs tended to keep an eye out for him, given many of the old gold mines run along compound boundaries." She swept a hand through her dripping hair. "This is not a good development."

"No death is, surely."

"Well, yes, but if we *are* dealing with a wolf gone rogue, we don't need him or her getting a taste for easy prey—and humans are certainly that."

It was also the very last thing this reservation needed. "Jackson's description of his attacker suggests we could be dealing with a kid."

"I very much doubt we are."

"Why?"

"Because the DNA fault wouldn't appear in a kid. It generally doesn't develop until midlife."

"Doesn't mean it can't happen."

"No, but given what he said about the speed and ghostly nature, I'm thinking it's more likely to be something supernatural."

I tended to agree, given Jackson hadn't seen what had gutted him despite the fact he'd been facing it when he'd spun around. That, at the very least, suggested there was magic involved—unless, of course, this thing was so small it had somehow slipped under his guard and sliced him open before he'd had the chance to look down.

Or it was simply super fast.

"Righto," Monty said. "Cover provided. I've set this one higher so you don't walk through it and shred the spell."

"Thanks." Her phone rang sharply, the sound strident in the cold night. She quickly answered it and, after a few moments, said, "We're down near the old crusher building."

She shoved her phone back into her pocket, then rose. "How long will the rain protection spell last?"

"Hopefully longer than this storm."

"Then you two might as well head back home. There's nothing more—"

"No can do," Monty said. "Not when that thing is still out there."

"Whatever it is, it's attacking lone people, not groups."

"Which means we can't leave at least until the others arrive," I said. "Besides, we don't know enough about the perpetrator to make a judgment like that yet."

She all but rolled her eyes. "Fine. Remain and get soaked. But do please tell Aiden I *did* try to send you home."

A smile tugged at my lips. "I daresay Aiden will be expecting me to be here. He knows I'm not sensible when it comes to things like this."

She snorted softly. "Let me tape off this area, then we'll go check the building for his belongings."

Once the area was secured, we headed into the building. The old conveyer that had once transported the rocks to the crusher was little more than a rusting metal skeleton and had become the springtime home of multiple birds if the number of old nests was anything to go by.

I followed Tala through the opening, carefully avoiding the jagged bits of metal sheeting that still covered most of the building. It was a vast and empty space; the wind howled through the various holes scattered along the roofline and walls, and the rain flooded in, spreading across the stone-covered floor in dark pools that again resembled blood. Beyond the odd bit of rusting metal, little remained of the vast crusher this place had once housed.

Monty swept the light around; in the far corner, near what appeared to be the remnants of an office, were a sleeping roll and backpack. Tala immediately strode over.

"He obviously liked sleeping rough," Monty

commented. "That sleeping roll wouldn't offer much in the way of comfort on this ground."

"Not everyone is as soft as you." Tala pulled on a pair of gloves, then grabbed his pack. After a quick search, she found his wallet and opened it up. "Jackson Pike, as you said."

"Has he family here?" I asked.

She nodded. "A sister, and this will hit her hard. I'm glad I'm not the one who has to tell her."

Because Aiden saw it as his job, though it was one I wished he'd share.

"Anything else in there?" Monty asked.

"No." Tala rose. "We'd better get back to the corpse."

"On the way there, we might as well check the trees to see if Jackson's tumbling bit of white rubbish is still around."

"If it was rubbish, that's unlikely." She nevertheless waved me forward. I led the way out of the building and headed for the base of the ridge. After pausing to scan the darkness, I spotted two elongated metal barrels laying at right angles to each other. The tubular boiler, no doubt. I walked around them and into the trees. I was barely five feet in when I found the track. Someone—something—had crashed through the undergrowth not that long ago.

"Good find," Tala murmured. She dropped to her haunches and carefully swept debris away from a footprint —one that was neither human nor wolf but a weird combination of the two. "It looks like we are dealing with a rogue, even if it isn't what killed Jackson."

"What makes you say that?" Monty asked.

Tala glanced up at him. "The size of the print—it's too big to belong to a kid."

"Aiden said the DNA fault forces them into a sort of wolf-human hybrid." I rubbed my arms—a somewhat useless gesture that did little to warm the inner chill. "Could the hybridization itself be faulty, causing them to morph between sizes as well as shapes?"

Tala wrinkled her nose. "Unlikely, but I'm no expert on these things."

"*Is* there an expert we could consult?" Monty asked.

"The boss has already been in contact with her." She rose. "Let me mark this off, then we'll keep going."

We got out of her way. By the time we made it back to Jackson's body, the storm had finally eased. Which didn't make the night any more pleasant, especially given the lower half of my body was wringing wet and water now squished out of my boots with every step. To say I was cold would be an understatement.

I think it's one of those cases of being careful what you wish for, Belle commented, mental tones amused. *Especially with winter coming in hard and early.*

Yes. And why are you following my thoughts rather than talking to your mom?

She's on the phone to Dad. This is the first time they've been apart more than a day for decades.

Why didn't he come down with her?

They can't—one of them has to be there. It's a recent alteration to their contract conditions.

Her parents had been in charge of the Psychic Advisory Commission—a government-sponsored service designed to help and advise psychics on all matters, be they legal or personal—for my entire life. I'd been under the impression that they could run it as they saw fit, but that obviously wasn't entirely the case. *That makes no damn sense.*

When did governmental decisions ever make sense?

But your parents are getting on—why wouldn't the government have a succession plan in place? One that involves possible replacements getting experience in the top seat while your mom and dad are still there to guide them?

Because again, that would make sense. Anyway, I thought you'd like to know that the luscious Samuel Kang left a message on the café's phone. He'd like to talk to you tomorrow at two, if that's convenient. And he didn't leave his number, so you can't actually refuse.

I snorted. *I wonder what he wants this time?*

The man's in lust with you, Lizzie. What do you think he wants?

I slapped her mentally. Her laughter ran down the line, bright and sharp. *I dare say it has something to do with his recommendations to the council.*

Probably. I glanced around as a twig snapped and saw Ciara and Maggie—who was the office receptionist and a ranger in training—emerging from the trees. *I've got to go. See you tomorrow.* Out loud, I added, "How bad was the car crash?"

"Don't know," Ciara said. "Luke's dealing with it."

Luke was her assistant and a recent addition to the team.

"So they're still out?" Tala said.

"Yeah. There were four cars involved. At least two deaths, from what I heard over the radio. People just won't learn to slow down in shitty weather." She stopped beside me. "Is it okay to go down there, or do you need to detangle a spell or something?"

"The latter. Give me a few minutes."

I collected my spell stones, then stood in the shadows of a tree, cold, miserable, and wishing I was home. Be careful what you wish for indeed.

It was close to midnight by the time we finally left. I'd

had no message from Aiden, so I presumed he was either still dealing with the car crash or now home waiting for me.

Sadly, the latter proved *not* to be the case. I had a hot shower to chase the chill from my body, then climbed under the mountain of blankets and went to sleep.

Only to have my dreams filled with the bloody rampages of a ghost-like creature who was neither wolf nor demon but a brutal mix of both.

The storm came back with a vengeance the following morning, so café traffic was almost nonexistent. Sam arrived at two on the dot, this time wearing a long black coat that emphasized the width of his shoulders while somehow defining the long and rather glorious length of his body.

He closed his umbrella, popped it into the stand, and then gave me a polite smile of greeting. "I do hope you don't mind meeting me like this again."

"It's not like you actually gave me a choice." I waved him across to the table in the corner near the window—one that had a conversation-muting spell already layered around it. "Would you like coffee and cake?"

His bright smile stirred inner warmth to life. I might be very happily involved with Aiden, but that didn't mean I was dead to the charms of other good-looking men. "A long black with whatever cake is on special would be perfect. Thank you."

I gave the order to Penny, then sat down opposite him and raised the muting spell. "I take it you've finished your investigations here?"

"I've still a few ends to chase up, but basically, yes."

"And?"

"And, after visiting Émigré's remains and talking to survivors, I agree—off the record, of course—with your earlier summation. The bastard deserved the death he received."

I glanced up as Penny appeared with our drinks and food and thanked her. "You surprise me."

Amusement lurked in his emerald eyes. "That's hardly unexpected given you don't know me."

"True." I picked up my fork and scooped up a large piece of salted caramel cake. "I take it one of the ends you need to chase is the vampire you refused to name?"

"Indeed."

"Care to explain why you won't name her? It is rather odd."

"Superstition." His lips twitched. "By saying evil's name, you invoke it into your life."

"Investigation wise, that's exactly what you want."

His smile widened. I had a suspicion he was simply teasing me. "We do need to get her statement, but in truth, there's no DNA evidence actually linking her to Clayton's murder."

I frowned. "But you have the recording of her stating she intended to kill him."

"Yes, and any decent lawyer would argue that it was nothing more than shock—an expected sentiment after watching both her establishment *and* half her staff being blown up."

And there was no doubt that Maelle would have a more than decent lawyer if they ever did manage to get her into court. "So, what will the official record say? Or aren't I allowed to know that?"

"It'll recommend that—pending an interview with Émigré's owner should she materialize at any point—the case be closed. Your actions in setting Clayton up as a target were a result of his kidnapping and torturing your familiar. Even if charges were brought against you, no witch court would ever convict you."

"The case being dropped is exactly the result Clayton's family wants."

"Yes, but my recommendations don't mean the end of all investigations. The Black Lantern Society is still pursuing the case against your father."

"At least they won't be swayed into dropping the case."

"*I'm* not being swayed, if that's what you're implying." He hesitated. "There is, however, something pertinent to the current situation you need to know."

The edge in his voice had my heart rate skipping. "And what might that be?"

"The *other* reason I'm here." He paused, plainly waiting for me to ask the obvious question.

I obliged. But deep in my heart, I already knew.

His gaze met mine, and there was an odd sort of anger in it. "I was asked to check you out as a potential wife."

CHAPTER SIX

I cursed and leaned back in my chair. "Well, it certainly hasn't taken the old fucker long to get back to his match-making ways, has it?"

"Given the resonance evident in the spells that protect this place *and* his notorious determination to maintain his power base," he replied, voice dry, "did you really expect anything else?"

"Yes, actually. I thought he'd at least wait until all the current investigations were finalized."

"Your father has little fear of consequences. There are more than a few in Canberra who hope the Society's case against him will change that."

"I take it your parents are *not* amongst that number?"

"Oh, they are, but just because they don't like the man doesn't mean they don't want the alliance."

I raised an eyebrow as the edge made another appearance. "I get the impression your dislike runs a whole lot deeper than theirs."

"That's because I've worked for the High Council for a while now, and I've seen what goes on behind the scenes.

But, that aside, I'm not keen on anyone who'd force an underage child into a marriage. Hell, *any* alliance in which there is no attraction or at least friendship should be outlawed, in my opinion. It very rarely leads to any sort of happiness."

A comment that had me remembering what he'd said earlier. "So who in your family was forced into such a marriage?"

"My sister, and in truth, the decision to go ahead with the arrangement was in the end hers." He grimaced. "She divorced after the first child, but for three long years she was utterly miserable."

"Why did she agree to the marriage then?"

A smile touched his lips. "Because she was young and romantic, and because she was a dutiful daughter. She was well aware it would increase the family's profile and reach."

"The divorce wouldn't have."

"The divorce was factored into the agreement. My parents were at least considerate in *that* regard."

Which was more than my damn father had done for me. But would it have made any difference if he had? Or would I have been so cowed after spending two years with Clayton that I wouldn't have dared walk away?

I'd never know, and for that I was damn thankful. "I gather there were suitable terms set for said divorce?"

He nodded. "As long as she produced a son and there was joint custody, he wouldn't contest."

Which, given how valued sons were, was rather surprising. "I take it she's okay now?"

He nodded. "It was hard on her for a few years, but her son is now sixteen and lives with her ex full-time. She's just started working for the Black Lantern Society with our older brother."

From his expression, it was pretty evident he'd been the shoulder she'd cried on—and that only made me like him more. "So given your very obvious opinion on contracted marriages, why are you even here?"

"Because I *am* the head investigator for the high council, and Clayton's murder falls into my purview. That my parents suggested I also investigate *you* has nothing to do with my presence here." A faint smile touched his lips. "Although I will admit that, after what I'd read in the various reports, I was intrigued."

I didn't ask the natural question, though I was vain enough—and, if I was being at all honest, attracted enough —to wonder.

"So why are you telling me all this? Why not simply leave and give your assent—or not—to begin contract negotiations once you got home?"

"Because I abhor secrets and lies. You deserve to know that your father is planning an alliance with the Kang line. If not my family, then others."

I smiled. "He can plan all he wants. I'm no longer sixteen, and he can no longer force me to do anything."

"In theory, yes. In reality? There are few able to resist the pressure he can bring to bear."

"Watch me."

He laughed. It was a warm, rich sound that escaped the muting spell and had the two customers in the café looking our way. One was a member of the notorious gossip brigade, which no doubt meant the whole town would be hearing the news of my new and very flirtatious friend.

"If the case against your father does make it to the courts—and I have every reason to believe it will—expect to see me in the front row," he said. "It'll be an interesting battle of wills to witness."

I frowned. "Why would I be called up to Canberra when they already have my testimony and a full recording of my memories?"

"Your father's lawyers would never forgo the opportunity to cross-examine you in person."

Of course not. But it did raise an interesting question—would I actually be able to get up there? I'd left the reservation on multiple occasions over the last few months, but never for any real length of time. A full trial might mean weeks—or even months—away, though I doubted my father would want all the media articles that would come with such a lengthy trial. It'd allow too much time for his reputation to be besmirched.

I hesitated and then finally asked the damn question. "Does that mean you plan on disappointing your parents in the matter of an arrangement?"

"Given my opinion on arranged marriages, I could hardly do anything else." He studied me for a second, his expression speculative. "Does *that* disappoint you?"

"No. I'm very happily involved at the moment."

"With the ranger." His smile bloomed again. "This reservation has the best gossip mill I've ever come across. It's an amazing font of information."

"That it is." My voice was dry. "And if you've been talking to any of the brigade, then your presence and motives for being here will provide much grist for their mill over the coming weeks."

"No doubt." He paused. "If your situation ever does change, do feel free to contact me. More than happy to go on a few dates and see where it leads."

As ever, Belle had been right about him being attracted. "I think we'd better get back to the matter at hand."

"Probably safer." He pulled a business card out of his

pocket and slid it across the table. "Ring me if our missing vampire does reappear. I've made the same request with the rangers, but whether they'll comply is unknown. This reservation does have a rep in Canberra for being ornery."

"They did have good reason."

"Maybe, but it's no excuse for not following the rules and thereby allowing this reservation to become a target."

"They've discovered *that* the hard way." I picked up the card and noticed he'd scrawled a second number on the back. I raised an eyebrow. "Your personal number?"

"Just in case." He shrugged. "It never hurts to show one's interest, even if the timing is utterly wrong. And before you ask, I couldn't give a fig about your connections."

"Of course, I only have your word on that."

"I wouldn't be head investigator for the council if my word wasn't worth anything. Trust is key up there."

"Here I was thinking power was key."

"There are all kinds of power, Liz. Not all of them are obvious."

"True." And if his family was my father's first choice when it came to a possible alliance, they were obviously major players in Canberra. I tucked the card into my pocket. "Don't expect a response anytime soon—not in either regard."

He smiled, finished his drink, and then rose. "If I have any further questions, I'll contact you."

I collected the plates and cups, then stood. "When are you heading home?"

"Tomorrow afternoon. Tonight I'm interviewing the trucker who made a delivery half an hour before the blast, and I'm talking to the council tomorrow morning." His expression was speculative. "Why?"

I hesitated. Instinct was stirring, and while it was sluggish and undefined, I wasn't about to ignore it. "Can I suggest you don't go out alone tonight?"

"Other than the interview, I wasn't intending to. Again, why?"

"This isn't local news, so don't repeat it, but we've had a couple of murders, and we're not sure whether the perpetrator is human or supernatural."

"And you think I'm in danger?"

"The psi radar is twitching. Which may mean absolutely nothing, but still ..."

His green eyes gleamed. "Thanks for the warning. It does bode well for future possibilities."

My eyebrows shot up. "And how do you come to that conclusion?"

"I'm a stranger and yet here you are, already getting prophetic dreams about me."

I laughed. "Hate to tell you this, but I get prophetic dreams about strangers all the time."

"I'm saddened to hear that."

I laughed again. He smiled, gave me a nod, and then left.

My mood remained decidedly upbeat for the rest of the afternoon. There was nothing quite like the interest of a good-looking man to make the day brighter, even if that interest was never destined to lead anywhere.

———

Belle leaned back in her chair and studied me over the rim of her glass of red wine. "You've a lovely buzz around you this evening."

I raised my eyebrows. "Implying I usually don't?"

"This buzz is different." She glanced at her mom. "Isn't it?"

"Indeed." Ava smiled. "I would in fact suggest it's the result of meeting with an eminently sexy witch this afternoon."

I rolled my eyes. "He's Dad approved. It ain't ever going to happen."

Belle straightened. "He was checking you out as a prospective bride? I didn't get that impression when I skimmed his thoughts."

"Then you didn't skim hard enough." I told them everything he'd said. "Which means, of course, my father has no fear that the consequences of the Society's case will in any way affect him."

"No doubt because historically men of his caliber very rarely get more than a slap on the wrist," Ava said. "This might be a little different, given the mood up in Canberra at the moment—and it may also explain why he's sent a Kang your way."

I frowned. "That's what I don't understand—why a Kang? They're generally spiritualists, and father doesn't have the time or patience for that sort of stuff."

"Technically," Ava said, "they're mystics rather than spiritualists. They believe all living things have an energy and a soul and that by connecting to that energy they can attain insight to both ultimate and hidden truths."

I blinked. "Which is a roundabout way of saying they talk to trees."

Ava laughed. "It's far more than that, and you well know it. Why do you think so many Kangs work as investigators for witch councils the world over?"

"I've never really thought about it."

"It's because they can tap into the power of the world

around them and 'see' the events of both the past and the present."

"That ability won't help them when it comes to situations that involve internal rather than external locations, though."

"Except some Kangs—and Samuel's linc is one of them —can connect to the resonance that remains in inanimate objects such as chairs. It might not give them as clear a picture, but if they take enough snapshots, they can certainly form an overall opinion on the truth of what happened in a set location."

"I wonder if that's why he spent so much time in Émigré?"

"No doubt," Ava said.

"It might also explain why he's recommended the case be closed," Belle said. "If he connected with enough inanimate bits of furniture, he might well have seen not only Clayton's hired bomber, but Clayton himself."

I frowned. "Clayton wasn't there, though."

"Yes, he was—he kidnapped me from there, remember, using the destruction as a distraction. Mind you, I'd love to know how he discovered Maelle's hidden rooms."

I shrugged. "He'd been in the reservation for at least a week before we realized it. It wouldn't have been hard to keep an eye on who was coming and going at the club and throw a tracker onto one of them."

"Maelle's magic aware, though."

"*Dark* magic aware. And the minute Clayton entered Émigré, he would have known what she was."

"True." Belle pursed her lips. "None of this explains why your father thinks an alliance with Samuel's family might help his case, though."

"Samuel's brother is second in charge of the Black

Lantern Society in Canberra," Ava said. "Perhaps he hopes an alliance would swing the verdict favorably his way."

I snorted softly. "Is there no end to my father's machinations?"

"Apparently not." Belle raised her glass. "Shall we make a toast to the old bastard getting his comeuppance sooner rather than later?"

I smiled and clinked my whiskey glass against theirs, though I personally doubted my father would *ever* be on the wrong side of either fate *or* the law. Recent shooting aside, he'd been extraordinarily lucky his entire life.

Ava took a drink, then leaned back in her chair and regarded me steadily. "So where is this ranger of yours, Lizzie? I think it rather rude that he hasn't taken the time to meet your other mother."

I smiled. "The reservation is a ranger short, so they're all working longer shifts at the moment."

"So it has nothing to do with avoiding parental inspection?"

I laughed and rose. "No. Anyone want a top-up?"

"You might as well bring the bottle over," Belle said. "Saves you getting up again."

I collected the plates and dumped them in the kitchen, then grabbed the bottle of red and flicked on the kettle. I had to drive home, so I couldn't afford to drink anything else. Sharing a bed with the head ranger would *not* get me out of a drink-driving charge.

But as I placed the bottle of red on the table, a moonbeam-bright flicker caught my attention.

Wild magic.

There was wild magic in the room.

And *that* could only mean something was wrong. Katie never sent the threads my way just to be sociable.

I held out a hand. The glittering thread wound around my wrist and pulsed lightly in welcome.

Danger stirs, Katie said. *You must come.*

Where?

Images spun through my mind—a forest, an old farmhouse. Two men. Samuel.

Fuck. Intuition had been right. I grabbed his business card and tried to ring him, but the call rang out. I left a message and hoped like hell he was okay.

You must hurry if you wish to save them both, Katie said.

Meaning if we were delayed in *any* way, one of them would die? I swore again, then spun and ran toward the reading room to grab the backpack.

A chair scraped against the floor. *I'll ring Monty,* Belle said. *You can't go out there alone.*

Thanks. To Katie I added, *Any idea what stalks the men?*

Nothing natural.

I grabbed the backpack, then moved across to the secret compartments behind the bookcase to grab an additional bottle of holy water. It was better to carry too much than not enough in this sort of situation.

So we are dealing with the supernatural?

Katie hesitated. *Uncertain.*

Unhelpful.

Her amusement spun from the glittering thread, sending gentle sprays of rainbow light through the room's shadows. *I know, but I cannot be in all places at all times, and this thing moves too fast for me to track. In case you've not noticed, the threads of wild magic do not move anywhere in any great hurry.*

I tucked the extra bottles of holy water safely into the pack, then headed back out. Belle had my purse and coat in one hand, and a tray containing two travel mugs in the other. "I rang Monty. He'll be waiting out the front in five minutes."

"Thanks. Could you also call Aiden? Let him know we'll call when we have more of an idea where we're going."

"You know that's just going to piss him off."

"Nothing much I can do about that."

I grabbed everything, then headed out the back, jumping into the SUV rather than the Suzi. I had no idea where Katie's information would lead me, and given how bad some of the tracks were around the reservation, it was better not only to have all-wheel-drive capacity but also decent ground clearance. Belle had keys to my car if she needed to go anywhere, so it wasn't really a problem.

I reversed out and sped across to Monty's. As he came out his front door, I jumped out and ran around to the passenger side. I couldn't drive and interpret Katie's information at the same time.

"Which way?" Monty slung on the seat belt. "Straight ahead, or a U-turn?"

"U-turn. It's over Campbell's Creek way."

He threw the SUV into gear and took off. "Which is a long way from the motocross site."

I glanced at him. "If we *are* dealing with a ghoulie, it's not going to be restricted to a certain area."

"But what if we're dealing with a mutation? It would want to keep under cover, surely, and there's a whole lot of farmland and housing estates between the motocross area and Campbell's Creek."

"Which could be crossed easily enough in the dark. Remember, this thing moves with unnatural speed, so it's unlikely to be spotted by most of those in the area."

He grunted. Whether that meant he agreed or not, I

couldn't say. "I don't suppose the wild magic gave any clarity on what it might be?"

I hesitated. "Whatever it is, it's not natural."

"That's not exactly helpful."

"It does erase the possibility of it being a compromised werewolf."

He glanced at me, eyebrow raised. "How did you come to that conclusion?"

"Because faulty DNA or not, they'd still register as a werewolf."

"I doubt the wild magic is sentient enough to recognize the difference." He glanced at me. "Unless, of course, there's more to the sentience than what you've been saying."

A smile twitched my lips. "Would I keep such a secret from you?"

"Very definitely."

I laughed. "Well, in some respects, you're not wrong. But the only secrets I keep are not mine to share."

"A statement that leaves me with *so* many questions."

"As soon as we get clearance, I'll tell you."

"And how will you get clearance?"

"Another of those secrets I can't say."

I couldn't see the eye roll, but I had no doubt it happened. "I take it Belle knows all?"

I gave him the "don't be dumb" look. "She's my familiar. It's rather hard to keep secrets from her."

Though I certainly had, more than a few times.

"That statement makes me almost glad my familiar is a cat," he commented. "At the very least, he has no interest in my thoughts, and there's no messy emotions to deal with."

"There may be no emotions," I agreed dryly. "But there *is* a whole lot of attitude and spite."

"Which is a statement that applies to cats in general, rather than those who are familiars."

"I've met other cat familiars. I'm thinking the attitude and spite are just Eamon's particular gifts."

He laughed. "That could also be true."

I smiled and directed him left onto Fryer's Road. As we sped on, the urgency pulsing through the thread of wild magic around my wrist increased. We were running out of time.

I bit back the urge to tell Monty to floor it. The lack of streetlights, the increasing thickness of the scrub, and the fact that roos were plentiful in this area made our current speed dangerous enough. There was a good reason many local cars and SUVs had bull bars installed—hitting a roo, especially one of the big buggers, could write a vehicle off. And that was the last thing we—or the two men we were trying to save—needed right now.

It draws close came Katie's comment.

Define close.

Five minutes, if that.

Five minutes at least gave us time. I leaned forward, peering into the darkness to the right of the high beams. After a moment, I spotted it—a driveway.

"There," I said, pointing. "Left there."

Monty swung into the drive. Mud sprayed all around us, momentarily blocking my vision. "A little more warning next time would be handy."

"Sorry." Though I wasn't.

The dirt road ran around the top of a large dam, then curved to the left. The headlights pinned a long, farmhouse-style redbrick house and the white Mercedes sitting out the front. Sensor lights came on as we pulled to a halt next to the Merc, spotlighting us in brightness but throwing everything else into deeper darkness.

I grabbed my pack, jumped out of the car, and slammed the door shut. The sound echoed loudly in the night, and the curtains twitched, revealing a pale, round face.

I had no immediate sense of danger, but the night was unusually quiet. Granted, it was winter and as cold as hell, but that didn't usually stop the night scavengers from moving around.

Monty moved to the front of the SUV. "I sent Aiden a text with our location. It'll be twenty before he gets here, apparently."

"Which will be seventeen minutes too late."

His gaze shot to mine. "It's close?"

"Yes, but I'm not getting any more feedback than that and I'm not sensing anything."

"Me either." He scanned the night for a second. "We might need to split up to have any hope of finding it."

I hesitated. Splitting up was dangerous, but given we had no idea what direction this thing was coming from, it was also the fastest way of finding it. "You go left, I'll go right. If you find anything, shout."

"If I find anything, shouting won't be my first option."

He strode off, the threads of a cage spell appearing around his fingers. As I slung my backpack over my shoulder, the front door opened, and the man I'd glimpsed through the window appeared. "What's going on out here?"

"We've reports of a possible intruder in the area," I said. "Go inside; keep your doors locked."

"You rangers?"

"No. Witches, working with the rangers."

"Lizzie?" Samuel stepped past the owner. "What's going on?"

"Remember that niggle I mentioned this afternoon?"

"It's proving true?"

"Yes. Lock everything down and keep the house owner safe."

Thankfully, he didn't argue; he just hustled the older man back inside.

I ran toward the end of the house, the threads of a repelling spell stirring around my fingertips; as the light from the spots faded behind me, the darkness closed in. Several large shapes loomed ahead, and I instinctively slowed before I realized it was a shed and a large water tank. I continued on cautiously. The near gale force wind that had plagued much of the day had fallen away, but it was still strong enough to stir through branches of the nearby trees, causing a rustling that sounded like the whisperings of the dead. I shivered and hoped it wasn't a portent of what was to come.

The wild magic chose that moment to untwine from my wrist and drift away. I'd either reached the limit of Katie's control or whatever she and the wild magic had sensed was no longer a threat.

I hoped it was the latter. I suspected the former was more likely.

I walked on, my heart racing so fast it felt like one long scream. I had no sense of anything untoward nearby, and there was no sound other than the whispering trees.

Then, from up ahead, between the shadowy outline of the tank and the larger structure that was the shed, something moved. I stopped, my fingers clenched against the instinct to unleash the repelling spell. The last thing I needed was to send some poor farm animal tumbling.

More movement, but it was gone almost as fast as it had appeared.

But that very brief glimpse was enough to have Jackson's words echoing through my mind.

I scanned the darkness, looking for something that resembled tumbling rubbish even if what I'd seen hadn't been tumbling—though it certainly *had* moved peculiarly.

Nothing.

I took a deep breath in a somewhat useless effort to calm the nerves and walked toward the tank. As I neared it, fading scents teased my nostrils—hints of magic.

Dark magic.

A twig snapped somewhere behind me. I spun around, the repelling spell buzzing brightly around my fingers, ready to be unleashed.

Another flash of white, this time moving away from the house and deeper into the trees. It definitely *wasn't* a scrap of rubbish drawn along on the breeze. It was moving with far too much intent.

It also held a human shape, even if small and misshapen.

"Monty," I yelled. "It's over here and on the move."

"Wait for me" came his response.

I hesitated, not wanting to lose the trail of whatever this thing was, but also knowing it would be nothing short of utter stupidity to go after it alone. I could protect myself—and had multiple times against all sorts of supernatural nasties—but, small or not, this thing had taken down a werewolf in his prime, and hadn't, if Jackson was to be believed, used magic to do so.

I swore and quickly flung a tracking spell after the fleeing form. But just as the spell was about to hit, the malformed figure darted sideways and disappeared.

Which left me wondering if it had sensed the spell. If it *had*, then definitely it couldn't be a werewolf. They weren't magic sensitive, even if there was magic in their souls.

Monty slid to a stop beside me. "Where is it?"

"Gone. I tried to place a tracking spell, but the damn thing sensed it."

"Fuck." He scrubbed a hand through his hair. "It'll no doubt come back the minute we leave."

"Doesn't that depend on why it was here?" I hurried toward the spot where I'd last seen the figure. If magic had been involved in its sudden disappearance, there should be some lingering evidence of it. "It's not exactly following the pattern of the last two kills, is it?"

Monty fell in step beside me. "The last two didn't have a pattern—other than being out in the bush."

"And the reports of a crying child in the area."

"There's no evidence yet that those reports are in any way connected."

I glanced at him, eyebrows raised. "Do you really think it's a coincidence that both Patrick and Jackson mentioned it?"

"Well, no, but my opinion doesn't make it fact."

"Until we uncover what we're dealing with, opinions are all we have."

"True." He stopped in front of the tree that held the fading remnants of my tracking spell and scanned the ground. It wasn't only muddy, but pretty chewed up. "It looks to me like something heavy caused that."

A distant siren began to cut through the otherwise quiet night. "The thing I saw was small, though. I wouldn't have thought it had the bulk to cause such deep impressions in the ground."

His gaze shot to mine. "You saw it? Clearly saw it?"

"Well, not clearly, but it was very definitely humanoid

in shape and just as clearly misshapen."

"Misshapen how?"

"It was small, ran with a limp, and was oddly hunched over." I shrugged. "I only caught a glimpse, Monty."

"Which is more than Jackson got, and he was facing the thing when it gutted him."

"And maybe the reason he didn't see it is because this thing uses dark magic. I smelled it over near the water tank."

"You *smelled* it?"

"Yeah." I grimaced. "The wild magic is enhancing my senses, remember?"

"Yes, but I've never read anything that has suggested magic has a *smell*."

"And the general stuff doesn't—at least as far as I'm aware," I said. "But dark magic has a definite and rather pungent sulfur aroma."

"Huh." He half turned as light briefly swept the strand of trees we were in. "That'll be Aiden, I'm guessing."

"And what gave that away?" My voice was dry. "Was it the red and blue lights, the siren, or the color of his truck?"

He raised his eyebrows, a smile twitching his lips. "Aren't you in fine form tonight? Any particular reason?"

"Nothing other than the fact I delight in making fun of dumb statements."

He snorted softly. "Watch it, or I'll return the favor."

I grinned. "Bring it on, Cousin."

Two doors slammed, then stones crunched as Aiden moved toward us. He'd obviously sent whoever was with him into the house.

He appeared a few seconds later; his gaze scanned us both, then moved to the torn-up ground at our feet. "Whatever left those tracks doesn't smell right."

"If you can smell it, you can follow it, right?" Monty

said.

Aiden nodded. "Is it safe to leave Jaz and John in the house without magical protection?"

"They're not unprotected," I said. "Samuel's in there."

His gaze shot to mine. "Why is he out here?"

"Said he needed to talk to the owner."

"About the bombing? Because John is the last person who would have ever gone into Émigré; trust me on that."

"Apparently he delivered some goods half an hour before the bomb went off."

Aiden grunted. It was not a happy sound. "When were you talking to Samuel?"

"He came to see me this afternoon."

Aiden studied me through slightly narrowed eyes. The alpha wolf, I suspected, didn't like having another male hanging around.

He didn't say anything, though. He just made a quick call to Jaz, then moved into the trees, following the muddy footprints. They drew us deeper into the forest and the shadows, but I had no sense of the being we were tracking, and the pungent scent of darker magic wasn't evident in the air. Of course, that could just be because the breeze was strong enough to draw it away, but something within me doubted it. And if that something was right, it meant that this thing was able to switch the dark magic on and off at will—and that was extremely unusual. For the most part, dark spells involved the use of blood—they couldn't just be spoken, not in the same manner as regular spells.

"Is it just me," Monty said after a while, "or do we seem to be looping back around the farmhouse?"

"We are." Aiden's voice was grim. "Perhaps its initial sighting was merely a means of drawing you two away from the house."

"Why would it want to do that, though?" Monty asked. "This isn't the only homestead in the area—why wouldn't he hit one of the others, instead of risking capture here?"

"Perhaps an easy kill is not what this thing is after."

"Meaning there's a connection between Patrick and Jackson?" I asked.

"They went to the same school."

I blinked. "They were the same age?"

They certainly hadn't looked it—though in truth, age was never an easy guess when it came to werewolves, thanks to their longer lives and their regenerative abilities.

"As is John," Aiden said. "I don't know if he was in the same class as the other two, but I wouldn't be surprised if that was the case."

"So our next task," Monty said, "is finding out what lies in the background of all three that might draw such a brutal death."

"Such a brilliant idea—why didn't we think about that?" Aiden's voice was dry.

"You've been hanging around Ashworth too long," Monty grumbled. "His snark has washed off on you."

Aiden's amusement stung the air, but he didn't say anything. The muddy ground continued to lead us in a wide loop around the back of the farmhouse and, after another five minutes or so, the glimmer of its lights became visible through the trees.

We were maybe a dozen steps away from the fence that divided the heavily treed area from the large paddock surrounding the house, when the pungent aroma of sulfur hit, the scent so strong it made me gag.

I stopped so abruptly, Monty crashed into me. But before either of us could say anything, gunshots shattered the night's hush.

CHAPTER SEVEN

A iden swore and ran. I followed, the repelling spell pulsing against my fingers, ready to be unleashed. Monty's magic surged, though I couldn't immediately place the spell and dared not risk looking over my shoulder lest I fall. But it wasn't another cage spell—it felt bigger than that. Deadlier than that.

Aiden cleared the fence in a bound. Monty and I were a whole lot less elegant but were nevertheless quickly on his tail. As we bolted across the grass that swept down to the house, the back door opened, and Jaz came flying out.

She saw us and slid to a halt. "Did you see it?"

"See what?" Aiden growled. "Nothing came out that door except you."

"It wasn't inside—it was at the window, but ran this way. I can't smell its trail, though."

Aiden swore again. "Get back inside, just in case it's doubling around. Liz, Monty, you sensing anything?"

"No," Monty said, even as I said, "Yes, this way."

I darted to the left, heading for the far end of the house. The pungent scent was tenuous, the breeze already tearing it apart. I placed a hand against the end of the house for balance as I slid around the corner, the rough bricks tearing my skin. A flash of white briefly appeared; it was on the bank of the dam, but winked out of existence almost as soon as I'd spotted it. *That* was the result of a shielding spell, rather than the ability to become invisible, if the brief flare of power across the night was anything to go by.

"It's over near the dam," I said.

Aiden sped past me, his form flowing from human to wolf. I swore and reached for more speed in a desperate effort to keep up. While the charm I'd made him should protect him from this thing's magic, it wouldn't protect him from a physical assault. He might be a werewolf in his prime, but Patrick had been too.

Monty ran past me, his longer legs giving him an advantage. He raced up the dam's bank, then tossed a twisted mass of green-and-silver spell threads across the water. Just for an instant, that flash of white appeared, and I saw its face. It was a grotesque mockery that was neither human nor wolf nor anything else I'd ever seen.

Then energy surged, and a black blot hurtled toward Monty's spell; the two met with enough force that the air vibrated. For a heartbeat, neither spell got the better of the other. Then fingers of black crept over the green-and-silver threads, containing them, erasing them. When there was nothing but darkness left, the blot exploded, and the two spells—as well as the creature—were gone.

I raced past Monty and continued on to the spot where I'd last seen the thing. Nothing. No smell, and certainly no tracks. Had it flown away? Just because I hadn't spotted anything resembling wings, didn't mean it couldn't have them. It could also have used a transport spell. I might not have sensed—or even smelled—the creation of one but that didn't mean anything, especially when the pungent remains of the black blotting spell still stained the air.

Aiden appeared out of the scrub, his silver coat shimmering as he regained human form. "Lost it about half a kilometer in."

"Did it stop abruptly or just fade?"

"The latter." He scrubbed a hand across his jaw, frustration evident in his expression. "What *is* this thing? Its scent is unlike anything I've ever come across."

"I don't know."

"Well, I've a bad feeling we'd better find out, and quickly."

"Things definitely aren't good when *you're* getting bad feelings," Monty commented.

He looked pale; backlash from the spell explosion, I suspected.

Aiden didn't look amused by the comment. "How likely is it that this thing will come back?"

Monty shrugged. "As you said earlier, it really depends on why this creature came here after John in the first place."

"We could ring the house with protections," I said. "But it would probably be better if John simply heads out of the reservation for a few days."

"Convincing him of that might take some doing. He's a stubborn bastard."

Aiden caught my hand and helped me back up the dam's bank, then kept hold as we moved back toward the house. Part of me couldn't help but think Samuel's presence was the main reason for this sudden bit of intimacy—especially given he generally avoided any such contact when he was working.

Maybe, I thought with amusement, it was the alpha's

gentle way of reminding me I was in a relationship with *him*.

He opened the back door and ushered me inside. I walked through the laundry, then followed the soft sound of voices down a long hallway.

Jaz looked around as we entered. "Did you get it?"

I shook my head. "Whatever this thing is, it's capable of magic."

"Light or dark?" Samuel asked.

He was sitting at one end of the leather sofa. At the other was a gray-haired, craggy-faced man—John, I presumed.

"Dark, though how that's possible given he or she didn't use blood sacrifice—"

"Not all dark sorcery needs a sacrifice," Monty commented. "And even when blood *is* required, sometimes a simple cut across the palm or the arm will suffice."

"Neither of which is easy to do when on the run."

"But not impossible if practiced enough." Monty glanced at Aiden. "Do you want us to run some protections around the place?"

"Unless John is willing to stay indoors twenty-four seven—"

"And he's bloody well not," the older man growled.

"Then it's pretty much useless. Patrick was killed in daylight, remember."

"Patrick? Dead?" John's obstinate expression dissolved into shock. "When?"

"A couple of days ago." Aiden moved past me. "I'm afraid Jackson was killed yesterday."

John swore and scrubbed a hand across his cheek. "Do you know why?"

"No, but maybe you can help in that regard."

John's confusion was evident. "But why? I haven't seen Patrick for months—and it's been years since I've seen Jackson."

"We don't think these kills are related to the present, but rather the past."

"That still doesn't make any sense."

As Aiden sat down near John, Monty touched my arm, drawing my attention from their conversation.

"Why don't you head home?" he said softly. "It's pointless us both being here."

"Except I can smell this thing. You can't." A smile twitched my lips. "Or are you just trying to save the council's coffers some overtime?"

"I don't care about costs. I do, however, care about you—and the bags under your eyes are large enough to carry a wallet."

I snorted. "Thanks for that lovely image."

"Go home."

"Before you do," Samuel said, rising. "Do you want to show me where you last saw this creature?"

"Sure, but why?"

He shrugged. "The trees might be able to clarify what was moving around out there."

"Seriously?" Jaz's expression was a mix of disbelief and awe. "You're going to talk to a *tree*?"

He smiled warmly, and Jaz blinked as something almost primeval crossed her expression. It was nice to know I wasn't the only attached woman affected by this man's charms.

"Not talk to them, as such. More ... connect to their energy and through it gather impressions of what passed through their resonance."

"Which sounds even more impressive."

Samuel laughed. "It's really not—especially when compared to the forces these two can bring to bear."

"Jaz," Aiden said, voice a little clipped, "go with them."

She nodded and motioned for me to lead the way. I hesitated, my gaze seeking Aiden's. "See you later."

"You will."

The sudden heat in his eyes suggested "seeing me" wasn't the only thing he'd be doing, and my hormones happily skipped around at the thought. I spun and headed outside.

The night seemed bitter after the warmth of the house, and I hurriedly zipped up my coat and then thrust my hands into my pockets. Samuel fell into step beside me, his big body moving easily through the darkness. But I guess when you could tune into the energy of all living things and basically "see" through it, tripping over the unseen wasn't so much of a problem.

I led the two of them around the top of the dam and then down the side to where I'd last seen the white figure. I stopped, but Samuel moved on, his fingers lightly touching the tree trunks as he passed them. An odd sort of energy stirred, one that reminded me a little of the wild magic, but richer, warmer. It ran across his hands and spun up from the earth, enveloping him in a golden-greenish light.

Jaz stopped beside me. "Am I imagining things, or is he suddenly glowing?"

"He's glowing."

"Is that because he's communing with the trees?"

"Basically, yes."

"You lot never cease to amaze me."

I smiled. "I could say the same about you werewolves."

She laughed. "I guess it's all a matter of what you grow up with."

"Yes."

Samuel continued to walk through the trees, his steps never missing a beat. I'd never had all that much to do with the Kang line in my time up in Canberra, and it was fascinating to watch his power at work.

After ten or so minutes, the glow faded, and he turned and walked back. His face was pale, and his eyes lacked their usual brightness. The cost of communing, no doubt.

"Anything?" Jaz asked.

"The energy that passed by the trees has been warped by dark magic," he said. "I think she—"

"She?" Jaz cut in. "This thing is a woman?"

"The radiated energy is feminine, so yes." His gaze came to mine. "The dark energy infuses her output in much the same manner as the wild magic infuses yours."

Given I was shielding my output these days, it was interesting that he could see it. "Does that mean the dark magic is a part of her DNA?"

He hesitated. "It is now. Whether she was born that way, or it's a result of a catastrophic event, I can't say."

"Anything else?" Jaz said. "Any idea how we catch her?"

Samuel scraped a hand through his hair. "Not really. She has an innate cunning—the trees could sense it. She also exudes a oneness with the wilderness, which is oddly juxtaposed against an underlying stream that speaks of humanity."

"Meaning we're dealing with something that's *human*?" I queried.

"Or werewolf. Unfortunately, she didn't linger long enough for her life force to make a deeper impression. There *was* a thread of anger—perhaps a shadow of revenge —in its output, however."

"If she's here for vengeance," Jaz said, "it means the three men must have had some contact with her in the past. That at least gives us a starting point."

Samuel hesitated. "I wouldn't be so certain, as it wasn't clear that the need for revenge is in any way connected to the catastrophic event that caused the twisted nature of her energy."

"And yet there must be some connection between her and the three men—why else would she specifically target them?"

"I have no idea." He took a deep breath and released it slowly. It was a sound of utter weariness. "I'd better go, otherwise I'll fall asleep at the wheel."

"Don't forget to set your wards when you get back to the hotel," I said. "Just in case."

The smile that briefly tugged at his lips was a pale shadow of its normally robust self. "I always do."

We all walked back around the dam. Jaz peeled off to go back into the house while Samuel and I continued on to the cars.

"Don't forget to give me a call if you hear back from Maelle," he said as he opened the Mercedes's door.

"Only if you promise to answer the damn call." At his raised eyebrow, I added, "I called to warn you this thing was after John. You didn't answer."

"Ah. Sorry." He grimaced. "The phone was dead, so I left it charging in the car."

"Best not to let it die too often," I teased. "Because you never know when I might change my mind about going out with you."

"I wouldn't let your wolf hear you say that."

"My wolf needs a reminder every now and again that there are other fish in the sea."

"Not sure whether to be pleased or offended about being compared to a mere fish. I'm far tastier than that." A sexy glimmer sparked in his eyes but just as quickly died. "Take care hunting this thing. It feels nasty."

"That's a very common theme when it comes to the things this place attracts."

"Yes, but you're not dealing with what I'd term a 'regular' type of supernatural being this time. It's something very different." He smiled. "And on that cheery note, I'll bid you goodbye."

I nodded and moved on to my SUV, starting her up and following him down the drive. I was halfway home when a vague vibration began along the psychic lines. It took a couple of seconds to realize what it was—the new perimeter alarms I'd set around the storage unit.

Someone was trying to break in again.

I swore and did a sharp U-turn, the SUV's tires squealing in protest. *Belle, you awake?*

It's ten in the evening. Her mental tones were dry. *Since when have I ever gone to bed that early? What's up?*

Someone's trying to break into our storage unit.

What? How do you know?

I set a new perimeter alarm after the first attempt—

There was a first attempt?

Yeah, sorry, forgot to mention it with everything else going on. Can you get over there and see what's happening? But be careful, because I have no idea who or what it is.

Why the fuck would anyone want to break into our storage unit? It's not like we keep much there other than books.

The would-be thieves wouldn't know that, though, and we do have one of the larger units.

She grunted. It was not a happy sound. *Mom and I will head over there now—*

I'm not sure it's wise to involve—

I'd like to see you try and keep her out of it, Belle said dryly. *Besides, she'll be handy to have around in the event there're more than a couple of them. She can mop up those that escape me.*

Just be careful, both of you.

As someone is wont to say, always.

I half smiled. *I'll be there in twenty.*

You're not home yet?

I was just on my way. See you soon.

I broke off the connection and concentrated on the road and getting back to Castle Rock as fast as I could. By the time I reached the self-storage premises, the lights were ablaze and there were several cars out the front of our unit—my Suzi, Harry's red four-wheel drive, and a ranger vehicle. I parked behind the latter and climbed out.

The first thing I noticed was the condition of the roller door. They hadn't bothered cutting the lock this time—they'd simply driven straight into it, punching the middle section of the door into the unit and ripping the sides away from the frame. Only the top section remained in place.

Anything taken, Belle?

The spells held, so no. She was standing to the left of the smashed roller door. Ava was nowhere to be seen, but the slight caress of movement across the protection threads suggested she was inside the unit.

How long has Mac been here?

He and Harry only arrived a few minutes ago.

"I can't understand it," Harry was saying as I approached. "I added extra sensor alarms—I should have been notified the minute there was any unauthorized activity."

"Did you check the other renters to see if anyone had lost a card?" I asked.

He turned around, his expression a mix of frustration and annoyance. "Yes, and no one had."

"Or they simply weren't willing to admit it," Belle said.

"Can you access the reader's data and see who entered in the last couple of hours?" Mac asked.

"Of course, but it didn't help last time."

"It happened before?" Mac's tone was sharp. "Why wasn't it reported?"

"Because I thought it was just kids up to idle mischief. Besides, nothing was taken." Harry grimaced. "It affects the insurance costs if we have too many incidents."

"Not to mention your reputation," Belle muttered.

Harry glanced at her, but didn't say anything, suggesting her comment was spot-on. Not that that was unexpected given she was no doubt skimming his mind.

"How did they get in the first time, then?" Mac asked.

"Via an unassigned card."

My eyebrows rose. "Unassigned cards are active?"

"Normally, no."

"Were any taken from your office?" Mac asked.

"No. I did check."

Mac's expression suggested he didn't entirely believe that. "Then how—"

"The encoding machine is in the office."

"And not locked away, I'm guessing?"

"Well, no, because I didn't think it necessary."

Mac rolled his eyes. "Were there any unusual incidents before the initial break-in, then?"

"No."

"Fine. Let's go check the records. Ladies, if you're confident nothing was stolen, you're free to go."

"I'll get the door replaced ASAP," Harry added. "At my cost, of course."

Suggesting he doesn't want to lose his best customers, I said.

Ain't that a fact. Belle pushed upright. *I didn't mention this to Mac, but the would-be thief didn't just use a car. They also used magic.*

My gaze snapped to hers. *What kind?*

The spell breaker kind.

Did you manage to snare a thread or two?

I didn't, but Mom did. Told you she'd come in handy.

She led the way into the unit via the new gap between the runner and the door. I studied the pulsing network of spells as I followed her across to the inner building. For the most part they were untouched, but there was a slight blot—little more than a smudge—along the lines of the new alarm spell I'd installed. They'd tried to disarm it; the fact they hadn't succeeded suggested we weren't dealing with professionals. Any witch with a good degree of training could have dismantled it easily enough.

I headed up the steps and followed Belle into the smaller unit. Ava turned and held up a small glass jar. Inside were two small spell threads. "These things won't last all that long—I haven't the skill to enhance their lifespan."

"We don't need to," I said. "We just need them to last long enough for me to try and get some sense of their creator."

Ava's gaze widened. "You can do that?"

I smiled at the surprise in her voice. She obviously knew it was possible to track threads back to their originator via magic, given it was a common process in Canberra when it came to rogue spells or spellers. She just hadn't—despite everything we'd told her—realized how much of a power jump I'd had since she last saw us. Or that it wasn't just my spell casting capabilities that had increased.

"In theory."

"So you've not tried it before?"

"Not with something this fragile," I said. "But we've certainly had success doing this with various other objects, including the bloody feather of a Empusa we were trying to stop."

Her eyes went wide again. "Dear God, an Empusa? You didn't tell me about that one, Belle."

Belle grinned. "There are some things a mother should never know."

"Meaning the Empusa wasn't the worse thing you've confronted?"

"Hell no." Belle patted her mother's arm. "Best you not ask, though, because you'll only get all worried and fretful."

"And a comment like that isn't going to have the same effect at all."

Ava's voice was dry, and Belle laughed. "We survived Clayton. Dealing with the supernatural world is a breeze by comparison."

"I wish the same could be said about Maelle." It was absently said. I plucked the jar from Ava's hand, then moved across to the desk.

Belle groaned. "You've had a dream? Or is it simply a very sensible fear of a very scary bitch?"

A smile twitched my lips. "No dream. Just a feeling."

"They're almost as goddamn bad."

"But nowhere near as accurate." I sat cross-legged on the table and placed the jar in front of me. The two threads inside the jar were pulsing, suggesting they were very close to the end of their active life. If I wanted to get any information out of them, I needed to be quick.

"Do you need us to do anything?" Ava asked.

I began unscrewing the lid. "Just keep an eye out for Harry and Mac. The latter will be annoyed Belle didn't mention a possible lead."

"It's not like they could have accessed it," she replied. "Not without our help."

"That, as Aiden would say, is not the point."

I placed the lid onto the table and then carefully shook the threads down into my palm. The caress of their power was faint, but it held no hint of shadows or darkness. The spell's construction appeared formulaic; the witch who created it had at least been trained at a base level.

None of which was all that helpful.

I took a deep breath to center my energy, then opened the psychic gates and reached. Nothing happened. I closed my hand around the threads and let the faint pulse of their energy beat against my skin. Slowly, ever so slowly, the image of a woman who looked vaguely familiar formed. She had gray hair, blue eyes, a happy smile, and an aura that glowed with a vivid mix of pink and green, the two colors most associated with healing.

Even as I frowned, the memory fell into place. Aiden and I had visited her shop in Woodend when we'd been searching for the witch who'd created the tracking and control bracelets being used to hunt and kill reservation werewolves.

The threads gave a final pulse of power and then faded away. I opened my hand and watched the threads disintegrate.

"Anything?" Belle asked.

I nodded and climbed off the table. "It was made by a witch in Woodend—her store is called Pot of Magic. Aiden and I were there briefly when we were looking for the witch behind the wolf trackers."

"Is she good or bad?" Ava asked.

"Her craft is healing. Not sure why she'd deviate into something like this."

"Money," Belle said. "It's the root of all evil."

"I don't believe *she* believed the spell was to be used in a nefarious manner."

Belle expression suggested she wasn't so convinced. "So a visit is in order tomorrow?"

I nodded. "Would you and Ava like to head out in the morning? Woodend's a lovely little town, and it's a nice drive down there. You could make a day of it."

"Deal." She smiled. "And it's not like the café's been flat out of late."

"The weather *is* supposed to improve tomorrow."

"Ha! Believe that when I see it." She turned and led the way out. "You'd better warn Harry our unit is protected by magic and that he'll need to contact one of us before the new door is installed."

I nodded. "You might as well take the SUV—it's the easiest to get out. I'll see you tomorrow evening."

"It'll be late. If we're going to make a day of it, we might as well have dinner out too."

"Sounds like a good idea."

I kissed both their cheeks, then, as the two of them climbed into the SUV, I walked across to the office. Harry was sitting at his desk while Mac leaned over his shoulder. Both were staring at a small computer screen, their expressions intent.

"Anything?" I asked.

"Yeah, bloody small writing," Mac grumbled.

I stopped behind them and looked over Harry's other shoulder. The writing was indeed tiny and gray on black, which made it even more difficult to see. "You can't enlarge the text?"

"No," Harry said. "Maybe you should both invest in eyeglasses."

Mac glanced at me and rolled his eyes. Obviously not the first time he'd heard that particular statement.

Harry continued to scroll through the files for several minutes, then stopped and pointed at the screen. "There it is."

I squinted at the screen. It was marked "unassigned keycard" and had a number and time stamp beside it. "Eight forty-five. When did they leave?"

He scrolled on a bit more. "Three minutes past nine."

"They weren't here long," I said.

"Long enough to make a mess of your goddamn roller door," Harry grouched.

"So why didn't the alarms go off?" Mac said.

"They wouldn't if the access was authorized."

"What about the cameras, then?" I asked. "Has the recording been checked yet?"

"No, because we had to grab a time first," Harry said. "Hard to tell who was actually authorized and who wasn't otherwise."

He swung around abruptly—forcing Mac and me to jump out of the way—and stalked across to the other side of the room. Next to the filing cabinets, on a long secondary desk, was a second computer, a printer, and an upright, foot-high black box with a number of wires sticking out of it— one of which was attached to the computer. He moved the mouse to reactivate the monitor, clicked through a number of programs and screens, and then typed the time in and hit enter.

The image blurred for several minutes and then settled. The gates appeared, the reader barely visible beyond them. Lights swept into the driveway, briefly flaring against the camera's lens, making it impossible to see anything.

"Need to fix that," Mac commented. "You'd only need to move the camera a foot or two to the right."

Harry grunted in agreement, though I suspected he had no intention of shifting anything. The gates slid open, and the fierce brightness of the lights dipped away. It was a nondescript white dual-cab four-wheel drive; my gaze dropped to the number plate. It had been blacked out.

The truck swung around so that its rear faced our roller door. Then, with a slight puff of smoke coming from the rear tires, the truck reversed back into our door. The truck stopped, and two men immediately jumped out. Not only were both dressed in black, but they both wore black gloves and brightly colored full ski masks. The driver was broad of shoulder and slim of hip, the other man smaller and built like a weightlifter or boxer.

"Well, this wasn't a random act of thievery, then," I commented. "They were fully prepared."

"What surprises me is that they didn't get in," Harry commented. "They should have, given the mess they made of the door."

"Watch," I said, amused.

The passenger kicked at the left edge of the door to widen the gap and then pushed through. There was an immediate spark of light, followed by a bright flare of red that punched him in the chest and threw him backward. He landed on his rump several feet away, close to the truck's rear.

Harry's gaze snapped to mine. "You've protected the place with magic?"

"Of course we have. Which reminds me, you'll need to contact us before the door is replaced. We made an exception in the spells for you, but we'll have to disengage them for the installer."

"You should have told me."

"Why? It's not like you can't get in there if necessary."

"But you just said—"

"Pay attention, Harry," Mac said. "She just said she made an exception for you and that means—unless I'm very much mistaken—that you can come and go as you want."

"Though not, as we've noted before, into the inner unit. Nothing and no one is getting in that. Not fire, not flood, not even a bug."

"I still think—"

"We've signed your waiver, Harry," I said. "So you've nothing to worry about in regard to the inner unit."

"With that sorted out, can we now get back to the image on the screen." Mac's gaze met mine. "I know both men are concealed, but is their build or the way they move familiar? Do you recognize the truck?"

I shook my head. "Sorry."

"Always a long shot. Harry, I'll need that tape."

As he set about making a copy, I said, "Mac, you'll keep us updated on progress?"

A smile touched his lips. "I daresay the boss will if I don't."

Or tell me off for not informing him of the problem earlier, I thought, amused. I touched Harry's shoulder lightly. "Don't forget to contact us when the replacement door arrives."

He grunted, his concentration more on what he was

doing. I bid them both good night, then left. Aiden still wasn't home by the time I arrived, so I made myself a toasted ham-and-cheese sandwich, poured a whiskey, and then settled down to read the books I'd taken from the storage unit earlier.

By the time Aiden's truck pulled in beside my car, I'd consumed another whiskey and had flagged two possible supernatural entities. While Samuel had said we were dealing with something that held a degree of humanity, it didn't totally discount the supernatural angle—especially since this woman was using dark magic. There were plenty of nasty entities out there capable of changing their appearance—and even the output of their life force—as necessary.

I glanced around as Aiden stepped through the door. Weariness haunted his expression and scent—my senses were definitely sharpening, and I couldn't help but wonder what else was changing. Katie might have said I would never become a full werewolf—and I did believe that, as not even the wild magic could make that sort of deep-level DNA change—but it was also fact that not even she could predict just how deep the alterations would go. Was it possible that I could become wolf in all ways except the ability to change?

Part of me hoped so. The other, more realistic, part was more inclined to think that holding such hopes would inevitably lead to heartache.

I snapped the book closed and put it on the table. "You're late. Was there another problem?"

"No, just the same one—John being ornery." He kissed the top of my head. "Would you like a coffee? Or a hot chocolate?"

"I never say no to chocolate. I thought you'd realize that by now, Ranger."

He laughed. "It's fairly late—I'd actually expected to find you in bed."

"I was reading up on supernatural nasties." I glanced across at the glowing blue numbers on the Blu-ray player and saw it was close to midnight. "If I'd realized it was so damn late, I would have been."

He flicked on the kettle, then made my chocolate and heated it up in the microwave. "Did you find anything in the book?"

"One likely and one remote possibility."

Once he'd made his coffee, he picked up both cups and walked over. "So, what is the likely?"

I quickly described the Tiyanak—which, according to one of the legends, was a dwarf-like being with one leg shorter than the other and knife-like claws that used the cry of an infant to attract his prey.

He frowned. "I thought Samuel said we're dealing with a female, not a male."

"Yes, but that doesn't mean there can't be a female version. Or that she's not using magic to change her appearance." I accepted my mug with a nod of thanks and took a drink. "You've nothing to fear on the Samuel front, by the way."

He half smiled. "I know, but I can't always control instinct."

"A werewolf getting all territorial over a witch? Impossible."

"Not when said witch has invaded every part of my life, physically and emotionally."

"Invaded is *such* a romantic word."

My voice was droll and he laughed. "Conquered? Possessed? Seeped?"

"Ew."

He laughed again, then leaned forward and kissed me, long and slow.

"I adore you, Lizzie Grace," he murmured eventually. "The day your path crossed mine was the best day of my entire life."

It was probably as close to a declaration of love as he was ever likely to get, and my heart did a crazy little dance. "That would be the day you arrested my ass?"

"And a mighty fine ass it is too."

"Here I was thinking you were too busy suspecting me of murder to notice such things."

"I followed you through the forest, remember. It was impossible not to notice. What happened at your storage unit?"

I raised an eyebrow. "How did you hear about that?"

"Heard the call come in when I was escorting John to his new digs."

"Ah." I took another drink and quickly updated him.

He frowned. "How many people know what you hold in that unit?"

"Only our immediate circle."

"What about the man Belle was dating? The one who was transcribing them?"

"Belle never told him about the storage unit, and he only ever saw a couple of the books."

"Were they valuable?"

I hesitated. "I'd presume so, given their age and the fact that there's nothing else around like them."

"I'll get Mac to talk to him, then, just in case."

"I guess it couldn't hurt." Though it would probably be quicker and easier if Belle did. If nothing else, she could skim his thoughts and tell truth from lie. Not that she'd seen him recently—their relationship had been casual, but it had definitely fallen by the wayside after Monty had flattened Clayton when he'd tried to attack Belle.

The conversation switched to other matters, and time slipped by. Once we'd finished our drinks, Aiden rose and held out his hand. "Shall we head up to the bedroom?"

I raised my eyebrows, smiling lazily. "That depends entirely on what's on offer in said bedroom."

"Anything you want, my dear."

"So the alpha is willing to let me take utter control over proceedings?"

Delight and desire shone in his eyes. "Absolutely."

I laughed, put my mug on the coffee table, and then let him pull me upright. He wrapped an arm around my waist, and we climbed the stairs, his body so warm against mine and his touch electric, even through my clothes.

In the warm darkness of the bedroom, I stripped him off —tasting and nipping him every step of the way—then pushed him back onto the bed and slowly, teasingly, undressed myself. His desire burned the air, drowning me in its scent, filling my nose and my lungs and making me ache in ways and places I hadn't thought possible. Once naked, I climbed onto the bed and straddled him. I caught his hands and held them lightly over his head before kissing him long and hard. After a soft warning not to move or touch me in any way, I worshipped his glorious body with lips and tongue and teeth, taking him to the very edge of release, then backing away, kissing him until the scent and urgency of his desire had banked enough to begin the whole process again.

When I finally took him deep inside, the air was so thick with need and hunger that it felt like liquid fire. He caught my hips, bracing me as he arched into me, driving upward again and again, his desperation matched by my own. I claimed every inch of him, wanting his heat, wanting his climax, wanting to feel it so very deep inside.

We came as one and, just for an instant, it felt as if this union was complete in a way that was more than *just* physical. Then that moment was gone and there was nothing but mind-blowing, body-shaking, utterly glorious satisfaction.

For several long minutes afterward I could barely breathe, let alone think or move. I simply rested my forehead against his, breathing in as he breathed out, feeling utterly as one with the man.

When my breathing and pulse settled to more normal levels, I lifted my face to kiss him and then slid to one side. He wrapped me in his arms, drawing me closer, and kissed my forehead.

"Sweetheart," he said softly. "Feel free to take control any damn time you want."

I laughed softly. "Prepare to be reminded of that—and not just when it comes to sex."

"You don't scare me, witch."

"One day I will," I murmured, even as my eyes closed. I was fast asleep within seconds.

As predicted, the weather did improve the next day, and the café had a steady flow of customers. Monty came in for his usual coffee and cake midafternoon and didn't seem surprised Belle wasn't there. That undoubtedly meant the two of them had spent time chatting on the phone either last night or this morning. I made myself a pot of tea, then sat down opposite him and updated him on supernatural possibilities I'd found.

"I don't suppose there was a suggestion on how to locate it?"

I smiled and poured my tea. "When have things ever been that easy?"

"I keep hoping that we'll catch a break one day."

"None of us are dead yet—that's probably as much of a break as we're going to get."

"And long may it remain that way." He clinked his mug against mine. "I was talking to Ashworth earlier—he said it might be worth laying a trap for this thing."

I frowned. "Aiden won't approve using John as bait."

"He doesn't have to. We can lay a scent trail using his clothes into a prepared trap."

"That's presuming we *are* dealing with either a rogue werewolf or a wolf twisted by dark magic. We may not be."

"But if we are, then it's a possibility."

"Have you mentioned it to Aiden?"

"Haven't seen him, so no."

I took a drink and leaned back in my chair. "Are you picking Belle up for the party tomorrow night?"

He nodded. "It's our first official date."

I grinned. "Is she aware of this fact? You *were* both invited separately, rather than as a couple."

"I asked if she'd like to come with me. She accepted. It is therefore a date in my books, and I will not be convinced otherwise."

"Wouldn't dream of spoiling your delusions, Cuz."

"And I appreciate that fact."

"So, what happened to all the grand plans you had for the momentous first date event?"

"They can wait until her mom has gone home. Although her mom has been rather helpful when it comes to the whole date thing." He finished his coffee, then pushed to his feet. "I'll see you tomorrow night, if nothing else happens in between."

"All things crossed it doesn't."

"Amen to *that*."

He left. I finished my tea, then collected the plates and cups and got back to work. Once the café had closed for the day, I spent a couple of hours doing prep, then cleaned up and turned out the lights. But as I picked up my purse, an odd scraping caught my attention.

It didn't repeat, but my trouble radar was now stirring. I shoved my keys in my pocket and carefully moved back into the café. While the pink fingers of sunset still tainted the sky outside, the café lay wrapped in shadows. There was no one in the room—the little bell above the door would have chimed had someone tried to enter—and no sign of anyone lurking beyond the windows, either at the front or in the laneway that ran along the side of the building.

I glanced up the stairs. The glow of the streetlights outside meant the darkness was not absolute. It also meant that if anyone *was* moving around up there, I should at least see their shadow. There was nothing.

And yet ...

I frowned and cautiously headed up. Magic stirred around my fingertips, the spell an odd mix of repelling and tracking magics. Perhaps my subconscious was a little more certain of trouble than it seemed. A tread creaked under my weight, and I froze, my heart beating somewhere in my throat, momentarily constricting my breathing.

There was no response.

I swallowed heavily, half wondering if the sound I'd heard was nothing more than the creak of an old place, then almost instantly dismissed it. While both the café and the upstairs apartment did have a chorus of nightly sounds as the building settled for the night, the noise I'd heard hadn't been one of them.

I walked on, only to pause again at a soft rattling. It was coming from the balcony area—or rather, from the sliding door. Someone was trying to get in.

I quickly—but quietly—went up the remaining steps, but stopped on the landing and cautiously peered around the corner.

And saw the shadow on the balcony.

CHAPTER EIGHT

H e had the build of a weightlifter and silver hair that glowed brightly in the streetlights. He was dressed in black, appeared to be wearing gloves, and had a large backpack slung over one shoulder.

If I wasn't mistaken, he was the shorter of the two men who'd reversed a truck into our storage unit.

I dragged out my phone, leaned back so that the glow of the screen wasn't immediately visible, then switched off the camera's flash and took a few quick photos. I debated whether to call it in or not, then decided to see what happened. I shoved the phone away and waited, my heart thumping so loud it seemed to fill the silence. The door rattled a few more times, then, with a soft click, slid open.

The thief stepped in, flashlight in one hand. I stepped out.

"What the fuck do you think you're doing?"

He swore, threw the flashlight at me, then turned and ran back out onto the balcony. As the flashlight landed near my feet and slid into the wall, I tossed the spell, then ran after him.

The tumbling threads of magic spun quickly through the air and hit his spine just as he was clambering over the railing. He made an odd gargling sort of sound, his arms flailing in an obvious attempt to gain balance, and then dropped out of sight.

I cursed, darted out the door, and leaned over the top rail. The thief hadn't disappeared down the street, as I'd half expected. He lay unmoving directly below.

I swore again, then grabbed my phone, calling an ambulance and then the ranger station.

"Ranger Jaz Marin here. How may I help you?"

"Jaz, it's Lizzie. Someone just tried to break into the apartment above the café and, unfortunately, fell over the railing when he was attempting to escape."

"Alive or dead?" she said calmly.

"Don't know, as I'm not down there yet. I've called an ambulance."

"Good. Don't touch anything—I'll be there in a minute."

She hung up. I slipped the phone back into my pocket and headed downstairs. The thief hadn't moved at all, and my heart beat a whole lot harder. I really hoped he wasn't dead, and that certainly *hadn't* been my intention when I'd thrown the spell. It had obviously packed quite a punch, and I couldn't help but wonder if the wild magic had something to do with that. Was it becoming a physical force as much as a magical? If it was, then it would certainly restrict what spells I could and couldn't do, especially when I was dealing with customers who came to the café for magical help.

I knelt beside the stranger and lightly pressed two fingers against his neck. His pulse was a little thready, but nevertheless strong, and relief stirred. Of course, whether he was simply unconscious or I'd done deeper damage, only time—and a thorough examination at the hospital—would tell.

I pulled my fingers back, but as they brushed the chain around his neck, heat rose, whispering secrets. I glanced around, but the immediate area was empty. That wasn't really unusual—it might be a Friday night, but most of the businesses around us only opened during the day.

As the sound of an approaching siren bit through the night, I wrapped my fingers around the chain then opened the psychometry gates and *reached*. The images hit so fast and hard they tore a gasp from my throat. I pulled back mentally and tried to control the speed and direction. I didn't want his whole history. I just needed to know what he'd been doing and who he'd been talking to over the course of the day.

The images pitched so violently that my stomach flip-flopped, before they abruptly settled into a watchable sequence. *A car. A hotel. A text saying "they're having dinner, you're clear to go. Grab whatever old books you see and we'll sort them later."* My pulse leapt into overdrive. Not only were they after Belle's books, but they were also obviously following Belle and Ava. I swore and tried to catch a number or name of the person who'd sent the text, but freezing specific images during a psychometry reading wasn't something I'd ever been able to do that successfully. Not that it mattered—the rangers should be able to grab that information easily enough.

I pushed the pulse of memories back a couple of days, but didn't glean much more other than confirmation he *was* one of the men responsible for the storage unit break-in. Which made it rather odd that I wasn't getting any informa-tion about his accomplice. Did he not know? I was tempted to push back further into his memories, but the ambulance had swung into the street and now sped toward me. I released the chain, rose to wave them down, then stepped back as they stopped.

The first medic grabbed her gear, then walked toward me. "What happened?"

I gave her a quick rundown, then got out of their way as they began administering help. The sound of footsteps had me looking around.

Jaz stopped beside me. "He's alive?"

The medic nodded. "Strong heartbeat and no immediately obvious signs of major trauma. We'll do a spinal and neck brace and take him to the hospital for tests."

"Tell them we'll have someone there shortly." Jaz's gaze rose to the balcony. "Did he leave anything upstairs?"

"He threw a flashlight at me. Other than that, I don't think so."

"Let's head up and grab it. He's wearing gloves, so there's no point in dusting for fingerprints on the door." She got her phone out. "You can tell me what happened on the way."

I did so and then added, "You wouldn't happen to know a motel that matches what I saw in his mind, do you?"

"Offhand, no."

"That's inconvenient."

A smile touched her lips. "It does at least stop you haring off to investigate it, now, doesn't it?"

I raised an eyebrow. "How long have you known me?"

"Lizzie, be sensible—you're not a ranger—"

"No, I'm not, so if I find anything, I'll call."

"You know full well Aiden wouldn't—"

"I don't run my life around what he might and might not approve, Jaz."

"I didn't mean it that way, and you know it."

I touched her arm. "Sorry, didn't mean to bite."

"I know." She squeezed my hand, then bagged the flashlight, checked both the door and the balcony for any other evidence, and left.

I immediately reached out for Belle.

I take it there's a problem? came her response.

Attempted break-in at the café and the possibility you're being followed.

Well, fuck. She paused. *Likelihood of it being connected to the attempts at the storage unit?*

Our would-be thief is one of the two involved, which means your tracker is likely the other. Keep an eye on things when you're coming home, just in case they attempt something direct.

Mom can scan everyone we pass while I drive.

Meaning anyone intending ill might well find themselves either not remembering what they were doing or suddenly going in the wrong direction. *Before I head to Aiden's, I'll extend the protections around the café to prevent unwanted human entry upstairs.*

It wasn't practical to do the whole building, especially when the wild magic was doing weird things to my spells. The last thing we needed was to have customers suddenly being ejected from the café.

Would it be possible to weave in a tracker? Belle asked. *That way, we're covered if they make a second attempt when none of us are there.*

I have no idea, but there's no harm in trying. Something Monty would have no doubt disagreed with had he been part of the conversation, given his constant warnings about the dangers of not playing by the spell "rules." *Enjoy the rest of your meal.*

I've crème brûlée coming, so I most certainly will.

Envious, I said, then broke the connection. After making sure the sliding door was locked, I went down to the reading room to weave the new exceptions into the already ponderous layers of spells that protected this place. It took a while and left me more tired than normal, but at least I could rest easier knowing Belle and her mom were protected from any further attacks.

I grabbed a brownie slice out of the fridge and munched on that while I googled motels in and around Castle Rock. There was at least twenty, but only two resembled the images I'd caught in the thief's mind. I rang Monty, but the call flicked over to his answering service. I didn't bother leaving a message and rang Ashworth instead.

"Lizzie," he said, the Scottish brogue in his voice deeper than usual. "To what do I owe the honor of this call?"

I smiled. He'd been away for nearly a week, working a case for the Regional Witch Association. He and Eli—his husband—had obviously been celebrating his return with a drink or two.

"I need some help—"

"We'll be there in ten."

"You don't even know what I want yet," I said, amused. "And there's no need for the two of you—"

"I've had a wee bit too much whiskey to be driving, but I'll not be left out of the adventure."

I laughed. "I think calling it an adventure is overhyping it. We're just going to break into the motel room of a would-be thief."

"How did you get involved with this thief?"

I gave them a quick rundown and then added, "And before you ask, Jaz is well aware of what I'm doing."

"Aware but not approving, I take it?"

I grinned. "But technically not *disapproving*, either."

He snorted. "Well, it sounds like the perfect evening jaunt. See you soon."

I hung up, a silly grin on my face. Both he and Eli had become—in the few months we'd known them—an important part of our lives. In very many respects, Ashworth was the father figure that had been so absent in my life, even if he was closer in age to a grandfather.

I made us all a coffee and then headed out to wait at the front of the café. Eli's SUV pulled up a few minutes later. Once I'd jumped into the back, I handed them their drinks, then belted up.

"Where are we headed?" Eli asked as he checked the side mirror and pulled out.

He was very much the opposite of Ashworth in looks—a tall, well-built, and very handsome man who looked to be in his mid-sixties but was actually a lot older. Ashworth was bald, short but powerfully built, with a heavily lined face and muddy silver eyes.

I gave them the address of the first motel—which was only a couple of streets away—and then said, "How'd the case in Mildura go?"

Ashworth snorted. "What was reported as a supernatural entity feeding off stock turned out to be a bunch of teenagers pretending they were vampires."

"Ew."

"Their parents were none too pleased when they discovered that not only would their delinquents face multiple charges, but they'd be held responsible for stock replacement costs."

"As they damn well should." I took a drink, then peered forward through the center console as Eli turned into the motel's parking area.

"Anything look familiar?" Ashworth asked.

I shook my head. "He was in unit twenty-four, so unless they've more rooms in another building behind this one, it's a bust."

"On to the next, then." Eli swung out of the driveway and headed down the highway. The next motel was only ten minutes out of town and substantially larger. Eli slowed and cruised past the rooms until we found the right one.

"I'm not sensing anything magic related," Ashworth commented.

"My thief was human, so that's not surprising."

"Humans are quite capable of purchasing spells, lass."

"And apparently *did*, as they used a spell breaker on our storage unit."

"Have you attempted to trace the spell back to its source?"

"Belle and Ava were doing that today." And I'd forgotten to ask them about it.

"Shall we break in or make it official?" Eli asked.

"Hardly worth expending the magical energy," Ashworth said. "I'll just go flash my credentials and grab the key."

"As long as your credentials are all you flash," Eli said, voice dry.

"Ah, there you go, spoiling all my fun again."

As Ashworth jumped out and headed for the reception area, I felt obliged to say, "Which begs the question, does he make a habit of flashing?"

Eli grinned. "Let's just say that Ira, a party, and too much alcohol, have sometimes led to various parts of his anatomy coming out to play."

I laughed. "He really doesn't look the exhibitionist type."

"There's a wild man lurking beneath that wonderfully craggy exterior," Eli said. "Why do you think I love the man?"

Because he's warm, caring, and generous, and he absolutely adores you. I didn't say that out loud, though, simply because it wasn't necessary.

Ashworth returned a few minutes later with the manager in tow. Eli leaned across to grab the backpack from the passenger footwell, then we both climbed out. The room was basic but clean, with a bed, a large TV, and a small desk and chair tucked to one side. A half-wall of glass bricks separated the bathroom from the main room, and there wasn't a door.

"Well, you'd certainly want to be utterly comfortable with your partner's toiletry movements," Eli commented, amused.

"A door isn't going to stop that sort of sound intrusion." Ashworth glanced at me. "Do you want to do a psychic skim before we start a full search?"

I nodded and proceeded to do so, running a hand across what little furniture there was, including the bed and the small carryall sitting on top of the desk.

"Nothing sets off the radar," I said, once I'd done the bathroom.

"Then we'll check the old-fashioned way." Eli zipped the backpack open. "Better wear these, otherwise the rangers will complain."

I caught the pair of gloves he tossed me and pulled them on as I walked across to the carryall. There wasn't anything more than a couple of changes of clothes inside; I ran a hand along the base of the bag, but nothing was hidden in the lining.

"Well, this is a bust," I grumbled.

"Maybe not." Ashworth picked up the small notepad near the clock and waved it lightly. "Someone wrote down a number on the page before this. I can see the indent."

"Give it a ring and see who answers," Eli said.

Ashworth tapped the number out on his phone and then put it on speaker.

"Professor Janice Hopetown," a pleasant voice said. "How may I help you?"

Eli immediately reached for his phone and began googling.

"Did you say your name was Hopetown?" Ashworth said.

"I did. Who's this? How did you get this number?"

"I was calling Margaret. I take it she's not there with you?"

"I don't know a Margaret. You've obviously got a wrong number. Good night."

"There's a couple of Janice Hopetowns," Eli said, "but the most likely one in this case works for the Department of Classics and Ancient History at Sydney University."

I frowned. "Why would a professor be involved in the theft of old spell books?"

"She might not know she's dealing with stolen goods," Ashworth said. "She also might have been approached simply to verify their authenticity and value."

Ashworth tore off the sheet of paper and handed it to me. "Get Aiden to ring her in the morning. It'd be better coming from an official source rather than you or me."

"You're official."

"RWA doesn't usually get involved in minor situations such as the theft of spell books, and she may think it suspicious—especially after my random call tonight."

"It does still leave the question of who might have

contacted her." Eli glanced at me. "Who knows about the books?"

I drew in a breath and released it slowly. "Aside from us? Only Kash."

"Have you spoken to him yet?"

I shook my head. "But I think Belle and I will have to do that tomorrow."

"He would have been my first port of call."

"Except we thought the first break-in was just a random event, and he doesn't match the build of either of the men caught on camera during the second attempt."

"Doesn't mean he's not the brains behind it all."

"I know." I just didn't really want to believe that either Belle or I could be so misled by a pretty face. Besides, he'd been telepathically restricted from either using or contacting anyone about the books. "Let's get out of here. I have a whiskey with my name on it waiting for me at home."

"You and me both," Ashworth said with a laugh.

We headed back to Castle Rock. Once Eli had dropped me back at the café, I jumped into my car and headed home.

"I take it," Aiden said as I walked in the door, "that you did go look for the would-be thief's hotel?"

I smiled, tossed my bag onto the sofa, and walked across the room. After dropping a kiss on his cheek, I peered into the pot he was stirring. "Spaghetti sauce. Your cooking repertoire is expanding."

"Yes, it is, and stop avoiding the question."

My smile widened. "You knew I would."

"Yes, but I do keep hoping you'll one day do the sensible thing."

"I did. I took Ashworth and Eli with me."

He rolled his eyes. "You three are as bad as each other. Did you find anything?"

"A phone number—it belongs to a professor who works in the Department of Classics and Ancient History at Sydney University."

"Did you talk to her?"

"Ashworth rang but pretended it was a misplaced call. We figured questioning would be better coming from an official source."

He grunted. "I'll do it tomorrow."

"You're still working?" I said, surprised. "I thought you were thinking about having the day off to prepare for tomorrow night."

"I decided it was better to take the day off after the birthday bash instead."

"Then I'll keep my fingers crossed work doesn't get in the way."

"Amen to that. You want to drain the spaghetti?"

I did so, then, while he plated everything up, made us both a drink. "Is your mother still refusing to be there?"

"Don't know, and don't care at this particular moment."

"Aiden—"

"Don't go there," he said. "I'm not in the mood."

I raised my eyebrows. The edge in his voice very much suggested he and his mom had had words sometime during the day, but as much as curiosity was biting, I resisted the urge to push. And yet I couldn't help the sliver of guilt; I was the reason for the fracturing of his relationship with his mother, and I could only hope it didn't become irreparable.

I quietly ate my spaghetti and, after a while, he sighed. "Sorry. I didn't mean to bite."

"It's okay—"

"No, it's not. Not when you—" The sharp ringing of a phone cut off the rest of his words. He groaned, collected the empty bowls, and then walked over to the kitchen counter to answer the call. "Ranger Aiden O'Connor—"

He quickly pulled the phone away from his ear. The person on the other end of the call was speaking both loudly *and* rapidly. It was a woman, and she was obviously frightened, but I couldn't understand much more than the occasional word.

"A fucking monster" did catch my attention, however.

I rose, grabbed my coat, and then swung my purse over my shoulder.

"We'll be there in ten minutes, Mrs. Sanders," Aiden said. "Make sure the door is locked and keep the kids in one room upstairs."

"What if this thing breaks in?" she screeched.

"Have you got a gun in the house?"

"Of course—"

"Then keep it handy and use it if necessary." He hung up and glanced at me. "You want to ring Monty and tell him to meet us at the Sanders farm?"

He gave me the address as we headed out the door. Monty still wasn't answering the phone, so this time I left a message.

"I don't suppose Mrs. Sanders described what she saw, other than it being a monster?"

"No. And she's been prone to exaggeration in the past, especially when her husband is away working."

"Do you think that's the case here?"

"Maybe, but she was in the same school as John, Jackson, and Patrick, so we can't afford to take a risk."

I shifted to study him. "Is that the only link you've found between them all?"

"So far, yes." He cast me a grim look. "But she wasn't in the same class, and isn't friends with them, then or now."

"How many classes were the three men in together?"

"Two—grade five and six."

"At least that cuts down the number of people you have to interview."

"It's still a monumental task, given half of them no longer live in the reservation. We have to check them all, just in case the two deaths here aren't the first."

We sped into the darkness, the red and blue lights giving the trees that lined the road an eerie glow. We weren't very far out of Argyle when he swung onto a long driveway that swept up to a double-story weatherboard farmhouse. Lights shone brightly across both floors and, on the upper floor, a curtain twitched and a pale face looked out. Mrs. Sanders, no doubt.

Aiden stopped and climbed out. I grabbed my purse and joined him at the front of the truck. The night was cold, but the drifting wind was free from the scent of foulness.

"Anything?" Aiden asked.

I shook my head. "That doesn't mean anything, though."

"No."

He touched my arm, then led the way across to the front door. It opened as we stepped onto the veranda. Mrs. Sanders was short and stout, with curly blonde hair and a pleasant face.

"About time," she grumbled. "I was about—"

"Has this creature tried to get inside?" Aiden cut in.

"No, but—"

"Where was it headed? Where did you see it?"

"It was over near the stables, heading toward the forest."

"Meaning it was probably just moving through. Keep inside, keep the doors locked, and we'll go check."

"Thank you." She immediately shut and locked the door.

"This way," Aiden said.

We moved to the end of the veranda and around the corner of the homestead. A number of buildings came into view—one a large machinery shed and the other a row of four horseboxes. We walked across the graveled driveway and strode toward the boxes. In the nearby paddocks, horses ran about, their tails high and their snorts filling the air. Something had stirred them up. I just hoped that something wasn't our beastie.

It was a hope that quickly died as we moved past the first horsebox and the acidic scent of magic hung on the air. It was a distant thing, but it nevertheless meant Mrs. Sanders hadn't imagined her monster.

"It was here," I said, voice grim.

Aiden's gaze snapped to mine. "Can you track it?"

I nodded and immediately took the lead, moving past the horseboxes, machinery shed, and then through a gate into another paddock. There were no horses here but there were a few cows, and they looked just as spooked as the horses. In the distance, a thick line of trees followed the fence boundary. Our beastie was heading straight for them.

"Is that forest part of this property?" I asked.

"No, it's a government reserve, although there are a couple of homesteads within it."

"Is it a big area?"

"Fifty or so acres, at least."

"Then let's hope this thing isn't simply on an evening jaunt through the bush," I muttered.

"A simple jaunt would be a better option than an attack."

Which was all too true. We reached the fence line.

Aiden held up the top two wires so I could climb through, then motioned me back into the lead. The shadows closed in once we were in the trees, but I could nevertheless see reasonably well thanks to the wild magic leeching Katie's werewolf senses to enhance mine.

The acidic scent of magic neither grew nor lessened. Wherever this thing was going, it wasn't yet in a hurry. We walked on, Aiden's steps light, mine heavier; neither would carry to our quarry, though, thanks to fact we were walking into the wind.

We'd probably gone just over a kilometer when Aiden grabbed my arm and hauled me to a halt. "Did you hear that?"

"Hear what?"

He cocked his head sideways, his expression intent. After a minute, he said, "*That.*"

I frowned, but after a moment, I heard it—a faint, child-like cry.

The creature was on the hunt again—and it was definitely a she rather than a he. Samuel had been right. "Can you tell how far away she is?"

"Half a K, at least. Can you run?"

"You lead, I'll try to keep up." I hesitated. "But please don't leave me behind. Not after what this thing did to Patrick."

"I'm not about to leave you roaming the reserve alone, even if you're even more able to protect yourself than me. Let's go."

He immediately broke into a run. I took a deep breath and followed. While I *had* been jogging of late in a vague attempt to get fitter, running at night on uneven ground was a very different matter.

We went as fast as was practical in the darkness and the

trees. The wind carried the soft, childlike cries to our ears even as it carried away the sound of our footsteps. We weren't getting all that much closer; the creature might be laying the bait, but it was also continuing to move.

Sweat began to trickle down my spine, and my breath was short, sharp pants of air. I concentrated on keeping up with Aiden, ignoring the ache in my side and the growing burn in my legs. We had to stop this thing before she claimed another life.

Another cry, this time shorter, sharper, and closer. It really *did* sound like a child, and that made me wonder if we were dealing with someone whose growth—through the use of dark magic—had been frozen at a youngish age even if it was far older in practical terms. It would at least fit with Jackson's comment that this thing was small, pale, and upright.

The cries grew louder as we drew closer. Then, from somewhere to our left came a shout—a male voice, telling the so-called crying child to stay put because they were on their way.

Aiden swore. "He's going to get there before we are."

"Shout to him."

"We do that, and this thing is gone."

"Then cut sideways and intercept him." The words came out as little more than harsh pants. Running and speaking clearly wasn't easy. "I'll continue on."

"Liz—"

"Don't Liz me. I can protect myself, remember."

"Yeah, but as you pointed out, I might not be able to."

He was right. But so was I. I sucked in a breath and then said, "Then let's try to correct that."

I quickly created a repelling spell, wove it into a net, and threw it across his body. The slender threads of silver and gold settled around his body, shimmering lightly with every movement. It looked to be in full working order. I just had to hope looks weren't deceiving, especially given this sort of net wasn't something I'd ever tried before.

"I just cast a protective net across your body. You've ten minutes, if that, before its force fades."

"Can I shift shape without losing it?"

"Yes."

"Good. Be damn careful, Liz. Promise."

"Always."

He snorted but leapt away to the left, his body blurring as he moved from one form to the other. I raced on, crashing through the scrub, not caring now if the thing ahead heard me.

In fact, it might be better if it *did*.

I sucked in another breath and then yelled, "I'm on my way! Stay still, and I'll find you."

Just for an instant, the cries for help stopped. It made me wonder if she recognized my voice. I'd been close to her at John's after all—perhaps she'd heard me speaking to Monty and Aiden when she'd looped around the back of the farmhouse for a secondary attack. Or maybe it was the fact that it was a *different* voice—I guess it depended on why she was out here hunting.

I continued on, crashing through the scrub and the trees, occasionally throwing a hand up to push away a branch or to protect my face. Another soft cry for help had relief stirring. She was on the move again, but heading closer to me rather than away. I hadn't scared her ... but now that she'd changed tack and was coming after me, I'd certainly better do something about protecting myself.

I began to weave a capture spell. The energy was fierce and bright, lighting the way even as the spell's heat pulsed across my fingertips. The inner wild magic was once again deeply embedded within the threads, and I had to wonder what changes it would make this time.

Another cry, this time slightly to the right. She was looping around me. I shifted direction and followed her, but the scrub got thicker and snagged at my clothes, hampering my speed.

Then, abruptly, there was a flash of white to my left. I slid to a stop, my breath a harsh rasp, my body shaking with a mix of tension and exhaustion.

More movement, this time to my right.

She was circling me.

I clenched my fingers against the need to release my spell and said, "Are you still out there? Can you hear me?"

There was no immediate response, but the back of my neck was prickling and every psychic sense I had was now screaming that she was close and I was in danger. I swallowed heavily, my gaze scanning the immediate area, looking for some sign of movement. The wind stirred past my nose but held no hint of her acidic scent.

And yet she was close. So damn close.

"Are you there?" It came out thick, deeply edged with fear.

No response.

The ever-hopeful part of me wanted to believe she'd either decided I wasn't worth the trouble or she'd realized I wasn't who she was after.

The ever-practical part recognized *that* for the stupidity it was.

She was still here. Still moving. Still sizing me up.

Then, from my left, came the faintest brush of air.

It was the only warning I got.

CHAPTER NINE

I dropped flat and grunted in pain as stones dug into my stomach. The sound of material ripping was followed by a sharp sting across my back. Then bare, grimy feet landed several meters ahead. I quickly unleashed my spell.

She spun as it tumbled toward her; just for an instant, I had a clear view of the mess that was her face. She thrust out a hand, her fingers ending in claws that were as sharp as razors. Energy surged, and a black blot similar to the one that had destroyed Monty's spell hurtled toward mine. The two crashed into each other, but neither spell immediately got the better of the other.

The bitch wasn't hanging around to see the winner; she ran on, moving swiftly through the trees and the darkness.

I scrambled upright and raced after her, a tracking spell forming around my fingertips. But just as I was about to throw it, the magic behind me exploded. The force it unleashed hit my back like a hammer and tossed me several feet in the air. I smashed into the ground and slid for several feet before coming to a halt inches in front of an old tree trunk.

I pushed up, wincing as various bits of me protested the movement, and scrambled on. But there was no trace of her now, either on the ground or in the air. Even the psychic lines were quiet.

I swore violently, then glanced down at my hands. The left one had copped most of the damage from the slide, and though only the scrapes on the fleshy section near my thumb could be described as deep, it was all bleeding quite profusely. My knees had at least fared better, as my jeans had protected them from the worst of the fall. I grabbed a tissue out of my purse and carefully wiped away the grit from my hand. It hurt like blazes, and I found myself hoping that the werewolf ability to fast heal asserted itself overnight. I wouldn't be doing a whole lot in the café tomorrow if it didn't.

The sound of light footsteps had me glancing around. Aiden appeared, his gaze quickly scanning me as his nostrils flared. "How bad are the wounds this time?"

"I skinned my palm, but it'll be fine."

"What about your back? Because the blood scent is more prevalent there."

"Her claws tore open my jacket and sweater, but I don't think she did too much damage given it's not really hurting—"

"You always say that when the opposite is generally true. Turn around."

I did so. He inspected the damage, his fingers so warm against my skin as he parted the various layers of clothes. "The cut's not deep, but it's long. You'll not be very comfortable sleeping for the next few nights. Hand?"

I turned and obediently held out my palm. "Who was our other searcher?"

"Jack Martin." He gently peeled away the tissue. "This

is certainly nastier than your back. The first aid kit in the truck contains some numbing salve. You're probably going to need it before the night is out."

I needed it now, but I wasn't going to admit that. He'd only fuss some more. "Is Martin connected to the other victims?"

"Unknown. What happened to our creature?"

"She threw magic at me and got away. But I did at least get a good look at her."

He raised an eyebrow. "Good enough to do a facial composite?"

I nodded. "She really *is* a mash of human and wolf, but it might be enough for recognition software to do a database search."

"That's presuming she's in our database." He wrapped the tissue back around my hand, then lightly touched my arm and guided me through the trees. "If she's human, she may not be."

That had my eyebrows rising. "Meaning you keep photo IDs of all the werewolves in the reservation?"

"In a manner of speaking, yes."

"Care to define that?"

"The council keeps a detailed register of all births within the reservation."

"That much I already knew." The High Witch Council did the same thing and for the same reason—to avoid inbreeding.

"Yes, but wolf registers are fully accessible to all other reservations, no matter where in the world they are. It contains not only lineage details, but descriptions, photo ID of the subject when they turn eighteen, and what they might or might not want in a mate."

I blinked. "So it's basically a dating site?"

A smile teased his lips. "Basically."

"And have you ever accessed this site?"

"Never needed to."

"Because you've already found your perfect woman?"

"I believed so."

Believed. It was a word that had my hopes stirring and yet it was an undeniable fact that until Mia *did* come back to the reservation, he and I would never know for sure whether she truly was his "one."

"Does Martin live in this area?"

"No. He was visiting a friend."

"So he might not have been our hunter's intended target?"

"Indeed. I've sent Tala over to interview them both. Monty will meet her there."

"So he finally answered his phone?"

"He did."

"Did he say why he had it switched off?"

"He did not."

The amusement in his tone had me glancing at him. "You have suspicions?"

"And you don't?" He tsked. "You disappoint me."

I raised my eyebrows. "He can't have been with Belle and Ava. They've been out all day, and he made his usual appearance at the café for coffee and cake."

"Doesn't mean he couldn't have joined them for dinner."

"True." I pursed my lips. "I shall have to interrogate Belle in the morning."

"I'm surprised you're not doing that now."

"It's easier to do face to face. She can't hide her reactions as well." Besides, my hand and my back were aching with renewed vigor, and I really couldn't be bothered.

He must have sensed my tiredness, because he wrapped an arm around my shoulders and tucked me close. "Let's get you home."

"Don't you have to meet Tala?"

He shook his head. "She's more than capable of handling the situation, and with Monty there, they shouldn't be in any danger."

I certainly hoped not. It took half an hour to get back to his truck, and by that time, my head had joined in on the pain party. I raided the stash of food he kept in the glove compartment, retrieving a small tetra pack of juice and a Mars Bar. After swallowing a couple of painkillers, I munched on the Mars Bar and watched while he spoke to a still animated Mrs. Sanders. It seemed to take an extraordinarily long time before she'd calmed down enough for us to leave.

Once home, I took a long hot shower that eased some of the aches but didn't touch the tiredness. After Aiden had applied more numbing salve on the various scrapes, I crawled under the comforter and was asleep almost as soon as my head hit the pillow.

"Did you manage to talk to the witch who'd created the spell breaker yesterday?" I asked as Belle propped her hip on the counter and took a sip of her coffee.

She nodded. "Lovely old lady she was, too. Absolutely horrified to discover her spell was used in a break-and-enter attempt."

"And the horror was genuine?"

"Utterly. She was told it was needed to unlock an old,

spell-protected safe because a missing will was believed to have been stored inside."

"And she believed that?"

"She said they looked genuinely upset. It was the woman's grandmother, apparently."

"So it was a couple?"

Belle nodded. "I got their description—"

"She didn't have security cameras installed?"

"No, unfortunately. Neither description sounded familiar."

"So it definitely wasn't Kash?"

"No." She frowned. "Why would you ask that?"

I quickly updated her on what we'd found at the motel and then added, "He was the only outside person who knew about the books."

"He didn't know about the storage unit, though."

"He could have followed you there easily enough. It wasn't as if you would have been watching out for that sort of thing."

"True." She hesitated. "If it was him, how did he get around the restrictions I placed on him? He shouldn't have been able to talk to anyone else about them."

"Maybe it was already too late by the time you did that," I said.

"Maybe." She grimaced and took another drink. "We need to go see him."

"I'm thinking right after we close. Penny and Celia can handle the cleanup and till." And certainly neither were averse to a bit of overtime.

She frowned. "That probably won't leave you much time to get back home and gussied up for the party."

"I'm changing here and meeting Aiden there."

"And he didn't object? Color me surprised."

My eyebrows shot up. "Why?"

"Because I got the impression he wanted you there for the meet and greets."

A smile touched my lips. "He did, but in all honesty, it's far better if I keep a slightly lower profile."

"Liz, the man is besotted with you."

"Yes, but his mother and at least some of his pack aren't. I don't want to cause any more problems than I already have."

"They're problems that will have to be confronted if you two ever do become a permanent item, you know."

"Yes, but let's not put the cart before the horse in the meantime."

She snorted softly. "Kash is usually at the gym between four and five on a Saturday. It's certainly the one place he won't be expecting a confrontation."

"Sounds perfect." I plated up a cake order, wincing a little as my palm protested the movement. Both it and the cut across my back had all but healed overnight, but the pale scars remained tight. They were also rather inconvenient—or, at least, the one on my spine was, as the low scoop of my dress's back meant it would be on full show. Then again, maybe it would remind certain members of his pack exactly what I went through to protect this place. "What's your mom doing tonight?"

"I suspect she'll be Skyping Dad. She's missing him something chronic."

And so was Belle, I knew. I touched her arm. "You should go up there and visit."

"What? And leave you without access to my sensible self?" She snorted. "That's not what a good familiar does when her witch is regularly faced with all manner of supernatural nasties."

"A week or two won't make that much—"

"Hey, I left you for a day, and what happened? Instant attack by a DNA-or magic-warped critter. Thanks, but no thanks."

"Oh, which reminds me—" I paused and studied her speculatively. "How was dinner last night?"

"You already know how it was—" She stopped. "Ah."

"Ah, indeed." I raised an eyebrow. "Why the secrecy?"

"It wasn't a secret, and it wasn't planned. And it's Mom's fault. She invited him, not me."

"You didn't object, though."

She sighed. "No. He's ... not as bad as I make out."

"We all know this. You're the one that's taking forever to admit the obvious."

A smile twitched her lips. "And yet, I can't make it too easy for the man—where's the fun in that?"

I laughed. "At least it explains his comment that your mom has been rather helpful when it comes to the whole date progression."

"She has that matchmaking twinkle in her eyes." Belle's voice was dry. "There's no convincing her that we really wouldn't be a great match."

I raised my eyebrows. "Why not?"

"Because I'm a Sarr and he's—"

"Absolutely determined to make you his wife."

"He says that—"

"He believes that."

She sighed. "I know, but his parents—"

"I think Monty abandoned the whole parental approval thing when they jettisoned him for failing to live up to their power expectations."

"Yes, but that doesn't mean they'd be happy—"

"Not to throw your own words back at you or anything,

but how about you concentrate on the relationship rather than what his parents might think?"

"But this is Monty. I mean—"

"He's not that annoying and scrawny teenager we knew at school anymore."

"Scrawny, no, but annoying? Hell yes."

A smile twitched my lips. "And we both know you don't really mind, don't we?"

"I refuse to answer that question on the grounds I may incriminate myself." She drained her mug and dumped it in the nearby sink. "But I would like to know what happened to all the grand plans he supposedly had for our first official date."

I grinned. "Put off until your mom goes home and there's a first official fuck."

She laughed, a warm, bright sound that ran across the soft babble of conversation and had people looking our way. "And *you*, my dear witch, will never know if and when that ever happens."

"Wanna bet? One look at Monty will tell me everything."

She groaned. "Damn it, you're right."

I echoed her laugh, then swung around as Penny approached with another order. Customers were few and far between for the rest of the day, though, thanks to the damn weather closing in again. Once we'd shut for the day, Belle and I jumped into the SUV and headed across to the fitness center. It was basically a big tin shed situated in a small industrial area.

We found a parking spot as close to the entrance as possible, then made a mad dash through the rain into the building. A long counter dominated the reception area, and the extremely well-built man behind it flashed a wide smile.

"Belle, wasn't expecting you here today." His gaze moved to me. "You've brought us a new victim?"

I laughed. "The day I lift a weight will be the day hell freezes over."

He grinned. "You wouldn't be the first to say that, and we do love a good challenge. What can I do for you ladies?"

"Is Kash here?" Belle asked. "We need to talk to him."

"He's in the weights room, as usual."

"Thanks, Joe."

He nodded. We walked through the double doors into the main gym area. It was, as expected, a big area filled with all sorts of torture machines. A glass wall divided this section from the next—a slightly smaller room that held all the weight equipment, as well as more machines and benches.

I couldn't immediately see Kash, but as we wove our way through the lines of treadmills, elliptical machines, stair climbers, and goodness knows what else, I spotted him. He was bench-pressing what looked to be an impressive amount of weight.

The door slid open as we approached. Belle strode over to his bench and stood behind the bar support. I stopped at the feet end. The three other men in the room got up and walked out, though not of their own volition.

"Hey, Kash," Belle said, her tone friendly. "How's it going?"

"Well, this is a lovely surprise." He hefted the bar onto the support. "You here to work out?"

"No. We're here to ask a few questions."

He sat up and swung around. He was, quite simply, a divine-looking man. At six-five, he was several inches taller than Belle—a rarity around these parts—and had dark hair, a neat beard, and the most amazing green eyes. A sexy

French accent completed the rather impressive package. "Why? Is there a problem?"

"There most certainly is. You want to tell us about your dealings with Professor Janice Hopetown?"

He frowned. "Who?"

Belle sighed. "Kash, I'm being polite right now, but if you don't answer my questions honestly, I'll force you."

His smile flashed. "Not to be impolite or anything, but you and what fucking—"

He didn't complete the rest of that sentence, and his expression morphed from one of gentle amusement to a mix of consternation and fear.

"There's one thing I forgot to mention during our dalliance," Belle said softly. "I'm not only a witch but also a strong telepath. You *will* answer my questions and you will do so willingly, or I'll scramble your mind so fucking badly you won't even be able to scratch your balls without help. Understand?"

He nodded. He couldn't actually do anything else given the fierce grip Belle currently had on his mind. And while she was perfectly able to simply delve into his thoughts and get every bit of information she needed, doing it this way not only saved her some energy but also ramped up his fear levels—and given how pissed off she was, *that* was something she was quite enjoying.

"Shall we try that question again?" Her tone was saccharine sweet. "What dealings have you had with the professor?"

She eased her grip on him, and he immediately tried to stand. Whether he was intending to run or it was simply an attempt to use his greater bulk to intimidate, I couldn't say. He didn't succeed either way.

He swallowed heavily and then said, "I haven't been in contact with her. I don't know her. I only know her name."

"And how do you know her name?"

"Belle, please, I never meant any harm—"

"Then answer the goddamn question and you won't come to any harm."

His expression suggested he was seriously regretting ever getting involved. I knew *that* went both ways.

"I was talking to a friend in Melbourne about the conversions we were doing, and he mentioned that maybe we could contact the professor to see if the books were valuable."

"When was this?"

He shrugged. "Before we broke up."

Meaning before Belle had placed her restrictions in his mind, which might explain why they apparently hadn't stopped him talking to the friend about the books. They'd been aimed at preventing discussions with *new* people.

"To what aim?" she asked.

"I wasn't intending—"

"To rip me off? To sell books you had no entitlement to and no understanding of?" She paused, her gaze narrowing as she dove a little deeper. "Fuck me, you're already *selling* e-copies? Do you know how dangerous these books could be in the wrong hands?"

Not to mention the possibility of the High Council getting wind of the copies and wondering where the hell someone like Kash got hold of them, I said.

I can order him to pull them down and erase all reference of them from his mind, Belle said. *But I can't do much about the copies that are already out there.*

"Oh, come on," Kash was saying. "Two were mythology

books, and the other three simple spell books—there's no great harm in any of them."

"And you say this as an expert in magic, do you?" She paused again, gaze narrowing. "Ah, so the *friend* is a witch."

"Half-blood—"

"And can he perform magic?"

"Not really—"

"How does this Roland know the professor then?"

"They went to school together."

"Was it Roland or you who arranged the break-in attempts on our storage unit and premises?"

"What break-ins?" He sounded genuinely confused. "Why would we do that when it's simply easier to keep playing the game as we were—"

"And get the rest with us being none the wiser?" Belle finished for him.

He sighed. "Yes."

"So when I suddenly stopped giving you the books to transcribe, you and Roland hatched this other plan?"

"No. I thought the lull was temporary." His lips twisted. "You did have trouble keeping away from this gorgeous bod. At least until very recently, anyway."

The surge of her anger blistered through my mind, though she somehow resisted the urge to smite him. "Is Roland currently in the reservation?"

"Yes. But I don't—"

"Are you *really* going to push that lie out there?" Belle said. "Because no one's buying it."

He grimaced. "Fine. But I really didn't know he'd go as far as robbery to get the rest of the books."

"While that *isn't* actually a lie, you certainly *did* suspect he'd take direct action if the seduction method kept failing. He *is* the brawn to your brain, right?"

He didn't say anything to that, which was probably just as well.

Belle sighed. "Ring him. Tell him you need to meet him urgently."

"My phone's in the locker."

"Then let's go get it, shall we?"

He didn't have any choice in the matter, and in very little time, he'd retrieved his phone and was making the call.

"On loudspeaker," Belle added.

He obeyed. The call was answered after a couple of rings. "Kash? What's up?"

"Plenty," Kash replied, his words courtesy of Belle's control over him. "We need to meet. Urgently."

"Why? What's happened?"

"I can't speak here. Can you meet me at Morrison's?"

Morrison's was a pub not that far away from his place, if I remembered rightly. Belle had mentioned it once or twice.

"Sure" came the easy reply. "What time?"

"Twenty minutes?"

"It'll take me half an hour to get there."

"Great. I'll order you a beer."

Belle forced him to hang up, then reached past him and grabbed his things. "Let's go."

"Where?"

"Back to your place, where you're going to take down every book you've uploaded and then utterly destroy both the files and the drives you've stored them on. You will never speak of said books again. To *anyone*, not even Roland. In fact, after tonight, you won't even remember me."

"Oh, come on—"

Belle shut him down, marched him outside, and climbed into his car. I followed them across to the old miner's cottage he lived in, then parked behind them and waited.

She came out twenty minutes later. Her expression was thunderous, though I suspected the anger was directed more at herself than at him.

She jumped into the SUV and pulled on her seat belt as I reversed out and headed for the pub. "How big of a number did you do on Kash's memory?"

"It wasn't worth the effort. I just forced him to erase every single book file, online and off. And then I repeated my threat to scramble his mind and provided a little reinforcement demonstration by making him pee his pants. He was suitably scared, trust me."

He might be scared, but would his partner be? "Were the books on sale in his name or Roland's?"

"Neither—it was some company called Black Arts, and from what I saw, they have a history of stealing and selling stuff. I daresay it'd be easy enough for a search to uncover their connection though." She shook her head. "But the worst thing is, they've been selling the e-versions in the university bookstore."

"Fuck."

"Yeah." She thrust her fingers through her hair. "I think the council realizing they're from Gran's missing collection will happen sooner rather than later."

"No doubt." I flicked on the blinker and turned into the pub's parking area. "I think our first course of action has to be moving storage facilities."

"That's not going to help, given it'll still be in our names."

"I'm sure either Ashworth or Eli will sign a new lease agreement for us."

"It would still be commercial premises though, and

that's probably the first type of place they'll check. We need to go private. Aiden might be able to suggest somewhere."

"I'll ask." I stopped the SUV, and we climbed out. "What does this Roland fellow look like?"

"He's a Waverley, and has a thick scar on his cheek from a motorcycle accident as a teenager."

The Waverley line was—like the Sarrs—a lower witch house and was generally pale of skin with thick brown hair and silver eyes. Their magic was of a healing kind, mostly with potions, though some were capable of physical healing, either through Reiki or sexual interaction.

We walked into the main bar but couldn't see anyone who looked like a Waverley witch. Belle glanced at her watch. "How long do you want to wait? We'll soon be cutting it fine if we want to get gussied up for tonight's party."

"The party doesn't start until eight, which still gives us plenty of time—even for you." I ordered us both a drink.

She grinned. "I was thinking more of you—you are, after all, the one intending to wear something so sleek and form-fitting it leaves very little to the imagination."

"It's not *that* formfitting."

"Hey, I was there when you bought it. Trust me, while you might have wanted to keep a lower profile, no man in that room tonight will be looking anywhere else."

I smiled. "It wasn't actually aimed at other men. It's more a big fuck-you to his mother *if* she happens to appear."

Belle picked up her drink and clinked it against mine. "Long may the bitch suffer."

We moved across to a table that had a good view of both entrances, but twenty minutes went by, and Roland never appeared.

"You think it possible he twigged something was up?" I asked.

"Possibly." She got out her phone and dialed a number. The call went to voicemail. "Change that to definitely."

"Did you happen to get his address?"

"He's staying in a motel not far from Kash's." She drained her drink and rose. "Shall we head over?"

I nodded and followed her out. Roland, it turned out, had checked out twenty-five minutes ago.

Belle swore. "What now?"

"We can't do anything more tonight. At least we've got his phone number, and we can get his home address from Kash if necessary." I swung out of the hotel parking area and headed back to the café. "Wonder if he's got electronic copies of the books?"

"Apparently not—Kash handled that side of it."

"At least that's something."

"Yes, although from what I saw of the man in Kash's thoughts, I wouldn't put it past him to go to the witch council and try to wheedle money out of them in return for information about the books."

"Then we really *do* need to do something about the storage unit ASAP."

But not tonight. Tonight was party time.

I opened my umbrella as I climbed out of the taxi, carefully avoiding the many puddles that didn't play well with sparkly party shoes. Monty had suggested I accompany him and Belle, but given this was an official date, I wasn't about to spoil their fun, even for such a short time.

The party was being held in the rear gardens of a grand old villa house. The main gate was open, and a path lit by fairy lights guided guests around to the Garden Room, a huge glass and wood conservatory situated behind the main house.

The place was ablaze with lights, and music was already thumping. I walked up the steps, then lowered the umbrella and dropped it into one of the many stands that lined the veranda. As I made my way toward the entrance, awareness zinged across my skin; a heartbeat later, the ornate glass doors opened, and Aiden stepped through. He wore a black dress jacket, a blue shirt that brought out the color in his eyes, and black pants that hugged the long lean wonderful length of his legs. He stopped when he saw me, his gaze all but devouring me.

"That dress," he said, voice so low it was almost a growl, "is absolutely stunning. As are you."

I smiled and sashayed toward him, the thigh-high slit on the right side of the dress revealing tantalizing glimpses of leg. He made a low sound deep in his throat, and the rich scent of wanting teased my nostrils even as it burned across my skin.

"Be careful, Ranger," I said, voice husky, "that you don't start a fire you can't quench until much later in the evening."

"If I'd known you'd be wearing a dress like *that*, I would have ensured a party of two."

I laughed softly and brushed my lips teasingly across his. "Happy birthday, Aiden."

He slid a hand around my waist, then ever so slowly down my spine. It felt as if I was being caressed by fire, and my breath hitched as desire surged.

It was a sound he echoed when his fingers slid under

the dark green silk that curved around the base of my spine. "You're not wearing panties?"

"Impossible to do so in this dress." I pressed my breasts against his chest. "I'm not wearing a bra, either, in case you didn't notice."

"Dear God, you're going to be the death of me."

And with that, his lips claimed mine. His kiss was all-consuming, all heat, hunger, and desire. I wrapped my arms around his neck, molded my body against the hard perfection of his, and returned his kiss in kind, not caring who might be watching. He was *mine*, not just tonight but also for the near future. I'd be damned if I'd in any way let the disapprovers stop me from enjoying either.

This dress was a declaration of that intent, and I didn't really care who knew it.

When we finally parted, the smell of desire was so intense it was almost liquid. He leaned his forehead against mine, his breath hot and rapid against my kiss-ravaged lips.

"It's just as well you're not wearing lipstick, because it'd be smeared all over your mouth *and* mine by now."

"That's the sole reason I'm not wearing it. I can hardly steal sneaky kisses if I'm forever touching up lipstick."

"To hell with sneaky kisses—they imply a lack of substance, and we're well beyond that." He took a deep, delightfully shuddery breath, then stepped back and buttoned his jacket. "Shall we go in? I'm looking forward to introducing you to a number of people tonight."

"That sounds rather ominous." I kept my voice light. "Are we talking disapproving siblings or disapproving friends?"

"If I said some of both, would you be worried?"

"Not at all. I did come dressed for a fight, after all."

He laughed, wrapped an arm around my waist, and

guided me inside. The room was large and decorated with more fairy lights and huge swaths of blue and silver material across the roof. Blue-clothed tables decorated with silver and gold balloons ran along the right side of the conservatory while the band was playing in an alcove at the far end. The bar and food servery area lay to the left.

"This is gorgeous."

"I let Myra handle arrangements." His voice was filled with wry amusement. "She has a fondness for extravagance."

Myra was eight years younger than him, if I remembered correctly. "No doubt you'd have preferred a tin shed, a lamb on the spit, and tree stumps to sit on."

He laughed. "Well, maybe not the tree stumps."

He guided me lightly through the crowd. People smiled and greeted us, many of whom I knew either from the café or from the few times we'd met with his friends at either the dances we went to or pub gatherings. I spotted Ashworth and Eli sitting talking to another couple on the other side of the room but couldn't as yet see Belle or Monty. They were here though—I could feel the buzz of Belle's happiness, even if our link had been firmly shut down by both of us.

As we moved deeper into the crowd, I realized there was a gentle but noticeable divide—the werewolves gathered on the left and humans on the right. Which I supposed wasn't entirely surprising. The two might intermingle on a daily basis, but it was rare that this sort of celebration—one werewolves considered a major milestone—was held off compound. It would undoubtedly take the consumption of a decent amount of alcohol before the intermingling truly began.

The introductions started with his family. Joseph, his dad—who was basically a grayer-haired version of Aiden—

greeted me warmly, dropping a kiss on my cheek and complimenting me on my dress. His siblings greeted me with varying degrees of friendliness, though Ciara—who looked stunning in a deep blue formfitting dress—grinned and said, "Word of warning—Mom's going to be here for the formal part of the night, but she's promised not to cause a scene."

"I wouldn't place a bet on that," I muttered.

Ciara didn't disagree, which made me think her reassurances might have been as much for Aiden as me. We moved on, and it quickly became obvious he very much was making a statement about my presence in his life. And while that warmed my heart, it also scared the hell out of me. Mia was coming, and she would make a mess of everything.

When the introductions were finally over, we got down to the business of having fun. It was an easy thing to do, given the music was fabulous, the food plentiful, and the champagne didn't stop. But as the night wore on, my inner tension increased. If Aiden sensed it, he didn't say anything. But then, the tension in him was on a similar trajectory.

At midnight, the music stopped and the "official" part of the evening began. As the speeches began, his mother appeared, stepping onto the stage without fuss, to take her place in the family line behind Aiden. She was rangy in build and wearing a long, flowing dress of deep blue that emphasized the sapphire of her eyes and the silver-gray of her short hair.

Her expression was one of pride, but her gaze, when it finally found mine, told a very different story.

The bitch was furious enough to erupt.

And she had every intention of doing so all over me.

CHAPTER TEN

I t wasn't just due to my continuing presence in Aiden's life, but also the indignity of holding what should have been a private ceremony in a very public place with people she considered undesirable.

How she intended to vent her displeasure without making a scene, I had no idea, but I nevertheless straightened my spine and returned her glare.

If she wanted a confrontation, she was damn well going to get it.

Her gaze narrowed and, after a moment, a small smile touched her lips. An acknowledgement of a challenge met and accepted.

The ceremony went on. Aiden winked at me a few times, but his speech, when his turn finally came around, made no mention of me. And while I'd been expecting it, it was yet another reminder of just how wide a chasm there was between his world and mine. He might have been making a statement about my presence in his life earlier in the evening, but when it came to "werewolf business," he wasn't going against custom. I couldn't help wondering if—

had he been in the same situation as Katie—he'd have made the same choice.

After the speeches finished, we were urged to party on while the family moved to a private area for the final step in the official "welcome to adulthood" ceremony. Aiden hadn't said much about it, other than it involved the whole council and some sort of blessing that traditionally could not be viewed by outsiders.

As the door closed, a somewhat familiar voice behind me said, "Lizzie?"

I turned. A pretty red-haired wolf dressed in black stood several feet away, an odd, almost apprehensive look on her face. It took me a moment to place her—she was a semi-regular customer at the café and had come into the reservation a few months ago as part of the werewolf exchange program. If memory served me correctly, she was staying at the O'Connor compound.

"Fawn," I said with a smile. "We haven't seen you for a few days—everything okay?"

Her smile didn't quite reach her blue eyes. "Yes, I've just been busy at work. I hate to interrupt your night like this, but Karleen asked me to guide you to a private room. She wishes to speak to you."

It was pretty obvious it had been an order rather than a request, and that certainly explained Fawn's uneasiness. "Isn't she in the private chambers with Aiden?"

"Her part ends in a few minutes. Please, follow me."

I briefly considered not doing so, but, in truth, I had no desire to get Fawn into trouble or spoil Aiden's night by publicly brawling with his mother. That sort of thing was probably best done in private.

I took a glass of champagne from the tray of a passing waiter and resisted the urge to gulp it down and grab another. I might have come prepared for a fight, but now that it was nigh, ice was forming in my veins.

Fawn led me into a small antechamber close to the entrance. The room was decidedly warm thanks to the log fire that burned gently in one corner. Several comfy-looking leather chairs were dotted about, and a French door opened out onto the front balcony.

The red-haired wolf motioned toward one of the chairs and gave me an uncertain smile. "Would you like another drink? Something to eat, perhaps?"

I smiled, despite the gathering tension. "I'm fine, Fawn, but thanks."

She nodded. "I'm sure she won't be long."

And *I* was sure the bitch would probably make me wait as long as she possibly could. Once Fawn had left, I moved across to the wood burner, placing the flute of champagne on the mantelpiece before hitching up my dress and warming my butt. It wasn't elegant, but I didn't really care. I wasn't about to face the O'Connor dragon with ice running through my veins.

The minutes ticked by. Threads of wild magic began to slip into the room, tiny threads of silver that didn't venture near me and yet whose presence gave me strength. I wouldn't ever use it against Karleen, but it was at least a visible reminder that—Aiden aside—at least one of the O'Connor clan was on my side.

My butt eventually grew too warm, and I stepped away from the fire. As the hem of my dress fell back down to the floor, the door opened, and one half of the alpha pair that ruled the O'Connor pack stepped in.

I retrieved my champagne and gave her a pleasant smile. "What can I do for you, Karleen?"

She closed the door, then walked into the middle of the

room, the storm in her eyes still belying her serene expression. "I came to give you some information and advice."

"Indeed?" I nonchalantly took a sip of champagne. "How lovely of you. Of course, I can't promise to take said advice, but I am willing to give you the courtesy of listening."

She smiled. It was an unholy thing to behold. *Don't poke the wolf too much*, whispered a voice that sounded an awful lot like Katie, *otherwise she might just attack, consequences be damned.*

I can defend myself. Whether that was said to reassure Katie or myself, I wasn't entirely sure. I took another drink. Sparks danced across my fingers—a showy reminder to my foe that I was not without defenses.

"It is never wise to ignore the words of an alpha, young woman."

"But as you've been so keen to remind me, I'm not a wolf, am I? Therefore, you may advise me, but I may choose to ignore it."

"There are always consequences for doing so." She took another step closer. With Katie's presence in the room further enhancing my senses, I could not only smell the thick waves of her fury but also feel it vibrating across my skin. "Are you willing to risk such a cost?"

"Are *you*?" I replied evenly. "Katie may be this reservation's guardian, but I am the means through which she—and the wild magic—acts. Are you really willing to risk the lives of everyone here in an effort to get rid of me?"

"I think you overestimate your importance, witch."

"And I think you underestimate it." I took another drink, but it wasn't doing a whole lot now to quench the rising tide of my own anger. Katie might be telling me to cool it, but I'd spent half my life running from parents who thought they knew what was best for their children, and I had no intention of doing that anymore. And it damn well didn't matter if it was my parents or Aiden's. "Like it or not, this reservation has become a target for both the arcane and the supernatural. If you think the death toll is bad now, then by all means, destroy my business and drive me out of the reservation. But the ghosts of every soul that dies as a result of your actions will haunt your days and nights for the rest of your goddamn life. And yes, that *is* a curse."

She made a low sound in the back of her throat, and the hairs on the back of my neck stood on end. She was close, so close, to shifting shape and launching at me. I didn't move. I barely dared to breathe. I might well be able to defend myself, but I also couldn't afford to physically hurt her—and given the volatile nature of my magic of late, that was a distinct possibility.

She didn't attack. She *did* clench her fists, but the immediate danger thankfully abated. It still bubbled away in the background, though, only one smart comment away from eruption.

"That being the case, I shall skip the advice and move on to the information." Her voice was low and flat. "I've contacted Mia Raines and invited her back to the reservation."

The anger that surged through the room wasn't mine—it was Katie's. It was so thick and violent that the threads in the air glowed white-hot for several seconds. Karleen must have felt the flow of heat, because her gaze widened as she looked around. While it was mostly surprise, I could taste the tiniest sliver of fear in her output now.

She was only just realizing how powerful I was—even if the heat show wasn't actually my doing.

"Then you're a bloody fool," I said, even as Katie whispered secrets in my ear.

"Mia is a wolf—perhaps one of imperfect temperament and breeding, but that is nevertheless an infinitely better choice that a *witch*."

"Mia was sent to this reservation for one purposes only —to gain status and gold for her pack by marrying into one of the three packs here. She didn't love Aiden."

Karleen's smile was disbelieving. "*That* is a lie."

Meaning she didn't know why Aiden had told Mia to leave? "Maybe you should have asked Aiden why they broke up before you took the step of re-inviting an already-spoken-for gold digger into his life."

"I've run a check on Mia, dear woman. She's currently unencumbered by a relationship."

"Which doesn't address the whole gold digger aspect of her nature." I moved directly into her personal space, only stopping when we were practically nose to nose. She bared her teeth, but otherwise stood her ground. "Mia was always destined to return. Aiden and I were always destined to break up. But by inviting Mia here—and doing so behind the back of your mate—to discuss a possible alliance, you have opened the pack's wealth to greedy eyes, and you *will* regret it."

She blinked. "How do you know *any* of that?"

"I didn't. *Katie* did. And let me tell you, she's mighty pissed. That surge of heat you felt a moment ago? That was hers. She did warn you when she spoke through me not so long ago to be wary of what you wish for, because you may just get it."

"A gold-digging bitch I can deal with. It is infinitely preferable over the prospect of another witch in the family."

Once again, Katie's anger heated the air, but this time it

was accompanied by such a wild surge of electricity that it not only lit the air around us but also shorted out the lights. In the orange glow of the fire, a figure formed, one that was little more than closely woven threads of wild magic and yet undeniably recognizable.

Grab her hand, Katie said. *Let her see me.*

She won't—

She will. The skill that allows you to feel emotions via contact will allow her to see.

I took a deep breath and then grabbed Karleen's hand. She growled low in her throat and yanked back, but the wild magic surged around my grip, locking us together. A pulse began deep inside—a beat that spoke of strength being drawn.

My strength.

The thread-wrapped being that was Katie stepped forward. *Mother, look at me.*

Though the words were not spoken out loud, they nevertheless vibrated through the air, thanks to the presence of the wild magic and my connection with Karleen.

Her head snapped around, and her eyes widened. "Kate?"

It was a hoarse sound, one that was a mix of disbelief and horror.

Stop this foolishness, Mother. Both your blindness and your interference will not only cause greater harm to those you love and seek to protect, but will also cost you dearly on a personal level.

Karleen waved a hand, obviously dismissing the warning. "You know the rules, Kate—"

And rules are made to be broken. They were for me. They can be for Aiden.

"The circumstances are very different, dear heart—"

Yes, but Liz is no mere witch. She is the voice and sword of this reservation. Don't break her, because you may well break the reservation.

Karleen's gaze came to mine. Hatred glimmered. She was never going to accept me. Never. It made me wonder what had happened to her in the past. It was more than just blaming Gabe for Katie's early death, of that I was sure.

"And how do I know this is not an illusion? How do I know she is not putting words into your mouth?"

You don't. But you know the sound of my voice; you've heard it often enough in your dreams of late, Mother.

"Dreams are not reality, but rather desires that can never come to be. Just as this"—her gaze raked me—"can never come to be."

Then I wish you well with what comes, even as I fear you'll live to regret your decisions.

With that, the wild magic unleashed our wrists and Katie faded away. I released Karleen and staggered back, somehow falling into a chair rather than on the floor. My heart hammered so hard it ached, and my whole body trembled. Katie might not have talked for very long, but she had nigh on drained me of strength. And while I knew she wouldn't have taken it that far, her actions could have killed me.

I sucked in a deep breath and lifted my gaze to Karleen. "You may have ensured that my heartbreak happens sooner rather than later, but be aware I will not give him up until I absolutely have to. And if you do anything or say anything to him *or* to anyone else in an effort to split us before Mia's arrival, I'll make your life hell. And rest assured, thanks to this reservation and the power it has given me, that is something I absolutely *can* do."

She smiled. It was another of those unholy things.

"Enjoy what time remains to you. Rest assured it *will* be brief."

And with that, she turned and left. The door slammed behind her, and the sound echoed across the fire-lit darkness. I sucked in air, but it didn't abate the trembling or the thick ache in my head. I gulped down the rest of my champagne; it didn't do a lot for either problem but at least eased the dryness in my throat.

The door opened again, and Belle stepped in. She took one look at me and told Monty to grab more champagne before striding toward me.

"What the fuck happened?" She knelt and took my hands in hers. Her fingers were warm compared to the ice of mine. "Why the fuck didn't you reach out for me?"

"Because I didn't want Karleen's hate spilling all over you." I sucked in another breath, then squeezed her hands. "Katie attempted to talk some sense into her, and the process drained my strength. I'll be fine in a few more minutes."

She didn't look convinced, but that wasn't really surprising. She might not be reading my thoughts but we'd been friends long enough now that she didn't need to. "Why can't the bitch just be happy that Aiden's happy?"

"I suspect there's been some sort of trauma in her past involving a witch."

"You mean other than the whole Katie and Gabe thing?"

I nodded. "Even if Aiden and I did become permanent, she won't ever accept me."

"You knew that going into the relationship, though."

"I did. I just—" *Hoped for a miracle.*

"So why did she corner you in here? Was it to impart more useless threats?"

"No. It was to tell me she's reached out to Mia and sent her an invite back to the reservation."

Belle sucked in a breath. "Why would she do that when Mia's a money-grubbing liar?"

A smile twitched my lips. "Because apparently she didn't know why Aiden sent her packing."

"Fucking men," Belle muttered. "Why do they all have to act so stoic and recalcitrant when it comes to emotions?"

"I'll kindly ask you to refrain from branding my entire sex by the actions of a few." Monty walked into the room carrying three flutes of champagne. "Some of us are very open and honest with our emotions."

"Some are even a little *too* open."

Belle's voice was dry. Monty grinned as he handed us both a glass. "At least you'll never be left wondering where I stand emotionally."

"I'm not entirely sure that's a good thing."

"Hey, you've got what most women would die for—a man who is ready and willing to tell you exactly what he's thinking and feeling."

She rolled her eyes and returned her gaze to me. She didn't, I noted wryly, disabuse him of the notion that he was her man. "Do you want me to shuffle through the bitch's mind and see what I can find?"

"As tempting as that is, no. It'd be pretty pointless right now anyway."

Especially given none of us—not even Aiden—knew what his reaction to Mia's arrival would be. If he *did* do the unexpected—if he decided to hold true to his emotions rather than his duty to his pack, their expectations, and his own desire to one day rule as his father does—then maybe we could investigate it further.

I gulped down my drink, but the bubbles caught in my throat and made me burp.

"You want another one?" Monty asked, amused.

I shook my head. "I *could* go for a thick piece of cake if there's any left."

"I'll go investigate."

As he plucked the empty glass from my hand and then headed out, I said, "I take it the private ceremony is still ongoing?"

Belle nodded. "While I haven't actively been scanning, I have caught a few waves of frustration and concern coming from both Aiden and his father. They obviously noticed Karleen had scampered."

"Noticed, but didn't stop," I muttered.

"She's an alpha, Liz. Alphas do rather than obey."

"She's joint alpha, and she didn't consult with her mate before inviting Mia or challenging me."

"I hate to be defending the bitch, but even in normal human relationships, that's quite common."

"Also true." I rose and moved back to the fire, once again lifting my dress to warm my butt. Ice still ran through my veins, though the trembling ache of tiredness had at least eased a little.

"How long have you got? Did she say?"

I shook my head. "I think she envisages it being a lovely surprise for Aiden." I grimaced. "And it may well be, given he still holds a torch for her."

"He holds a bigger one for you, Lizzie."

"Yes, but will it be enough? I'm not a wolf, and never will be, no matter—"

I stopped as pain speared through my brain. The source wasn't tiredness but rather the new threads I'd woven into

199

the magic that protected our café. It seemed tonight's surprises had not finished with us yet.

I swore. Loudly. "Someone's just attempted to break into our café. We need to get over there."

"Mom's there," Belle said, frowning. "If there'd been any trouble, she would have contacted me."

"Unless she's taken one of her sleeping draughts. She used to take of a lot of them to help her sleep when her migraines hit, if I remember right."

"Possible. I'll go grab our coats."

"Monty?"

"Already on his way back."

I followed her out the door. She handed me Monty's coat, and I tugged it on as he strode toward us, a plastic-wrapped piece of cake in one hand. "Figured you might still need it, especially if we *are* dealing with something other than a stupid thief."

He handed me the cake, then opened the front door and stepped out onto the veranda. The wind was fierce and cold, tugging at the end of my dress and flinging it sideways, freezing my legs and other exposed bits. I drew the coat tighter across my chest, then shut the door and hurried after the two of them.

Belle, can you reach out to Ashworth and ask him to let Aiden know where we've gone?

She immediately did so. *You know he's not going to be happy with us disappearing like this.*

Nothing we can do about that, and I'm certainly not waiting around for his grand reappearance.

Karleen will no doubt think she's run you off.

Let her. Her victory will be short-lived.

We jumped into Monty's classic 1967 V8 Mustang, with me—being the smallest of the three of us—inelegantly squeezing into the rear seat of a car that was never really designed to carry backseat passengers. The big engine rumbled as he started her up and then eased her gently down the old stone driveway. Once out on the main road, he unleashed her full power. In the wet conditions, it was a hair-raising experience.

The café remained wrapped in darkness when we arrived, and there was no immediate indication that anything—or anyone—had tried to enter.

But as I clambered out of the back seat and looked up at the first floor, I spotted a few faint wisps of broken spell threads. Something *had* at least tested the magic.

"Doesn't look as though they got in." Monty stood in the middle of the road gazing up at the first floor balcony. He didn't seem to care about the pelting rain or the fact he was getting soaked. "I'm not sure it was our book thief, though."

Belle pulled the keys out of her small purse and opened up. "Only one way to tell."

She opened the door and then motioned me to precede her. I hitched my dress up, running quickly through the tables and then up the stairs, my heels clattering on the wooden steps.

The gentle glow of the streetlights washed through the glass doors at the far end of the room, highlighting more tiny threads of shattered magic; this time, the edge of darkness that still crawled around them was plain to see. Monty was right—our book thief hadn't done this. Our magic-capable DNA-broken werewolf had been here.

I strode across to the room, unlocked the sliding door, and then stepped through. A tiny sliver of thread drifted past me and I gently captured it in one hand. A pulse of evil briefly caressed my skin—confirmation of our culprit. Thankfully, the spell she'd destroyed belonged to the tracking layer I'd recently added. That she hadn't succeeded in breaking the rest was no doubt thanks—at least in part—to how integral the wild magic was to the spells that now protected this place. She certainly wouldn't be the first witch who'd looked at our deeper protections and decided not to risk them.

But the fact she'd been able to pluck a particular line of magic free from the other threads and then destroy it spoke of her knowledge and strength. Whatever she was—however her body had become so twisted—her magic was decidedly strong.

But how was that possible, if she was a werewolf? Magic might be an inherent part of their souls, but they'd never been capable of *any* sort of spell work.

Monty stepped out onto the balcony and stopped beside me. "If she's here for revenge, why is she coming after you? Why not me? And how did she even find you?"

"She saw me clearly at the farm *and* in the forest. She might also have used the blood that was no doubt on her claw when she sliced open my back to do a tracking spell."

"I very much doubt there would have been enough to develop a decent tracking spell," Monty said.

"And it would have led her to either the party or Aiden's rather than here, surely," Belle said from the doorway.

I opened my hand and let the tiny broken thread drift away. "Except my resonance is stronger here than it would be at Aiden's—especially with the weight of all the spells."

Monty frowned. "That still doesn't explain why she came after you rather than me."

"She may not be aware you're the reservation witch."

"I doubt *that*, given it was my magic that attacked her at the farm."

"Maybe she's after you both." Belle crossed her arms. "That would make more sense, especially given you're both the reason she's out two victims."

My gaze shot to Monty's. "Have your spells been tested tonight?"

"How would I know? I'm not there."

"You didn't weave an alarm in?" I said, surprised.

"Didn't see the need. I'd feel any attack if I'm there and don't really care what they do to the place if I'm not."

Belle snorted. "There speaks a man who not only has a ton of money, but also cares *so* much about the safety of his familiar."

"Eamon is canny enough to get the hell out of there at the first hint of an assault," Monty said. "Besides, he's a cat. He has nine lives."

"And how many has he used to date?"

"Thanks to the fact my life was extremely boring until I came to this place, only one—and that was due to the age of his flesh form, rather than accident." He motioned to the fading threads. "Shall we head over to my place and see if she's attempted to do something similar to my spells?"

As we retreated and I relocked the door, a tall figure in a pale nightgown appeared from the shadows haunting my bedroom. "Is there a problem?"

"Attempted break-in," Belle said. "You didn't feel anything?"

Ava shook her head. "But I did take a sleeping draught, so that's not surprising. The protections still feel to be in place, though."

"They are. Mostly." Belle touched her mom's arm. "Go back to bed. We're heading over to Monty's to see if his place was also attacked."

"Be careful, all of you."

As she headed back to bed, we clattered down the stairs and squeezed back into the Mustang. I unwrapped the cake and munched on the creamy goodness while being very careful not to drop crumbs. Monty would have been most displeased.

His place was a small but beautiful brick terrace, with off-road parking out front and a small garage. He rarely used the latter for his Mustang, preferring to keep her offsite in a specialty storage unit. It was certainly a move that had paid off when, only a few months ago, a soucouyant had kidnapped him and utterly destroyed the temporary accommodation he'd been staying in.

"I'm not seeing any indication of an assault," he said, as the garage door slowly rose.

"You might not from here," I said. "Especially if she came in through the forest."

He grunted in agreement. Once the Mustang was safe in the garage, we all climbed out and headed inside. The terrace basically consisted of a long hallway off which most of the main rooms ran. There were two bedrooms—both with en suite—a separate powder room, a TV room and, at the rear of the place, a large open-plan kitchen and living area.

I followed Belle down the hall, our heels clattering loudly on the shiny wooden floorboards. Eamon—an orange tabby with a pale, fluffy mane that made him look like a miniature lion and a coat that had random tufts of fur sticking out at odd angles—stalked out of the second bedroom, his mismatched eyes scanning all three of us and narrowing as his gaze settled on me.

"Attack me," I growled, holding out a finger in warning. "And I'll burn your furry ass with wild magic."

A look that was pure disdain crossed his face. Then,

with a flick of his tail, he turned and went back into the bedroom.

One win for me, I thought, relieved. The bastard had sharp claws and wasn't afraid to use them.

"You know why he attacks you, don't you?" Belle said, amusement evident in her voice.

"Because he's cranky and mean?"

She laughed. "No. He senses your fear."

"I wouldn't fear the bastard if he didn't unleash his weapons of mass destruction at the smallest opportunity."

"I'll admit he's a wee bit grumpy," Monty said. "But hey, he's got the right, given he's older than Methuselah."

He meant the spirit within the cat rather than the body he inhabited, which was only a little over three years old. "Age is no excuse for meanness."

"I'll remind you of that when you get old and cranky." He moved past me and walked across to the sliding glass doors that led out into the patio and barbequing area. "There's no sign of interference. Eamon says he would have informed me if someone had made such an attempt."

"Maybe attacking our place drained her," Belle commented. "But given you've not got the wild magic to boost your protection spells, Monty, you might want to add a few additional layers to take care of any unpicking attempts she makes."

"Are you having a go at my protection spells?" he said, eyebrows rising. "I'm wounded to the core."

"I'd rather see you wounded that way than have this bitch get her mitts on you." Her voice was dry. "How can I have the pleasure of proving you wrong, if you're not actually around?"

"See?" Monty nudged my shoulder with his, a delighted grin on his face. "She really does care about me."

Belle rolled her eyes. "How about you change out of that wet suit so we can get back to the party before we're—" She stopped as Monty's phone rang. "Sirens? You have police sirens for a ringtone?"

"Only for the rangers."

"Dare I ask what ringtone you have for me?"

"I wouldn't." He hit the answer button. "Monty speaking—what can I do for you, Duke?"

Though I couldn't hear exactly what was being said, the urgent note and Monty's expression both suggested it was pretty bad.

"I'll need to change, but I'll be there in roughly ten minutes."

"*We'll* be there," I corrected as he hung up. "You're not going after this thing alone, Monty. It's not only dangerous, it's damn fast—and I have the scars to prove it."

"Liz, don't be ridiculous. I'll be fine."

"Now *you're* being ridiculous," Belle said. "And if either of you think you're escaping without me, you can think again. Besides, me talking to the dead might be the only way we'll uncover any real information."

Monty blew out a frustrated breath. "Fine. I'm not arguing because we haven't the time. But neither of you can go dressed like that. Follow me."

He turned and stalked toward his bedroom. We hurried after him.

"What are we dealing with this time?" I asked.

"It's not a simple murder." His voice was grim. "Not this time."

"Then what?" I asked with more than a little trepidation.

"This time, it's a fucking massacre."

CHAPTER ELEVEN

"Oh God, *no*," Belle murmured.

"Yeah." Monty threw open his wardrobe door and tossed us sweatpants and sweaters. "You can change in the spare room. Shoe wise, mine will probably fit you, Belle, but you'll have to stuff them with socks, Liz."

"That's fine." I gathered everything up then hurried into the other room. I didn't bother stripping off my dress but instead pulled everything over the top of it, then tucked the swaths of silky material into the waist and tied the drawstrings up tight. As predicted, I swam in the shoes, but shoving socks into the toe area and then lashing the laces around my ankles certainly helped.

We were back on the road—this time in Monty's old Ford—in record time.

"Where did the attack happen?" I asked. "Not that far, I take it, given you said we'd be there in ten."

"It happened over at the old scout hall."

Dread clutched at my throat, making it difficult to speak. "Not kids. Please don't tell me she's killed kids."

"No, thankfully. But that doesn't make it any better, given six kids have probably lost a parent."

"How on earth did she kill six people?" Belle said. "We're in a goddamn werewolf reservation—surely one of them would have had time to react and defend?"

"Unless they're all human or she used magic." He hesitated. "Apparently, it's pretty bad."

Mass murders generally were. But I kept that thought to myself. It was pointless saying what we were all no doubt thinking.

The scout hall was a long, tin-roofed weatherboard building with two old metal water tanks sitting at the rear. The front section facing the parking area was obviously a new addition, as it had been built using those horrible gray concrete bricks. Three ranger vehicles were parked close to the entrance, one bearing a Coroner's Office sticker. Given Ciara was at the celebration, it meant Luke was here.

Monty stopped beside the coroner's vehicle, and we all climbed out. I wrapped my borrowed coat closer and tried to ignore the thick scent of blood and death drifting from within the hall. Werewolf senses—especially in a case like this—sucked.

Jaz appeared, her face pale and expression haunted. "I'm not sure there's a lot either of you can—" She stopped when her gaze fell on Belle. "Oh."

Belle grimaced. "Yeah. It's not something I'm looking forward to, though."

"And with good reason. This way."

She led us into the building. The thick scent of death grew stronger, and the air crawled with confusion and fear —emotions that emanated not only from the violence of these deaths, but also the souls who now haunted this space. Their deaths had not been ordained.

"Fuck, it's going to take some strength to move all of them on," Belle muttered uneasily.

I gripped her arm and squeezed it lightly. "Between the two of us, we should be alright."

It was confidently said, though in truth, moving these souls on to their next life very much depended on their lucidity, their willingness to accept what had happened, and their being able to understand that their only other option was forever lingering in this hall.

We strode through a short hallway that had smaller rooms on either side, then into the main room. It was a big space with metal roof trusses and wood-clad walls. Two further rooms lay at the far end, one obviously a kitchen, the other bathroom facilities.

The destruction of life had happened in the middle of the main area around several long wooden tables. My gaze swept the violence almost unwillingly, quickly taking in the blood, the gore, and the body parts that had been spread in a wider arc around the main grouping of bodies.

It really *was* a massacre.

But what was far worse than the physical destruction was the thick wave of disbelief, horror, and pain emanating from those who'd died here. It wrapped around me like a cloak, smothering fresh air and making each breath feel as if I was swallowing death.

Belle made a low sound of distress and stopped abruptly. "I can't go any further."

"Will you be able to contact the souls from another room?" Monty immediately asked.

Belle nodded. "I'll need you to make a protection circle though, as neither of us have our spell stones with us."

"No problem at all." He lightly cupped her elbow. "Let's get you out of here."

"Call me when you're ready," I said, then followed Jaz deeper into the destruction zone. Luke was examining the body of a woman. Duke was in the process of photographing and tagging everything. It was going to take him quite a while.

I took a deep breath and regretted it immediately, as the thick scents that filled the room clawed at my throat. I'd seen some pretty horrendous deaths in my short time within the reservation, but this was the first time I'd not only seen it on such a large scale, but also felt it so strongly, both psychically *and* sensorially.

I swallowed heavily, but it didn't do a lot to ease the sick churning in my gut. Five of the victims had a look of horror and disbelief forever etched onto their faces. The sixth—a man—had obviously been the first to die, as not only was his expression one of surprise, but his body was the most intact of all. Our rogue wolf had gotten more violent as she'd moved on. The last victim—a blonde woman in her later years from the look of what remained—had been utterly torn apart.

I stopped several feet away from the end of the table and tried breathing through my mouth. It didn't help. The scent of blood and death and utter rage—

The thought stalled as I caught a faint but familiar scent. I drew in a deeper breath and there—barely—was the pungent aroma of sulfur.

And it was coming from the rear of the hall.

I backtracked around the circle of destruction and strode down the hall, carefully avoiding the outlying puddles of gore and blood.

"Lizzie?" Jaz said. "You all right?"

"Yes. But there's something else here."

She hurried after me. "What?"

"Magic. *Her* magic."

I pulled down the sleeve of my jacket and carefully pushed open the kitchen door. It was small but modern, with gleaming stainless steel benches and appliances, a surprisingly large fridge, and open storage that contained all the cooking and serving necessities.

The sulfur scent pulled me on through a second door that led into a storeroom. Shelves lined either side, and directly in front were a padlocked rear door and a window.

The latter had been smashed, and on one edge of the glass were two scraps of blood-soaked material.

My heart beat a whole lot faster. If she'd used my blood to find me, there was no reason why I couldn't return the favor.

"Well, at least we know she left via the window," Jaz said. "And we should be able to get some DNA evidence from those bits of material."

"Yes, but would you mind if I collect them both first and make an attempt to trace her through them?"

"Is that possible?"

"I won't know until I try."

"Then wait until I record the find."

She did so, then handed me a pair of gloves and an evidence bag. "I'm sure the boss won't object to you at least trying, as long as there's no cross-contamination."

I plucked the two bits of material free; even through the gloves, I felt the dark pulse of her presence. How long it would last, I couldn't say. The last time I'd used blood to track someone, it had been a supernatural being and the connection faded pretty fast. I had to hope that wasn't the case here, because I couldn't go anywhere until Belle had talked to the ghosts.

I carefully constructed a spell that would both contain

and also "freeze" the blood in its current state; hopefully, that would hold the pulse in a useable state until we actually had the time to access it. Once the threads of magic were tightly wound around and through the evidence bag, I activated the spell. The dark connection fluttered briefly and then beat on. For how long was anyone's guess, but relief nevertheless stirred. At least I hadn't killed it.

"Don't lose that," Jaz commented, "or Aiden will have my hide."

"Only after he has mine."

A smile twitched her lips. "But in a very different manner, I'm thinking."

I snorted softly and followed her back into the main room. Duke looked around at us. "Anything?"

"Yeah, she went out through the rear window and left a couple of material strips behind. Liz is going to attempt to trace her through them."

"But not," I added quickly, "before Belle makes her attempt to contact the souls in the room."

Duke's eyebrows rose. "How many souls are we talking about?"

"All six. We're hoping one of them might be able to tell us something."

He nodded. "Jaz, you want to record that?"

"Will do."

We made another wide circle around the destruction and walked into the smaller of the two rooms at the front. Monty glanced around as we entered and motioned toward the spell-wrapped evidence bag. "What's that?"

I tossed it to him. "Scraps of blood-soaked material our murderer left behind. Thought we might try tracking her through it."

He frowned down at the bag. "I'm not feeling a pulse or anything emanating from it."

"You might not—the magic was coming from her blood and it was really faint. I think it was more my psi skills than magic that allowed me to feel it."

He grunted. "It does at least indicate that dark magic is a part of her DNA, in much the same manner as wild magic is with you."

"But if something like that was possible, there would have been evidence of it before now," I said. "Blood magic *isn't* wild magic—it's been used for eons by black witches."

"Except there probably *is* evidence of such in the archives—"

"Can we skip this discussion until afterwards?" Belle cut in. "I really need to get this over with ASAP before it all overwhelms me."

"Sorry," Monty immediately said. "Liz, once you sit, I'll raise the circle."

I stepped over his spell stones and sat opposite Belle, my knees lightly touching hers.

As Monty's spell rose around us, I said, *You okay?*

For the moment. She wrinkled her nose. *But this is going to be a dark journey into hell.*

Referring to the fact that she'd be battling the emotional outpouring that came with the moment of death. In normal circumstances, when there was only the one soul to deal with, it wasn't such a problem. Her shields were well able to deal with such a small influx. But with six, they'd take a hammering.

I hesitated, and then said, *Perhaps the key to uncovering anything is talking to the soul of the woman who died last.*

Belle raised an eyebrow. *I still have to talk to the others to move them on.*

Yes, but if we can get all our information from the last victim, you won't have to go through the questioning roller coaster with the others.

It would certainly help. I take it you know who was the last?

The destruction got more frenzied as she went on. I quickly described what was left of the woman and then added, *Of course, given she witnessed everything that happened, it's also possible she'll be the hardest to deal with.*

Maybe, but worth trying. She glanced across to Jaz. "You ready to record?"

Jaz nodded. Belle took a deep breath to clear her thoughts and gather her energy, and then closed her eyes and lightly gripped my fingers. While some spirit talkers used personal items to make contact, or objects such a Ouija board or even a spirit pendulum, Belle had never needed such props. Her ability was so strong that she was able to contact them direct.

With our hands and minds linked, everything she felt and saw echoed through me. The minute she reached out, a thick wave of ghostly terror hit like a club, forcing me to suck in air in an effort to both smother and control the incoming sensations.

Sorry, Belle said as the output muted. *They got the better of me for a moment.*

Unsurprising.

I closed my eyes and, through our connection, studied the ghostly forms in the other room. Two were little more than pale wisps of energy, which perhaps suggested this death was close enough to their ordained one that they would be easy enough to move on. The form of the other three were almost solid; only the faint blurring of their limbs as they moved around the room in obvious confusion gave away their true condition. At the very far end of the table, close to the remnants of her body, was the last victim. She was definitely elderly and, despite the confusion on her ghostly features, appeared a whole lot calmer than a couple of the others.

Belle carefully reached out to her. She swung around, her ghostly features briefly disintegrating before resolving into an expression of surprise. *Oh, I didn't expect to see or hear anyone in this state.*

You know what's happened? Belle asked.

Obviously, I'm dead. Horribly, violently dead.

The shudder that ran through the woman's form was a heated wave of pain that washed through Belle and into me. I gripped her fingers a little tighter and silently bolstered her strength. She was going to need it, even if this woman appeared more aware and emotionally controlled than many ghosts.

Your name? Belle asked.

Jenny. Jenny Brown. She looked around again. *Why have we not moved on?*

I repeated the questions and answers for the recording Jaz was making; it was something that had become almost second nature, given we'd done this far too many times now.

Because this death wasn't ordained, so you need help to do so, Belle said. *That's something I can help you with, but I need to ask some questions first.*

So the date of your death really is *written in the stars on the day you're born?* Jenny asked.

In a sense, yes, though many things can alter it. Fate is not an unmoving timeline—the things we do and the decisions we make always have an effect.

Huh. She drew herself upright, and I had the sudden impression that she'd been a headmistress at some point in her life. She had that look—that no-nonsense manner. *What can I do to help you?*

I'm afraid I need to know what you saw before your death.

Why?

Because it may help track down this thing before it kills again.

It all happened so very fast. One minute we were arguing about decorations, and the next ...

A shudder ran through her and, just for a second, her horror was thick and overwhelming. Belle smothered the wave as best she could, but it nevertheless left us both gasping. Having to shield out the emotions of the other five was definitely making things harder.

The first I knew of the assault was Derry's screams, Jenny continued, a catch in her voice. *By then, the creature was tearing into Marian.*

Can you describe the creature?

Jenny's nose wrinkled. *She was a mix of wolf and human—it was almost as if her shift had gotten stuck at midpoint.*

Did you recognize her? Was she young or old?

Jenny hesitated. *The human portion of her face reminded me of Leesa Rhineheart, but she was far too young to actually be her. Besides, Leesa wasn't a wolf.*

Did you know Leesa?

I taught her, though that was at least thirty years ago now, if not more. Her brief smile was tinged with sadness. *She was barely sixteen back then, but you always remember the children with serious behavioral problems.*

"Ask her if Patrick or the others were in Leesa's class" came Jaz's comment.

Belle did so, and Jenny nodded. *They weren't what I call on friendly terms though.*

Do you know why?

Students rarely confide in their parents when it comes to being bullied, let alone their teachers. She hesitated. *I suspect there was more than that to it, though.*

As in, physical violence? Like rape?

I honestly can't say. I wouldn't have thought any of the boys capable of such a thing, though.

How many times had that been said over the centuries, I thought, when plenty of them had?

Is there anything else you can tell me about her? Belle asked. *Anything unusual that caught your eye?*

Once again Jenny hesitated. *I won't swear to this, because she moved with blinding speed, but I think she had some sort of mark on her cheek—her human cheek, not wolf.*

What sort of mark?

It looked rather like a scythe with a snake woven around it. I remember thinking it was a rather odd place for a tattoo.

Given our rogue was capable of dark magic, I was betting it *wasn't* a tattoo. At least, not an ordinary one. A few months ago we'd confronted a dark practitioner who'd taken over the body of his much younger apprentice—something only the most powerful dark witches could do. That apprentice had been wearing a maker's mark—a tattoo on the cheek that signified who his master was.

Why didn't you run? Why didn't the others run?

I certainly tried, but it felt like my feet were glued to the floor. The others did run, but they were moving incredibly slowly. She grimaced. *Of course, time always seems to slow when disaster strikes.*

And sometimes, the impression of time slowing was in fact a reality, courtesy of magic.

Was there anything else?

Other than the madness in her eyes? No.

What color were her eyes?

Gray. Which means it couldn't have been Leesa. If I remember right, her eyes were mismatched—one brown, one blue.

You can remember that tiny detail?

Jenny smiled sadly. *The smallest details are often the only things that you do remember. In Leesa's case, it was her mismatched eyes and diminutive stature that caused the bullying. There wasn't much I could do, as it never happened within my sight and Leesa refused to report it.*

I appreciate the help, Jenny. Are you ready to move on?

Yes. Looking forward to it, in fact. Anything would be better than lingering in this place.

Then I bid you health, happiness, and good fortune in your next life, Jenny. And with that, Belle began the spell that would guide her soul onwards.

As Jenny's presence shimmered and began to fade, Belle took another of those deep, somewhat shuddering breaths. It wasn't over yet. She still had five other souls to move on.

In the end, she only managed three more before the pull on her strength *and* mine became too dangerous. She broke our connection and pushed back unsteadily, her breath a harsh rasp and her body shaking.

"I'll have to do the remaining two tomorrow, after I've had some rest. They were ... problematic."

"How?" Jaz asked curiously. "I mean, do they actually want to stay in this place?"

"They refuse to accept their deaths." Belle scrubbed a shaky hand through her damp hair. "If that continues tomorrow, then their souls will be doomed to remain in this place forever."

"Even in death, some people aren't big believers in sensible thinking." Monty dismantled his protection circle and began collecting his spell stones.

"So that's how haunted houses happen?" Jaz said. "People refusing to accept their death?"

"That, or believing they have unfinished business to attend to."

I pushed a little unsteadily to my feet, then offered Belle a hand. She accepted it gratefully but didn't immediately release me. She really *had* pushed herself to the limit.

And taken you to the edge with me. It was little more than a hoarse whisper. Even something as simple as telepathy was an effort. *I don't think you should be going out there hunting—*

It's not like we really have another choice, given I have no idea how long the pulse will last. I half shrugged. In truth, I would have liked nothing more than to curl up in my bed and let sleep take me, but that wasn't really an option. Not if we wanted any chance of catching this thing quickly. *Besides, it sounds like she used magic to freeze—or at least slow—her victims. Confronting her in a weakened state might be our best option.*

Not when you're also weakened.

I might be, but Monty will be with me, and he's not. And I can always call on the wild magic.

Because that never takes a toll on your strength. Her mental tone was wry. She waved a hand in frustration. *Just be careful, okay?*

A smile tugged at my lips as I answered with my usual, *Always.*

She rolled her eyes and glanced over to Jaz. "I don't

suppose someone will be able to give me a lift home? These two are heading out after the rogue."

Awareness surged across my senses, and a faint but familiar scent teased my nostrils. I mentally steeled myself against the annoyance that was no doubt about to be deployed. Damn it, why couldn't the man have stayed at his party?

Jaz frowned. "That won't be a problem, but I'm not sure Aiden would approve—"

"You can ask him yourself," I cut in. "Because he's about three steps away from the door."

She raised her eyebrow. "I know that, but how the hell do you?"

"Magic." Which wasn't actually the truth, but it was an answer I knew she'd accept without question.

He stepped into the room, his body practically vibrating with annoyance and tension. His gaze unerringly came to mine, and I raised both hands. "The call came in while we were checking the rogue hadn't attempted to break into Monty's after doing so at the café. We wouldn't have left without informing you if the call had come in at the party."

Which was a partial lie, and we both knew it.

All he did was raise an eyebrow and glance at Belle. "I take it you've contacted the souls of the dead?"

She nodded. "Jaz recorded it."

His gaze returned to me, his blue eyes sparking. The man really *was* annoyed, but I had a suspicion it wasn't directly aimed at my actions. "And what was it that I'm not going to approve?"

"We've got a small opportunity to track this thing down, but we need to do it now," Monty said.

"Then let's go." He swung around and headed out the door without waiting for an answer.

"Well, that at least solves one problem." Monty tossed Belle his keys. "I'll collect the old girl tomorrow."

She caught the keys with a nod. "To repeat, be bloody careful. This thing really doesn't feel right."

"To echo your earlier words, I'm hardly going to get dead before you can prove me wrong." He motioned toward the door. "After you, dear cousin."

I followed Aiden outside. The night was dark and, despite the thickness of my borrowed coat, chills ran down my spine. Whether they were the result of the icy air or the trepidation of what we were about to do—and find—I couldn't really say.

Aiden opened the passenger door and helped me into his truck. "You look rather ridiculous in those clothes, you know."

Though his voice was light, I could feel the tension in him. The anger and frustration bubbled deep within, but I was becoming surer that it really wasn't aimed at me.

"We were about to head back to the party from Monty's, but when the call came in, we had little other choice. I wasn't about to wander about a crime scene in that dress or shoes."

"A sensible move that shocks me given your past exploits running through forests in inappropriate clothing." He slammed the door shut before I could reply, then ran around to the driver side.

Monty climbed into the back, then leaned forward and handed me the evidence bag. "You still feeling the pulse?"

I hesitated and gently probed the magic protecting the two scraps of blood-soaked material. "Yes, but it's fainter. I'm not sure how long my magic will keep it viable."

"Then we'd better get moving." Aiden started the truck. "Where to?"

I carefully deepened my connection to the magic and probed the pulse with my "other" senses. "Right at the gate and then right again."

"How far away is it feeling?" Monty asked.

"Not far." I frowned down at the evidence bag, watching the faint flutter of the protecting magic reacting to the blood's pulse. "I doubt we'll even be heading out of Castle Rock."

"Given what we know about this thing's looks," Monty said. "It really makes no sense for it to be holed up within town limits. Too many people to see her."

"Sometimes the best place to hide is the most obvious place," Aiden said. "Those in rural areas are generally more likely to notice unusual activity than those in main hubs."

"I wouldn't exactly call Castle Rock a main hub." Monty's voice was dry. "And it's not like the gossip brigade ever miss a trick."

"But the gossip brigade are not nighttime warriors."

"Thank God for that," I muttered. "Otherwise we'd never be able to do anything interesting."

Monty laughed. "Luckily, I don't hold their interest."

"Oh, I wouldn't bet on that," Aiden said, voice dry. "Especially at the moment."

"Why on earth would the gossip brigade—" Monty stopped and laughed. "It's not so much me, is it?"

I directed Aiden left onto Barker Street and then added, "They're currently running a betting pool on engagement dates."

He laughed again. "Our first official date was tonight, and our second is on Friday. That's hardly a basis to be betting on a relationship, let alone anything more serious."

"That's never stopped them before," Aiden said. "They were doing the same when—"

He cut the rest off with a grimace, but it didn't take a genius to guess what he'd been about to say.

"When you were with Mia." I gave him a lopsided smile. "She was part of your past and may well be your future, but avoiding any discussion about her isn't going to help anyone."

He glanced at me; his expression gave little away, but his eyes were fierce. "I just thought you might have heard enough of that name for one night."

I hesitated and then said, "Have you had words with your mother?"

"Not as yet. But I will, trust me, especially after learning she skipped out of my rite of passage to go harass you." He paused, his grip tightening briefly on the steering wheel. "What did she say?"

"You don't know?"

It came out surprised, and he frowned. "I never got the chance to ask her."

Meaning the bitch hadn't yet told him what she'd done? That not only sucked, it put me in a rather dicey position. As tempting as it was to tell him all the gritty details, I honestly didn't want to get in the middle of any argument between mother and son.

"Then perhaps you'd better talk to her first."

"Liz," he growled. "Stop playing games—"

"I've never considered our relationship a game, Aiden."

"Implying I have?"

"That's not what I meant, but let's be honest here—you've never treated it as permanent, either."

"Guys," Monty cut in, a hint of steel in his voice. "That sort of discussion is better had in private."

I twisted around in the seat to look at him. "You're right. Let's talk about you and Belle going out Friday instead.

223

Does this mean your big plans for a momentous evening are about to happen?"

"I would certainly hope so." He smiled, but there was sympathy in his eyes. For me, and for the situation I was now in. "But I don't want to count my horses and all that."

"Says the man who has told all and sundry he's going to marry that girl." The magic around the bag stirred, whispering its secrets. "Turn right at the next street, then slow down. We're close."

"She certainly has some balls," Monty said. "We really *are* in the middle of goddamn Castle Rock."

"It could be her ancestral home." Aiden's voice held only a vague vibration of the anger that swirled through his aura. I might have changed the subject, but a discussion *would* be had later. "A lot of the houses along this section of Doveton Street have been in the same family for generations."

"So most are werewolf owned?"

He nodded. "There're only two that are human owned. The brick one down the other end of the road close to the church and—"

"That rather overgrown-looking one up ahead on our right?" I guessed.

His gaze shot to mine. "Is that the place?"

"It certainly is." I studied it for a second, uneasiness stirring even though I wasn't immediately sensing anything or anyone. "Do you know who it belongs to?"

"Not these days." He halted on the other side of the road, just down from the house. "I do know it's been abandoned for quite a while. The neighbors were complaining about rats recently."

"It looks the sort of place rats would love." Monty

leaned forward. "I'm not seeing any sort of major protective spells, though."

"You probably wouldn't, thanks to the thickness of those tea trees on the nature strip." I glanced down at the evidence bag. The pulse was little more than a vague flutter now; while it had led me here, it wasn't giving me any further information. "The signal's now too faint to say whether she's inside or not."

"Then we find out the old-fashioned way." Aiden opened the truck's door and climbed out.

I tucked the evidence bag into the glove compartment and then scrambled out after the two men. It had at least stopped raining, although the scent in the air suggested another thunderstorm wasn't far away.

Aiden retrieved his gun from the weapons locker in the back of his truck and quickly strapped it on.

"I'm not entirely sure you're going to be faster at drawing that thing than she's able to move," I said.

His smile held little in the way of humor. "There's only one way to find that out, too."

"I'd really prefer it if we didn't."

"So would I. But nothing else so far has stopped this bitch, so maybe a bullet will. Monty?"

He immediately strode across the road. Beyond the tea trees, on the other side of the footpath, was a thick hedge. It was unkempt and uncut, which meant all that was visible of the house were its moss-ridden red roof tiles. The property had no driveway; the only entry point was via the very old metal gate barely visible in the middle of the hedge.

Monty stopped and peered through the greenery. "You smelling anything untoward, Ranger?"

"Only neglect."

"Might be worth trying a probe spell," I said. "If you use

a low-grade one, she may not sense it, especially if she used most of her magical strength earlier."

"The only problem with *that* being if she does sense it, she'll run."

"I'll head around the back," Aiden said. "If anything moves, I'll shoot first and ask questions later."

"I'll go with you—just in case the shoot first plan fails." I glanced at Monty. "Remember what Belle said."

He grinned. "Stop worrying, Liz. I'm going to be around to annoy you for a very long time yet."

I raised an eyebrow. "Is that also written in the stars?"

His grin flashed. "Text when you get in position."

Aiden turned and moved into the neighboring property. The driveway was lined with red-tipped lilly pillies that provided a thick shield from the old house. The gate dividing the front yard from the back made no sound when Aiden pushed it open, and no dogs came running at us. Luck, it seemed, was feeling friendly tonight.

We found a slight break in the lilly pilly screen and swiftly climbed over the fence. My movements were a little hampered thanks to the length of Monty's shoes, but thankfully Aiden was on the other side to catch me.

The rear yard was as overgrown as the front. Not only was the grass at least three feet high, but scotch thistles and several other thorny weeds grew with wild abandon. An old metal shed lay to our immediate left, and across the other side of the yard were remnants of a clothesline. The house itself looked to be in reasonable condition, although thick clumps of weeds dominated the spouting and the steps onto the porch had, at some point in the past, given way.

Aiden sent Monty the text. The faintest spark of magic rose, then immediately fell away. I had no idea what spell he was using, but surely if I could no longer sense its presence, the rogue wouldn't.

Tension wound through me all the same, and it was all I could do to keep still. Time ticked by, but nothing stirred within the house. It remained as dark and as silent as a grave.

Goose bumps crawled down my spine; I really, *really* hoped that *wasn't* what we were about to find.

A message flashed up on Aiden's phone. I peered around his arm to read it.

No magic, no sense that anything living lies within.

Then we go in, Aiden replied.

Meet you in the middle.

Aiden tucked the phone away, then glanced at me. "Ready?"

I nodded and followed him across the yard, keeping in his footprints as much as possible to avoid tripping over whatever the grass might be hiding.

We avoided the broken section of the steps easily enough and walked over to the back door. The screen door creaked as Aiden opened it, and he froze, his body tense.

There was no response of any kind from within the house.

Either she wasn't here, as Monty's spell had indicated, or she was wrapped in some sort of disguising magic, waiting to attack. Although she didn't have to do *that* magically—not given how fast she apparently was.

The back door was locked. Aiden moved to one side and motioned to me to proceed. I quickly spelled it open and then stepped through, a repelling spell forming around my fingertips. This auto spell-creation feature I seemed to have gained was both disturbing *and* handy.

The air was old and smelled faintly of rot and damp—

both suggesting that perhaps the roof was leaking. Very little in the way of moonlight came through any of the nearby windows, but I could nevertheless see well enough to pick out the broken bits of furniture from the other drifting piles of rubbish.

We'd entered into what was basically a sunroom that separated the bathroom to our left and another room to our right. A quick check proved both were empty of anything other than mold and rubbish.

We moved up the three steps that led us into a hallway that ran the full length of the house. The front door opened, and Monty stepped through. He gave us a thumbs-up, then motioned toward the room on his right and went in.

We checked the nearest room—it had once been a galley kitchen with windows that looked into the sunroom, but only a few cupboards and what looked to be one of those old-fashioned wood stoves remained. The room on the opposite side of the hall was a largish living area with an old, smoke-stained fireplace that hadn't seen recent use.

We moved back into the hall. Monty came out of a different room, shook his head, and slipped into the last room. We followed.

And found not only death, but also the rogue's lair.

CHAPTER TWELVE

O n a grimy mattress that didn't quite cover the metal bedframe lay the bones of a woman. Or I presumed it was a woman, given the remnants of the nightgown that still covered part of her body. A pile of blankets and a pillow lay beside those bones, and both looked far newer than anything else in the room. A second, much grimier-looking pillow lay across the woman's skull, hiding it from sight. Which was a little weird—why hide the skull and not the body?

Tins of food and discarded food wrappings lay around the base of a dressing table, while a camp stove and a range of cooking utensils and plates sat on top.

The air in the room was rank, though its cause was more unwashed humanity rather than putrefaction—no real surprise given the woman had been dead long enough for her body to become skeletal.

"Why hasn't anyone found her before now?" Monty said. "Surely the neighbors would have smelled it? A rotting body isn't exactly a pleasant aroma, and we are dealing with werewolves."

"Couldn't say until we talk to them." Aiden moved across the room and squatted beside the bed. "But they did complain about the rats, and maybe this is the reason for the infestation."

"Is there any indication of rat feasting?" Monty asked, a mix of horror and fascination in his voice.

"At first glance, yes."

"Hopefully *not* when she was still alive." I shuddered and scanned the rest of the room in an effort to take my mind off the grim images that rose.

If our rogue had been hiding out here, then she didn't have anything in the way of personal possessions. Given no one had mentioned her being naked—and she'd certainly been clothed when we'd chased her—that had to mean she had another hideaway. So why risk coming here at all? Did it have something to do with the bones she apparently slept beside?

Aiden snapped on a pair of gloves and carefully lifted the pillow. "There's a bullet hole in the side of her skull, which suggests either murder or possibly suicide. Can't see anything that suggests it happened here, though."

"Would you, with a mattress that grimy?" Monty asked.

Aiden glanced up. "You'd see the blood stain at the very least, both soaking into the mattress and the spray of it across the wall."

My gaze immediately went to the wall behind the bed. It was as filthy as the rest of the place, but there was nothing that even vaguely resembled blood splatter. I rubbed my arms and walked across to the dressing table. "There's left-over baked beans in a pot on the camp stove, and they don't look that old."

Monty walked over. "Cooked last night, I'd say."

I glanced at him, eyebrows raised. "And you know this how?"

He smiled. "A long history of leaving leftover baked beans in pots."

I tugged the sleeve of the jacket over my fingers and then carefully opened the first of the two drawers. Aside from a selection of ancient-looking makeup containers and lipsticks, there was a slightly newer-looking brush and comb. "What color is the victim's hair, Aiden?"

"Gray—why?"

"There's a brush in the drawer, and the hair in it is dark. It could belong to our rogue."

"Which we can confirm by comparing it to the DNA in the blood we found at the hall," Monty said, "It'll be interesting to see if there's a familial connection between the rogue and this woman."

"At the very least, there's an emotional connection. Otherwise, why would she be sleeping with the bones?" I left the drawer open and turned. "Did Leesa Rhineheart ever live here? Could the bones belong to her?"

"I really can't answer either question right now," Aiden said. "Why?"

"Because Jenny Brown—one of the women murdered in the scout hall—said our rogue resembled her."

"Then that's certainly an option we'll be investigating." He pushed to his feet. "I'll have to call a team in—Liz, do you want to take my truck and go home? There's nothing much else you can do here."

I frowned. "What if she comes back?"

"I'll deal with it." Monty touched my shoulder lightly. "Go home. Your eye bags have bags."

"Thanks for *that* charming image." I walked across the room and accepted the keys Aiden held out. "Given you're likely to be here for a while and I'm likely to be fast asleep when you do get home, I'll see you tomorrow sometime."

"Try not to grind the gears too much," he replied, a smile tugging his luscious lips. "The box is new."

"You give me the keys, you have to accept the consequences." I blew him a kiss, then headed out.

The journey home was uneventful, and I avoided grinding the gears, though my hate for manual gearboxes continued. The outside sensor light flicked on when I pulled up, lighting the path as I shivered my way to the front door. Inside, that chill crept through the air, no doubt due to the fact the fire had burned down to embers. I added a couple of logs to ensure I wasn't shivering my way through breakfast, then headed upstairs for a quick shower. It would not only save time in the morning but allow me to sleep in that little bit longer.

Although sleep hit me fairly quickly, so too did the dreams. They were filled with shadowy figures that loomed large and threatened destruction. One of those figures was twisted in body and soul and marked by a deal with the devil. The other was tall and slender, and while not marked by evil was every bit as dangerous.

One was female, the other male. Both had the power to destroy those I cared about, even if in very different ways.

If the dreams were to be believed, I'd not only be uncovering the identity of that second figure but feeling the impact on my life very, very soon.

I had no idea what time Aiden got home, but he slept through a good part of the morning. I'd taken the day off to be with him, but found myself restless and angsty, unable to concentrate on anything. Part of that was the feeling of guilt —Sunday was a busy day for us, and I really didn't like leaving Belle to run the place alone, even if both she and our crew were more than capable of handling it.

The other reason was the discussion about his mother that we'd delayed.

He came down just as I was making ham and cheese toasties for lunch. "You want one?"

He nodded and walked over to the coffee machine. His face was drawn, and there were shadows under his eyes. I guess even a werewolf had to hit a wall sooner or later.

I plucked the toasties free, put them onto two plates, and slid one across to him. "How'd things go last night?"

"Routine at the murder scene. Less so at the party."

"You went back?" I said, surprised.

"It was expected."

"Ah." He didn't elaborate, and I didn't ask. It would no doubt come under the "werewolf business" tag. "Did you talk to your mother?"

"Yes, I did." He handed me a mug of coffee, then leaned his butt against the counter and contemplated me through narrow eyes. "What did she say to you?"

"What did she say she said?"

"Liz, I'm not in the mood. Just tell me what she said."

I took a deep breath and released it slowly. Decision time. Should I be honest? Or did I simply wait and see what happened when Mia finally appeared?

The coward in me opted for the middle ground. "She basically just warned me off again."

"There's more to it than that. Ashworth was fucking furious."

"Ashworth wasn't in the room. He has no idea what was said."

233

"Perhaps not, but he said you were pale and shaking after she'd left."

"Because we weren't in that room alone. Katie was there, and she spoke to your mother through me. You know how badly that drains me."

He clearly wanted to believe that's all there was to it ... and just as clearly knew it wasn't. He picked up his toastie and took a bite. "What did Katie want?"

I shrugged. "She was just warning your mother once again to be careful what she wishes for."

"That being you out of my life?"

I nodded. "I'm Katie's mouthpiece in this reservation, remember. She doesn't want to lose that."

"And could she?"

It was flatly said, with little emotion, and I desperately wanted to believe that was because he was tightly controlling himself. And perhaps he was. He cared; I knew he cared. Hell, he might even love me in his own way. But would that ever be enough for him to break tradition and go against his pack?

In my heart and my soul, I knew the answer was no.

I smiled, though it felt as if something was breaking inside. "No. You and I will have to learn to live with each other's presence in the reservation when this relationship ends."

"At least that is something we don't have to contemplate for a long while yet."

I smiled, though my heart really wasn't in it. "Which will piss your mother off no end."

He raised his coffee mug. "To pissing my mother off for many years to come."

I picked mine up and lightly clinked it against his, even

though I knew we had at best months rather than years ahead of us. "A resolution I can utterly get behind."

Once we'd finished lunch, he took my hand, led me up to the bedroom, and made love to me. It was full of heat and hunger, passion and unspoken emotion. But entwined within it all was a hint of desperation and sorrow; he knew, like I knew, that we were coming to an end, even if he had no idea how or why.

I headed back to the café the following morning. There was a steady flow of customers over the course of the day, which meant Belle and I couldn't get across to the scout hall until after we'd closed at three. Jaz met us there and ushered us into the small front room again. As I set up a protection circle, Belle carefully probed the atmosphere in the main hall.

"There's less confusion and disbelief today," she said. "That will at least make things easier."

"Maybe they've had time to think about—and accept— what has happened," I said.

"I'm not so sure of that. At least one of them is feeling belligerent."

"Do you come across many belligerent spirits?" Jaz asked.

Belle grimaced. "More than you'd think, unfortunately. In this case, he was the first to die, and in these sorts of situations, they're often the most obstinate."

"I really am going to have to sit you down over a drink or two and quiz you. It's all really fascinating." She got out her phone. "Ready when you are."

Belle stepped into my circle, then sat and crossed her

legs. "There may not be much to record, as the two who remained were the first to die and might not have seen or heard much."

"I've still got to record it."

I raised the protection circle, then sat opposite Belle and shuffled forward until our knees touched. "Ready?" I asked, and held out my hands.

She nodded and placed her hands in mine. Contact with the souls in the other room was almost instant.

What the fuck is going on? Why the fuck am I still here?

Belligerent was certainly an apt term for *this* particular soul.

I explained all that the last time I spoke to you, Belle said.

I wasn't listening last time.

I'm well aware of that. Only the slightest hint of an edge in her otherwise calm mental tone gave away her annoyance. *You're dead, Morris, and it happened before your allotted time. That means you can either stay here, permanently haunting this hall, or you can accept my assistance to move on.*

I'd rather be fucking alive.

I'm sure you would, but that's not an option.

And what about the bitch who killed me? Can I go after her? Kill her? Ghosts can do that sort of thing, can't they?

It's a rare ghost that can interact with the real world, and you, I'm afraid, are not that special.

Well, aren't you a charmer? He looked around. *Where are the others? I only see Dorothy.*

The others chose to move on. Belle paused. *Tell me, what exactly did you see or hear before you found yourself in this situation?*

This situation? That's a pretty mild term for it, isn't it?

I was being polite.

He grunted. *Well, don't bother on my account. It won't change a goddamn thing, will it?*

Belle's mouth twitched. *What can you tell me about your killer, Morris?*

He growled, though it was a sound of frustration rather than anger. *Not much. Heard a noise, turned, and she was on me.*

And there was nothing unusual about her that you remember?

Well, her face was a fucking mess. Other than that ... He paused. *There was a sweetie stuck in her hair.*

Belle blinked. *A sweetie?*

Yeah, you know, a lolly. One of them humbug things they used to make over at Butterworth's.

They no longer do? Belle asked.

No. Old man Butterworth had a heart attack six months ago, and production ground to a halt. Haven't been able to get fresh humbugs since. And I guess I won't now, will I?

No, I'm afraid not. Is there anything else you can remember about her?

She was fast. Other than that, no

Then what do you want to do, Morris? Stay here, or move on?

Well, it's not much of a fucking choice, is it? Despite the lingering anger, there was an undercurrent of acceptance in his tone now. *Move on, I guess. I certainly don't want to be hanging about this maggoty old hall for eternity.*

Are you certain?

Of course I'm fucking certain. I said yes, didn't I?

Another smile twitched Belle's lips. Once she'd moved him on, she turned her attention to the more fragile-looking Dorothy. The other woman had nothing much to add, but she also obstinately refused to move on, even after Belle explained the consequences. Belle sighed, wished her peace, and broke the connection.

I squeezed her fingertips. "You did the best you could."

"I know, but I always hate it when they refuse help like this."

"She made her choice. You can't deny her that."

"I know." She took a deep breath and then glanced at Jaz. "What do we know about this sweet factory Morris mentioned?"

"Nothing more than what he said—though it does explain why we randomly found a humbug on the floor." She stopped recording and put her phone away.

"Is it worth us going over there to check?" I disbanded the protection circle and then collected my spell stones. "She must have been there at some point recently, given none of the other souls we talked to mentioned the humbug."

"There've been no reports of a break-in though, and trust me, there would have been, especially given Ingrid and her son live on site."

"It won't hurt to check, though, surely?" I shoved my spell stones safely into my backpack and then offered Belle a hand up. Although today hadn't sapped a huge amount of energy, her weariness pulsed through me. She hadn't yet fully recovered from her previous efforts.

Jaz's eyes glimmered with amusement. "It might if anything goes wrong and you get hurt."

I snorted. "I do wish everyone would stop worrying about what Aiden might or might not do or say whenever I suggest a course of action when he's not around. Seriously, it's getting annoying."

"I'd rather you're annoyed at me than him." She held up

a hand, forestalling my reply. "But I agree—we should go check it out. He and Monty will be updating the council right about now, anyway."

"Good." I glanced at Belle. "You should head home and rest up."

She frowned. "I'm not sure that's a good idea when you're just as tired—"

"But I can call on the wild magic to help, if needed." I smiled. "Besides, you need to be at full strength for your date with Monty on Friday."

She groaned. "For fuck's sake, can he not keep anything to himself?"

"Apparently not." I handed her the keys. "I'll bring dinner back for the three of us—if Jaz doesn't mind stopping before she drops me off, that is."

"She doesn't." Jaz motioned to the door. "We right to leave?"

When I nodded, she spun and led the way out. Belle headed for our SUV, while I climbed into the passenger side of Jaz's truck. Once she'd locked the hall, she jumped in and we took off. After weaving our way through a number of smaller side streets, she eventually stopped on the side of the road opposite a large, multi-building factory complex. "Butterworth's is the red-brick building with the big chimney."

Aside from that chimney, its only other difference to the multiple other buildings in the complex was its length and proximity to the creek. I glanced at the old weatherboard house on the other side of the creek. It had been wedged onto a triangular bit of land overgrown with weeds and blackberries. "I take it Mrs. Butterworth and her son live in that house?"

"Yes, and we'll need to get the keys off them, as I don't want to be setting off any alarms if this thing *is* inside."

"Good idea."

She drove back over the bridge to the small house, then undid her seat belt and opened the door. "You'd better stay here. The old girl has this weird thing about strangers—she seems to think everyone is out to steal their sweet recipes."

"If the sweets are as good as Morris implied then I just might."

Jaz laughed and climbed out. The curtains twitched, and a few seconds later, the front door opened. Mrs. Butterworth was a stout-looking, curly-haired woman with a stern, rather humorless face. I wound down the window and listened as Jaz explained she'd had a report of an intruder and that we needed the keys so we could check out all the factories. Which obviously meant Mrs. Butterworth owned the whole complex, not just the sweet factory. A bit of haggling followed, then the keys were handed over. Jaz tossed them to me before reversing back onto the road.

"It sounded like you practically had to promise her your first-born child to get these things."

Jaz laughed. "Just about. I had to promise to stay for a cup of tea and a scone when I returned them."

I raised eyebrows. "She didn't seem the tea and scone type to me."

"She isn't. She's trying to set me up with her son—he still lives with her despite being in his late thirties."

"She knows you're married, right?"

"Yes, but she's convinced I'd be the perfect partner for her good-for-nothing lazy offspring." Jaz glanced at me, expression amused. "I'm not entirely sure what that says about her opinion of me."

"You've never asked?"

"Never dared. It's not like I see her outside her annoyingly regular reports of break-ins. Aiden, I must point out, takes great delight in sending me over here."

"I'd have a word with him on your behalf, but it's not like he'd take all that much notice."

"You'd be surprised," Jaz said. "He did move heaven and earth so that you could attend his initiation, remember."

I was hardly likely to forget, given Karleen's input on the whole matter.

The main gate into the complex was open. Jaz drove around to the left and parked out the front of the Butterworth's building. I grabbed my backpack and swung it around my shoulders as I joined Jaz at the front of the SUV.

While the old brick chimney dominated the skyline, the building itself was less than impressive. It was little more than a long brick shed with a tin roof, double metal doors at the front, and not much in the way of windows. A second, somewhat newer brick building stood off to the left, with a large Factory Direct sign emblazoned on the front.

There was no immediate sign of either a break-in or magic. No hint of the pungent sulfur scent associated with our rogue.

Which didn't really mean she wasn't here—especially given there were spells that could contain scent, and that was certainly something she'd want to do in an area such as this. This factory might be closed, but the complex overall was quite busy. Werewolves *would* notice such an odorous scent coming from a sweet factory.

"Anything?" Jaz asked.

I shook my head. "You?"

"Nothing that shouldn't be here. Let's do a circuit and see what we find."

She moved off to the right. I followed, my gaze on the

building and every sense humming with tension. There were a few windows on the long side of the building, but none were broken. The raised loading dock dominating the rear section was large enough that several trucks could load or unload at the same time. They'd obviously sold a whole lot of sweets at one point in time.

Jaz ran up the steps to test the roller door leading into the building. "Locked."

"Let's check the other side before we go in."

I moved on. A small and somewhat shadowy lane divided this building from the next. Nothing moved, and the putrid scent of sulfur remained absent.

After a brief hesitation caused more by a flicker of unease than any immediate sense of trouble, I continued. Stones crunched softly under my feet, and the drifting wind took on a whistling note, suggesting that somewhere up ahead a window might be broken. I couldn't see any glass on the ground, but there was a pile of twisted metal lying halfway down.

The deeper we moved down the lane, the more unease grew, and the more forceful the inner response became. I clenched my hands against the magic once again pressing against my fingertips; the surest way of alerting her to our presence if she *was* here would be to allow that magic to escape my skin.

The pile of metal turned out to be the rusty remnants of a ladder, the top half of which remained attached to the building. No one—aside from a very athletic werewolf— would ever reach it.

I glanced at Jaz. "You think the destruction was deliberate?"

She knelt and studied the pieces on the ground. After a few seconds, she picked up what looked to be one of the supports that had held the bottom portion of the ladder to the wall. "This has been cut, as have several other bits."

"Recently?"

"Fairly." She pushed upright. "What I can't say is whether our rogue did it or someone else."

"Do you know if there are skylights or even a roof entry point up there?"

"No." She motioned to the rest of the lane. "And there's only one way to find out—let's get back to the main door and go inside."

That, instinct was suddenly suggesting, wasn't really such a great idea. Or maybe *that* was simply fear. Sometimes it was hard to tell the two apart.

As we neared the other end of the building, the unease faded but didn't entirely go away. Whatever I'd sensed, it had centered on the portion of the building near the ladder.

"You might want to grab your gun, Jaz, just in case. I'm getting a really itchy feeling things could go wrong in there."

She frowned. "Then maybe I should call in—"

"No, because it could just be my natural propensity to think the worst will happen in any given situation."

She snorted and walked around to the rear of her SUV. "From my experience, your instincts are generally spot-on."

She strapped on her weapon, then unlocked the double metal doors and pushed one open. The air inside smelled as sweet as fairy floss, and my stomach rumbled a reminder that I hadn't actually eaten much over the course of the day.

There was an office area to our right and a locker and bathroom area to our left. The corridor led us down through a series of other rooms—storage, refrigeration, and the like— before opening into a large room that held a multitude of different types of machinery and processing lines. Metal grating and non-slip mats lined the walkways and would make moving without making much noise a little more difficult.

Light filtered in from the regularly placed skylights along the roof, but none were broken. An internal wall ran the length of the left side of the building, and a number of doors led off it. My gaze unerringly went to the third of the five.

That's where the ladder was.

That's where my percolating unease was centered.

"I'm not smelling anything other than sugar," Jaz murmured. "And there's no indication of a break-in."

"I doubt she'd be here—it's not exactly the most comfortable area to bunk down in." I motioned to the left. "This way."

I moved on, my gaze on the door and my hands still clenched against the pulse of magic. The unease ratcheted several notches when we once again neared the midpoint of the building. I stopped to the right of the door and motioned toward Jaz's gun. She silently drew it, then wrapped her fingers around the handle and raised an eyebrow.

I nodded. Tension crawled through me, and I half raised a hand, ready to throw the magic that now burned across my fingertips.

She thrust open the door, then flowed through to the left, her gun raised as she scanned the hall beyond. I went right and pressed back against the door, gaze sweeping the shadows, looking for the source of the threat and finding nothing.

Nothing *here*, anyway.

There was a door to Jaz's left and two more to my right. Whatever I was sensing, it was coming from the last on the right.

I motioned toward it. Jaz nodded but held up a finger, bidding me to wait as she moved left and slipped into that room. She reappeared a few seconds later and shook her head.

Relief stirred, even though I'd expected nothing else.

I took a deep breath that did little to ease the tension, then turned and walked quietly down the hall. Jaz touched my shoulder as I passed the second door, and I paused, waiting while she checked out the room. My gaze remained on the final door; if our quarry *was* in there, she'd surely be aware of our presence by now. We were being as quiet as possible, but the metal grating meant our footsteps were audible to anyone with wolf-keen hearing.

Jaz came back out into the hallway and touched my shoulder again. I moved on, gaze still on the door, half expecting it to open and unleash hell and fury on us both.

That it didn't only ramped up the tension.

We reached the door. I gripped the handle, my fingers trembling and my gut churning. Jaz moved to the other side and held up three fingers. As the last finger dropped, I thrust the door open, and we went in as one.

No response.

No immediate sign that anyone or anything had been in here recently.

It was a large plant room, packed with pipes and tubing of all sizes, boilers, backup generators, and who knew what else. I studied the area, my back pressed against the wall and sparks spinning across my fingertips. I couldn't restrain it, so if she *was* here and *did* sense the energy, I hoped she'd think it was something to do with one of the nearby machines.

Unlikely, but still ...

A quick look at the ceiling proved my earlier guess had

been right; while the skylight in this room wasn't broken, it *had* been propped open with a rusty bit of metal, allowing easy entry and exit without being too noticeable by whatever security guards this place had.

I pointed up. Jaz nodded, then touched her nose and motioned me to follow her. She obviously smelled something. I drew in a deeper breath but couldn't find the pungent scent I'd come to associate with our rogue. Nor was there any hint of magic, dark or otherwise.

Which didn't mean it wasn't here. Not at all.

Jaz padded past a generator, keeping close to the wall and carefully scanning the space between each of the machines before moving on. The cool evening air stirred past my nostrils as we moved under the skylight, and I glanced up again. Even for a werewolf, it was a fair drop down to the ground. My gaze swept the two large machines that sat slightly off to one side of the skylight; a thick crust of grime coated both, but the one to the right held several cleared patches that suggested someone might have slipped down its side. I glanced at the floor; it was concrete, and though it wasn't exactly pristine, there was no sign of footprints.

I flexed my fingers; the sparks spun through the air again and, from somewhere up ahead, came a flare of responding energy.

She *was* here.

Fuck.

I touched Jaz's shoulder. When she stopped and looked around, I quickly pulled out my phone and then typed, *she's here. Thirty or forty feet to our left, near the outside wall, close to where the ladder was.*

She nodded and repeated my actions. *How do you want to handle this?*

In truth, I didn't. Every instinct screamed we needed to turn around and get the hell out of here. But if we did that, we'd lose her again, and that could lead to yet more deaths. I did *not* want that on my conscience.

I quickly typed, *I'd better go first, just in case she attacks magically. But keep close and be ready to shoot.*

She nodded and motioned me forward. I breathed deep, then carefully crept past her, my gaze flickering between the area ahead and the walkways between each of the machines. Tension rode me, and it was all I could do to keep going, to keep breathing normally. To not turn around and run.

A soft sound whispered through the air. Nails against metal, I thought, and quickly looked up. The nearest machine wasn't much taller than me, and our rogue would have been visible if she'd been creeping along its top. Unless, of course, she was shielding herself with magic.

I pressed a little closer to the wall and moved on, carefully scanning each of the big machines as we drew closer. She wasn't on top of them, but she remained in the room. Of that, I was certain.

Another scrape, this time accompanied by a surge of magic. It rose and fell—a swift, dark wave that gave me little time to understand the intent of the spell before it was gone. But I doubted she was planning anything good.

I got my phone out again and typed, *she's on the other side of the room from us, about twenty feet ahead. But I don't think we should leave the protection of the wall, because this is feeling a little too much like a trap.*

Agree. Let's go the long way around.

We'd barely moved a few more feet when another surge of magic washed through the room. Though it didn't fade quite as quickly, I still had no idea what its intent was. It wasn't a spell I was familiar with, that was for sure.

It had come from further down the room and made me wonder if she'd decided to run rather than risk confronting us. If so, then there had to be another skylight propped open toward the end of the room.

But even as that thought crossed my mind, I dismissed it. I had no doubt that she'd come to the café in an attempt to either erase or nullify my presence, so why would she run now, when I was not only close but in her territory?

She wouldn't.

She wasn't.

The air behind us stirred ever so faintly. We both swung around, Jaz raising her gun. There was nothing there ... except there *was*.

A faint shimmer was all that gave her presence away.

"Jaz, shoot now, one o'clock," I yelled, and unleashed the inner wild magic—but not at our rogue. I didn't understand enough about my wild magic and its connection to the reservation's wellsprings to risk killing the rogue and perhaps forever staining the purity of the magic here. Instead, I raised a protective shield around the two of us.

Jaz fired. The shots echoed loudly in the enclosed space, but the first three missed, pinging off nearby machinery and throwing sparks into the air. Jaz shifted aim, obviously scenting her now. Another shot, followed by a high-pitched squeal. Blood sprayed across the nearby machine, but it didn't stop the bitch. She hit the shield hard enough to press the magic toward Jaz, and pain fizzed through my brain as she was flung away.

"You've shielded us?" Jaz said, surprised.

"Yes, so keep close to me in case she attacks again."

I ran into the walkway between two machines, a tracker

spell spinning around my fingertips. There were drops of blood on the floor, a gleaming path that led around to the right.

Again, it was the shift of air that warned us. Jaz fired; the sharp noise so close to my ear was painful, but I ignored it and flung the tracker spell. Magic surged, and the spell was batted away, but the rogue couldn't so easily bat away a bullet. Blood sprayed through the air, splatting across my face and the nearby machine. She didn't attack. She ran.

I swore and bolted after her, Jaz so close on my heels I could feel her breath on my neck. As we half slid around the end of the machine and headed for the end of the room, claws scraped against metal. The last skylight in the room was flung open, and the dripping trail of blood disappeared from sight.

"Fuck, we can't lose her now," Jaz said.

"I don't aim to. Boost me up."

She did so, then leapt up beside me. I grabbed the edge of the skylight and hauled my butt up onto the roof. The protecting shield shimmered and stretched, but didn't snap.

It was the only thing that saved me.

CHAPTER THIRTEEN

Her claws tore across the surface of the magic protecting my spine; it briefly bent with the pressure, then responded, flinging her across the rooftop and over its edge.

I swore, scrambled upright, and raced to the end of the building. There was no sign of her, but her blood left a trail we could easily follow.

If I could jump from the rooftop without breaking something, that was.

"This way."

Jaz grabbed my hand and led me across to the half-destroyed ladder, then held it steady while I climbed down the portion still attached to the building. When I reached the broken end, I released my grip and dropped the rest of the way to the ground. It was far enough that the impact shuddered up my spine, but I didn't break anything, and that was definitely a bonus. Jaz leapt down beside me, then raced on, pulling ahead all too quickly.

"Jaz," I said as the shield began to unravel, "we need to keep together."

She growled, a low sound of frustration if ever I'd heard one, but her speed nevertheless slowed enough for me to keep up.

We raced through the maze of factories, following the rogue's blood more than her scent, but getting no closer to catching the bitch. Then, from up ahead, came a sharp yelp of pain followed by the thud of a door slamming and the squeal of tires.

"Oh fuck," Jaz said and raced ahead again.

This time, the shield did shatter, and the force of it rebounded through me, tearing a gasp from my throat. I stumbled, my fingers brushing the ground for several seconds before I caught my balance and chased after her.

By the time I'd caught up, she was on the phone and kneeling in the middle of the road. Beside her was a well-dressed, gray-haired woman who looked to be in her mid-sixties. The side of her face was scraped and bloody, and she was nursing a wrist that—if the swelling already evident was anything to go by—was probably broken.

I squatted beside her and pulled my backpack around. "I've got a pain potion in here—would you like it?"

Her brown eyes were a little unfocused. Shock, probably. "You're one of the witches that runs the café."

I nodded. "The pain potion is natural but strong. It'll subdue the throbbing in your wrist."

"The face scrapes are worse."

Her voice was barely audible, suggesting she might be on the cusp of fainting. I shifted so I could catch her if she did and then uncorked the small vial. "Here, drink this."

She didn't reply, but when I raised the bottle to her lips, she swallowed it. "The potion is fast-acting, so you should start feeling better within a couple of minutes."

"Thank you."

Jaz hung up and shoved her phone back into her pocket. "I put an APB out for the stolen car, but I'm betting she'll abandon it long before we find her."

There was no question about *that*. Our rogue might be many things, but stupid wasn't one of them. "If the amount of blood she's losing is any indicator, her wounds are really bad. She'll have to seek help—"

"That would depend entirely on whether she has the werewolf ability to heal."

"That happens during shifting shape, though, and everything we know about her suggests she can't."

"Except we *don't* fucking know a whole lot about her." Jaz sighed and thrust a hand through her hair. "Sorry, don't mean to bite."

I smiled. "It's okay. I get the anger."

The older woman leaned back against my knees, but a quick look revealed she was simply getting a little more comfortable. The potion was obviously kicking in. While it did do an amazing job of curtailing pain, this particular one also had a "floaty, I'm on a high" side effect. "You okay, Mrs. —?"

"Grantham," she said in a much stronger voice. "And thank you for that potion—I'm feeling much better."

"That's good, but I wouldn't be moving around too much, as I think you've broken your wrist." Jaz squatted down beside her. "The ambulance should be here in a few minutes. In the meantime, are you able to tell me what happened?"

"There's really not that much to tell—it was all over so very quickly."

"You still need to recount what happened. Even the tiniest detail might help us track her down."

"She ran straight in front of me from the side of those

buildings over there." She motioned briefly with her good hand to two nearby metal sheds on the other side of the road. "I hit her—couldn't help it, you know? I wasn't going fast, but still—"

"It's okay, Mrs. Grantham," Jaz said soothingly. "We know the accident isn't your fault."

"You'll say that to my insurance company?"

"Yes, of course. What happened next?"

"Well, I hit her, didn't I? Sent her tumbling. But before I could get out and see if she was okay, she was ripping open my door and hauling me out."

"Can you tell me anything about her? Her looks, her build, any outstanding features?"

"Well, as I said, it was all too fast." She paused. "She did have a tattoo on her cheek—a snake wrapped around a scythe."

Which at least confirmed what Jenny had already told us. I glanced around at the sound of an approaching siren and saw the ambulance turning into the nearby entrance.

"Anything else?" Jaz asked.

"Not really. But you might want to check the Thaumaturge Society. They should be able to track down whose mark that is."

My gaze snapped back to her, and I blinked in surprise. "You're a witch, Mrs. Grantham?"

She laughed. "Of course not. But I am a former magician and was a card-carrying member of the society back in the day. I do believe they have an index of black arts marks, though it wasn't something a general member like me had access to."

"I don't suppose you could give us a contact name or number of someone we could speak to in the society?" I asked.

She shook her head. "It's been a good ten years since I was involved with them. Most of the people I knew would have long retired. Sorry."

"That's no problem, Mrs. Grantham," Jaz said. "At least you've given us somewhere to start."

"Glad to have helped." She waved her good hand again. "I do believe you'll be seeing me at your café more often, young lady. That potion is absolutely brilliant—might need some for the rheumatoid."

"We do have a couple of specific options for arthritis that'll probably suit you better." And without the floaty side effect—although maybe *that* was what she liked.

"Excellent news."

The ambulance pulled up, and the two paramedics climbed out. Once Jaz had filled them in, I told them what I'd given her and then got out of their way.

"So, what the hell is the Thaumaturge Society?" Jaz asked.

"From what I understand, it's a private society that promotes and celebrates all things magic."

"Human or witch?"

"I had thought witches, but Mrs. Grantham's comment suggests they're more human illusionists—though I wouldn't be surprised if some of them were part witches."

"That happens?"

"Yes, but more with the lower witch houses than the royal." One of the medics slammed the ambulance's rear door closed, then hopped into the driver seat. As the engine roared to life, I added, "If the society *is* cataloging maker marks then they're obviously a whole lot more than what they let everyone believe."

"You think they'll help us track down the rogue's mark, if that *is* what she's wearing on her cheek?"

"I really have no idea, but it's certainly worth a shot."

"At least something good appears to come out of losing her. How do we go about contacting them?"

"They're not a hidden society, but I'll talk to Ashworth —he might have a contact we could use."

She nodded. "Let's get back to Butterworth's and check what she's left behind."

I followed her back through the maze of buildings. While our quarry was long gone, I nevertheless took the lead again once we were inside. There had been several spell surges, and only one would have been for invisibility. Strangely, the only other spell I found was an alarm, and it was easily disconnected.

So what had the other spells been for, if not a trap?

I frowned and stopped in front of a small, partially walled alcove that had obviously been built as an additional storage area in the plant room. The right side of the small area was lined with metal shelving and held the various bits and pieces that were no doubt necessary to keep the machines running properly. To the left were a couple of lockers and a makeshift bed consisting of two old wooden pallets as the base and flattened cardboard boxes as the mattress. A sleeping bag provided warmth.

I waited while Jaz took photos to catalogue the entire area. Once that was done, she handed me a pair of gloves, snapped on a pair herself, and walked across to the bedding. "This safe to touch?"

I nodded and moved across to the lockers; the first one held an army-green carryall. I pulled it out, then knelt and carefully unzipped it. Inside was a small selection of soiled clothes and undergarments, but little else. I zipped it back up in an effort to contain the stale, acidic scent and moved to the next locker, discovering boots, a coat, and a toiletries bag. A quick look inside the latter revealed soap, a pack of disposable razors, a toothbrush, and a somewhat mangled tube of toothpaste.

"Is it possible to pull DNA from toothbrushes?"

She snapped a photo, then carefully bagged some hair. "Sometimes, though a buccal cell test is considered the gold standard for DNA profiling."

"Somehow, I can't see her agreeing to us doing a mouth swab."

Jaz laughed. "No."

As she probed the sleeping bag, I noticed a phone charging cable at the back of the locker. I took a photo, then carefully bagged it and moved onto the next locker. There was a jacket in this one, so I took it off the hook and checked the pockets. One was empty, but the other held a ticket stub. "Looks like she got here via the train."

"That would take some gumption, given what we know of her face. What date?"

I glanced at the stub. "A couple of days before the first murder."

"She didn't take much time to settle in and scout the area, then."

"Maybe she didn't need to. Maybe she was born in the reservation."

"Surely if she'd spent any amount of time here, we'd know of her. It wouldn't be easy to hide the deformities she has."

"Unless that's what the bulk of her magic does—it presents a more 'acceptable' appearance."

"She wouldn't have that ability from a very young age, though, would she?"

"Probably not." Some witches certainly could call on and control major magics from a very young age, but they were rare. Even my sister—who'd been one of the most promising and powerful witches in Canberra before she'd been murdered—hadn't truly stepped into her full strength until she was in her teens.

But concealing magic could explain the other energy surges. Mrs. Grantham might have mentioned the tattoo on our rogue's cheek, but she hadn't noted either her half-formed facial features or claws for hands.

Jaz glanced at me. "I know we've had demons and the like capable of altering their forms, but she appears to be a wolf, even if a mutated one. She shouldn't be able to perform magic."

"And yet she can." I shrugged. "For every rule there is a rule breaker."

Jaz's expression suggested she didn't think that was the case, but her phone rang, interrupting any reply she might have made.

As she answered the call, I checked the remaining lockers. There was another carryall in the last one; this one contained a pair of clean jeans, several pairs of fresh undies, a couple of bras, and an oversized sweater. Which wasn't a whole lot and obviously meant she hadn't planned to dally, but rather to track down and murder her targets as quickly as possible.

But why these people? And if she *was* Leesa's daughter, and therefore human, how did she become so genetically twisted?

Was she, perhaps, the result of a wolf-human union?

Karleen had certainly warned me about the dangers of it. Even Katie had said that the offspring of such a pairing didn't usually survive all that long.

But what if our rogue *had*? And what if—for some as yet

undefined reason—she was now going after all those who'd bullied and rejected her mother?

"Aiden and Monty should be here in ten minutes," Jaz said.

I rolled my eyes. "Anyone would think Aiden was the only ranger in this reservation capable of handling murder investigations."

"He *is* head ranger and an alpha. They like to be across the top of every single thing." She shrugged. "He won't ever change—remember that."

I half smiled. "I get daily reminders of it. I'm just worried he's going to burn out."

"He won't—unless, of course, these damn supernatural nasties never stop coming." She eyed me for a second. "They *will* stop coming, won't they?"

"Yes, but I couldn't give you a timeline. It very much depends on how far the vibrations of an unprotected wellspring went."

"Well, here's hoping they only lapped at the shores of darkness rather than reached the interior."

"Amen to *that*." I placed the bag back into the locker. "Has any information been uncovered about Leesa Rhineheart?"

"Don't know, as Maggie's been assigned the task and I haven't talked to her today."

Maggie was the station's receptionist and ranger in training. "You might want to mention that it's possible we're dealing with Leesa's daughter."

Jaz eyebrow's rose. "What makes you think that?"

"My gut, mostly, but also Jenny's comment that our rogue reminded her of Leesa."

"Then I shall definitely mention it."

We checked the rest of the small room, but there really

wasn't much else to find. Our rogue might have been staying here on at least a part-time basis, but she certainly wasn't eating here. There was no takeout trash, no camp stove, and no utensils of any kind.

The thud of doors slamming indicated Aiden and Monty had arrived—a fact backed by the gentle stirring of awareness across my senses. While I didn't believe in the whole soul mate thing, I *did* think there were some pairings that were so right it was possible to form a bond so instinctual that awareness of the other person was hyper increased.

Which in my situation—with this man—was both a good and bad thing. It gave me hope of future possibilities, if only because that stirring awareness seemed to go both ways. But it also meant that if Aiden *did* hold duty and expectation above emotion and heart, the pain of breaking up would be that much fiercer.

And perhaps not just for me.

The door down the other end of the plant room opened, and footsteps echoed. A few seconds later, the two men appeared.

Aiden's gaze immediately met mine, and the smile that tugged his lips had my pulse skipping a beat or two. Sexy did *not* do it justice.

"Maybe the easiest way of tracking down this killer is to just stick by your side twenty-four seven."

I crossed my arms in an effort to stop the almost instinctive need to wrap my arms around his neck and kiss him senseless. To enjoy his lips and his body while I still could. "I wouldn't mind, but I'm not sure your team would be impressed with the increase in workload."

"If it meant grabbing this bitch before she kills again, I'm all for it." Jaz quickly updated him on everything we'd discovered. "I've asked for the hospitals and medical centers to be put on alert for anyone presenting with gunshot wounds, but I personally don't think she'll risk either."

"It would depend on how bad her wounds are and whether she's werewolf enough to fast heal." Aiden stopped beside me, his big warm presence flowing across my senses as sweetly as any caress. "We'll need to dust this area for prints on the off chance she's in a database somewhere. Monty, once we're done, will you be able to set up a snare of some kind, just in case she comes back here?"

"Yes, and if I make it complex enough, she might not be able to unpick it."

I frowned at him. "What makes you think that when all the evidence points to the fact she's magically proficient?"

He shrugged. "It's a gut feeling, but it's based on the fact that the most dangerous of her magic is an energy *force* rather than a spell."

"And yet she knew enough about magic to unpick the alarm spell around the café."

"She didn't touch the rest, though."

"Which was no doubt due to the presence of the wild magic."

"*If* she can sense it. There's no evidence that she can."

"She's been marked by a dark practitioner. She can sense it."

Aiden cleared his throat. "Can you two argue about this on your own time? We really need to lock down this area and collect evidence if we're to have any hope of getting home at a decent hour tonight."

"Sorry," Monty said, though the amusement in his eyes suggested he really wasn't. "I'll wrap an alarm around the capture spell; even if she does dismantle it, I'll get a warning that she's here."

"Thanks." Aiden's gaze returned to mine. "Do you need a lift home?"

A smile tugged at my lips. "In other words, shove off, my love; you're no longer needed now that Monty is here."

"I'd personally choose you over Monty, if only because you're far prettier. However, he's head witch, you're only part time, and I think you've done more than your fair share of work over the last few days."

Though it was lightly said, concern glinted in his eyes—not surprising given he could probably smell my weariness. In truth, I was damnably glad to be getting the heave-ho; right now, I wanted nothing more than to zone out for several hours with Belle and Ava and talk about anything other than death for a while.

I rose up on my toes and dropped a quick kiss on his cheek. "I'll walk back to the café—it's not far."

He gently brushed his knuckles down my cheek, then stepped back—just in case temptation got the better of him, I thought with amusement.

"I'll catch you at home."

I said my goodbyes to Jaz and Monty and headed out. Dusk's flags of pink and orange were already giving way to darkness, and the air held the promise of rain. I zipped up my coat, shoved my hands into the pockets, and followed the old road out of the complex. I detoured around to the Chinese café to grab dinner, so by the time I arrived at our café, darkness had well and truly set in. But the downstairs lights were on and music was playing. I unlocked the front door and entered, discovering not only had a table been set, but also Belle pouring drinks.

I walked over and dropped the bag of food in the middle of the table. "I take it you're hungry."

"Starved. It *is* close to seven, you know."

"And this old woman," Ava said, as she came out of the kitchen with a selection of tongs and serving spoons, "is very used to eating dessert at around this time. The stomach is not amused, let me tell you."

I chuckled and began pulling the lids off the various containers. "I'll remember that for next time."

"Good." She sat down and handed me one of the serving spoons. "I've been trying to convince young Isabelle here to come back to Canberra with me to see her dad."

A smile twitched my lips. Ava only used Belle's real name when she was displeased. "I absolutely agree that she should, but I'm not sure now is the right time."

Ava's eyebrows rose. "Why would you— Oh, your father."

I nodded. "I wouldn't put it past him to make a grab for Belle when she's up there."

"Even your father wouldn't be that desperate—especially when your mother is already displeased with him."

"And yet she won't divorce him." I scooped up some fried rice and dropped it with a little more force than necessary onto my plate. "She values her position and standing in the witch community far more than she does her daughter."

"That's a trifle unfair," Ava admonished. "Granted, she was never what *I* would call a good mother, but she was never neglectful, either. I have no doubt that, in her own way, she really does love you."

"You'll have to forgive my skepticism, if only because she hasn't even bothered to contact me since Clayton's death and the investigation into my father's actions deepened."

"Perhaps she fears an approach wouldn't be welcome."

"It wouldn't, but that's beside the point. She hasn't even *tried*."

And that hurt, more than I really wanted to admit.

Ava caught my hand and squeezed it lightly. "Not all mothers are as perfect as me—"

Belle laughed, and Ava gave her a severe look, though the effect was somewhat spoiled by the amusement in her eyes.

"But your mother never needed to be, Liz. She was well aware you were getting your emotional needs met by me."

I blinked. "What?"

Ava sighed. "She thanked me once—only once, I'll admit—for providing you with a stable and happy environment when you were growing up."

My mother? Thanking a Sarr for *anything*? But even as I thought that, I recognized the unfairness of it. While my mother had been as annoyed as my father when the familiar selection ceremony had given me Belle rather than the more acceptable spirit or animal, she'd never been rude or abrupt with her and had, in fact, welcomed her into the house on numerous occasions, even if that was only when no other family members were there.

"When was this?"

Ava wrinkled her nose and released my hand. "Not that long before the whole Clayton mess went down. And I sincerely believe she played no part in that."

"She said she didn't, and I do believe it. But I'll never forgive her for not standing up to my father or for not breaking the marriage contract once she *did* know. She *had* to have realized I'd never willingly agree to such a thing."

"Did you ever think that perhaps you were not the only one forced into compliance?"

I laughed. "My father wouldn't dare to spell my mother. She'd kick his ass."

263

"Undoubtedly, but there are other ways to force compliance."

"You think a telepath messed with her head?" Belle said, surprised. "Have you been near enough to test that theory out?"

Ava smiled. "Eleanor walks in very different circles to me, so no."

"What about when you were interviewed after our disappearance?" Belle asked.

"They were well aware of my gifts, so it happened in a telepathically null space. I could barely hear my own thoughts, let alone peer into anyone else's."

"Then why do you think someone's gotten into her mind?"

She hesitated. "It came from her recent reaction when the news of Clayton and Lawrence's actions broke."

"She walked out on him." But even then, that had only been *after* the Black Lantern Society had interviewed them both.

"Yes, but not only has she never confronted Lawrence over the mess, they haven't even talked about it."

"No one can really be sure what is said behind closed doors," Belle said. "And I daresay that in this day and age, all royal houses are regularly swept for listening devices— both mechanical *and* spell."

"Yes, but permanent staff always know the inner workings and dynamics of a house and they *always* talk."

"They're magically inhibited from speaking publicly to anyone without permission." Or at least they had been when I'd been a kid, and I doubted that had changed.

"But *not* from talking to each other. It's not hard to uncover exactly where certain members of the Marlowe household meet for coffee with those from other royal residences. It's also not hard to be there at the right time and place to peruse the minds of said staff and uncover what they know. Unfortunately"—she touched Belle's arm—"they had no knowledge of where you'd both been found, otherwise I would have been here long before Monty contacted me."

Belle briefly slipped her hand over her mom's. "I know."

Ava nodded and returned her gaze to mine. "You do realize the ongoing case against your father will probably mean you'll be called up to testify in person at some point."

I nodded. "Samuel warned me."

Ava raised an eyebrow. "Samuel?"

"Kang," Belle said before I could. "Think a well-built and divinely handsome man who has a hard-on for Lizzie."

I rolled my eyes. "Whose parents were approached by my father regarding a possible match between me and him."

"Which means the old bastard has at least learnt one lesson—this time he sent someone worthy of your good self." Ava paused, her expression speculative. "And were you interested?"

"The lust was definitely mutual," Belle said.

I picked out a pea from my fried rice and tossed it at her. "I'm in a relationship, but even if I wasn't, I wouldn't consider anyone my father sends my way."

"You could be biting your nose off to spite your face," Ava mused. "That particular branch of the Kangs is well respected."

"That still doesn't alter the fact he carries my father's recommendation. I have no intention of ever pleasing my father with an 'appropriate' marriage."

Ava laughed and raised her whiskey glass. "Here's to overcoming the hurdle of interfering parents and finding your happy ever after with an inappropriate man."

Belle and I clinked our glasses against hers. The conversation moved on to reminiscing about the past, and we were on coffee and cake when Belle's phone rang.

She rose to collect it from under the counter and glanced at the screen. "It's Kash."

"Why would he be ringing you?" Especially given our last encounter with the man.

"I don't know."

"Put it on loudspeaker."

She hit the answer button and then walked back to the table. "What do you want, Kash?"

"Roland," he said, voice hoarse and filled with agony. "Please, help. He's trying to—"

The rest of his sentence was cut off by two sharp retorts.

Gunshots.

CHAPTER FOURTEEN

"Oh fuck," Belle said. "Kash? Are you there? Are you all right?"

There was no response, and the call cut out a second later.

I scrambled upright. "This is very possibly a trap, but on the off chance it's not, we'd better get over there. I'll grab the backpack; you call the rangers."

I ran to the reading room for the pack, then came back out to get the SUV's keys from under the serving counter.

Ava came racing back down the stairs, two coats in her hand. I frowned. "I don't think—"

She raised a finger in warning. "Don't complete that sentence, because I'm coming with you whether you want it or not. You have no idea what you're about to face, and an additional telepath might well come in handy."

I hesitated, tempted to argue, but I knew that tone well enough from childhood to know there was little point.

"Tala's on her way," Belle said. "Let's go."

We ran out the rear door, Belle ensuring it was locked before jumping into the passenger seat. I threw the SUV into reverse and accelerated out of our spot; stones flew from under the tires, smacking loudly into the rubbish bins on the other side of the parking area. I threw the car back into drive and sped out, hitting the horn as I neared the street to warn any pedestrians thinking of crossing the parking area's exit.

It didn't take us long to get to Kash's. Tala was just getting out of her SUV as we pulled up.

"What type of threat are we dealing with?" she said, her gaze on the cottage rather than me. "Human or supernatural?"

"Human, we suspect," I replied. "You heard about the break-ins at our storage unit?"

She nodded. "This connected?"

"Yes, as is the guy who fell off my balcony." I paused. "Did you ever interview him?"

"Yeah, but he didn't say much. Claimed he didn't know who hired him. He was lying, of course." She shrugged. "He's been charged and is out on bail."

"And has hopefully learnt his lesson."

"He's a career crim. He won't." Her gaze flicked to Belle. "How many minds are inside?"

"Just the one—Kash."

"Meaning his attacker has probably scarpered. I'll head around the back. You two go in the front." She paused, eyeing Ava warily. "You as strong telepathically as Belle?"

"Yes."

"Then you'd better come with me, just in case the attacker's hiding out the back and needs to be neutralized."

The two of them headed down the somewhat overgrown path that led around to the back of the cottage. I went through the front gate and stepped up onto the veranda. The door was locked; a quick spell soon fixed that.

It swung back gently, but I didn't immediately enter; just because Kash had mentioned Roland, didn't actually mean that was who or what we were dealing with. And it certainly didn't mean there was no other sort of trap waiting. Not in this reservation.

Like most of the old cottages in Castle Rock, this one consisted of a long hall that ran down the center of the building. Several doorways led off it, and there was a combined kitchen-dining area at the rear. There was no sound or sign of life, but there was no hint of death either, which suggested we might have arrived in time. The air *did* hold the metallic scent of blood, and it was coming from the second door on our right.

I glanced at Belle. *Anything?*

She nodded. *He's alive, but in a whole world of pain.*

In the bathroom?

Yes. There's no one else here, though. If Roland did this, he's long gone.

We nevertheless moved forward cautiously, checking the other rooms before stopping either side of the bathroom door. I tugged the sleeve of my jacket over my fingers and carefully tested the handle. It wasn't locked.

After a deep breath that did little to calm the tension, I carefully pressed the door open. Kash lay on the floor, his back against the vanity unit. His face was pale and sweaty, his breathing fast and shallow. Blood seeped through the fingers that were pressed against his shoulder, and more blood pooled under a second wound on his thigh.

I handed Belle the backpack and then rang for an ambulance. She squatted beside him and hastily unzipped the bag. While we didn't have any potions that could fix these sorts of wounds, we did carry a regular first aid kit. First order of the day had to be stopping the bleeding.

"What the hell happened, Kash?"

"The bastard shot me." His tone was angry. "The bastard actually *shot* me."

"Why would Roland do that?" Belle pressed a thick wad of gauze onto his shoulder wound, then added, "Press this—hard."

He obeyed. "He was pissed."

"Because you erased the files?"

"No, because I transferred the funds out of the business account and then closed everything down."

Belle swore silently. *This is my—*

No, it's fucking not, I cut in angrily. *He's the one who abused your friendship and profited in the process. He's the one who decided to rip off his friend, not you.*

Yes, but if I'd—

You can hardly be responsible for his decision to milk the business accounts. I daresay if you dug into his mind deeply enough, you'll find it's not the first time he's done this.

Probably not. To Kash, she added, "For a smart man, you show an amazing lack of intelligence."

He snorted, then made a gargled sound of pain. Sweat popped across his brow, and for several seconds he did nothing more than suck in air. His reply, when it came, was faint. "I knew you were just after my body."

A smile tugged her lips. "A fact I made no secret of. How did Roland escape?"

"Car."

"Plate number?" I asked.

He rattled it off. "He said something about a storage unit. He was yelling that no bloody witches were going to get the better of him."

She glanced at me. *Why would he be going back to the storage unit? He knows he can't get in.*

Maybe getting in isn't his intention.

True. Her gaze returned to Kash. "Did he say why he was going there?"

"No, but he's the type to destroy what he can't have." Kash grimaced. "It's actually not the first time he's shot me. This time it was totally uncalled for, though."

Which only made me wonder exactly *what* he'd done the first time.

"And you're still in business together? Why?" Belle asked.

"Because we're a good team."

"I think your definition of a good team and mine are miles apart."

Footsteps echoed on the old floorboards, and the wild magic stirred briefly across my fingertips. But the soft scents flowing toward me said it was Tala and Ava, and the sparks faded.

"Anything out back?" I asked.

Tala shook her head. "Only a trail that led over the rear fence. He obviously had a car parked in the rear lane. You called an ambulance?"

"And got Roland's plate number." I gave it to her. "He's apparently headed across to our storage unit for some no doubt nefarious reason. Can you get someone to meet me there?"

"I'll order Duke across, but you're not to go in until he arrives. Understand?"

I nodded. "Magic is pretty useless against bullets, and Roland seems a little too trigger-happy for my liking."

"I'm coming with you," Belle said. "Mom, can you keep the pressure on this?"

"As long as you both promise to be careful." She squatted beside Belle and placed her hand on the gauze covering the wound on Kash's thigh. "I do *not* want to lose either of you just when I've found you again."

"Careful is my middle name," Belle and I intoned together.

"I don't think there's anyone in this room who actually believes that statement." Tala's voice was dry.

I grinned, not bothering to deny it.

We quickly jumped back into the SUV and drove across to the storage facility. There was no sign of a vehicle, either on the road or inside the complex. The alarms we'd layered into the spells protecting the storage unit hadn't been triggered, and the facility's main alarms were also silent.

I didn't pull into the driveway, but instead cruised slowly past. We had no idea where Roland was, and until we did, we couldn't risk entering the storage area. Not when he was armed.

"I have no sense of him in the front portion of the complex, but that doesn't mean he's not hiding out at the back," Belle said. "It's also possible he had second thoughts and decided to get the hell out of the reservation. A sensible person certainly would."

"We're talking about a man who has shot his partner several times and yet remains in business with him, so I don't think the term sensible can be applied. Besides, I think it's a setup."

Belle glanced at me. "Why?"

"The fact that Roland told Kash where he was going. Why would he do that when he had to be aware that Kash had called us? It makes no sense."

"True." She wound down the window and peered back at the facility. "If he *is* waiting for us to appear, then we can't go in through the main entrance. What about the fence behind our unit?"

"We can't go over it, because it's topped by razor wire, and we can't go through, because we haven't got wire cutters."

"We could still walk down there—"

"Given he could be anywhere inside—including on a rooftop—it's not worth the risk. Besides, that isn't what your mom would call careful behavior."

"No, but it's pretty normal by your standards."

I grinned and once again didn't deny it. In truth, had he not been armed, I'd have been tackling that fence in an instant, razor wire or not.

I turned off the headlights and pulled over to the side of the road to wait for Duke. He appeared a few minutes later —lights and sirens both off—and came to a halt beside us.

After winding down his window, he said, "You been in?"

"We were told not to."

"Yes, but how often does that matter?"

"You seem to be getting something of a reputation," Belle murmured.

I ignored her. "He's armed, and I'm not silly."

He grunted. I wasn't entirely sure whether it was a sound of agreement or not.

"I'll pull off road and do a quick run around the perimeter. Wait here."

He parked behind us and got out. In wolf form, he moved into darkness and quickly disappeared.

The storage facility remained silent. There were no shouts, no movement, and no gunshots. Nothing to indicate Roland lay in wait.

I had no doubt he was here, but where? And what was

he up to? Retrieving the books he and Kash no longer had access to? Kash had said he was the type to destroy what he couldn't have, but that didn't mean it was the truth. And it certainly didn't mean the two of them hadn't jointly hatched this bloody plan to make a final grab for the books.

Duke reappeared out of the shadows and stopped beside the passenger door. "I can't tell if our suspect is there, because the wind's going the wrong way and the only scent I could smell was damn petrol."

Alarm ran through me. Though our spells would protect our unit from fire, the last thing I wanted was the whole complex going up in flames.

"There's no petrol stored on the site," I said. "Not as far as I know, anyway."

"There isn't—we do regular safety check across all the storage places in the area. He's obviously brought it in with him."

"Roland didn't have the time to fill containers after shooting Kash." Belle glanced at me. "Whatever they're up to, it's something they've pre-planned."

That was becoming obvious. "How bad is the saturation, Duke? Is it the whole complex or just around our storage unit?"

"Right now the latter, but there's no saying he's not busy pouring it around the rest of the units as we speak."

"The whole facility has alarms and sprinklers," Belle said, "It's a pretty pointless action."

"Unless it's nothing more than a means of drawing you two out."

Duke had barely finished that sentence when Belle's phone rang. She glanced down at it. "Unknown number."

"Answer it," he said. "I'll do another loop and see if I can locate him via voice."

As Duke disappeared into the darkness again, Belle hit the speaker button, then answered the call. "Hello?"

"I take it you've now seen what has happened to Kash?"

The voice was cool and calm. This definitely wasn't a man acting in anger.

"According to what he said on the phone, you shot him. I dare say the rangers and the ambulance officers are in the process of dealing with it."

Roland paused. "You didn't go there?"

"Why should I? He was using our relationship to steal my books and profit from them."

The pause was longer. He obviously wasn't expecting her to be so blasé. *Threaten to come after him, Belle.*

She raised an eyebrow. *Is that really wise?*

He obviously doesn't know we're parked up the road. It gives us an advantage.

I'm not seeing how, she grumbled, before adding, "And if I were you, I'd be hightailing the hell out of the reservation."

"The rangers don't worry me."

"It's not the rangers you should be worried about, Roland."

He laughed. "You can't touch me. I'm wearing a band to protect me against telepathic intrusion."

And that's why I couldn't sense him, she said. *We need to get closer if I'm to have any chance of getting past the band's electronic wall and freeze the bastard.*

It's too big a risk, given he's armed.

It's not if we go through the factory next door. If kids can break into it, surely a ranger can. To Roland, she added, "And you think telepathy is my only skill?"

He laughed. "I think your other skill isn't really up to

scratch if all the books you're collecting on magic is any guide."

"You're quite welcome to think that if you want, Roland. Now, is there a point to this call? Because otherwise, I'll bid you goodbye and hope the rangers catch your ass and throw it in jail for a very long time."

"You hang up, and I'll destroy that fine collection of books that you've been so secretive about."

"You and Kash can't make money from them if you destroy them."

"True, but I'm thinking you care a little more about them than I do. They were a gift from your dead old granny, weren't they?"

Belle shot me a gaze. *How the fuck did he know that? It's not something I ever told Kash.*

I'm betting Professor Janice Hopetown did some digging and discovered the likely source. It was no secret that Nell kept an extensive library on the occult and magic, so it's possible one of the volumes Kash and Roland converted was recognized by one of the blue bloods.

Belle grimaced. *If that's true then we really do need to hide the library elsewhere ASAP.* "So, what do you want, Roland?"

"The books, of course. Ten minutes should be just enough time to get here from your café. Any later, and I'll burn the whole fucking place down."

"And if I *do* appear, you'll no doubt shoot me like you did Kash."

"I won't kill you, if that's what you're worried about. A murder charge is not something I want hanging over my head anytime soon." There was amusement in his voice. "Why do you think I only pinged Kash?"

"Maybe because he was stealing from you?"

He paused. "How did you know that if you didn't ride to his rescue?"

Damn, caught by my own lies, she said, then added, "How do you think? I'm a telepath, remember? And, by the way, we passed all information about your scam, your company—Black Arts, in case you think I'm bluffing—and your Canberra contact—one Professor Janice Hopetown—to the Witch Council. Given their views on theft of ancient articles, I daresay you'll be hearing from them soon."

"Bitch," Roland growled. "Ten minutes. Not a moment longer."

He hung up. Belle snorted. "Part one of the plan down."

"What plan?" Duke said, reappearing at the side window.

A squeak escaped my lips as my heart landed briefly in my throat. "Fuck, way to give a girl a heart attack, Duke. Did you locate him?"

"He's on the rooftop of the unit diagonally across from yours. Now, answer the damn question."

I quickly filled him in. "Can you get Belle into the factory next door without making much noise?"

"I've bolt cutters in the truck, so yes, but given he's already shot his partner, I'm not sure putting you in the line of fire is a good idea."

"He won't know I'm not Belle until I step out of the car, and he won't immediately shoot me, because he wants the books."

"And with any sort of luck, I'll have him disabled before then," Belle said.

Duke hesitated and then nodded. "How much time we got left?"

I glanced at the clock on the dash. "Eight minutes."

"Then let's move."

Belle dropped her phone onto the center console and then climbed out. Once they'd moved away, I locked the doors and tried not to think of all the things that could go wrong with this plan.

Time ticked down so very slowly.

We're in the factory next door, Belle said eventually. *I can feel him—or rather, the buzz of the shield protecting him.*

How quickly do you think you can break through it?

Four or five minutes.

We've only three before I have to go in there.

Then drive slowly through the gate.

I snorted softly but didn't bother replying. She needed to concentrate on the task at hand. As the clock hit the one-minute-to-go mark, I started the SUV, made a U-turn, then switched on the headlights and drove back to the storage facility.

I took my time at the gates and waited until they'd fully opened before driving through. The SUV's high beams washed brightness across the whole area but didn't quite reach the rooftops.

Belle?

Almost there.

So am I.

I know. Can't help it.

I took a deep breath and kept the SUV crawling forward. The brightness of the lights at least meant he wouldn't immediately notice it wasn't Belle driving, but I was running out of room and would have to stop soon.

Belle's phone rang. I jumped and glanced down. Unknown number again. I hit the answer button and hoped like hell the glow of the screen wasn't enough to give the game away just yet.

"Stop the car, then get out," he ordered.

I stopped and pulled on the handbrake. *Belle?*

A minute or so.

"Get out of the car, Belle, or I'll shoot you through the fucking door," Roland said. "I don't need you fully mobile, remember. I just need you alert enough to detangle your magic."

I took a deep breath, then slowly got out of the SUV and raised my hands. Magic sparkled across my fingertips, but I didn't unleash my weapon. I couldn't. It was pure energy and just as likely to kill as maim; I couldn't risk that until I was sure an attack resulting in death wouldn't somehow rebound back into the reservation's wild magic, forever staining it.

I scanned the rooftops opposite but couldn't immediately see Roland. Tension tightened my muscles as I instinctively readied to react or run. Of course, me being faster than a bullet was highly unlikely, no matter what changes the wild magic might be making to my DNA.

"Why the fuck are *you* here?" he said.

He was still hidden, which I hoped meant he didn't have a great line of sight on me, gun wise.

"The magic protecting the storage unit is mine, not Belle's. You want it open, you deal with me."

Just a few seconds more came Belle's comment.

"Why would your magic be protecting it when they're not your books?"

"Because I'm the stronger witch."

He rose from the shadows, his gun aimed at my body and utterly steady. He was obviously proficient enough with the weapon that his movements didn't affect his aim in any way.

"Then go open the roller and dismantle it."

"And present my back to you? I'm not that stupid."

"As I said, I don't want you—" He stopped, his eyes widening even as light flared around his neck.

Oh fuck, Belle said, even as Roland swore and unleashed metal hell. The wild magic exploded from my body even as I threw myself down and away. Bullets pinged all around me, accompanied by multiple mini explosions. Sparks flew from the asphalt and thudded into the SUV far too close to my head.

Then, just as suddenly, the assault stopped.

Lizzie? came Belle's silent scream. *You okay?*

Amazingly, yes. I pushed upright and dusted the grit from my hands. The wild magic rippled around me, a fierce white glow in which metal glittered. *Melted* metal. I blinked. It had not only stopped the bullets, but rendered them utterly useless.

And *that* scared the hell out of me. If it could do that, what else could it do?

As the bright glow faded, the mangled bullets fell to the ground. The soft sound of paws padding on the ground had me quickly turning and, just for a second, the world spun and my stomach rose up into my throat. I swallowed heavily and pressed a hand against the SUV to remain upright.

Duke flowed from wolf to human form and strode toward me. "Any damage?"

"A few bullet holes in the SUV, but that's it."

Relief flickered across his expression. "Good. I did *not* want to get the boss offside."

I half smiled. "Thanks for the concern."

"You know what I meant." He touched my arm lightly, then walked across to the unit and stared up at Roland. "Can you ask Belle to order him to release his weapon and get down the same way as he got up?"

I did so. There was a clatter, then Roland spun and

walked away. Duke headed around the side of the building and reappeared a few minutes later with Roland in tow. His hands were secured behind his back, but his expression remained slack.

"She can release him now," Duke said.

The minute she did so, Roland's expression regained its animation. "Bitches. You utter double-crossing bitches. I'm going to fucking make sure—"

The rest was cut off as Duke shook him hard. "The only thing you'll be doing is going to jail for a very long time. Now shut up, or I'll damn well make you."

"You can't threaten me—it's against the damn law."

"Not in this reservation it's not." He glanced at me. "Are you sure you're okay? You're looking a little pale around the edges."

I *felt* a little pale around the edges. In fact, it felt as if my body had been utterly and completely drained by the force that had exploded from me.

I waved a hand, a small movement that had my head pounding. "I'm fine, but thanks."

His expression suggested he didn't believe one word of that particular statement, and I couldn't say I blamed him. "You'd better head home, then. I'll take care of this scum and lock down the area."

"I'll drive you home." Belle reappeared out of the gloom. "You're certainly in no state."

I didn't argue. I simply didn't have the strength. I carefully made my way around to the passenger side of the vehicle and climbed in. As Belle drove out of the storage facility, I opened the glove compartment and fished out several chocolate bars.

"What was that flash at the very end, just before he started shooting?"

"A goddamn warning alarm had been woven into the circuitry. I wasn't expecting it." Her expression was grim. "My inattention could have killed you."

"But it didn't, so stop stressing." I bit into a Snickers Bar, but the nutty nougat goodness didn't immediately make me feel any better. I rather suspected it'd take a whole lot more than a couple of chocolate bars for that to happen. "I'll have to get Monty to raise the urgency on his search through the archives for any more information on wild magic. The stuff that's happening is goddamn scary."

Belle glanced at me. "I did feel the surge of power, but I thought it was the reservation's wild magic rather than yours because of its sheer force."

"It melted the goddamn bullets, Belle. *Melted* them."

"Which is as scary as fuck, but also somewhat comforting."

"Except it feels like it's aged me ten years."

Her gaze swept me, and concern stirred through our link. "You do look gaunt, but that's not unexpected when you think about it. It's obviously drawing on your personal strength, and that means the bigger the force, the bigger the cost."

"And makes me wonder if it could actually kill me."

She wrinkled her nose. "It's sourced from your DNA, so surely self-preservation mode would kick in before that happened."

"I'd like to think so, but given I don't appear to have full control over what's happening, who actually knows?" I took another bite of the Snickers. "All magic costs, and the greater the spell, the deeper the cost—how often were we told that in school? There certainly have been witches who were killed by their own spells."

"Yes, but it's a rarity."

"I think it's safe to say that being born with wild magic fused to your DNA is something more than a mere rarity."

"True." Her expression was grim. "I'll stick a fire under Monty's ass and get him motivated."

"I think the promise of hot and heated—"

"Do *not* finish that thought."

I chuckled, then winced as pain stirred anew. It felt like there were dozens of tiny men gleefully stabbing red-hot pokers into my brain. I reached for the backpack and grabbed some Panadol, though I seriously doubted the tablets would make all that much difference.

"Maybe you need to take tomorrow off," Belle said in concern. "It's not like the café will be flat-out given the storms they're predicting."

"You know putting a statement like that out there in the world means fate will take it as a challenge."

"And we'll cope if she does. Seriously, you need to rest; you've been overdoing it magic-wise of late, and you need to take more care of yourself."

"I'm fine—"

"Tell that to someone who can't feel your bone-deep weariness."

Her voice was dry, and I held up a hand. "Okay, I give in. But you'll ring—"

"I will not. Besides, it takes you twenty minutes on a good day to get from Argyle to Castle Rock. Any rush we experience might be well over by then."

"Fine." I paused. "I might just use the time to contact Ashworth—"

"*That* is not my definition of resting."

"A five-minute conversation won't matter one way or the other, and you know it."

"As long as that's *all* it is." She paused to overtake a slow car. "And Monty will be informed not to call on you if our rogue makes another appearance."

"I doubt she will, given how badly she was wounded."

"To echo your words, now that you've put that out there, fate will accept it as a challenge."

I hoped not. I actually hoped her wounds would knock the thought of revenge out of her mind and that she'd do the sensible thing and get the hell out of the reservation.

Of course, when did those who lived in shadows and darkness ever do the sensible thing?

Belle pulled up in front of Aiden's house. "Aiden's truck's not here—you going to be okay?"

"I'm not going to collapse into a coma or anything, Belle. Honestly, stop worrying."

A smile tugged at her lips. "It's a familiar's job to worry —especially when it's been just you and me for such a long time."

I reached out and gripped her hand. "No matter who else comes into our lives, or how much our lives might diverge thanks to family and children if we're both so blessed, you'll always remain the most important person in my life, and not just because you're my familiar."

She reached across the console and gave me a fierce hug. "I do love you, you know."

"I know." I blinked back the silly tears and pulled away. "Drive home safely."

"To echo someone else, always."

I chuckled and climbed out of the SUV, watching her leave before moving inside. The fire had burned out, so I relit it then made myself a herbal tea in the vague hope it would help stop the crazy men with pokers attacking my brain.

After putting on some music, I curled up on the sofa,

sipping my tea and watching the flames. Weariness soon caught up with me, and I drifted to sleep. Soft steps had me stirring who knew how many hours later. Strong arms slipped around me, lifting me up and then holding me close to a body that was warm, muscular, and smelled delicious.

I pressed my face into his chest to draw in his scent and murmured, "What time is it?"

"Just after midnight. Why aren't you in bed?"

"Was waiting for you." I shifted my head and kissed his neck. "Happy now. To bed, Ranger."

"And to sleep."

"That's no fun."

I ran my tongue around his ear, and he made a low sound deep in his throat. "We can have fun another day. Right now, your cheeks are crazy hollow and your weariness is so strong it's all I can smell."

"I'm sure some gentle loving will fix all that." I trailed light kisses along his chin. "If you're worried about my strength, you can do all the work."

He laughed softly. "I have absolutely no problems doing all the work, but I do prefer a partner who's not going to fall asleep on me."

"Work it well enough, and she won't."

"Says the woman who hasn't yet been able to open her eyes."

"A minor inconvenience." I yawned hugely. "We can get over it, I'm sure."

"Not tonight we won't." He placed me onto the bed and then efficiently undressed me. When I tried to return the favor, he caught my hands and then captured my lips with his, kissing me long and deep. "Sleep, Liz. We'll talk in the morning."

I sighed but nevertheless accepted the inevitable and

snuggled deeper into the blankets. I was back asleep within seconds.

A deep rumble of thunder woke me. I yawned and stretched, then glanced out the windows. The sky was dark and the rain pelting down so hard I could barely see the trees that lined the lake. The house was silent, suggesting Aiden had already left, but the air was warm, so the fire was at least going.

I tossed the blankets off, pulled on a sweater, then padded barefoot down the stairs. Aiden had left a note on the counter: *Be home at five. I'll cook.*

No doubt meaning steak and chips again—not that I was about to complain, given how few of the few men in my past had ever deigned to enter the kitchen, let alone cook for me. Besides, I'd gained a deep hunger for steak—and meat in general—in recent weeks, but that was probably a good thing if using the wild magic was going to exhaust me to the point of collapse.

I glanced at the clock on the stove and saw it was well after two. I'd slept for over twelve hours—no wonder I felt a whole lot better.

I fried up some bacon and eggs, made a coffee, then headed over to the sofa and plopped down directly in front of the fire. It had burned down considerably over the course of the day, but the heat coming off it was just right.

Once I'd eaten, I grabbed my phone from the backpack and called Ashworth. Eli answered.

"Hey, Liz, Ira's in the shower. Is this a social call or is there something I can help you with?"

"The latter, I'm afraid."

He laughed. "That'll actually make his day. He's been somewhat out of sorts, what with the limited number of cases requiring RWA intervention of late."

I chuckled. "It's actually not a case but rather information I'm after, and you might well be able to help me anyway."

"Always happy to try." There was a smile in his voice. "What do you need?"

"Do you know anything about the Thaumaturge Society? Other than the fact they're some sort of private fellowship for human illusionists?"

"Many of whom actually have at least some true magical ability thanks to their ancestors—near or far—having a link back to witches."

Because while blue bloods would never marry a human, they certainly didn't mind bedding them. "Is the fellowship its only purpose? Because it's been suggested to me that they have a library catalogue of dark art maker marks in their possession."

"I've never seen it, but I believe that's true. I also believe maker marks are not the only items relating to dark arts that they collect."

My eyebrows rose. "Meaning spells?"

"Apparently so. The council does regular inventory checks, of course, because that sort of information could be dangerous in the wrong hands. Nothing has ever been found on site, however."

"What about off-site?"

"They have always denied there is such a thing."

I snorted. "And the council believed them? Seriously?"

He laughed. "No, but they can't legally react without reasonable evidence."

"Since when?"

He laughed again. "Despite your experiences, there are some very good people on the High Witch Council."

"I'll bow to your greater wisdom when it comes to that."

I took a sip of my coffee then added, "I guess my next question is, do you or Ashworth have any contacts who might be able to do a search through their archive and let us know whose mark is on the cheek of our rogue?"

"If the rogue is a wolf, she can't possibly be marked by a dark sorcerer. Only witches can be."

"I know, but the witness we talked to was convinced it was a maker's mark, so we need to follow it up."

He grunted. "Well, I've been retired long enough that I've few usable contacts these days. You want Ashworth to ring back?"

"Please."

"It won't be immediately. He does love long hot showers —we've had to install a larger hot water service just to cope."

I laughed. "Tell him he's unattractive when he's all wrinkly and prune-like."

"I have. Trouble is, he knows it's not true."

I laughed again and then hung up. Once I'd finished my coffee, I pottered about doing the washing and some cleaning, then headed up for a shower.

The phone rang just before five; the tone told me it was Aiden. My stomach plummeted. I took a deep breath and then answered. "I'm gathering dinner is on hold."

"Yeah." The edge of weary frustration in his voice tugged at my heart.

"For a bad or a super bad reason?"

"The latter. I'm afraid the rogue has hit again."

CHAPTER FIFTEEN

"So much for the hope her wounds would hamper her movements for a couple of days," I muttered. "Who was it this time?"

"Jack Martin."

"The man she was tracking in the forest behind that horse place?"

"Yeah. We'd explained the situation to him and did in fact escort him from the reservation as he didn't live here, but either he didn't believe us or considered sex with his girlfriend a higher priority than his life."

"So it happened at the girlfriend's place?"

"Yes. They were postcoital, apparently, and didn't hear the rogue break in."

"Was the girlfriend also killed?"

"No, just Jack. Thankfully, we've managed to get a list of everyone who was in the same class as John and the other three victims. We'll be attempting to contact them all tonight in an effort to hamper the bitch's progress."

"She may not be going after the entire class," I pointed out. "She may just be going after those who bullied Leesa, either because they're related or they have some other connection we haven't found yet."

"While that might be the case, we can't take any risks at the moment. I have no idea how late I'm going to be, so don't wait up for me."

"Okay." I hesitated, biting back the instinctive need to add "love you" and simply said, "Talk tomorrow."

"You will."

I'd barely hung up when the phone rang again. This time, it was Ashworth.

"Don't tell me you've been in the shower all this time," I said, amused.

He laughed. "Indeed I haven't, lass. Been hunting up some old contacts, and I've managed to get a viewing at the Thaumaturge Society tomorrow morning at eleven. Thought you'd like to come along."

"That would be fabulous."

"I'll pick you up at the café just after nine, then. That'll give us enough time to get down to Melbourne and find parking."

"Thanks, Ashworth."

"No problems at all. And I daresay Eli will be glad to get me out of the house for a while."

"That's a surety," came the response in the background.

I grinned, bid them both good night, and hung up. After making myself ham, cheese, and spaghetti jaffles for dinner, I spent the rest of the evening flicking through the TV channels in a vague hope of finding something decent to watch. Eventually, I just gave up and went upstairs to sleep.

The lack of an indentation on the pillow next to mine the next morning suggested Aiden hadn't made it home. I hoped it meant he'd decided it was easier to sleep at the compound rather than drive all the way here, but knowing him as well as I now did, it undoubtedly meant they'd worked all night.

I made a quick breakfast, then jumped into the Suzi and headed up to Castle Rock. Belle was just clattering down the stairs when I stepped through the back door.

"Didn't expect you here so early," she said. "What's happened?"

"Ashworth's made an appointment with the Thaumaturge Society to look through their archives. He's picking me up at nine, so I thought I'd get here and do some prep work." I slung my bag under the counter. "How was yesterday?"

"Steady, which was nice. Coffee?"

I nodded and updated her on the rogue. She swore softly. "How the hell are we going to stop her?"

"We?" I said, amusement twitching my lips.

She waved a hand. "A general we. You know, the whole damn gang."

"I'm guessing it'll depend on what we uncover about her at the society."

She handed me a coffee, then leaned a hip against the counter. "Why would they have a record of her existence?"

"They may not, but to me it seems practical to not only keep a record of the marks, but also who's received them."

"I guess." She wrinkled her nose. "You know, this whole rogue episode feels a lot different to all the other entities we've had through here."

"That's because it is. Not only is her killing spree personal, but she appears to be a wolf capable of magic."

"Which is why I think the final action we take against her should be different."

I frowned. "Meaning what?"

She hesitated. "Mom and I were talking about it last

night. If she does want revenge for how badly her mother was treated—and I suspect we're dealing with more than bullying here—then surely she deserves our pity rather than our hatred? Plus, what sort of upbringing must she have had? She's been marked by a dark sorcerer and consumed by her mother's trauma and need for revenge. She may not be playing on the same footing as the rest of us."

I thought *that* was a safe bet. "Trouble is, she's now killed nine people."

"I know, and I'm not saying she shouldn't be brought to justice. I'm just saying that our usual method of dealing with dark entities—that is, killing them—may be neither right *nor* appropriate in this particular situation."

"What happens in that regard will depend entirely on what she's capable of and how she reacts to us when we finally track her down."

"I know, and I'm just putting my thoughts out there."

A smile twitched my lips. "Have you put those thoughts out to Monty?"

She raised an eyebrow, knowing exactly what I was actually asking. "No, I have not, and you well know it, given he was with the rangers last night, not me. Go do some prep, evil woman."

I laughed and headed into the kitchen. We worked steadily for the next couple of hours, with me handling the knife work and Belle readying cakes and slices. Ashworth arrived right on the dot of nine. I swung my handbag over my shoulder, then picked up the coffee I'd made us both and headed out.

The trip down to Melbourne went without a hitch, though things got a whole lot slower once we entered the city. We might have arrived well past peak hour, but the traffic still seemed on a go-slow.

The Thaumaturge Society was located in a grand old building at the top end of Collins Street. As we walked under the ornate arches that lined the building, a blue-clad security guard stepped in front of the door and said, "May I help you?"

Ashworth dug out his RWA credentials and showed them. "We've an appointment with Marian Jennings at eleven."

"Please wait here while I check." He stepped to one side and spoke quietly into a two-way radio.

"Rather tight security for a place that supposedly supports and promotes illusionists," I murmured.

"Oh, I think it's safe to say it's more than that. How much more, of course, is a question we've never been able to answer."

"If there's doubts over their legitimacy, why has no one investigated?"

"One needs a reason to investigate, and they've never provided one."

"So they're cagey."

"Extremely."

The guard stepped back in front of us and swept a card across the reader. "Okay, you've been cleared to enter. Miss Jennings will be waiting for you in the second-floor foyer. The stairs are to your right, and the elevator directly ahead."

"Thank you," Ashworth said, then motioned me to precede him.

We headed right, our footsteps echoing hollowly on the crisp white marble. There were a number of comfortable-looking chairs dotted about, but otherwise the foyer was boringly pristine. Just beyond the small bank of elevators was a wall of blue-tinged glass bricks that gave no hint as to what might lie beyond them. They gleamed under the bright lights above but lent no warmth to the overall feel of the place. Stark sterility certainly wasn't what I'd expected from an organization representing illusionists.

We bounded up the wide steps and quickly reached the second floor. A tall, thin woman who appeared to be in her mid-forties waited in the middle of the foyer, her hands folded in front of her and her expression somewhat bored. Her crisp white shirt, black skirt, and sensible black shoes might have been old-fashioned but her hair certainly wasn't. It was short, spikey, and a startling blue in color—the same blue as her eyes, in fact.

She held out a ring-lined hand. "Marian Jennings, at your service."

Ashworth shook her hand and then introduced me. Marion's grip was cool and efficient. Much like the woman, I suspected.

"This way, please." She turned and led us past the elevators and through a security door. "We've done a quick search for the mark you described and found several active possibilities."

"Meaning there were also inactive possibilities?" I asked.

She glanced briefly over her shoulder, her expression giving little away. "Yes. I'm not sure how much you know about the marks—"

"The reservation recently dealt with a heretic witch and his apprentice," Ashworth said.

"Ah." One word that seemed to speak volumes. "Then you're well aware that it's rare for dark witches to take on an apprentice and mark them in such a manner."

"If you've got a library filled with records of said marks, I'm thinking that's not quite true." We followed her through a second security door and into what appeared to be a reading area.

The look she cast me was somewhat disdainful. "Our collection is centuries old, young woman, and a maker's mark can be handed from master to apprentice through multiple generations. We have recorded all such events, hence the number of volumes in the library."

"Handed down" was something of a misnomer, given the only reason many dark masters took on an apprentice was to steal their bodies—ousting the apprentices' souls and replacing them with his own—once they were approaching their own mortality.

But it was interesting that the society was able to catalogue such exchanges, especially given how secretive dark witches generally were. It was undoubtedly another reminder that the society was far more than what they claimed on all the advertising.

We walked down a short corridor into the library, which was a lot smaller than I'd expected. Shelving units lined the three walls, with a nest of tall tables in the middle. There were no chairs. Obviously, you were not meant to get comfortable in this room.

The nearest table held three books and three sets of gloves. Marion motioned toward them. "Please."

We dutifully donned the gloves and then moved to the first book. Several paper bookmarks stuck out at the top of it. Marian carefully opened the book at the first tab. The first mark she showed us was more a moon than a scythe, though a snake was very definitely wrapped around it. I shook my head, and she carefully folded over the ancient-smelling pages to the next tab. This time it was a scythe, but there was no snake, just a rope that rather weirdly ended in a noose. And if *that* hadn't warned the apprentice of his ultimate fate, I'm not sure what would have. The third one in this book was another scythe, but I had no idea what was wrapped around it. It certainly wasn't a snake.

I shook my head again. She carefully closed the book and moved on to the second one. This only had two paper tabs, and the second one was a scythe with a snake wrapped around it.

"That's the symbol our witnesses described," I said. "Who owns it?"

She flipped several pages, then ran a gloved finger down the records until she came to the last name on the list. "According to this, Henry James."

"Dead or alive?" Ashworth asked.

Her finger slipped across several columns. "Still alive. Retired and living here in Victoria, apparently."

I blinked. "Dark sorcerers retire?"

She gave me a severe look. "Not all dark sorcerers are evil, young woman. Some simply use the darker forms of magic."

"I was under the impression—"

"Is there any chance of us speaking to him?" Ashworth cut in, sending me a warning look. "The woman who bears his mark has been causing chaos up in the Faelan Reservation, and any information he might be able to give us could help capture her."

She pursed her lips. "I can contact him and see if he's willing to talk to you, if you wish."

"Would it be possible to do so today?"

"I'll check. This way, please."

She led us out of the library, killing any hope I had of snooping through the other books. We were deposited in the reading room, given a quick, "I won't be long," and left to our own devices.

I walked over to the nearest sofa and plonked down. "I had no idea dark witches weren't always evil."

"That's certainly not my experience, but I guess in my line of business that's not entirely unexpected."

He strolled to the rear wall and made a small upward motion with his hand. My gaze followed the movement and landed on the camera—one that had an odd round bulge underneath it, which no doubt meant they were also listening in. No wonder Ashworth had given me a warning glance earlier.

I crossed my legs, got out my phone, and scrolled through Twitter in an effort to catch up on whatever shit-storm was currently overtaking the day. Ashworth continued to walk around the room, but the gentle wash of his magic suggested he was probing the spells surrounding this place. Spells I could feel but couldn't see.

Marian returned ten minutes later and handed Ashworth a piece of paper. "He has agreed to meet at this café. He'll be there at midday and will wait no more than fifteen minutes for your arrival."

Ashworth glanced down at the note, then nodded and shoved it into his pocket. "I appreciate your help in this matter, Marian."

She smiled, though there was little sign of warmth or sincerity. "We're always happy to help on matters such as this. This way, please."

We were led through the final security door and then politely motioned toward the stairs. The security guard opened the front door as we approached and bid us a good day as we headed for the parking lot.

"Where are we meeting Henry?"

"A café in Carlton. It'll only take ten minutes or so to get there."

"Given it was eleven-forty when we left, he has to live close by."

"I'd say so. I am surprised he agreed to meet, though. Those who survive to retirement tend not to."

"Because of past activities?"

"Yes. No matter what Marian might espouse, there're very few dark witches who don't slide into evil. The forces they deal with on a regular basis generally ensure there's little light left."

I frowned. "Then how dangerous is meeting going to be?"

"It'd pay for us to be on our guard, but I doubt he'd actually try anything, given I'm on official business and he wouldn't, in any way, want to bring RWA attention down on himself."

"That's only semi-comforting," I muttered. "Especially given the record I have when it comes to the dark side trying to kill me."

"Lass, the charm around your neck is strong enough to cope with any minor spell he throws." He hesitated. "I would, however, fully raise your muting shield so that he doesn't sense the wild magic. That could well cause a problem in the future."

I immediately did so. Like all witches, I'd been taught the basics of controlling magical output at school, but with the discovery that I'd been born with wild magic entwined through my DNA, I'd had to learn how to create an inner shield that would stop other witches sensing its presence. It was basically active whenever I was awake, though I'd begun lowering its output in an effort to conserve some strength whenever I was with witches who knew about the wild magic.

The café was situated near the corner of Lygon and

Faraday Streets, an area where it was notoriously difficult to park. It probably would have been easier to catch a tram up, but neither of us had a smartcard Myki ticket and time was too tight to source them.

In the end, we were lucky and found a center strip parking spot only two blocks away, which meant we arrived at the café with five minutes to spare. The building itself was a small, two-story Victorian terrace, and quite popular if the babble coming out of it was anything to go by.

Ashworth stepped through the door first, holding it open with his fingers as he scanned the room, no doubt looking for our dark witch.

In truth, he wasn't all that hard to spot, though not because he in any way stood out physically. The actually opposite was true. He was small, balding, and crumpled looking, but there was nothing simple or harmless about the energy he radiated. It felt like a wave of tiny fire ants crawled across my skin, making it twitch and burn.

If this was muted, God help us if he decided to unleash.

Ashworth wound his way through the tables and stopped in front of the dark witch. I stopped just behind Ashworth, unrepentantly using him to shield some of the waves of dark energy.

"Henry James?" Ashworth said.

"I think we're both well aware I could be no one else, but I appreciate the politeness." His voice, like his appearance, was mild. Unremarkable. Utterly deceptive. He motioned to a chair. "Please, sit."

Ashworth did so. I remained exactly where I was. Henry's gaze flicked over me and just as quickly dismissed me. Relief stirred. Obviously, it meant the inner shields were working, even if it felt like a storm raged deep within. Of course, that might well have been fear rather than magic.

Henry interlaced his fingers and leaned forward slightly. His expression was unconcerned, but his energy was ramping up. The ants had become hornets, and my breathing hitched a little.

"How may I help you?"

"We're having problems at the Faelan Reservation with a woman who bears your mark on her cheek, and we'd appreciate any information you might be able to give us about her."

Though Ashworth's tone was ultra polite, the wash of his power increased sharply. He'd also lowered his shields a fraction, no doubt as a warning to the man sitting opposite. And while Ashworth would never be a match for a dark witch in his prime, Henry had fallen over that particular ridge a long time ago.

The dark waves eased, but my breathing didn't. This man scared the hell out of me, and all I wanted to do was run for the door and get well away from the stain of his magic. The urge was so damn strong that I had to grip the back of Ashworth's chair to remain still.

"There have been a few women over the years who've born my mark." He raised an eyebrow, his black eyes glittering. He knew well enough who we were talking about. "I will need more information than that."

"We believe she could be the daughter of Leesa Rhineheart."

"Ah, then you could only be talking about little Honor." A smile touched his lips, though there was nothing in the way of amusement or warmth. He picked up his cup and took a drink. "I want a guarantee that in providing you with the information you require, I will be given immunity for my actions. I've reached an agreement with my demons and now wish nothing more than to live what remains of my life in peace and without consequence."

"I cannot give you such a blanket guarantee, Henry, and you're well aware of that."

He leaned back in his chair, his fingers playing lightly across the rim of his coffee mug. Darkness briefly rose and then fell away. "Are you willing to guarantee no investigation or repercussions for my actions in this particular case, then?"

"That I'm willing to agree to."

"You swear this?"

"If you'll swear that the information you give us is utterly truthful, then yes." There was amusement in Ashworth's voice. "I take it you're recording our conversation?"

"By regular means and magical." He reached into his pocket, drew out his phone, and placed it on the table beside his coffee. "You're no doubt aware of the consequences of breaking an oath witnessed by darkness?"

"I am."

"Then I also vow to this agreement." Henry pressed the "end record" button on his phone. "Leesa Rhineheart hunted me down some thirty-five years ago. She wished to become a werewolf."

"That's not—"

I cut the rest off, but Henry's gaze nevertheless rose to mine. I shivered. Now that he'd gotten an agreement about not being prosecuted for his actions in this matter, his mild-mannered projection had fallen by the wayside. What I saw in the darkness of his gaze was the souls of all those he'd killed in the long years of his life.

There were *hundreds*.

His mouth ticked, though the movement was too small

to call it a smile. "Anything is possible if you have the power and knowledge, though something like this is not without its risks for the receiver. She was made well aware of this."

I was betting that wasn't the case, but I kept that thought to myself.

"Did you grant her request?" Ashworth asked. "And did she pay your blood price?"

"Yes and yes."

"Did she say why she wished this?"

"She believed being a werewolf would make the man she desired both love and marry her. I daresay a love spell would have been easier in the end, but she wished the full journey." He shrugged. "Who am I to shatter such dreams?"

"And was the spell successful?"

"In that she could shift shape, yes." Another twitch of the lips. Another chill stole through my soul. "Unfortunately, neither of us were aware she was pregnant at the time. Powerful magic, be it light or dark, can sometimes invade and twist the cells of embryos, and the price paid can be horrendous."

His gaze met mine again. He knew, I thought with horror. He knew about the wild magic. My grip on the chair back tightened yet again, but I met his gaze evenly and tried to restrain the fear churning through me. There would be consequences for that knowledge; perhaps not now, but definitely sometime in the future.

"This is what happened to Honor?" Ashworth said.

"Yes. She was born in a state of incompletion—neither human nor wolf, but a mix of both."

It was a statement that immediately had me thinking about any children I might have with Aiden if our relationship *did* get that far. While Honor's state was a result of the dark magic used to alter her mother's DNA, it did present a rather stark reminder of what we might one day face.

Did I have the right to risk that? As much as I eventually wanted children, perhaps Katie's statement that it would be better not to risk such a fate was in truth the only way to move forward.

But Aiden was an alpha. The desire—need, even—for offspring to continue his lineage was paramount. He would never have that with me.

I swallowed the bitter pill of realization and tried to concentrate on the ongoing conversation.

"And you raised her?" Ashworth was saying, "Trained her?"

"Of course. That was the price." He hesitated. "Though I will admit I wasn't expecting her to be infused with darkness, which of course made her far more useful."

Meaning blood-wise, no doubt. Was it any wonder Honor was so screwed up?

"Was she also capable of using dark magic?" Ashworth asked.

Henry nodded. "It was more a force than a spell, though she was in the end quite capable of manipulating it into certain spells."

"Such as appearing to disappear?" I asked.

His gaze rose to mine again, sending another shiver through me. "Yes."

"What about Leesa?" Ashworth said, drawing the dark witch's attention again. Deliberately, I suspected. "What happened to her?"

"She initially returned to the reservation but I believe was rejected most brutally by her man."

"Do you know what happened to her after she gave birth and fulfilled her part of the bargain?"

"She stayed with me, of course. She had no place to go, and I had no desire to raise a child until she became useful."

Meaning grown enough to become a source of blood and maybe even magic, given it also ran through her veins. "Is Leesa still alive?"

His gaze rose briefly. "No. The magic that enabled her to transform began to physically tear her apart, and she killed herself. Honor took her back to the reservation and buried her. I believe it was then that she vowed to take revenge on those who had so brutally rejected her mother."

I hesitated, not really wanting to draw any more of his attention but nevertheless needing answers. "Do you know why Honor would be seeking vengeance now rather than when her mother died?"

He made a somewhat dismissive motion with his hand. "It was simply a matter of timing—she was too young and had little control over her power ten years ago. That is not the case now."

"And have you unleashed her on a temporary or permanent basis?" Ashworth said.

"Given the current situation, I think we both know my ties to the woman have been severed." A faint smile touched his lips. "That will, of course, make her more dangerous. Do not, under any circumstances, underestimate her."

"Oh, I make a habit of never underestimating anyone."

"Which is why, like me, you have lived to a grand age." He collected his phone and then rose. "It's been a pleasure talking to you. If you'd be so kind as to take care of my tab, it would be appreciated."

"One more question before you leave," Ashworth said. "Have you any suggestion as to how we track her down given her familiarity with magic and protection?"

Henry smiled. It was a cold, dark, and cruel thing to behold. "How do you think? With blood and bait."

With that, he left. My legs buckled as relief swept through me, and I hastily sat down. "Fucking hell, he was *scary*. More so than the one we dealt with on the reservation."

"And canny too, given it's doubtful he ever made it onto the Heretic Investigations Center's fifteen most wanted list."

I frowned. "What makes you say that?"

He motioned for the bill. "The fact he had no fear of meeting us here today."

"Except he *did* make you swear not to take action against him on this matter."

"He wouldn't have agreed to providing any information on any matter if he'd in any way feared it getting back into HIC's hands."

Huh. "What did he mean when he said his severing ties would make her more dangerous? I'd have thought the opposite."

"It would suggest his hold over her—via his magic and his demons—was the only thing keeping her on an even keel. She'll either go full psycho or slip into full incoherence and be unable to function."

"I'm hoping for the latter, but I'm thinking we'll get the former."

"On that, we agree." He paid the bill and then rose. "We'd best be getting back. The rangers will need a full report on what we've learned."

"I'll ring Aiden now and get him to meet us at the café."

Ashworth opened the door and ushered me through. "Why there and not the ranger station?"

"Because it feels like I've been bathing in a slick of evil.

I need a long hot shower followed by several large glasses of whiskey to feel normal again." I glanced at him as we moved toward his truck. "I was under the impression dark or blood witches were all eventually consumed by the forces and the demons they did business with, so why has Henry been able to retire?"

"Because he obviously made a far better contract with his demons than many others." Ashworth said. "As I've said, he's a canny one."

"And someone I hope we never have to go near again."

"Indeed."

We jumped into his truck and headed out of Melbourne. My call to Aiden went to voicemail, so I left a message saying Ashworth and I had information about the rogue and needed him—or one of his rangers—to meet us at the café at three. I then sent a similar message to Monty.

It was near two-thirty by the time we made it back to Castle Rock. Ashworth dropped me off with a promise he'd be back in half an hour. There were half a dozen customers inside the café, which was pretty good given it was that awkward midpoint between lunch and afternoon tea. I wound my way through the tables, greeting everyone I knew, and then bounded up the stairs to the apartment.

"Well, someone's in a hurry—" Ava's gaze widened. "That's a rather nasty magical aftertaste you've got lingering around you, Lizzie."

"Yeah, and I'm about to do something about it." I glanced past her. "Belle, Aiden, Ashworth, and Monty will be here at three."

She nodded. "You wanting alcohol after the shower?"

"Hell, yes."

By the time I was clean and dressed, it was close to

three. I raked a brush through my hair, then twisted it up into a ponytail and headed out into the living area.

Belle handed me a large glass of whiskey. "I've asked Penny to stay back and close up for us. She'll send the men up when they arrive."

"Excellent thinking, Ninety-Nine." The ice clinked softly as I took a long drink and then sighed in happiness. "That feels decidedly better."

Ava laughed. "Drink the rest of that so fast, and we won't be getting any sense out of you for the rest of the evening."

"After being so damn close to a dark witch, I'm thinking that's a good thing." A shudder ran through me. "He was *nasty*. Polite, but nasty."

"I daresay that's why they're called dark witches," she replied solemnly, but with a twinkle in her eyes.

I picked up a cushion and threw it at her. She caught it with a laugh. "Sorry, couldn't resist."

The sound of footsteps had me looking around, though I was well aware it was Aiden even without seeing him.

"Perhaps we should just make you a ranger and be done with it." He stopped inches away from me, filling my nostrils with his warm, smoky scent. My pulse rate leapt as desire flared between us, thick and strong. "You seem to be better at tracking down information than we are at the moment."

"As interesting as that prospect sounds, we both know that would likely lead to less work being done than more."

He laughed. "A truth I cannot deny."

With that, he wrapped a hand around my waist and tugged me close for a kiss that was hot, hungry, and all-consuming.

Belle coughed. "Seriously, Ranger, hands off our girl

until you're home and alone. You are, after all, the one with all the rules when it comes to the kissy stuff during working hours."

His laugh vibrated against my lips. "As Monty would say, sorry not sorry."

"That depends entirely on what exactly I'm talking about," Monty said as he bounded up the steps.

"He was referring to kissing during working hours," I said helpfully. My pulse rate remained decidedly high, and wasn't at all helped by the continuing press of Aiden's warm hard body against mine.

"Ah, well," Monty said. "I happen to believe such a rule is nothing short of utter foolishness."

He strode past us and headed for Belle. Her eyes widened, and she put up her hands as if to fend him off. But it was only a half-hearted effort, and we all knew it. He rather grandly swept her into his arms, kissed her passionately, and then stepped back with a grin. "Long may the 'sneaky kiss while working' reign."

Belle didn't comment, and her thoughts were ... interesting on *so* many levels. She immediately cast me a warning look; I grinned, but resisted the urge to tease.

"Do either of you want a coffee?" I said.

Aiden shook his head, but Monty nodded. "And cake, if there's any up here."

"Double that for me," Ashworth said, appearing on the landing. "It's been a long day with no lunch."

"A point I forgot," I said. "Maybe I should grab something before I consume any more alcohol. Or you, Ranger, will be forced to drive me home."

Amusement twitched his lips. "A hardship I think I can endure."

He brushed his knuckles lightly down my cheek and

across my lips, his expression briefly intent, as if considering kissing me again. Sadly, he didn't. Instead, he moved across to the sliding door and dragged in a couple of our outdoor chairs while I made the coffee, then cut the cake we kept up here for emergency indulgences. This week, it was a salted caramel chocolate cake.

Monty, Belle, and Ava had claimed the sofa, leaving the rest of us with the plastic chairs. As I handed out the drinks and cake, Ashworth quickly updated everyone on what we'd discovered.

"And we can trust the word of this dark witch?" Monty asked.

Ashworth's gaze flicked to him. "Aye, because we swore a pact on his demons. If there's bad faith on *either* side, there will be consequences."

"Ah, good." Monty scooped up a large portion of the cake and munched on it thoughtfully. "Have we any idea who Honor's father might be?"

Aiden shook his head. "The DNA results haven't come in as yet, though we have asked for them to be expedited."

"Have you talked to John about Leesa?" I asked.

Aiden nodded. "He denies any involvement in what might have happened to her."

"So he denied being involved in the bullying?" Monty asked.

"Yes." Aiden's mouth twisted. "It was pretty obvious he was lying though."

"Then maybe," Monty said, "Belle needs to have a good ramble through his memories."

"At this point, we have little other option." Aiden glanced at Ashworth. "Did your dark sorcerer have any suggestion as to the best way to capture Honor?"

"Yes," Ashworth said heavily. "But it's not an option you're going to like."

"Using John as bait?" Aiden guessed.

"And blood to draw her in. *His* blood."

"He won't agree to that."

"He may not have a choice. Not if he wants to survive this bitch." Ashworth drank his coffee. "And it doesn't have to be much blood. We can use magic to amplify its range and draw her in."

"The only problem with all that," Monty said, "is the fact she's magically proficient; we can't offer John any real means of protection, because she'll sense it and stay away."

"She won't sense me," I said. "If I'm with him—hidden, but with him—then—"

"No," Aiden growled. "Definitely not."

I met his gaze and raised my eyebrows. "Really? You've a better plan, then?"

He glared at me. It was a full-on "the alpha is unhappy" type glare, and the sensible part of me definitely quailed. Thankfully, the unsensible part was in full control.

It usually is in matters like this, Belle commented dryly.

He's being unreasonable.

He's imagining you dead, and it scares the hell out of him.

I'm not going to get dead.

I daresay he'd find that statement as comforting as I do, given just how close you've come on several occasions.

You exaggerate.

You are altogether too cavalier about your own safety for comfort sometimes.

Only when there's little other choice, Belle. This is one of those times.

She mentally grunted. It was not a sound that suggested agreement. *Then you won't be there alone.*

I briefly thought about arguing, but in truth, it was actually a damn good idea. Telepathy was probably the better weapon in this particular case.

"Why you?" Aiden growled. "Both Monty and Ashworth—"

"Need to create their spells before they can use them. I don't have the same restriction with the wild magic. It's becoming a weaponizable force."

Monty frowned. "When did this start happening?"

"Recently." I gave him a deadpan look. "If only we had someone with access to an ancient book on the wild magic, we might learn why."

He grinned. "It's not my fault that the reservation is considered country and it therefore takes extra days for a parcel to be delivered here. Which it will be in the next day or so, if tracking is to be believed."

"Which doesn't help the current situation," Aiden growled. "Besides, if Honor *is* part wolf, she may well scent the presence of anyone else in the room, concealed or not."

"Not if Lizzie's in the roof," Ashworth said. "It'd be easy enough to drill a small hole through the ceiling and stick a peephole spy camera through to keep track of everything."

Aiden made another low sound deep in his throat, his expression one of frustration. He knew what we were proposing was the logical course of action. He just didn't like it.

"Before anything is decided, we need to talk to John. Would you be able to sift through his memories this afternoon, Belle?"

She nodded. "The sooner the better, I'm thinking."

"I agree." Ashworth leaned forward and placed his now

empty plate on the table. "She'd know by now that the ties that bound her to Henry were severed, and there's no accounting how she will react. It may just send her mad."

"Which raises another point," Belle said. "We can't treat her like any other dark witch or supernatural entity. She's not. She's been twisted and controlled from the very beginnings of her life, and she should be treated with pity rather than death."

Monty frowned. "Except, she's as dangerous as any other supernatural—"

"There *are* jails capable of holding even the strongest of dark witches," Belle said. "Just as there are witch psychiatric hospitals. She's a human-wolf hybrid rather than a supernatural entity, and we have to treat her as such. Otherwise, we're no different than darkness itself."

"And what if Liz's containment doesn't work?" Aiden said.

"It will," Belle said simply. "Because I'll be there right beside her, freezing Honor's goddamn brain."

"You two are as bad as each other," he muttered and then pushed to his feet. "I'll go ring Mac and warn him we're on our way."

As he moved out onto the balcony, Ashworth said, "If this is the course we're set on—and I do agree we should at least try containment before destruction—I'll contact the specialist psych hospital in Melbourne and get them to send up a team this evening."

Belle's eyebrows rose. "They have teams for this sort of thing?"

"Well, not exactly *this*, because it's rare for a blood apprentice to survive their master." He shrugged. "But insanity is not an unknown side-product of witches who attempt spells beyond their capability."

Because all magic had consequences, I thought, and wondered again what price the wild magic would ultimately draw from me.

Aiden came back into the room. "Okay, we're set. Monty, Ashworth, I'd feel better if you're nearby when we try to pin this bitch down, just in case things go pear-shaped."

Ashworth nodded. "Let us know where you're setting the trap, and the laddie and I will meet you there."

"I do so love it when you make decisions for me," Monty said, his voice dry. "I mean, it's not like this is my job rather than yours."

"It may be your job, but you're but a babe when it comes to experience." Though Ashworth's tone was stern, amusement creased the corners of his eyes. "But I'm more than willing to share my knowledge in the hope that one day you'll make a decent reservation witch."

Monty grinned but didn't bite back. Instead, his gaze went to Belle, who immediately raised a warning finger. "One step, and there'll be brain freeze."

He laughed. "I'm thinking our marriage is never going to be boring."

"And I'm thinking you remain delusional."

He laughed again and headed out. Ashworth quickly finished his coffee and then followed him down the stairs. I glanced at Aiden. "Are we going to set the trap immediately after talking to John?"

He nodded. "I'll head over to the station to grab all the electronics we'll need. I'll meet you out the front in twenty."

"Well," Ava said as he left, "you four certainly have an interesting dynamic."

I smiled. "They're family on so many levels."

"Young Monty is definitely thinking about family, but not, I suspect, in the sense you meant that, Lizzie."

"Mom," Belle groaned. "Can you just quit it?"

Ava's smile grew. "Unlikely. He's perfect for you in every way, my dear, and I will nag until you see sense."

"Just as well you're going home in a couple of days then," Belle said.

"I'm quite able to nag long-distance and have no doubt Monty will keep me updated on progress." She paused, expression thoughtful. "Although I'm not really after graphic details when it comes to the consummation of your relationship. There are some things best left to imagination."

"He would do that, too, wouldn't he?" Belle said, with another groan. "The man has no shame."

"When it comes to you, none at all. But be warned, dear heart, he's also no fool, as much as he plays it. He won't hang around forever."

Belle didn't reply, but her expression was thoughtful.

I scooped up the last of my cake, then rose. "I'll head downstairs and pack everything we might need. You might want to change, Belle—remember we'll be up in the rafters."

She shuddered. "If there're rats, I'm not going to be happy."

"Rats tend to be scarce during winter," Ava said.

"That might be true for the wider world, but in this reservation, anything is possible." She glanced at me. "I'll meet you downstairs."

I nodded and headed down. But as my foot hit the bottom step, an odd sense of awareness stirred. My heart skipped several beats and then raced.

Someone was here. Someone I knew.

Someone who stank of anger.

CHAPTER SIXTEEN

I froze and scanned the café. While I did know several of the couples sitting at various tables, they were regular customers and not the source of the gathering trepidation.

I stepped down and walked slowly through the café, absently smiling and greeting people as I looked for the presence I was sensing.

Still nothing.

"Everything all right, Liz?" Penny said.

I jumped slightly and turned around. As I did, a flicker caught my eye—magic. *Concealing* magic. Outside, in the lane between our building and the next.

"Yeah," I said, and ran past her for the door. *Belle, there's someone in the lane disguising themselves with magic. Can you read them?*

Hang on. She paused. *Found them, but they're wearing a shield and moving away too quickly for a concerted attempt to break through.*

Fuck. The bell chimed loudly as I threw the door open and darted for the lane. *Does the magic surrounding him or her feel familiar?*

Not really. Why?

Because according to my psi senses, I know whoever it is.

I reached the lane and spotted the trailing end of the spell disappearing around the corner. I swore again and belted after it, desperate to catch whoever it was before they utterly escaped. A scent caught in my nostrils, one that spoke of subtle floral undertones warmed by woody notes and a hint of rosewood. Not the scent of anyone I knew here in the reservation. Whether it was the scent of someone from my past, I couldn't say. Not just because my memory wasn't that detailed, but also because it was only recently that my sense of smell had become close to werewolf sharp.

Your watcher is heading for the lane that runs down the side of the old theater.

Thanks.

I ran through the parking area and into the lane, leaping over puddles and the various bits of rubbish that generally accumulated in old lanes like this. There was no sign of trailing magic now, and the scent was fading fast. Whoever it was, they could definitely run.

I hit Hargraves Street, did a quick two-step to avoid a woman with a pram, then stopped and spun around.

Nothing. Absolutely nothing.

I swore and stalked back into the lane.

Anything? Belle said.

Nope. Lost the trail.

Fuck ... do you think it could have been Honor?

No. The scents staining the air weren't hers. I think they were male in origin.

It wouldn't be your dad, would it?

Why would he hide? He'd march right in, announce his presence, and demand whatever the hell he was here to demand.

Which suggests your psi senses believe our unknown watcher is here to demand something.

Who knows? It's not like they've ever been overly generous with information.

True. She hesitated. *Could it have been Juli?*

Why on earth would my brother come down here? He never cared all that much about me when I was a kid, and I doubt that's changed.

Except you now have wild magic and might well be useful.

It was a totally possible supposition, of course, but I just couldn't see my pampered and rather spoiled brother leaving the safe confines of my father's "kingdom" up in Canberra.

That kingdom teeters on the edge, remember. Maybe that motivated him.

Then why would he run?

Maybe he wasn't ready to confront you just yet. Or maybe he simply didn't want witnesses and decided to try again later.

I still think hell would have to freeze over before my brother moved his butt out of Canberra. Although with my family, anything was possible.

As I neared the café again, my senses twitched. I stopped and studied the surrounding area. The usual amount of traffic rolled down the street, but shoppers were a little sparse, no doubt thanks to the bite in the wind. There was nothing to indicate anyone was watching and no visible sign of magic.

I'm not sensing anything untoward now, Belle said. *There's certainly no one within scanning range that has any interest in either you or the café.*

And yet my senses continued to twitch. I did another

sweep of the area, but couldn't spot whatever it was setting off the internal alarms.

I sighed in frustration and headed back into the café. Penny glanced at me, her eyebrows raised in query. I gave her a smile, said, "It's all good," and then headed into the reading room. Belle rattled down the stairs and followed me in. After placing a number of charms that would ward off evil—none of which Honor would sense until she was close —into the backpack, we headed out. Aiden appeared a few minutes later. I tossed the pack into the footwell and then climbed into the front seat. Belle shoved several boxes across to the other side of the back seat and then climbed in.

"Where are we headed?" I asked.

He checked the side mirrors and pulled out. "We've got him in temporary accommodation in Louton."

"And is that where we'll set the trap?" Belle said.

Aiden shook his head. "The place belongs to a friend, so I'd rather not, just in case things get nasty."

"And it might," I said. "It just depends on what her mental state is."

"Which does nothing to ease my concern." He cast another of those dark, broody expressions my way, but it probably had the opposite effect to what he wanted, given how damn sexy it made him look. "We'll set the trap back at his house. The roof is high enough to move around in with some ease, and there's plenty of spots for the rest of us to lie in wait out of immediate sight."

"Immediate may not be good enough," I said. "Remember what she is."

"Oh, trust me, I'm not forgetting."

Neither was I, even if he seemed to think so.

The safe house turned out to be a small weatherboard miner's cottage with a rusting tin roof and very little in the way of tall shrubs and trees around it—which no doubt made it easier to spot intruders.

Once Aiden parked out the front, we all climbed out and headed through the old picket gateway. The front door opened as we stepped up onto the veranda, and Tala appeared. "He's in a mood. He wants out."

"Well, we're about to offer him a means of that happening."

Tala's eyebrows rose. "There's a plan?"

"Yes, there is."

"Well, it's about fucking time," came the belligerent reply from inside the living area. "Being cooped up like this is intolerable."

"It's better than being damn dead," Aiden growled. "So sit back down and shut the fuck up."

The big man glared, but nevertheless did as he was told. Aiden stopped in the middle of the room and crossed his arms. "Right, you've got one last chance to tell us what you know about Leesa Rhineheart."

"I told you," John growled. "I didn't have all that much to do with her, and I'm certainly not sure why you're so fixated on the dumb bitch. Besides, it was ages ago, so what has it got to do with anything that's happening now?"

"Plenty. It appears Leesa's daughter is the one behind the attacks."

John's eyebrows rose. "Leesa's *daughter* killed Patrick? A human girl against a full-grown wolf?" He snorted. "You're stretching, Ranger."

"Not if we're talking about someone who's half wolf and capable of dark magic. Now, are you going to come clean or not?"

Aiden's voice held a final note of warning, but John wasn't listening.

"I've nothing to come clean about, Ranger, and you'll be hearing from my damn lawyer. This is nothing short of harassment."

"You're a werewolf in a werewolf reservation. The rights that apply to humans in the reservation do not apply to you. But by all means, feel free to complain to the council." Aiden pulled out his phone and hit the record button. "Belle? Your turn. Don't forget to verbalize what you're seeing."

John's gaze darted from Aiden to Belle and back again. "What the fuck is going on now?"

"You had your chance," Aiden growled. "Now, we'll simply grab the information by force."

"No, you fucking—"

The rest of that sentence froze as Belle rolled his mind. For several minutes, there was little sound other than the crackle of the nearby fire and the gentle ticking of the clock on the mantle above it.

"Okay, despite protestations to the contrary," she said eventually, "he was very definitely involved in the gang harassing Leesa."

"How deeply?" Aiden asked.

"Very. It was basically a scam they played on humans."

"Such a charmer," Tala muttered. "Maybe we should just release him and let him take his goddamn chances."

"As much as I personally agree, I doubt the council will," Aiden said. "How far did the scam go, Belle?"

"All the way—dates, declarations of love, the whole deal." She paused. "Once the two of them had fucked, the game was revealed, and she was told in no uncertain terms that she was just another human notch on the bedpost."

A muscle in Aiden's jaw ticked, and his fists clenched. But his voice, when he spoke, held none of the anger.

"Which doesn't explain Leesa thinking becoming a were-wolf would fix anything."

Belle's concentration deepened. "He apparently made an offhand remark suggesting it would have been a very different outcome if she'd been a werewolf. They all had a damn good laugh over *that*, let me tell you." Her gaze flashed to Aiden's; the anger boiling through her mind made her silver eyes glow. "Can I make sure this bastard never uses his damn dick for anything more than pissing ever again?"

Aiden's mouth twitched. "As much as I'd love that to happen, it's another of those things the council definitely wouldn't approve. What happened after Leesa came back? Because she obviously did."

Belle returned her attention to John. After a moment, she said, "She was brutally rejected, of course. And it wasn't just because of the foul stink of magic or the fact she remained human regardless of the ability to shift. The trans-formation spell wasn't as advertised—her ability to shift was more along the lines of the traditional Hollywood werewolf than the full wolf transformation she'd been after."

"Which isn't exactly surprising, given she was dealing with a blood witch," I muttered. "Those bastards never play fair."

"Anything else?" Aiden asked. When Belle shook her head, he added, "Then hold him steady while I grab the blood we need."

"You *can't* take my fucking blood without a permit."

"And you might want to revisit my earlier comment about human laws not applying. Tala, can you grab a knife and a small container from the kitchen?" As she walked around the sofa and disappeared through the doorway, Aiden squatted in front of John. "While there's no specific crime related to scamming someone for sex, you'll certainly be charged with making a false statement and hampering an investigation. And if I can at all make a case against you for being an accessory after the fact to the six murders in the scout hall, you can be damn sure I will. In the meantime, you *will* help us capture Leesa's daughter. Understand?"

He couldn't nod because he remained in Belle's control, but the stink of his fear filled the air. No real surprise, given he was being faced down by an alpha in full fury.

Tala returned and handed Aiden a knife and what looked to be a small plastic specimen container with a screw-top lid. He glanced up at me. "How much blood do we need?"

I hesitated. "To be honest, I have no idea, but I wouldn't think much more than a quarter of that little tub."

Aiden grabbed John's hand, carefully sliced open a finger, and then held it over the container. When enough blood had dripped in, he held the finger up while Tala stuck a couple of Band-Aids around it.

"Okay, Belle, release him."

"You sure? He's not exactly in a great frame of mind at the moment."

"He won't attack. He's not that stupid." Aiden rose and handed me the blood, though his gaze remained on John. "If he does, I'll throw every damn charge I can think of at him, and he'll be stuck in a prison cell for ages. Understood, John?"

John glared at him for several seconds and then swallowed and looked away. "Yes," he muttered sullenly.

Belle released him and then took a deep, somewhat shuddery, breath.

You okay? I asked.

Surprisingly, yes, though I certainly shouldn't be given

I've never gone that deep into someone's thoughts before. Her gaze met mine. *Maybe some of the wild magic's strength is bleeding over to me.*

Another of those things that shouldn't be possible, but at this point, probably is.

"Right," Aiden said. "We'll head over to John's and set up. Belle, you'd better go with Tala, as there won't be room for both you and John in the back seat with all those boxes."

She nodded and followed Tala out the door.

"You want me to call Ashworth and Monty?" I asked.

"No, I'll do it once we're in the car." He grabbed John's arm and led him outside. I locked the door and then hesitated, my gaze searching the area. My instincts were prickling again, but as usual, weren't giving me any concrete reason why. There was certainly nothing to indicate any sort of danger, and yet …

I frowned and hurried after Aiden. As he handcuffed John into the rear, I jumped into the front seat. Again, that vague unease stirred, and I glanced to the right. Whatever I was sensing, it was hiding somewhere back down the road. Was it the stranger I'd chased down the lane? Or was it perhaps Honor?

Aiden jumped into the driver seat and, after he'd made the calls to Ashworth and Monty, reversed out onto the road and followed Tala's SUV. I flicked down the visor and used the vanity mirror to check the road behind us. There were no cars immediately behind us.

"Problem?" Aiden asked.

"Twitchy instincts."

"How twitchy?"

"On the scale of these things, it's about thirty percent."

"You think it's Honor?"

"I don't know. Maybe."

I flicked up the visor ... and almost immediately, my spider senses switched direction, this time suggesting the problem lay to our right.

Which made utterly no sense, as there was nothing but a small housing estate to our right.

If Honor *was* tracking us, wouldn't Katie have sent the wild magic out to warn me? Especially given I was with Aiden? Or had talking to her mother through me utterly drained her? The threads of her wild magic *had* been unusually absent the last couple of days.

Aiden's gaze flicked to the rearview mirror. "There's no indication that we're being followed."

"We're not now."

His gaze shot to mine. "She's moved away?"

"For the moment, yes." I studied the houses for a second. "If her current trajectory is anything to go by, it's possible she's heading toward John's."

Aiden grunted and immediately hit a button on the center console. When Tala responded, he said, "It's possible Honor is heading for John's. Don't go anywhere near the place until we all get there."

"We're already close, so we'll pull over up the road from his driveway and wait. Call when you're near. Out."

We turned onto Fryer's Road. Aiden slowed as he drove onto the dusty sections, and my gaze went to the trees on the left. The tingling sense of wrongness was no stronger than before and yet ...

That's when I felt it—a surge of magic so thick, foul, and *close* that I had no time to do anything more than scream, "Brace!"

The dark wave hit hard, sucking away the air, making my brain and lungs hurt. The world turned end over end, and the sound of breaking glass and groaning metal competed with the high-revving scream of the engine. There was blood on my face, fear in my heart, and white-hot heat in my veins.

That heat could save us ...

Protect, I said, and imagined a curtain of power enveloping the entire truck.

The wild magic erupted from every pore in my body and rolled through the vehicle, wrapping it in a wiry net of powerful moonbeams. The truck slid to a stop on its side, the roof pressing deep into the car. The wild magic briefly bent with it and then rebounded, pushing the roof back with it. Pain tore through my brain, leaving me gasping, making my vision blur and eyes water.

I sucked in air and tried to concentrate. The truck was on its side, driver side down, and the roof was crushed around a tree. The only thing stopping me from falling was the seat belt cutting deep into my chest and stomach. Aiden lay unmoving beneath me, and there was blood all over his face. For an instant, fear filled my heart, then I saw his chest rise. Unconscious, but alive. I swallowed the thick rush of relief, then twisted around as best I could. Though John's seat belt was keeping him in place, his body was limp, and there was a deep bruise near his temple—maybe a result of his head being smashed into the side window as we rolled. There were minor cuts across the rest of his face, but his eyes were fluttering, suggesting he wasn't that far from full consciousness.

I turned back around and peered through the front windscreen. Dust plumed around the truck, a thick brown curtain through which nothing—

Eyes suddenly appeared—eyes that were bloodshot and filled with rage.

Honor.

She snarled, raised a fist, and smashed it down, cracking the windshield. I swore and pulled my net of wild magic to the front of the truck, pressing against the glass in an effort to protect us.

Another fist down. More cracks in the glass. I swore again and began to spell, but red-hot pokers immediately dug into my brain and threatened to overwhelm me. I let the spell fade. It seemed I could have one or the other—either spell or the net—but not both. Not at the moment. And the wild magic was the only thing saving us right now.

Lizzie? came Belle's scream. *We're on our way back!*

Be careful. God, speaking hurt. *Everything* hurt. The wild magic might be protecting us but at what cost to my body? It felt like it was utterly draining me. *She's in full-on fury, and I have no idea how much dark energy she has left.*

A third blow. This time the glass shattered, and with a scream, she thrust her claws through and slashed wildly. The wild magic bent around her fingers and then rejected her. Forcefully. As she disappeared into the dust, I flicked the wave back around the rest of the truck. More pain. More crazy people armed with pokers digging into my brain. My vision blurred again, and the vague wetness became a torrent down my cheeks. I closed my eyes and used my other senses.

Footsteps moving around to the truck's exposed under-belly. Fear hit again, and my breath caught. God, if she punctured the fuel tank and set a fire, we were goners. She stopped just behind me, and for several seconds, there was no sound other than the high revs of the engine, her thick, rapid breathing, and the frantic beating of my heart.

Then her magic surged again, a foul force that poked and probed both the truck and my protecting wave. More pokers and weakness washed through me, threatening to send me tumbling into unconsciousness. I swallowed heavily. I *had* to hang on. I had no idea if the wild magic could or would remain if I *did* lose consciousness, and it was the only thing keeping the bitch at bay.

Something thumped heavily on what was now the top of the truck. I twisted around again, trying to see what she was up to. The dust was settling, and her shadow loomed large. A fist came down on the side window, and the glass shattered, spraying wildly through the truck. Again she slashed with her talons. Again the wild magic bent around them. This time, it wasn't fast enough, and she managed to sever the belt holding John in place. As he flopped awkwardly down onto the pile of boxes, blood sprayed across my face.

I gagged, even as panic set in. Obviously, she cut far more than just the seat belt. And if she'd hit a main artery and we didn't help him, he'd bleed out fairly quickly.

Aiden groaned. My gaze darted down. He raised a hand and brushed the blood from half-open eyes. "Aiden, John's been hurt. You need to grab something and staunch the bleeding."

He blinked at me for a second or two before awareness sharpened in his eyes.

"You okay?" he asked, even as he unclipped his seat belt.

I nodded, but a sharp, inhuman scream had my head whipping around. Honor had grabbed the edges of the door and, with another spine-chilling scream, pulled the thing off its hinges and tossed it away.

Need you here fast, Belle!

We're almost there, but it's not easy given the thick forest you're in.

Meaning we must have been thrown a *long* way in.

Maybe that was why she was using sheer strength rather than magic against us. Maybe she'd all but burned herself out hitting the truck so hard.

She leapt down into the gap. Again the magic bent and then rebounded, but its response was even slower. As she was tossed back out, the pokers in my brain began to spread, washing weakness through my body even as my heart rate skyrocketed.

It was then I knew the cost of using the wild magic this way: it would kill me. It would put so much strain on my heart that it would literally tear it apart. I had to release it soon if I wanted to survive.

And if I *did* release it, we were all dead.

Belle ...

Close

Hurry.

Am.

Honor jumped back into the truck. The bending was greater this time, and a gargled cry of pain was torn from my throat. Aiden swore, the sound thick and full of anger, then the air sang with sudden movement.

"Don't!" I yelled, but far too late.

His fist punched a hole through my magic and smashed into Honor's legs. She howled, but her claws nevertheless tore into the hole, trying to make it bigger even as my magic tried to stop and repulse her. Pain shot through my body, my breathing now so harsh and ragged it filled the air. Every heartbeat was one long scream.

I couldn't go on. I just couldn't ...

I sucked in air, closed my eyes, and fought with every ounce of strength I had left, not only to keep what remained of our shield active, but also to resist the instinctive need to reach for Belle. To draw on her strength now that mine was so close to failing.

Then, abruptly, Honor stopped screaming. A heartbeat later, she climbed out of the truck.

Belle.

She was here.

Too fucking right I am, and this bitch is now mine.

Thank fucking God.

I'm thinking you also need to thank my fabulous legs and the speed they produced to get through the forest so damn fast. I outran Tala, you know.

A smile tugged at my lips, as she no doubt intended. *It's amazing what a little fear can achieve.*

It is indeed. The backwash of her telepathic energy ran through my mind, a thick, strong wave that was doing far more than merely controlling.

I sucked in more air and released the shield. What remained of the moonlight threads washed back into my body, and a sliver of strength returned. It didn't ease the madmen with pokers or the quivering weakness in my body, but my heart no longer felt ready to explode, even if its beat was still uncomfortably high.

"Tala?" Aiden said. "Get the medics out here ASAP. John's throat's been cut."

I carefully turned, but the movement nevertheless had the madmen doing a crazy dance. I blinked back tears and then said, "How bad is it?"

"She missed the carotid but got a jugular." His gaze swept me. "You okay?"

I half smiled, despite the pain. "You already know what my answer is going to be."

His mouth ticked upwards. "Yeah, but I keep hoping that one day you'll actually be honest."

"It'd only make you worry more, and you're bad enough already."

A couple of thumps on the side of the truck had me looking around. Tala. She pushed my battered door open and peered in. "You want help getting out?"

"I have to keep pressure on John's neck," Aiden said. "But get Liz out."

Tala's gaze met mine. "You look like pale shit."

"Thanks."

"Welcome." Her eyes gleamed with amusement. "If I grab under your arms, will you be able to release the seat belt?"

I nodded. Once she'd maneuvered into position, she said, "On three," and then counted down. I released the catch, and she grunted as my weight dropped into her grip. But within seconds, she was hauling me out onto the top of the truck and then helping me down to the ground.

She got out her phone, called in the ambulance, and then said, "Won't take them long to get here. I'll head back to the road so I can guide them in."

"Hopefully, John will last that long." Aiden's grim tone suggested he didn't think that would be the case.

As Tala disappeared into the trees, I slowly made my way across to Belle. Honor sat cross-legged on the ground a few meters in front of her, her face a grotesque mix of human and wolf that had been fused together in a random and brutal pattern. Her body was little better, and for the first time, pity stirred. It couldn't have been easy living in flesh so twisted.

The closer I got, the worse her scent. Foulness emanated from every pore. It wasn't just her flesh that had been twisted by the spell. It had altered her entire being, even her smell.

330

Belle's gaze swept me. "You look worryingly gaunt."

"I feel it." I stopped beside her and crossed my arms. "How bad is her mind?"

"She has lived and breathed revenge. She is a weapon raised, and she wouldn't have stopped killing even if she had gotten John."

I hesitated and then asked softly, "Can you help her?"

Belle's gaze came to mine, silver eyes troubled. "I could erase her mind, but doing so would basically leave her a vegetable, and she doesn't deserve that."

"And yet she's too dangerous to leave as she is." I hesitated. "I think there're two problems here. One, while I'm sure Ashworth gave a full explanation of the situation to the psych people he's called in, the minute she's out of your control range, she may well go full-on ballistic again."

"Possible, given that her rage still beats at the cage I've placed around her mind. What's the second problem?"

"The fact that, while her dark master might have said he'd severed his ties with her, was that the truth? Would he really risk losing such a powerful source of dark magic, whether or not he was retired?"

Belle wrinkled her nose. "From the little I know of those bastards? Not likely. But I can't erase her magic—not when it's as much a part of her being as the wild is with yours."

"What if, instead, you erase all that she's been taught about it? Henry did say the only reason she hadn't come here earlier was because she was too young and had no control over her powers. If you erase the learning, then at the very least, she'll have to relearn it all."

"And if I fudge the implanted hate and her memories of where she was raised, she might have no reason to do so."

I nodded. It would give her some chance of normality,

even if I doubted she'd ever leave the walls of the psych facility.

Belle took a deep breath and released it slowly. "Right then, let's do this."

As her telepathic energy surged and its force washed through the back reaches of my mind, the sound of sirens bit into the air, drawing close. I hoped the crew hurried, because even though I couldn't see John from where I stood, I was well aware the shadows of death were closing in fast around him.

I rubbed my arms and kept my gaze on Honor, watching as the thick light of fury slowly faded from her eyes.

Tala stepped back into the clearing, followed by the medics and rescue. A few minutes later, Ashworth, Monty, and two men I didn't recognize appeared. The psych specialists, I guessed, given the strength of the barely concealed witch energy that rolled around them.

"Looks like we've missed all the fun," Monty said as he strode toward us. "You two okay?"

"We survived."

He stopped on the other side of Belle and studied Honor for a second. "She looks docile. I'm guessing there's a little brain rearranging happening?"

I nodded. "It's the only way anyone was going to be safe in her presence."

Belle took a deep, shuddering breath and then said, "Done."

"What did you do?" the taller of the two strangers said.

Belle explained and then said, "Her magic is still there and still very strong, and there's no guarantee that she won't accidently unleash it."

"There never is when it comes to this sort of stuff," the other man said. He reached down and gently touched

Honor's shoulder. "Up you get, lass. We need to get you home."

Honor obediently rose. The two men stood on either side of her and gently raised a cage of restricting magic around her. Then, with a sharp nod at us, they left the clearing.

"Will they be okay?" I asked.

"Oh, aye," Ashworth said. "Even if Belle hadn't curtailed her memories, I'm guessing she probably spent most of her energy attacking you." His gaze swept me critically. "And I'm also guessing you spent most of yours defending. You're not looking well, lass."

"It's nothing a few days and a few hearty meals won't fix," I said.

He raised a skeptical eyebrow, but didn't gainsay me. I glanced back to Aiden's truck and saw one of the medics climb in. The high revs of the engine finally cut off, and Aiden climbed out. He spoke to Tala softly for a few minutes, waved away the medics' suggestion he be checked over, and then walked across to us. Aside from the multitude of small scratches over his face and the forming bruise on his cheek, he looked relatively unharmed. Even if that *hadn't* been the case, he was a werewolf and would only have had to shift shape to heal his body. That was one damn benefit of being a wolf that I wouldn't have minded the wild magic passing on ... and of course, it probably never would.

"What's happened to Honor?" he asked

"The Blackwing psych guys will transport her straight down to the hospital," Ashworth said. "You wouldn't have gotten any sense from her, laddie."

"As long as she's locked up for a very long time, I'm happy with that solution." Aiden's gaze came to mine. "Let's get you and Belle home."

I frowned. "What about the crime scene? And John?"

"Unfortunately, John died a few minutes ago. Tala is well able to take care of the situation from here."

My gaze went to the truck, but there was no sign that John's soul lingered. This death must have been destined. And while part of me regretted being unable to save him, I also couldn't deny it was utterly justified given what he and the others had done to Leesa and the horrific upbringing Honor had suffered because of it.

"I take it I'll be dropping you all home?" Ashworth said.

"I'm taking Tala's SUV," Aiden said, "but I'd appreciate you dropping Monty and Belle off. That way, I can get my girl home and look after her."

Ashworth nodded. "This way, then, the pair of you."

He took off without waiting for either of them. Monty caught Belle's arm, tucked it through his, and then said, "Shall we go, my dear?"

"Call me that again, and I shall fry your brains." She didn't, however, make any attempt to free her arm from his.

He laughed and, as one, they followed Ashworth. Aiden smoothly scooped me into his arms and strode after them.

"I *am* capable of walking, you know."

"No doubt, but I'd prefer to get home sometime in *this* century, not the next."

I smiled and leaned my cheek against his chest. "So, this pampering ... what, exactly, does it involve?"

He raised an eyebrow. "I'm taking a few days off, so I'll be cooking you meals, running you baths, and generally doing whatever your heart might desire."

"I like the sound of that last bit."

Despite the smile that tugged his lips, there was a seriousness in his eyes that warmed my heart while somehow emphasizing just how close to death I'd come.

"Your heart's desire will *not* include sex," he said. "Not until your cheeks look a whole lot less skeletal, at least."

I raised an eyebrow. "And you really think you have the strength to resist my wicked wiles for more than a day or so?"

His smile grew. "I do."

"Would you like to bet a bottle of Glenfiddich on that, Ranger?"

He laughed. "Sure. It's not like I'm actually going to lose either way."

As it turned out, he was right.

I might have won the bottle of whiskey, but when it came to the satisfaction game, we were both winners.

ALSO BY KERI ARTHUR

The Witch King's Crown

Blackbird Rising (Feb 2020)

Blackbird Broken (Oct 2020)

Blackbird Crowned (June 2021)

Lizzie Grace series

Blood Kissed (May 2017)

Hell's Bell (Feb 2018)

Hunter Hunted (Aug 2018)

Demon's Dance (Feb 2019)

Wicked Wings (Oct 2019)

Deadly Vows (Jun 2020)

Magic Misled (Feb 2021)

Broken Bonds (Oct, 2021)

Kingdoms of Earth & Air

Unlit (May 2018)

Cursed (Nov 2018)

Burn (June 2019)

The Outcast series

City of Light (Jan 2016)

Winter Halo (Nov 2016)

The Black Tide (Dec 2017)

Moon Sworn (May 2010)

Myth and Magic series
Destiny Kills (Oct 2008)
Mercy Burns (March 2011)

Nikki & Micheal series

Dancing with the Devil (March 2001 / Aug 2013)
Hearts in Darkness Dec (2001/ Sept 2013)
Chasing the Shadows Nov (2002/Oct 2013)
Kiss the Night Goodbye (March 2004/Nov 2013)

Damask Circle series
Circle of Fire (Aug 2010 / Feb 2014)
Circle of Death (July 2002/March 2014)
Circle of Desire (July 2003/April 2014)

Ripple Creek series
Beneath a Rising Moon (June 2003/July 2012)
Beneath a Darkening Moon (Dec 2004/Oct 2012)

Spook Squad series
Memory Zero (June 2004/26 Aug 2014)
Generation 18 (Sept 2004/30 Sept 2014)
Penumbra (Nov 2005/29 Oct 2014)

Stand Alone Novels
Who Needs Enemies (E-book only, Sept 1 2013)

ABOUT THE AUTHOR

Keri Arthur, author of the New York Times bestselling Riley Jenson Guardian series, has now written more than forty-eight novels. She's won a Romance Writers of Australia RBY Award for Speculative Fiction, and two Australian Romance Writers Awards for Scifi, Fantasy or Futuristic Romance. She was also given a Romantic Times Career Achievement Award for urban fantasy. Keri's something of a wanna-be photographer, so when she's not at her computer writing the next book, she can be found somewhere in the Australian countryside taking random photos.

for more information:
www.keriarthur.com
kez@keriarthur.com